P9-DBT-208

MY SECOND DEATH

A NOVEL

LYDIA COOPER

TYRUS BOOKS

F+W Media, Inc.

Published by
TYRUS BOOKS, an imprint of F+W Media, Inc.
10151 Carver Road, Suite 200, Blue Ash, Ohio 45242
www.tyrusbooks.com

Hardcover ISBN 10: 1-4405-6126-5
Hardcover ISBN 13: 978-1-4405-6126-9
Trade Paperback ISBN 10: 1-4405-6129-X
Trade Paperback ISBN 13: 978-1-4405-6129-0
eISBN 10: 1-4405-6127-3
eISBN 13: 978-1-4405-6127-6

Printed in the United States of America.

10 9 8 7 6 5 4 3 2 1

For Joanna: now you're in a book I wrote.

Acknowledgments

I would like to thank the best and kindest agent in the business, Amy Rennert, and Robyn Russell, editorial superstar, without whom this book would not exist, or at least would not exist in a form that any sane person would lay claim to. Robyn especially demonstrated uncanny and superwomanly patience, insight, and sense of humor through the book's evolutionary process.

And of course, in a purely physical sense, this book would not exist in the form it currently takes without my publisher, Ben LeRoy, who has incredible energy and great vision. I am truly lucky to have him as a publisher. I would also like to thank Ashley Myers at F+W Media for her keen editorial eye, Arin Murphy Hiscock for her brilliant (and incredibly quick) copyediting, and the talented production department at Tyrus Books.

I was so fortunate to study writing with Bob Pope and Greg Garrett, who are magnificent teachers and writers and mentors and yet I still don't have a big enough vocabulary to thank them properly.

And I have to acknowledge Emily Kolbe. I wouldn't write if it weren't for her. Even though she is dead now, she taught me about why people write and so in a way, everything I write is for her and because of her. I also want to thank my wonderful friends who have adventures with me in foreign countries and in weird parts of the U.S., and who have, all of them (you know who you are), taught me how to be a better person. And finally, my family, which defies adjectives, with a special shout-out to Kara and Beatrice for having such delightfully perverted tastes in television shows.

ONE

I gasp and wake up, damp with sweat, to a dim gray dawn and the gentle murmur of a late autumn drizzle. Rain crawls in shifting patterns across the windowpane as I wait for my pulse to slow. It's always like this when I dream about my brother's afterbirth: panic, something between lust and terror.

I was almost eleven when he was born. My older brother and I were waiting in the hallway. My mother lay exhausted on crinkly white sheets, and she turned her head to the doorway where the nurse stood like a guard. *You can come in, come look,* the nurse said, and I went into the room. I looked down. A lucent, pulsing cord of blue and gray sprouted from the baby's taut belly. The doctor clipped the cord and lifted the heavy sac of placenta into a stainless steel surgical bowl, a blood-dark jellied anemone. He saw me watching and he raised his eyebrows a little, and then he winked, as if he could tell how much I loved the smell of the rich, metallic blood. But what I loved best was the neat snick of the scissor blades. It was seventeen years ago today, but I can still hear the sound of the scissors like an ache in my molars. That sound, that smell.

I'm not an idiot. In my relatively short life I've been through enough shrinks and therapists that I am well acquainted with the convoluted machinations of my psyche. I know better than to lose myself in visions of my younger brother's afterbirth.

I scrub my thumbs against my eye sockets and get out of bed. The concrete floor is cool under my bare feet. Because there isn't a bath in the garage where I sleep, I have to go into the house to shower.

The kitchen is quiet when I let myself in. The silent tableau looks like a postmodern Vermeer masterpiece, the pristine domestic scene full of shiny metallic objects—a coffee pot, a microwave, an electric can opener—but devoid of humans. I go upstairs.

The bathroom is still hot and steamed and smells of a man's cologne. My father must have already left for work. Condensation drips down the mirror, dragging clear lines so that it looks like the mirror's stripping itself off in pieces. Slices of my face appear. I check my watch. I've got fifteen minutes to shower, brush my teeth, and assemble the strips of my face in the right order. I grin at the mirror and see one eyeball, one incisor grinning back.

After my shower, I wrap a towel around my hair, pulling on a threadbare Jane's Addiction T-shirt, a pair of jeans, and a black hoodie that I zip up to my throat.

The bedroom door to the left of the bathroom is tilted open. I stop in the hallway and listen for his sleepy grunts and the rustle of sheets. My little brother. He's a junior in high school, small and acne-chinned.

With my fingertips I brush his door in, and it swings on silent hinges. The shadows cling to his rumpled sheets, to the lines of his outflung limbs. One bare arm stretches over his pillow, his fingers curled against the headboard. I imagine running my fingers across his knuckles, the downy hair on his forearms, the rubbery tubes of veins. I imagine taking my pocketknife and peeling back skin to see the rich gelatinous blood, latticed muscle, and pearl-white tendons.

I rest my forehead against the wooden doorframe and wait for him to draw another breath. Then I go back into the bathroom and in the condensation on the mirror I write, *Happy Birthday, Kid.*

I pour coffee into a thermos then head out to the carport, ducking against a sudden spatter of cold rain. Dried leaves hiss across the tarmac. The sky swarms with roiling clouds, lavender and steel.

Under the canted carport roof a faded blue tarp covers the car. Not a car, *the* car. I drag the tarp off a 1971 Chevrolet Chevelle with a 350 cubic-inch V8 engine sitting under its sloped hood. In this case, the V8 engine is more of a V7, one cylinder misfiring. I need to sit down and order parts sometime.

The cracked vinyl seat is cold, and I set the thermos between my thighs to drive. I roll down the driveway, the car's broken insides heaving and bucking against the strain. Windshield wipers screech metronomically, swish-screek, swish-screek. My parents' house is on a brick-paved street and when I pull onto the street the car's suspension creaks and rattles through pocked cobbles filled with rainwater.

The house is in west Akron, a maze of brick streets and old houses with turrets and leaded glass windows, solariums and Tudor-style wood frames. The city of Akron, Ohio, is, as everyone knows, an ugly city, a plastic and rubber city with dirty streets and abandoned factories and warehouses. Goodyear and Firestone built Akron a century ago; the sky darkened as greasy factory smoke billowed out into the wind, and now, a century later, gritty rain weeps down on us ten months out of the year. To the north, Lake Erie is a gray sea floating with soggy trash, yellow McDonald's wrappers, iridescent skins of oil, and pale dead fish with raw white bellies and staring eyes.

But *this* is west Akron, cloaked in ancient oaks and maples, aristocratic, quiet, something slightly removed, a swath of archaic rectitude and decaying beauty. Long ago the Seiberlings and all the wealthy tire-factory-owning families lived here. They built their mansions and now the biggest mansions are sub-divided into apartments and the smaller houses are dreary, cracked relicts of a noblesse long gone. The families who live here today are a different aristocracy, a poor, working-class aristocracy.

Like the faded paradise in which they live, my parents are gods in ruins. My father is an academic dean at the university. My mother teaches piano lessons. They are quiet, respectable, successful people whose lives are free of blemish. They use the correct silverware when they eat and they are unfailingly polite to each other. Unassuming, educated, urbane, they err perhaps on the side of decorum rather than happiness.

Like the rest of the city of Akron, however, the other members of my family are more tarnished, a faintly sordid smell clinging to the corners of their lives. My older brother, Dave, recently moved back to Ohio from New York. He now lives in a bohemian studio apartment littered with cigarette butts, twists of aluminum foil, a threadbare volume of Ginsberg's "Howl." He published a short story when he was in high school, a chapbook of poetry in his first year at college, and another critically received book of poems before he was twenty-three. His charm is manic, addictive, and because he makes almost all of his editors' deadlines and usually manages to walk without a stagger he is forgiven his tawdry aura and loved by all.

My younger brother, Stephen, is an honor roll student at a preppy mostly Jewish high school where he pretends that his Jewish genes outweigh his Presbyterian ones. Chameleon-like, he becomes Presbyterian when my mother forces him to attend church. He is an atheist when he visits our father at the university. His cosmology, his colloquialisms, and his convictions switch at the speed of light, adapting mercilessly to his environment. His only constant is a quiet yet determined smile, shining so brightly that no one suspects he has an older sister who lives in the garage behind his house and who, like crude oil drillers, coal factories, and logging companies, has the dubious honor of being a dark catalyst for adaptive genius. I'm not proud of it.

And then there's me, the middle child. I live in the garage and say "fuck" too much, but I never whine about the rain or the cold, I rarely eat dead animals, and I haven't killed a man since I was ten.

I park in a gravel lot at the university. The rain has faded and the air is thick with the smell of car exhaust, ozone, and wet soil. Sunlight breaks through mottled shelves of clouds, striated bands of gold making the packed rows of cars glimmer like subaqueous stones.

The glass doors of the humanities building open onto a hallway packed with hurrying students. Eddies of voices, fragmented shouts, giggles, curses, and the swirling smells of bubblegum and chalk. Speckled linoleum flickers under the glare of fluorescent runner lights. Nausea bubbles like rotten sewage in my gut.

Elbow tilted out, chin ducked, I brandish my thermos in front of my face and press through the crowded hallway to my classroom. The students have already arrived. They sprawl behind tiny pressboard desks and watch the doorway with sullen eyes. A few of them have fixed their gazes fervently on the second hand ticking round the clock that hangs over the teacher's podium.

I am out of breath. I dump my backpack on the seat behind the podium, turn to the chalkboard and scrabble along the metal rim for a piece of chalk. The chalk squeaks. *Acrasia, Amavia, Ruddymane.*

I turn around and dust my fingers on my legs. Papers rustle. A pen scratches. I face a gulf of four feet and then rows of blank, expressionless eyes.

"Okay, so we've got through Book Two of *The Faerie Queen*," I say. "We're going to talk about Ruddymane today. Anyone want to start us off by defining anagogical allegory?"

A student leans over and whispers. Quiet snickers.

I suck down a mouthful of coffee, then set the thermos under the teacher's podium. The bitterness sticks to teeth, my tongue. The clock ticks in the silence.

"All right. Pop quiz."

I grin. They hate this. The hatred sizzles on their post-adolescent faces. They take their heavy textbooks and shove them back into backpacks. The multiple thuds of book spines hitting the floor sounds like a flock of dead birds falling from the sky.

A hand rises in the back.

"Yes, in the back. Question?"

"Are these terms going to be on the exam?"

I lean against the chalkboard. "Let's get one thing straight, Mr. Back Row. I get paid a stipend to teach this class while I work on my dissertation. I am here because I want lots of letters after my name, letters that mean I don't have to talk to people, or spend any more time breathing their air than I have to. *You* are here because you want a degree that means you won't have to flip burgers the rest of your life.

But with the state of the economy right now you will likely settle for some minimum-wage government job, like, say, delivering mail, that will provide you with a modicum of security and health insurance. Disappointed by your life work, you will drink yourself into a coma every night in front of *American Idol* reruns. You will sink into a stupor from which you will be barely aware of your own insignificance in the world, far less the insignificance of esoteric terminology you failed to memorize in your sophomore-level literature class at college. So even if I say yes, they are on the exam, would it make a difference?"

Twenty-five pairs of doughy lidded eyes, twenty-five moist, slack mouths. Silence. The guttural tick of the clock.

A hand from the back row.

"So, you're saying they *will* be on the exam?"

After class, I cram the heavy volume of Spenser's collected works into my bag and go upstairs to the fourth floor where the graduate students work in a windowless room overstocked with broken swivel chairs and outdated computer monitors. In addition to teaching one class a semester, we are required to hold six office hours per week so that our students can come to us with complaints or for help understanding course material. I spend an average of six minutes a week in the office, but I rarely get reported for dereliction because my students don't feel the need to seek my sage advice, and my fellow graduate students do not exactly miss my less-than-sunshiny presence.

The room is almost empty. Two grad students sit at a computer sharing a pair of headphones. The one sitting awkwardly on the arm of the chair leans against the other's shoulder. They are bobbing their heads back and forth and singing along with some video clip. I've seen them do this before. They told me it was "poor man's karaoke," but I still don't get it. I wonder what it would feel like to plant a palm casually on someone's shoulder, to feel the rise and fall of a person's breathing synchronized with your own. They look so oblivious, like they don't know I'm standing here. Like they don't know how lucky they are that they find it so goddamn easy to be happy. I inhale as if I want to say something, but I don't know what I would say. I don't even know why I would want to join their cat-neutering wail. I breathe out and back out of the doorway.

Because life is short and graduate student offices are boring, I sign my name on the spreadsheet of hours and turn to leave. On my way through the front office the secretary lifts her head from behind her laminated desk.

"Ms. Brandis? You've had a lot of calls. I've got the messages here. The dean wants to see you."

She holds up a sheaf of small pink notes, my missed messages. I flip through them. The dean. My dissertation director. The dean again. I crumple them. One note is written in a different script, a slanted downstroke of black ink. The words make me pause.

Even gods decompose.

I look up. The secretary is behind her desk unwrapping a kielbasa croissant, her phone headset moved away from her mouth.

I look back at the message. *Message for: Michaela Brandis. Time and date: 3:20 p.m., Wednesday, 10/06. Message: Even gods decompose.* And then numbers and a name. *411 Allyn.*

I frown, and fold the note and put it in my pocket. For some obscure reason I feel the need to hide it. But I honestly have no idea who left it for me, or what it means.

"Michaela Brandis!"

I startle.

"Sorry to jump out at you like that. I didn't see you here all week."

Dr. Robert Telushkin, my dissertation director, scuttling into the office smelling like rain, an umbrella beaded with mist pinned under his tweed-sleeved arm. He's a small man with brown liver spots on his forehead, and eyes that are metallic green-gold like a bullfrog's. He wears heavy gold rings on his fingers, untucked shirts, and sandals even in winter.

"So! Have you thought about what I said, Michaela?" The loose skin under his chin ripples when he talks.

I scowl at him. "Oh, I've got a *great* idea. Why don't you fuck off and leave my personal life alone?"

His chin waggles. He waves a gold-banded finger back and forth. "Now, I've told you. I know academia, the ivory tower, all that seems ideal for the social recluse, but what did I say?"

Last week, he returned one of my essays with a penciled lecture on my behavior. He wrote that graduating depended on being a great student, which I had the potential to be, but getting a job depended on politics, which I sucked at. I paraphrase. His point was that my writing was good, my research was great, but I'd been getting too many complaints about my attitude from students, from my peers, and from the dean.

When I don't answer him right away, my dissertation director says, "Getting a job depends on *politics*." His voice is damp, plummy, an old-man whiskey voice. "Playing the game. Part of which is, you don't tell your dissertation director to fuck off." He makes air quotes when he says "fuck."

I grin. "Oh," I say. "Okay." I make air quotes around "okay."

"See? That's another example of what I was talking about. You get away with as much as you do because you're a great student. But you'll never become a great *academic* until you learn a little respect."

At least he didn't say I got away with as much as I did because of the dean.

"I respect you," I say.

He smiles suddenly. The soft leathery wrinkles of his cheek fall into creased folds like a well-worn map. "I know," he says. "That's why I know you'll think about what I said. Right?" He gives my backpack an awkward pat and then turns to go into his office. He stops in the doorway. "And I believe the dean wanted to see you."

"I know."

"All right, then. Tell him I send salutations."

He disappears into his office.

I stand in the hallway and ball my fists in my pockets. The folded pink slip rubs against my skin. I could go see the dean.

Or I could investigate the message.

I decide to take the bait. I've got nothing better to do.

Allyn is the name of a street near campus. I have driven past it before, but it exists outside the periphery of my small world of classroom, car, and assiduously avoided office.

I walk out into decay-spiced autumn air and hike down the cobbled slope of the main campus, then turn down an alley behind a parking garage. A warren of shabby houses, all crackled paint and slanted ridgepoles, swarm the southern bank of the university like a scabrous architectural infection. I glance again at the pink slip in my hand, at what I assume must be an address, and a cryptic quote from Friedrich Nietzsche.

Cars hurtle down Exchange Street. I cross at the light and walk up a block past a blood plasma center, a pawnshop with barred windows, a bar whose neon brew signs flicker dyspeptically. I stop at the street corner where Allyn, a cramped alley, runs into Exchange Street.

I turn down Allyn. Weeds sprout through the cracked sidewalk. Collapsing houses crowd each other, their yellowed, overgrown lawns reaching across boundary lines like jaundiced fingers. I walk slowly, looking left and right.

And stop suddenly.

411 Allyn is indeed an address, but the house occupying the plot of land is a structural carcass. Plywood nailed over the windows, a yellow plastic streamer across the front door, paint chipping off aluminum siding, and bald patches of tar showing through shingles.

I believe this edifice is what is known in the vernacular as a "crack house," a building once used but now condemned for its role in the sale of cocaine or, more likely, the refining, cooking, and selling of methamphetamines. Because I live in my parents' garage, and have done so for most of my twenty-eight years, I have never had the opportunity to view even the remains of such a den of vice.

This lack of experience suddenly seems wrong, a deficit that must be immediately rectified.

Half-smiling, intensely curious, I go up the drive, the fine gravel like crushed shells under my feet. A side door stands partially open, hanging crookedly on two broken hinges. I reach out to touch the door. And such a *feeling* suffuses my bloodstream, adrenaline rushing through veins and arteries. I can't believe how cramped, how stultified, my life has become, my God, how *bored* I've been since—oh, since I moved into my parents' garage ten years ago.

My chest expands and constricts.

Even gods decompose.

I push open the door and step inside. Darkness closes around me like a shroud when the door swings closed after my entrance. I blink and wait for my eyes to adjust, for the pale rainy light outside to reach into the cavernous gloom.

A chalky smell has leeched into the concave walls. The house sounds empty, the sort of dull stillness you only notice when the electricity and water have been long turned off. A faint musty, mammalian stench, as if wild animals have camped out in here at some point. A couple of empty rooms to the left and right. And straight in front of me, a narrow flight of stairs that climbs into shadow.

I walk up the stairs slowly, the fingers of my left hand running along the wall, my feet delicate, searching each stair before I lever my weight onto it.

A hallway. A thin carpet, creaky floorboards.

A door to the right. I reach out to open it, then hesitate. I don't know what lies inside. I don't even know what kind of hide-and-seek game I'm playing at. Is my mysterious message-leaver a chess player, intrigued by mental gymnastics? He, or she, I suppose, could be sending me on goose chases, trying to see how much influence over my actions he can wield. But what if my Nietzsche-quoting stalker is actually dangerous?

I know that this is a bad idea. I push the door open anyway.

For a second, I hesitate, every muscle tensed, waiting for something—anything. But the room is empty.

Another door on the left, latched shut. I touch the door handle. It turns. The door creaks and sighs. A smell, the cold touch of wind on my skin and the smell. A sweet reek, like raw sugar and mold-softened tomatoes.

I reach into my pocket, feel the cold teeth of my car keys. Find a thin plastic tube, a miniature flashlight attached to the keychain. I click on the flashlight. Iodine-yellow light trips across the room. Wooden floorboards, an antique bureau with clawed feet, the veneer chipped and faded in patches, each porcelain knob stenciled with tiny violets.

In the opposite corner of the room, a twin-sized mattress on a metal bedframe. Something is lying on the bed. I inhale sharply.

The flashlight blinks off when my hand momentarily loses all messages from the neurons frantically misfiring in my brain.

I can't breathe.

My thumb presses on the flashlight button again. The beam pins the bed in its single-eyed gaze.

A man lies facedown on the mattress, his arms cuffed at the wrists to the bedposts. His legs are duct-taped at the ankles. The skin of his back is slit down the spine and spread like wings across the bed sheets.

TWO

My heart kicks against my ribs and electricity fizzes through my veins. My pupils dilate. I have to, *fuck*, I have to leave.

My feet shift. A step closer to the bed. And then I am bending over it.

My hair swings down. The strands brush against the body's cold skin. I pull my hair back, wrap the length around my fist and tie the hank into a knot.

The corpse has been flayed, his back skin pulled apart like fabric. The skin drapes white-clotted against persimmon-red sheets. The red sheets are bleached pinkish-yellow in patches as if some acidic substance splattered them.

Knots of vertebrae like sea sponge, slender yellowed laths of ribs. Clumps of macerated pink flesh cling to the bone. The head and neck are intact, the skin split from the protruding curve of spine at the base of the shoulders down to the lumbar vertebrae at the top of the swell of buttocks.

Venetian blinds stir as rain-scented wind snakes in the cracked windowpane. Broken slats clack against each other like teeth. I take a breath. The smell of blood, cold soil and coins.

I reach out two fingers of my left hand and brush lank strands of hair from the corpse's neck. The skin there is the color of milky tea. I press my fingers against the skin. The knobby vertebrae shift under the skin with a gritty sound. A thin fluid wells up from an almost-invisible slit.

I look at the man's head. His face is turned to the wall, his right cheek pressed against the sheets. His left eyelid is visible, but the skin is puckered where it droops over the drained sac of his eyeball. The jaw is distended, the left cheek tented. I see a glimpse of fabric between his lips. With my forefinger and thumb I tug at the tiny corner. The teeth are locked tight. My tug jolts the head. A handcuff clinks against the metal post.

The wad rips as it comes free, stiff and clotted with dried saliva. A handful of crumpled pages, a fuzzy archaic type. I try to separate the wad and the paper crumbles in my hand. I pull free a large fragment with a section of print and realize that the text is not in English. There can only be a handful of citizens in the decrepit burg of Akron who would be able to read this foreign text, but I am one of them. Even more uniquely, I know the book from which it comes, Nietzsche's *Die fröhliche Wissenschaft* (*The Gay Science*), that contains the (translated) phrase "even gods decompose," as well as, more famously, the expression *Gott ist tot*.

All I can make out of the blurred type on the scrap in my hand is "*wenn dir eines Tages oder Nachts*." I feel a prickle of sweat along the back of my neck. In English, this section reads something like: *What if, some day or night, a demon were to steal after you into your loneliest loneliness and say to you, This life as you now live it and have lived it, you will have to live once more and innumerable times*. It's a section where Nietzsche describes a demon calling into awareness the darkest parts of a man, so that he can throw off the constraints of civilization. So that he can be free.

I make a fist around the wad of paper and wipe the back of my wrist across my mouth. Turn to the mute messenger on the bed.

In this instance, the god is not only dead but quite literally decomposing.

I try to focus, to be objective. I am meant to see this. What am I meant to see? I step back and look at the mattress, at the sheets spattered with blood already oxidized and brown, a few congealed clots of skin and fatty tissue. The lack of blood spatter and the relative smallness of the pooled bloodspill make me think that the man on the bed was killed and then skinned. I wonder how he was killed. Drugged first, maybe. And then the body, lax, under the killer's nimble hands—

Wetness pools in my mouth.

I swallow and blink. The pages in my fist waver and I realize the tremor is in my hands. And like waking up, I think with sudden and fierce clarity that I am standing over an exquisitely mutilated corpse.

I turn and collide with the door. My fingers slip on the knob. I run down the steps. My left shoulder bangs into the wall. I elbow open the side door.

The air is cold, shocking and fresh after the fetid sweetness inside. I grip my fingers around my knees and squeeze. The underside of my hair is damp with sweat.

Defying all odds that I can calculate, the body upstairs is only the second human corpse I have seen or touched. It is this sole fact that has kept me walking free among the sane.

I bend over and cough and spit onto the gravel.

Then I get up and run. I run fast, my lungs making scissoring noises. I run through backyards and gravel alleys, across the busy four-lane street dissecting the hovels of poverty from the university campus, between towering brick buildings alight with morning sun. I get to the car, start the engine.

My fingers shake when I uncurl them from the clutch of paper.

I put the wad from the dead man's mouth into my jacket pocket and reach for the gearshift. My palm itches. I turn my hand and see crescent-shaped nail marks, oily beads welling up from slit skin.

I put my head against the steering wheel. Shit. Shitshitshit.

I imagine grabbing whoever wrote that fucking note and screaming into his face. What do you think will happen, I want to ask him. What do you fucking *think* will happen now?

Somehow I drive home. I don't remember the trip.

I sit on the bare mattress in my cinderblock garage cell. A small pile of ash on the white-painted floor where I burnt the pink message slip and the pages of Nietzsche. It occurs to me that the decision to burn the message is forensically intelligent but of course I have little interest in establishing my connection to the corpse or in hiding it. All I want is the smell of burning paper to overpower the memory of blood-stink. My mouth keeps filling with spit. I wipe my hands on my knees and breathe smoke and can't stop smelling the body and imagining my fingers exploring the vertebral ridge, each knob a fossilized cauliflower blossom. What it would feel like to dig a serrated blade into a spinal column, metal teeth catching on bony joints.

I clench my jaw and rock and squeeze my eyes closed. Focus on the darkness. Focus.

I breathe in slowly, exhale.

Calm seeps into my muscles. My diaphragm relaxes. My breathing slows. My heartbeat decelerates. I have been forcing myself through this pantomime—under tamer circumstances and with lower stakes, to be sure—for, well, for close to all my life. Some people practice yoga. I pose formulaic dialogues in my head, Glaucon to my own Socrates. What is good? What is justice? What is beautiful is most loveable, Glaucon. Do you not agree? Therefore right love has nothing mad or licentious about it.

So: What is the proper thing to do?

The civically responsible individual would call in the cops, who would investigate. The cops would inevitably question that civically responsible individual. But any investigation into my past will uncover my unfortunate encounter with a man that ended in his falling down a flight of steps in my parents' basement and cracking his neck. The judge said that the murder was self-defense. The shove down the stairs wasn't what got me the rapt attention of psychiatrists. Mutilating the corpse did that.

I spent a couple weeks in a juvenile psychiatric unit under observation. Lots of valium. I have watery memories of crosshatched pink patterns on the backs of my thighs from sitting on hard plastic chairs. The first diagnosis was schizophrenia. It was accompanied by little pills that went by exotic names like Haldol and Prolixin. They made me sleepy and my mouth dry. After I got out of the psych unit my parents took me to a shrink who asked me questions like, "Do you hear voices?" And, "Does it make you angry when people ask you questions?" The shrink was a large woman with a chest the size of a coastal shelf and smile-crinkles by her eyes. The Mrs. Claus of prescription drugs. She dropped the schizophrenia diagnosis, downgraded me to "borderline personality disorder," and gave me anti-anxiety meds. My older brother called the diagnosis "crazy lite." The new meds were supposed to stabilize my moods but they made me scratch the skin on the backs of my hands and bang my head against the wall. So I got a new shrink and a couple of Rainbow Bright Band-Aids. The next psychiatrist, a man who stroked his fingers slowly across his mouth while he talked, gave me the MMPI and an IQ test and announced that I was too bright for school so I was bored, and that was why I had killed and mutilated a man. The following morning my parents deposited me at a different therapist's office.

By the time I was twelve the collectors' set of psychologists and psychiatrists in the greater Akron area had ruled out emotional neuroses and decided that all that was wrong with me was that I lacked the capacity to experience guilt or love or compassion. In short, I was a highly intelligent borderline sociopath. Dave said that was shrink-speak for "evil." There are no pills for evil so, at the recommendation of a couple of child therapists and a psychologist, my parents pulled me out of school. My dad gave me exams in analytic geometry and the history of Western civilization each week. My mom listened to me play Chopin etudes on the Steinway while she breastfed baby Stephen upstairs. When I was fourteen Dave moved to New York to study Marxist poetry at New York University. I would go days without speaking to other people. It was the closest I've ever come to being content.

When I was sixteen I got one last shrink who downgraded me for the final time, said I had "antisocial personality disorder" and that he'd send my parents a bill. I've been drug- and shrink-free for the last twelve years.

But even after so many years of legal purity, I can't imagine that claiming to have "discovered" a corpse in a condemned house on whose premises I had no reason to be would go over well with Akron's finest. If I decide to play the civically responsible individual, in all likelihood what freedom I now have would end with my being abruptly returned to closely monitored living quarters and mandated psychotherapy.

Finding a corpse and not calling the cops is wrong. I know that.

But. Finding *that* corpse . . .

I think of my hands wandering over the wallpaper, the stair railing, the doorknobs, at 411 Allyn Street. My hair falling across the corpse's naked vertebrae. In addition to the inevitably uncomfortable questions I would face if I, with my preadolescent psychiatric record, reported finding the corpse, there is the one other little problem as well: I was set up. That note was intended to make me curious, to make me explore the condemned house, leaving fingerprints all over the place. It's not like I would necessarily get convicted, but at the very least I would be a suspect.

If I don't report the body, I could be in worse trouble once the Akron police department steps in and finds those prints. Then again, there's nothing to connect me to the site except for my fingerprints, and my fingerprints would only bring up a sealed juvenile record. Besides, the corpse has been there for at least a day, probably more, by the smell. The note left in my message box was dated yesterday. So far there hasn't been any hue and cry. If I wait—just don't say anything, or do anything unusual for a few days—well, I don't know what will happen next.

I pick at dry skin on my lower lip until I taste salt. I drop my hand to my knee and stare at the limb. Because all of this is pointless, really. I don't want to do the therapy circuit again, and I won't risk going near any more corpses. Which leaves me with exactly the same option I faced ten years ago when I decided to move into my parents' garage and live like a saint in a monk's cell. I know what I will do and it is what I have done since I was ten, what I will always do, world without end, amen. I will do nothing.

The worst part is, I don't know what this decision means, if it shows the strength of my resolve to be civilized, or if it makes me monstrous. I get up and hold my hands under the hot water tap in the industrial sink until my fingers have stopped shaking. Above the sink a flyspecked mirror reflects a pale-skinned ovoid face with two eyes, one nose, one forehead, two lips and approximately thirty-two teeth. The human face, unblinking, looks away while the human hands turn off the tap, dry themselves on a towel, and two human feet walk steadily to the door. I go back out to the car, sitting patiently under a white-scabbed sky.

THREE

I drive back to campus because the only rules for normalcy I have involve going to the university. I need to find out who left the message in the box. I climb the stairs to the English department floor. My palm squeaks against the over-polished metal railing. Outside the glass door with the stenciled words "Department of English" in some faux-Old Germanic script, I stop and wipe my palms on my thighs. Then I stick my iPod earbuds in my ears and push through the door. I don't know how to ask. The office is open from 8 A.M. to 5 P.M. every day and the department secretary won't necessarily have seen everyone coming and going. She takes long breaks, heading across town to Panera to chat with her friends, while a student worker sits behind the desk and reads *Us Weekly*.

Maybe the graduate students will know. Maybe it was one of them. I have almost reached the graduate student office when a finger touches my scapula. My whole body flinches. My heartbeat thuds in my neck and pain grips my scalp like fingernails dug hard into my skull. I take a breath and let it out.

I pull out an earbud and turn around. It's the department secretary, wearing blue polyester and smelling like overripe peaches and greasy sausage. Her little shiny marble eyes stare up at me and her mouth is moving. "—Brandis?"

I realize she has been saying my name. In my left ear, Tchaikovsky's Symphony No. 4 in E major swells to a crescendo.

"The dean called again. He wants to see you at your *ear*liest convenience."

I can almost hear the dean's inflection in her voice.

I swallow. "Okay." It comes out faint, cracked in the middle.

Her little face crumples when I answer. She starts to smile. "He's been calling *all* morning, you know. I'm so glad I finally caught you! I'll just tell him you're on your way."

She trots off. Her small bottom twitches under the shiny synthetic fabric of her suit skirt. I watch her go. I didn't mean, "Okay I will go see the dean." I can't go see the dean.

She doesn't understand.

But she's on the phone already. She glances up and smiles at me. Her mouth is moving, the lips pushing in and out like she's chewing.

"Who else leaves me messages?"

The sound of my voice is loud. It sounds metallic, echoing. I wonder if something is wrong with my ears.

The secretary ignores me, just holds up one finger and keeps talking.

After she hangs up the phone she leans forward. Hair falls over her left eye.

"What was that now?"

"The dean and my dissertation director," I say. "Who else? Who else leaves me notes?"

"No one that I know of," she says. She smiles at me. Her lips are shiny with semiliquid gloss. She looks fake, painted.

"Someone else left me a message," I say. "Was it one of them?" I point to the grad student office door.

Her little mouth wrinkles around the edges. "As far as I know, Ms. Brandis, the only person leaving you messages all day is the dean. Maybe you should ask *him*."

I imagine talking to me feels like licking soap to her. She is not helpful. I think that she would walk a far distance to avoid noticing anything about me, or talking to me. She is not likely to be an observant source of information.

I turn and walk down the hall toward the stairwell.

One time—I must have been thirteen or so, down to one psychiatric visit a week—my shrink *du jour* asked me if I ever felt happy, or sorry for someone else, or scared. I told her she was wrong to imply I didn't feel things. "It's just that other people feel with their emotions," I told her. "And I only feel with the nerve ends under my skin."

She gave a snort of laughter so hard her glasses slipped down her nose. Then she straightened her glasses and smoothed her hand over her mouth. "That was a good one," she said. "You got me with that one."

But I hadn't meant to tell a joke. My face felt hot and I wanted to punch her in the mouth.

In retrospect, I should have explained it better. It's not that I don't feel things. It's that the emotional center in my brain feels like it's a million galaxies away but the world around me is pressing in on me, hot and sticky and loud, full of bright colors and breathing and textures. By the time I figured out how to explain myself I was seeing a different psychiatrist who didn't care about feelings, only about dosages and fifty-two minute sessions. In my adolescence I went to more psychologists and psychiatrists than most kids go to football games or sleepovers. I understand the way my mind works better than tax attorneys understand the month of March, but sometimes I wonder if a big part of my problem isn't just that I never learned the basics that most kids learn at those games and parties. I mean, I figured out how to tell jokes. I just never learned how to laugh at them. Sometimes I think I could have turned out so much closer to normal if I had just been forced to act like a normal kid.

I thought going to college would help me learn to blend in, find my rhythm, my way through the feelings other people translate as emotions. But it didn't work out that way.

As I walk down the hall, snatches of conversation from open office doors drift out. Faculty isolated in small offices with a single windowpane, a few plants, seventeen thousand books, and a rotary telephone that went antique in the '90s. Someday I will live in one of those offices. It will smell of damp mold and dust and I will leave the door shut.

The dean's office is in a red brick building with wide white-painted steps. I climb the steps and go inside, my sneakers squeaking on polished parquet. My footsteps slow. I know it's illogical, but I am convinced that as soon as I walk in he will see it in my face, the fact that I've gone closer to the edge than I've been since I was ten. He knows me well enough that he should be able to see it. I almost turn around and leave. But I tell myself that he's not a very perceptive individual. And that's true. He's a solitary man, the dean in his glistening dean's aerie. In many ways he's as close to antisocial as a normal person can get.

I walk down a carpeted corridor to an office sporting a brass plaque that reads *The Office of the Dean*. The dean's secretary looks up when I come in, one hand pressed to her ear. "I'll tell him you're here, Mickey."

I go over to a rack of magazines and glossy brochures. Travel in Spain! Summer Abroad in Scotland! Declare a New Major!

"Mickey? He can see you now. Just go on in."

His office door is a big wooden slab fitted flush in its frame. I wipe my palms on my pant legs and push it open. The office has tall windows on two sides, but the blinds are pulled, the only light an amber glow from a frosted glass globe to the side of the desk. Waxed plastic plants in woven planters, rows of leather-bound books with uncreased spines, and dust-free cherry wood bookshelves. It is good, in short, to be dean.

I pull out the chair facing the desk and sink down onto a faux-leather seat cushion with brass tacks. The leather lets out a fart-like sigh, and I let out a nervous laugh.

The dean sits far back, one leg crossed over the other, his elbows pressed to the armrests of his orthopedic swivel chair. His hands rest loosely in his lap, knuckles like walnuts under papery skin, small polished fingernails.

He leans forward and his face emerges from shadow a piece at a time, like a geographic puzzle sorting itself out, lines and creases and planes and hollows. An aristocratic forehead and neatly combed graying hair. Wire-rim glasses. And his dark heavy-lidded Semitic eyes that always look on the brink of tears. I've never seen him cry.

He clears his throat. “It’s your brother’s birthday tonight.”

I unzip my hoodie, then reconsider and zip it halfway up. “To be precise, it’s his birthday this morning as well. But don’t worry, I understand the subtext here. You want me to play big sister tonight. You’re sounding the depths, testing the waters of crazy. The ebb and flow of hysteria. Am I right?”

He clears his throat again, a syncopated two-syllable rearrangement of phlegm. “So, how are you.” A proposition, not a query.

I zip my hoodie up to my neck.

A flash of bone and stringy flesh, a smell like old fish and maple syrup.

I look at one of the fake plants. The woven planter has a plaster base like a real planter, ready to catch the life-carrying water that will never be poured out on this polymer construction. I wonder if anyone has written a psychological study on the verisimilitude of fake plants. I stare hard at the plant. My eyes burn.

I’m not good at this, at lying. I cough. Then I spread my mouth wide, separate my teeth. I’m going for happiness, but for all I know I look like a badger having a stroke. “I’m peachy,” I say. “Dandy. Absolutely tip-top. How are you?”

My father watches my face then sits back, dissolving into darkness.

“I’m—doing well.” He pauses. “So you . . . I mean to say, will you be present tonight? For your brother’s birthday?”

I hunch my shoulders. “Mom already told me in no uncertain terms that I’ll be present and accounted for. Say, separate bedrooms seem to be hell on your marital communications.”

“Yes,” he says.

I look at him.

He doesn’t say anything else.

The glossy desktop reflects his shadowy image. I don’t know what to say. “Um, if you need a shoulder to cry on—”

He turns to look directly at me. His face, disembodied by shadow, moves into the sepia light. The skin near his eyes wrinkles. “A shoulder.”

"Well. It's the thought that counts. That's what they tell me anyway."

"That is what they say."

"Okay. So, I'll be there tonight." I reach for my backpack.

"One other thing," the dean says.

"Come on, a*nother* complaint? Dad, seriously, they're a bunch of assholes."

"No, not that. I just wanted to say that I spoke with Robert Telushkin."

The dissertation director. The bullfrog with a whiskey voice.

I don't say anything.

"About what Bob Telushkin said, ah, you should know that—he and I may differ in many viewpoints, but your—your scholarship is good. You should know that."

I don't know what he means at first. And then I figure it out.

"It's okay, Dad. You don't have to console me. I know I'm not like the other kids." I sigh. "And he's not wrong. I'm not going to succeed much in life with my, uh, problems. But I'm fine with that."

He doesn't say anything.

I stand up. "Seriously. I am." I don't know if he believes me. I don't think I believe myself. *Even gods decompose.* "Don't worry about me."

"No," he says.

I don't know if he means that he won't worry or if he means to negate my adjuration, that he *must* worry. As I leave his eyes follow me, a glimmer of white from the gloom.

When I go outside a light rain has started to fall in drifts like seaweed. Mist beads on my eyelashes. When I blink cold dribbles race down my face. I think of the plants in my father's office and realize that the rain on my face is my own mummery, the verisimilitude of tears that I will never produce on my own.

I stand outside the administrative building watching students hustle past. They call to each other, wave, fling arms around each others' necks or slap each others' backs. A skateboarder leaps the fountain to a scattering of applause.

Beyond the fountain is the university library, a brick and concrete monstrosity that looks like a Cubist ziggurat. I look around but no one seems to be studying me. Whoever left me that note was on campus, knew my campus schedule. Knew where my office was.

I check my watch. Hours to kill until my brother's birthday dinner. The library is safe. No corpses in the stacks, no incriminating questions that people will remember when the city detectives arrive at some point in the future. Just . . . information. The blank substance of knowledge encoded on a page.

I head past the fountain to the library and push through the security alarms, metal detectors to prevent the theft of the mildewing tomes that exist in multiple copies in every academic library in the lower forty-eight states. The library always smells musty and acrid, like sweaty shoes and Xerox machine toner. I've heard my graduate student colleagues joking that the only reason people come here is to fornicate in the stacks, but that has always struck me as suspicious. The library's fug is no aphrodisiac I would recognize.

I go up the winding steps to the third floor where pale light filters through flyspecked windowpanes, the mustard-yellow carpet is worn thin as old linen, and the stacks of books smell like damp paper. Unlock my study carrel, log onto my laptop, and sort through stacks of printed-off digitalized illuminated manuscript pages from a ninth-century book.

I put my thumbs on either side of my nose and press. A calcified knot of pain sits just behind my left eye.

The slick threads of his hair against my fingers, the spongy feel of his bloated skin when I pressed on the slit at the base of his skull.

My fists convulse. I sit back sharply and bump into the desk. The pen rolls across the desk and falls to the floor.

I open my laptop, pull up the library catalog, and scroll through entries for Nietzsche's works. Then I leave the carrel and wander through the stacks, running my fingers over the crumbling spines. The library carries very few foreign-language copies, and I don't see any copies of *The Gay Science* in the original German. When I turn to leave, I see a book wedged beside a Germanic translation of the Bible and a travel guide to Vienna. A thin blue volume with faded letters. I can only make out the "*D*" and the "*issenschaft*."

My cell phone rings. I blink. Look at the phone.

My mom.

Shit.

She's calling about the dinner. You would think, from how much energy they are expending to enforce my presence at my brother's birthday dinner, that I am wildly unpredictable. But I'm like clockwork. Dysfunctional, broken, and self-isolating clockwork, but still. I always come home at the same time every day. Then I go for a long run. Then I shower. Then I study or work on my dissertation. Then I check my e-mail and go to bed.

I look at my watch. I am usually running at this time.

I silence my phone and open the book. Flip through a few pages.

The pages are stiff, the binding crusty with disuse, and there is a broken part of the spine that the book wants to open to. When I separate the book at the broken place, I see that a page is missing.

My breath seizes.

When I trace my fingers over the faded script, sounding out the words, the words sound familiar. *Und wir—wir müssen auch noch seinen Schatten besiegen!*

And then the faint ruff of a ripped-out page. But I know what that missing page says. I just don't know how it got from the book to a dead man's teeth.

I close the book. The tips of my fingers are dusty and itch. I almost slide the book back onto the shelf where its OCLC number belongs. But instead I take it back to my study carrel and put it under a stack of books on old English land reform laws.

The book was misshelved for a while and no one noticed. The shelvers here at the library are mostly undergraduate students on work study. No one cares if a volume is missing.

When I come out from the carrel and lock it behind me, the buzzing fluorescent lights give my skin the yellowed cast of ageing paper.

And we—we must throw off his shadow.

But I don't know whose shadow to throw off. I don't know whether I'm being hounded by gods or demons, or how to find my way out from their shadow.

I can't go home yet. Not with the smell of book glue and burnt paper on me. Not with my mind caught like a stuck needle on German phrases. I grab my duffel bag out of the trunk of the Chevelle and go into the campus gymnasium to change into running gear.

FOUR

After my run, I return home, shower in scalding water, and watch my skin flare red. Steam billows up and chokes the bathroom with the scent of apple blossom shampoo. Outside the bathroom window the rain comes and goes in waves, applause dimming to a gentle hush.

Everything is wet and clean. I towel off and dress and take a breath. Then I go downstairs, twisting my wet hair into a rope and draping it over my shoulder. The kitchen is full of smells, sweet basil and olive oil sizzling on the stove, rosemary bread baking in the oven. My mother stands over a simmering pot, stirring, droplets of condensation beading her upper lip. She startles when I come in, but she turns toward me. "Oh, honey, hi! I didn't see you come in. I didn't know if you were—I'm glad you decided to come."

Her hands are clasped under her breasts. She pauses, smiling, watching me. Her life is punctuated with strange pauses and verbal ellipses. I have always felt that in her head she plays an edited footage of her own life and in these moments she is blocking in a scene of familial warmth. A kiss to my cheek, perhaps, or a brief maternal embrace.

"Where's the birthday boy?" I say.

"In the living room. We haven't had this in a while, have we? The whole family together for a birthday."

"The whole family?" I realize this is the first family birthday since Dave moved back to Ohio a couple months ago. "He's coming?"

She's smiling but the tendons under her translucent skin are tight, carving dark ridges down her neck. "Aren't you going to be glad to see him?"

"Are you?" I want to know why she looks anxious.

She says, "Of course I am. I'm always glad to see him—to see my whole family. I love all of you."

I raise my eyebrows a little but don't say anything to that.

I go into the living room, a wide wood-floored room with brown leather couches and a white shag rug. Separated from the living room by an empty foyer is the solarium, a flagstone room with vast windows and a jungle of green plants, lush sun-house for the mirror-shiny grand piano which sits like a black goddess in the center of the otherwise empty room. I want to go into the solarium where it smells like eucalyptus and orange-scented wood polish. I hate the smell of human bodies, the clammy sweat, and the way human eyes and voices crawl all over me, sticky, brutish, *bruising*.

The TV is on, mumbling to itself. Flashes of blue light reflect off an evening-dark windowpane. Stephen lies on the rug in front of the TV, a game controller in his hand, eyes fixed on his screen avatar. The human-shaped cartoon lurches across rooftops with the graceful stop-motion of a praying mantis.

I sit on the far end of the couch and clear my throat.

"Happy birthday."

His thumb joints move but the pupils of his eyes remain fixed. "Yeah. I got your message on the bathroom mirror. Classy."

"Sniper," I say.

"Yeah, I see it."

Graphic gunfire rattles the screen with flares of yellow and orange. Red blood like a paint can flung in a slow-motion arc. I think of Stephen's blood spooling from the sliced umbilical cord.

"I dreamed about your afterbirth last night."

Without looking around he wrinkles his nose. "Gross."

I sit forward, my elbows on my knees. "Yeah. You were pretty gross too. When you were born."

"Some would say," he says without looking around, "that I still am."

I smile.

The front doorknob rattles and opens and along with a swirl of ozone-scented air a silvery voice calls, "I'm home! Hello! I'm *hee-eere*!"

Stephen drops his controller and twists around.

Dave comes into the living room, unwinding a red knit scarf. A man comes in after him, turning to shut the door after them. Dave advances into the wood-floored foyer, pausing under the halo of the glass-shaded lamp with an almost-unconscious theatricality. His hair is untrimmed but he is clean-shaven. Faint red veins splay across the shadowed hollow under his cheekbones.

He holds his arms wide. Stephen goes to him and they hug, Dave cupping Stephen's face and kissing his forehead loudly before releasing him. Mom comes out wiping her hands on a towel and he kisses her as well, his lyrical voice in cadenced ecstasies over how beautiful she looks. Her eyes catch his fevered sparkle, and her tired lines disappear into a haze of pure happiness.

"Sweetie," she says, "you're *thin*."

"Sweetie," Dave says, "you'll feed me." They both laugh. Stephen crosses his arms around his middle and shifts his weight.

The man behind Dave edges into the room. Mom says, "Hello!"

My elder brother is often drunk, is not morally averse to drugs, and despite his publication record and reviews, is less than normally intelligent in some ways. So it is not surprising when he walks in with random strangers, which he frequently does, of both sexes. My parents are overly polite. They think they are being open-minded, that Dave is a bisexual whose proclivities are a test for their middle-class morality. I told them once that Dave was not bisexual, that he just liked to fuck. They thought that I, in my pristine virginity, didn't know what the hell I was talking about and they smiled kindly at me.

Dave laughs now, an affected yet oddly addictive giggle.

"Oh, God, I'm an asshole, I *totally* forgot. Mom, Stephen, this is Aidan. Aidan, this is my family." He raises his eyes to mine. They are bright with laughter and he's holding his mouth tight, like he's sharing a secret joke with me. Like he's about to say something that will send us both into peals of helpless mirth like stock characters in a Jane Austen novel. But he just says, "Oh, and that one is my sister. Michaela."

The stranger moves around Dave's side for the first time.

A dark buzz of hair covers his skull like moss. His eyes are wet-dark, bright, almost feral. One iris holds steady and the other zigzags like an unmoored boat in a storm. He looks right at me, as if I'm the only one of interest. I wonder if Dave has told him about me.

"Hey." He speaks so softly I have trouble hearing him.

Mom says, "Welcome, Aidan. Come in. Dinner's ready in five minutes."

"Thank you for your hospitality, Mrs. Brandis." The words are small and compact and appropriate, like a child reciting from a politeness grammar. He even looks at my mother when he talks, his solitary good eye moving reluctantly to her face. But as soon as he finishes talking he looks back at me, his singular eye focusing like a compass needle honing in on north. The wild iris swivels sideways, a shivering dark disc in a milk sea.

Dave comes into the living room, one arm around Stephen's shoulders. "What are you playing? Oh, excellent. What's the high score?"

I stand by the couch, palms pressed against my thighs, watching Dave fold his limbs as gracefully as a crane and Stephen throw himself down on the couch like a beanbag. Dave rests one hand on the back of Stephen's head and with his other hand grabs a second game controller from the coffee table.

The stranger takes a step into the living room and hesitates. He is wearing a brown plaid shirt faded to translucence over a green T-shirt. Crusty patches of white and blue paint speckle the worn fabric.

He looks at the television. Then he looks up at me, the force of his stare reaching across the space between us. He holds out a hand to me. I notice Band-Aids on two of his fingers. He says, "Hi again. I know you."

I look up at his face. We watch each other in silence.

Finally his fingers fold in on themselves and he pulls the hand back.

"You don't," I say.

Aidan's eyelids open wide, startled, apparently, that I speak. "I'm sorry. I meant, we met before. I don't know if you remember?"

"Are you a cutter?" I ask.

"What?"

I nod at his fingers. "I asked if you're a cutter."

There is a short silence. Stephen twists his head away from Dave's hand, where it rests against his neck. He says, "Dave, stop it! *Geez.*"

Aidan says, "What do you mean?"

I smile a little. "No need to sound so anxious, dear stranger. I've got no problem with cutters."

"Yeah, you really *like* cutters, babe, don't you? Like your roommate when you moved into that dorm, she was a cutter, right?"

I didn't know Dave was listening.

"Shut up."

"I already told him about you, babe. Had to, you know? Had to warn the poor kid before he met you. I just told him about whatsername, your first roommate." He snorts, as if the person in question were somehow barely relevant, scarcely worth the breath to speak her name. "First *and* last roommate." The person whose name he doesn't speak is the reason I moved into my parents' garage ten years ago.

Stephen doesn't say anything. He pretends he can't hear a lot of the time.

There's a short silence. Then Aidan says, "If you mean, do I cut myself on purpose, then no. I don't."

"Guess you're just clumsy then."

He frowns and looks down at his fingers. He folds them under his thumb and looks back up. "Guess so."

I look at the TV screen.

After a while Aidan perches carefully on the edge of the couch. He leans forward, hands clasped between his knees. Dave, transfixed by the television screen, ignores him and shrieks in glee when his avatar shoots Stephen's.

Aidan rubs his fingers over his knees, making a soft scratching sound. Then he says, "Stephen—you're Stephen, right? Um, there's one of those cop guys, behind the trashcan."

"Yeah, I saw it," Stephen says, surly. Then, more mellow, "Thanks."

Mom comes back into the living room. She looks at us, at the walleyed stranger stiff on the couch, at Dave and Stephen entranced in vicarious bloodshed, at me standing like a sentry by the fireplace.

"Honey, have you met Aidan yet?"

"I might not enjoy the presence of others, Mother, but I do at least *notice* them. I am neither blind nor mentally deficient."

"I'm sorry, honey. Aidan, can I get you anything? A drink? I'm making a spaghetti Bolognese for dinner."

"I'm fine, Mrs. Brandis. Thank you."

Mom goes back into the kitchen. From the kitchen, the clink of metal pot lids, the spicy tang of a simmering tomato sauce, a sweet cinnamon smell, maybe a pie baking. My stomach growls.

Dave says, "Shit! I almost had that one."

Another quiet.

The air feels thick with human pores oozing urethra and my throat convulses like I'm going to gag. I get up and walk out of the living room.

The piano lid slips like satin under my sweaty fingers. I run my hands over the oil-slick keys and start to play. I never got very good at piano because I can't sit on a bench with another person. I can, however, make my way through some easier Beethoven and Mendelssohn and Mozart. I like the way notes are precise and clean, the purity of sound produced by metal cables stretched so taut they are on the brink of snapping.

"Dinner's ready! Honey, dinner's ready."

I keep playing, washing out the clinks of silverware and scrapes of chairs and shuffle of bodies. My mom comes into the doorway to tell me dinner's ready but I let a staccato run erase her voice.

A hot hand claps down on my shoulder. I jump and the piano clangs atonally. I slam the lid shut and shove back the stool and lurch to my feet, spinning to face Dave who grins, sloppy-mouthed, like an idiot. His eyeteeth are crooked and yellowish.

"You're such a fucking *ass*hole!"

"Dinner's ready," he says.

He's still chuckling when I yank my chair back and sit down at the end of the table. Mom carries in a wooden bowl of salad. She sets it down and says, "Dave, wait till we're all sitting," because he's reaching into a basket of buttered rosemary rolls. He pulls his hand back and sits down.

The front door swings open with a clatter. My father is nothing if not endowed with the innate capacity to make an entrance. He comes in balancing a briefcase, stacks of free papers, a few heavy tomes, and rain-fogged glasses. He nods at everyone, his eyes catching on Aidan, and says, "Pardon my tardiness. Cynthia."

This last to my mother.

She smiles at him, but her eyes move away from his face before the smile reaches them.

He goes into his office, unloads his briefcase and books, and then his feet tread upstairs, each step firm, irrevocable. The crank of a spigot. Water thrumming in the old pipes. He comes down a few minutes later, buttoning a beige cardigan. He hitches his trouser legs and sits, leaning for the basket of rolls.

Dave claps his hands once and then cups them around his mouth like a trumpet. "Birthday present time!"

Dad frowns but withdraws his hand.

Dave pushes his chair back and goes over to the sideboard where a small collection of gifts in shiny silver and blue wrapping paper sits. He picks up the largest box and turns it, finds a card by the large bow. His eyebrows go up and his face creases into glee. He lifts his eyes to us and says, solemnly, "For my baby boy."

Stephen's ears turn pink.

"Oh shush," Mom says. "Just give it to him."

In my head I play through a Chopin nocturne. My fingers move across my thighs, picking out chords. This is taking too long. I snap my fingers to get Dave's attention and point to a card lying on top of the other presents. "That green card is mine. Give him that one next."

Dave pushes out his lower lip. "Patience, grasshopper. You can't rush me. I have a *meth*od."

I roll my eyes. "The silver present is Dad's. It's a watch. The other card is yours. God knows what you wrote in it. It's cash or a gift card, but my bet is cash. Now give him the green card, okay?"

Dad clears his throat. "Michaela."

"It's okay," Stephen says. He shrugs and reaches for Mom's present. "It's not like I didn't know. No offense, but none of you are, like, creative geniuses when it comes to gift giving."

Mom says, "You don't know what mine is."

Dave snorts like he's going to laugh, but swallows the sound.

Stephen bends his head to open Mom's present. He slits the tape, unfolds the paper without tearing it, and sets the ribbon neatly by his elbow. He is careful and slow.

Dave picks at his fingernail and shifts his weight and finally says, "*God*, boy. I'm evolving."

Stephen smiles a little. "Don't rush me. I have a method." He says it softly, almost absently, and Dave makes a face. But I am impressed with my little brother. It's not easy to upstage a man who steals the spotlight in a family of actors.

Mom's gift is sweaters.

Stephen looks surprised and lifts out the one on top. "This is awesome, Mom. Thanks!"

Mom always gives clothes. It's the only gift she gives. For all the years that Dave lived in New York, she sent him a box of ties and button-down shirts on his birthday and sweaters for Christmas.

"I'm glad you like them," she says.

Dave brings over the other present and the cards.

I say, "I got you iTunes."

"And *I*," Dave says, "gave you *cash*."

Stephen reaches for the card on top of the pile Dave hands him. It's Dave's card. He pulls out a twenty. "Hey, great! Thanks!"

"He's so easy to please." Dave looks at Aidan. "It's *cute*."

"Dave, honey," Mom says.

Stephen's mouth tightens but then he relaxes and smiles at Dave.

Dad clears his throat. "If the gift-giving is done, may I suggest we eat?"

Stephen pushes his cards to the side and puts the clothes and watch on the floor near his chair. "Thanks, everyone."

Mom gets up to bring in a bottle of wine.

Dave turns to our younger brother with eyes shining like a saint who has seen God. To anyone else his glittering teeth and eyes would mean genuine interest, but I recognize the latent cunning in his wide smile, his elegant, joy-pitched voice.

"Well, *this* is nice. The family, together at last. Why, the last time I was home for your birthday, you were so little! And all you wanted—what was it you wanted?"

Dad clears his throat. "David."

Dave sighs and sits back in his seat, linking his fingers over his chest. "I remember now. It was a puppy. Remember that? You wanted a new dog so bad, you cried for *weeks*."

Stephen's eyes flick from Dad to Mom and then to me. Mom says, "Well, look how fast those rolls went. There are more warming in the oven."

Aidan watches her leave and then turns an inquiring eye on Dave. And that as much as anything makes me decide to play along.

I smile at Dave and say to Stephen, "What's the matter, kid? Still pissed off I ate your dog's liver?"

A sudden silence hovers over the table.

Mom comes into the room. I turn and reach into the basket to get a roll. Her fingers brush mine and I jerk my hand away. She catches the roll and sets it on the edge of my dish.

Aidan's eyes are fastened on my hand as if mesmerized by that violent instinctive reaction to my mother's accidental touch, as if the gesture has startled him into recognizing some darkness lurking behind the awkward conversational gambits.

Dave turns to Aidan. "She ate the family dog," he says. "This was when she was, like, twelve. We come into the kitchen because we smell something burning, and there's Mickey frying a piece of meat at the stove. We go, What's that, Mickey? And she says, Buster's liver."

"Buster," I explain, "was the dog."

Aidan looks down at the red sauce swirled across the dinner plate that Mom hands him.

She says, "Did everyone get pasta?" She smiles like a deaf mute.

"Mother, for God's sake. You're throwing us off. We're performing for our guest, you see." To Aidan, I say, "I've got APD, not Down syndrome. They act like I'm a moron."

Aidan lifts his head.

"APD is antisocial personality disorder," Dave says.

"Right. Anyway, that's the final diagnosis. All those shrinks, and that's what they end up with. It's supposed to be better than schizophrenia, which is what they first thought I had. But the way I look at it, Joan of Arc was a schizophrenic and she managed to get canonized. Whereas APD is what most serial killers have. So go figure, right? Not much of an improvement as a diagnosis."

Aidan's eyes flick to my mom, then to my dad, who is picking industriously at his pasta. Aidan's mouth looks strained.

I smile. And relent to social pressures, the shade of Emily Post whispering in my ear. "But I'm not a serial killer. I just dislike people." I incline my head in Dave's direction. "The dog thing wasn't that bad. He can explain the difference."

Dave says, "Hundreds of people have APD and most of them grow up to be perfectly ordinary citizens. Accountants and janitors and doctoral students studying medieval literature, just for example." He winks at me. "Serial killers have other traits in addition to being antisocial. For example, a lot of serial killers start off killing animals, you know, like gutting cats or killing a dog and eating its liver."

I rip off a flaky bit and blow on it, then put it in my mouth. "This is terrific, Mom."

She smiles a little. The muscles by her mouth contract, at least. "I'm glad you like it, honey."

"But Mickey," Dave says, "as far as we know, didn't kill Buster."

I tear off another piece of croissant. "Bingo. I didn't kill Buster. He was already dead. Died of old age. He was stiff as a board when I cut him open. See the difference? The fine distinction?"

My father's lips are pale. He has surrendered his fork and knife on his dish and sits with his hands balled beside his plate, skin bleached white in patches around his nose.

"But that's old history." I look away from him. "I don't mutilate animals any more, living or dead. And I don't even like meat that much. I mean, I might have a hot dog for lunch, but that's it." I don't explain that hot dogs are made of spleens and gristle and tendons mashed up by huge metal teeth, churned into a lumpy pinkish mash of semi-liquid ooze. Normal people eat hot dogs. Normal people don't *think* about hot dogs. As far as I can tell, that's the difference between normal people and me. Normal people also do not particularly like other people. Take the way Dad's eyes are burning into the table right now. But normal people don't admit to themselves how violent their fantasies of murdering their fellow humans can be. This is why I don't consider myself the victim of a disorder, the carrier of a genetic disease. No. Me, I'm just radically honest. Someday they will erect statues in my honor.

"So. No serial killing for me." I smile at Aidan. "Now tell us something about yourself. Do you enjoy birthdays? Attend every one you can?"

His eyelids flicker. He looks over at Dave.

Dave says, "Mickey doesn't go for the small-talk thing. She's not good at it. But she doesn't lie. She hasn't killed any animals—" He looks at me. "—that we know of. And if she asks a question, she's interested in the answer."

"Right," I say. "He's right."

Aidan's lips part. They are dry and a waxy seam splits when he opens his mouth. He doesn't look distressed, though. Most of Dave's dates would have gagged by now, or would be showing the whites of their eyes. He says, "I enjoy birthdays."

I grin at him. "Like what part? The cake and ice cream? Those poky party hats? Scotch tape?"

"Scotch—? Oh, you mean, like on presents? Well, I guess I'd have to say I like the cake and ice cream."

I look at him for a while. He looks back. He smiles, a faint tuck of the lips at the corners. I clear my throat and look away. "Good choice. That's my favorite part too."

After a brief silence, my father asks Aidan a question in a formal voice. Dinner conversation returns to its melodic pitch. They talk about the sort of banal shit most families discuss at dinner tables—subjects one is studying at university (fine arts), whether or not one enjoys those studies (he guesses so, yes), and what one intends to do after graduation (he doesn't know, thinks he might run an art studio).

My parents are experts in facilitating normalcy, just like Dave is the family Puck, stirring his delicate fingers in the waters to disturb the strange creatures lurking below. Dave can control the monsters, and at my advanced age I have become a well-trained, well-behaved, barely monstrous monster. But the whole charade strikes me as supremely stupid. Things can change in an instant. They should know that.

I want to raise my head and scream at them, *I touched a dead body today. I pressed my fingertips into the ripped dead skin of a man handcuffed to an iron bedpost.*

My father comments on an exhibit at the art museum that he saw while at a banquet for a visiting speaker. My mother apparently was there as well—this event must have fallen serendipitously during a thawed moment of détente in the polar ice cap of their relationship. My mother gets up to open a new bottle of wine and for a minute there is silence while my father and Dave sip their glasses of wine, their mouths pursed in identical moues of qualified approbation.

Stephen is frowning at his dish. I think about asking him a question but can't think of anything to say.

I swirl my fork through the pasta. The spaghetti sauce is leaching into a half-eaten roll resting on the side of the plate. Red creeps slowly up the soft white underbelly of the roll.

My mother says, "Aidan, did you get enough to eat? Do you want more of anything?"

When I was six years old, my mother left Dave to babysit while she went to the store. Dave turned on the TV. An old film was showing on one channel, a movie about a vampire with long white teeth and a shiny black cape. Dave got me a plastic sippy cup of grape juice. I told him I didn't use sippy cups any more but he said to shut up or he wouldn't let me watch the movie.

We watched the movie in silence. An old man in a tweed jacket stabbed a silver spike into Dracula's chest.

"Why did he do that?"

"You have to stab their hearts or they won't die," Dave said.

"Why not?"

"Because the heart is what keeps you alive."

"What's the heart?"

Dave put his fingers against his chest and said, "It's a muscle that beats—you can feel it."

I put my fingers against my ribcage. Silence. Bone.

"Move your hand. To the left."

And then I felt it. Tha-thump. Tha-thump.

"That's your heart."

I smiled.

Dave said, "If you spill that juice, I'll kill you."

It was summer. A brief, sudden rain came hard while Mom was out shopping. When the clouds shifted, steam spiraled up from the driveway blacktop. A heady scent of lilacs and dogwood hung thick in the damp. At night, Mom put me to bed with a window fan blustering moist air across the moon-slatted room. I lay on my sheets in red panties and a white eyelet nightie. I could hear the house breathing and I felt the patterned thump of my heart against my ribs, against the mattress.

They woke up in a blued room with the shadows silver against the kitchen knife.

I saw the whites of their eyes flare in the dark. The glisten of lips.

My father made a hissing sound.

Neither of them moved.

"Is she awake?" my father whispered.

I squatted on the sheets between them, my nightie ruched around my waist, the kitchen knife in my sweaty grip. My hair hung in my face.

My mother said, "I don't know."

"Jesus Christ," he whispered.

"Don't," my mother said. She put her hands on my arms. Her skin was sticky with heat. I gripped the knife and put the point on her sternum. My mother gasped. Her fingers, bony, strong, squeezed my wrist and my childish flesh, soft and yielding, weakened in her grasp. She took the knife away from me. My father reached over and clicked on the bedside lamp. Sweat stained the hair by his temples. His sagging cheeks were dark with prickles of beard. He took the knife in his fingertips and got up. The bed creaked when he left. His bare feet made pat-pats on the linoleum of the bathroom. A cupboard door closed.

The tap turned on. He came back into the bedroom with a glass of water.

My mother pulled me into her lap. Through the fabric of her nightgown I could feel the hard lumps of her nipples, the soft pouch of her belly. She smelled faintly of red wine and fabric softener. She combed my hair away from my forehead with her fingernails.

I put my hand against the side of my mother's breast. Through the skin, I could feel the solid thud of a spasming muscle.

"Tha-thump," I said. "Tha-thump."

My mother's arms tightened around me.

"What?" she said against my hair.

"That's your heart."

"Yes." She put her palm against my back and rubbed in slow circles. The nightie bunched under her hand. "Yes."

"What was she doing?"

"Shh. I don't know. A nightmare, maybe."

I pushed my mother's hand away and leaned out from the damp heat of her body. When she tried to gather me against her chest again I got off the bed and scampered back to my room. I lay down in front of the fan and the wind fluttered across my face and neck.

They came into my room and my mother stayed there until I fell asleep. I woke up with a pillow under my head and a sheet over my body.

The next afternoon I went into the kitchen but the knife drawer was latched. I rattled the drawer but it wouldn't budge. Dave was sitting at the island eating a bowl of Lucky Charms and reading a Punisher comic book. He put the book down and watched me trying to claw the knife drawer open. He said, "Did you seriously try to stake Mom and Dad?"

I turned around and ducked my head.

He said, "Well, you can't do that. Okay?"

He got down from his stool and fixed a bowl of Lucky Charms for me. I dragged a stool over to the island and climbed up, put a spoon in the cereal and began stirring the milk into a pinkish-brown saliva-thick swirl. He leaned his elbows against the countertop next to me. Then he said, "Listen, Mick. You can't do crap like that. You'll get put in prison if you do. In prison bad stuff happens and I swear you wouldn't like it."

I sucked on a marshmallow and looked up at him.

"That guy who staked Dracula was old, remember?" he said. "*Way* old. Because when you're old, you're smart about stuff and you don't get caught."

"Okay." I took a bite of cereal.

"Promise?"

"I said yeah."

"Okay." He sat down and opened his comic book.

I push my plate away and pinch the skin of my forehead between my two clenched fists. I need to get out of here, go somewhere I can breathe. Time for Elvis to leave the building.

I put my napkin on the table and go into the kitchen. I rinse my hands at the kitchen sink, scrubbing them in water so hot that curtains of steam waft upwards.

In the dining room, Dad says, "Thank you for a wonderful meal, Cynthia. If you'll excuse me, I need to go over that FIDC report. Aidan, a pleasure."

A chair scrapes. The rustle of wrapping paper.

Mom says, "Stephen, honey, did you want more dessert?"

He mumbles a reply, apparently committed to collecting his stash and retreating again to his lair, which is equipped with headphones and an Internet connection to the world beyond his home. I figure he's earned his retreat.

Mom calls after him. "Don't forget that you're taking the PSAT on Saturday. Are you still planning to ride with the Rosenbergs?"

Stephen's voice fades as he moves up the stairs.

Mom comes back into the kitchen with a stack of used plates, her lower lip pinched between her teeth. Then Aidan comes in carrying his own and Dave's used bowls to the sink. I back away and lean against the counter, watching him.

He turns on the faucet.

Mom says, "You don't have to, Aidan."

"It's okay. I kind of like doing dishes."

Mom scrapes marinara sauce into a glass bowl. "So you two go to school together," she says. "Have you been in any classes together?"

"Oh yes," I say. "All of them. At recess we plait flowers into each other's hair."

Aidan gives a small cough. "It's a pretty big place," he says. "But actually I did meet Michaela—"

"Mickey."

His eyes flick up at me. "—Mickey. We met at Dave's poetry reading, the one on campus a couple weeks ago. You came in at the end."

I frown. Because I do remember the night in question. About a week, maybe a week and a half ago, my much-vaunted (in certain select, poetry-reading circles) brother gave a reading at the university. Being my brother, he's lost his license due to a third DUI. He required the services of a pro bono chauffeur, which inevitably ends up being me. I waited two hours in the parking lot but there were still people clustered around him when I went in to fetch him. He was leaning an elbow on the podium, his hair falling in his eyes, laughing. He may have pointed this wall-eyed stranger out to me. He could have pointed Elijah reincarnated out to me. I was too busy concentrating on dragging him away from his personal paradise of wattle-chinned geriatric poetry fans to notice.

"Oh, that's nice," Mom says. "Michaela, you didn't tell me you knew him."

"How odd," I say. "He made such a lasting impression."

But Aidan is watching me. He doesn't blink, doesn't look away. He's holding a half-rinsed dish, and soap suds plink into the sink basin.

I shrug, but it feels more like a squirm. "Sorry." I don't even know why I'm apologizing

He blinks then, and turns back to the sink. "No problem." He starts rinsing again. Slots the bowl in the dish drainer.

"I asked your brother about you," he says. "Earlier. After we met."

"Oh, Jesus. You're not obsessed with me, are you? Do you want to have sex with me or something?"

"Honey," Mom says.

"What? It's a legitimate question." To Aidan, I say, "*Are* you?"

"No."

"Michaela, sweetie, that's not—"

"He doesn't mind," I say.

"I don't mind," Aidan says. "It's just part of your condition. Right? Saying things that are offensive?"

There's a brief silence.

Mom says, "Oh, well, that's not—"

"Mom," I say, "Go away. You're doing that thing, that *gooey* thing. Everything's fine."

She tosses the towel on the counter and walks out of the kitchen. She makes a wide path around me and she doesn't look back. Her mouth is so thin it looks like a pink thread stitched across her face and the skin around her eyes is flushed like an overripe peach.

Aidan says, "Did we offend your mom?"

I sigh and rub my hand over my mouth. I pick up the towel and wipe off the counter. "I don't understand why people take offense. If something's only going to upset them, they could just not care."

"Unless their feelings got hurt," he says. There's a short pause. He rinses off another dish and puts it on the rack. "Dave said that you don't really—you don't really *do* feelings."

For a second I don't know what to say. "I have them. Feelings." But that seems inadequate, somehow. Untruthful. So I add, "Sometimes."

Aidan looks over his shoulder. The left side of his face is toward me and his bad eye dances crazily.

I'm uncomfortable with his staring but it doesn't feel as awful as other people's. He looks like he's waiting, like he's a chess player watching for my next move, not like he's trying to peel my skin back and break open the plates of my skull. For some reason, I find myself talking, the words pouring out like I've unstoppered a drain. "People don't feel the right things. That's the problem. They get—you know, everyone feels all this, all this junk, just messy, squabbly emotions over the smallest things. Like if someone says a political word at dinner, or forgets someone's name. Those are stupid fucking things to care about. No one cares about the bigger things. You can—people just, you know, they watch all this shit on TV every night, bombings, and drone attacks, and disease, and no one melts down over that. But that's—at least that's *real*."

My voice fades.

Aidan doesn't say anything for a while. He turns back to the sink and starts washing spoons.

"So you're getting a PhD?"

It surprises me, the question. Like some art major is more interested in the higher echelons of my intellectual ability than in my sordid, dog-mutilating psychoses. People are usually more morbid. I nod. But his back is to me now. So I say, "Yes."

"Dave said you were the smartest person he knows. He said you could've joined Mensa."

I laugh.

Aidan looks up.

"I'm not that smart."

He looks at me like he's trying to figure something out. "Are you being modest?"

"No. I don't do modest. I'm smart. I'm really smart. Just not, you know, Mensa-smart. I'm not a genius."

"Dave said you were."

Dave has always had an inflated sense of my capacities. I think it's just part of his love of cheap melodrama. "Well then. I must be."

He nods once and goes back to washing off the spoons.

"Seriously." I put my hands in my jeans pockets and lean against the counter. "What's your deal? Why the twenty questions? They're not—you're not like most people."

For one, he didn't run out shrieking and crying in the middle of dinner.

"I told you," he says. "I remembered you. From the reading."

"Bullshit." I've had this happen a few times. People noticing how I look. Then they talk to me. That's usually when the interest wanes, and it wanes like that Roadrunner cartoon where the Coyote runs off the edge of the cliff and then notices there is nothing but air beneath him. "You shouldn't still be interested, not after Dave told you about me."

Aidan shuts off the water and shakes his fingers over the sink. He comes over to the refrigerator to grab a hand towel. I step away from him. He looks at me, one eye straight and fierce, the other a dark aimless orb. "You want the truth?" he says. He's standing so close I can feel his body heat, smell garlic and wine on his breath. I want to back up but I can't. My ass is already pressed up against the counter. "I want you to solve a murder."

My chest feels empty and then my heart starts to beat, each convulsion burning. My mouth goes dry.

"Jesus," I whisper. "*Christ*."

He looks a little surprised. His eyebrows rise and he takes a half step back.

"Not an open case." He starts talking quickly. "It's not illegal. It was a while ago, like a cold case. The cops already closed it. But—"

I shake my head. "Wait. Stop."

He stops talking.

"The cops know about it?"

For a second he looks even more confused. His forehead wrinkles slightly. "Sure. It was a long time ago. It—my mother. It was when I was a kid. My mother died. The cops say—well, it's technically unsolved, they thought it might be homicide but they didn't have evidence to—"

"No."

He backs up another step. "What?"

I push myself off the counter. "I don't know what you're talking about. There's no—there's no dead woman."

"What?"

We just stare at each other. I try to figure out what's going on. Who he is, this frail, pale-skinned art student with a broken eye. And the incalculable odds that his fascination with me and his mysterious murder have nothing to do with the pink message slip, with 411 Allyn Street.

I take a breath. "You're talking about—about someone who died a long time ago?"

"Yes," he says. "My mother. She died ten years ago."

I look down at the floor, then back at him. "You're mentally fucking challenged. Dave *told* you about me. Why the fuck would you think it's a good idea to come to me, to try to—to get me involved with a dead body? With fucking murder, or suicide, or whatever it is? This is—you're playing with, not fire, God, you're playing with unstable isotopes in a nuclear reactor. Do you understand that? Do you *get* it?"

"I get it." He doesn't even blink. "I didn't really buy most of what Dave said. And now I've met you, I think it was mostly just crap. I think you're more normal than he said. You've got emotions. You just don't . . . you know. Coddle people."

"I don't—what the fuck are you talking about?"

He says, "I want someone who's not afraid of truth. Of hurting people."

I take a step toward him. My heart is pounding and my head feels weightless, my skull like crepe paper. "This isn't a joke. You should be afraid of me."

And his face cracks into a smile. He gives a snort that turns into a laugh, a cough-like bark of happiness surprised out of him.

"Are you kidding?" He grins. "Why would I be afraid of you?"

I can't breathe. And then I reach out and shove my hands against his chest. He stumbles back a step, his eyes opening wide with shock.

I go around and him fling open the door.

It's cold, the air snatching at my skin. My sneakers hit the gravel drive with a crunch.

I'm halfway down the drive when I realize I didn't even shut the door behind me. When I look back over my shoulder he's standing there in the door, looking after me, hugging his arms around his chest like some penitent cenobite. The kitchen light limns his silhouette in gold.

FIVE

I startle awake. A milky glaze of moonlight across the ravaged sheet. My shirt is soaked through. Even my hair is damp. His skin felt rubbery, moisture seeping through the dead pores. I can feel crusted spinal fluid and coagulated blood under my fingernails. I showered and washed my hands three times and they still have that salt and damp soil smell.

I jerk upright and kick off the sheet. Wipe my hands on my T-shirt. My neck and chest itch. I scratch at my skin. It feels gritty. I'm still in my clothes. After I ran out of the house, I just kept running until the cold made me turn back.

And then I must have fallen asleep without undressing.

I bury my face in the pillow and try to calm down from the dream. But with my eyes closed the only thing I can see is the raw pink-gray sheet of veined skin, the only thing I can smell is that syrupy sweet rot of dried blood.

I scramble up and change into running shorts and a warm sweatshirt and I run through the darkest hour, the hour when humans' circadian rhythms ebb lowest, when the world is asleep and I am alive. I run beneath a piebald predawn sky. I run until my lungs are burning, until the inside of my head is finally calm, swept clean in a breathless gray haze of oxygen deprivation and glycogen depletion.

My calf muscles twitch. Sunlight turns the insides of my eyelids a pulpy reddish-orange. I open my eyes. I'm lying on my mattress, my sports bra and running shorts crisp. My arms powdered with a white salty residue from dried sweat. I sit up. My left calf spasms. I rub my knuckles into the muscle and remember going for a run at, what was it? Five in the morning? And I remember suddenly what woke me up before. The smell. Viscous fluid, my fingernail peeling the—no, the eye belonged to the man I killed when I was ten.

I lie back on the mattress and rest my forearm over my eyes. Dried sweat crystals burn the mucus membranes around my eyes. Fluid collects in the corners of my eyes and leaks down my nose. I'm too tired to run anymore. My legs hurt. Christ.

It doesn't matter how much I run. How much I follow rules and teach my classes and write my dissertation. How much I show up for family dinners and make conversation. The dreams come back.

I used to think that every year that passed, every year that I lived like an ordinary person, I was like a snake growing larger than its skin. Like I could walk out of one life and into the body of a different person, like a snake sloughing off its papery shell.

But the dreams always come back. And I always wake up the same.

When I was eleven, I died and came back to life.

My life the previous year, after I got out of the psych unit, had been a series of frantic visits to psychiatrists who laid tattered stuffed bunny rabbits on my lap and told me to talk to them, then prescribed medications. Long hours in gray offices spent staring at primary-colored Lego and Fisher Price toys. I asked for my brother but he was in school, dear, he can't come play with you now. What do you play, when you are with your brother? Does your brother *touch* you when you play?

Assholes.

The visits faded in intensity. Days between shrinks grew longer. My parents' voices regained a measure of lucidity. My brother's laughter grew less manic, his eyes less wary and white-rimmed.

At the end of the year the baby was born. Grandparents in the house. Fat happy women from Mom's Pilates class and gourd-dry academics from Dad's department. I stayed in my room. Only Dave ventured inside. He budged out the rocking chair I'd shoved in front of the door to bring me white cake with chocolate frosting and to laugh at the decapitated stuffed animals under my pillow.

Months passed. And then in June, a year, more than a year since my first murder, we packed a lunch of pastrami and cheddar sandwiches, baked chips, apple slices. We drove north to Lake Erie to have a picnic on the dirty sand of Mentor Headlands, a cigarette-strewn beach flocked with squabbling seagulls. The water greenblack and vast under a serried gray sky. Cold and endless. Icy yellow foam raced along the sand and we ran through it, my brother and I, our bare feet aching in the cold water. Cloud-shadows skittered like animate inkstains over the crinkled skin of the water.

When they called us in from the water we came flushed, seaweed lacing our toes and our fingers pruned and smelling like rancid fish and old cheese. My mother sat with her knees tilted to the side, a nubby cotton sundress tucked between her thighs, a soft blanket draped over her shoulder. The baby underneath. My father with his pants rolled to his calves, bulbous blue veins prominent on his thin legs. He was reading a book on analytic geometry, his glasses lying in the sand at his side. They looked at us, lips stretching, pushing skin into shapes and angles that were unfamiliar to me. I thought it was happiness.

"You were having fun."

"Is that a crime?" Dave flung himself by my mother and reached his cold fingers to touch the baby's toes. The baby's leg kicked. My mother touched Dave's face.

"Watch it, young man," she said and smiled.

He kissed the baby's toes. Smiled up at her with eyes like Loki, full of a canny joy.

I went away from them down the shore.

And I saw the shape of me walking, growing smaller and smaller on the filthy beach. The earth tipped sideways and I slid off into an airless abyss.

Heat swept over me. I burned from the inside out. My bones shimmered through clear gelatinous flesh. The luminescent sac of my body, emptied of its flesh, slipped off the pebbly sand and drifted up and up through darkness and white light and more dark blacker than the center of nothingness.

And I gasped and opened my eyes. A sick pain bubbled up in my gut. My intestines were a wriggling mass of diseased worms. The taste of vomit caked the insides of my teeth. Everything hurt, a raw weeping pain at the base of my jaw emanating out like tidepool ripples.

And noise, and the stench of burning tires.

The paramedics said it was a seizure. My mother was crying and patting the baby, bouncing it, heedless of the tiny chin knocking against her collarbone.

A woman who smelled like strawberries and talc, her nipples pressing out against her pastel green smock, bent over me in the emergency room and shone a small light in my eyes. A doctor with breath that smelled like peanut butter said it was an idiopathic tonic-clonic seizure, that four out of every hundred children experience them before adolescence. They put me through an MRI and I didn't mind it. It felt cold and smelled like plastic and aerosol bleach. I knew that the universe smelled like bleach and charred bone and the scent reminded me of my miracle.

A medical attendant asked why I was smiling and I said that I had died and been raised again and my soul was clean.

On Monday I was back in the psychiatrist's office with a stuffed rabbit on my lap.

I am a pragmatist and so—at least during my waking hours—I no longer believe in miracles or in resurrection. It was a fantasy my mind created to cope, not with the murderer lurking in my eleven-year-old brain, as the shrink suggested, but with my inability to remain on the same stretch of sand with a smiling mother, a nursing brother, a contented father. I think I realized then, in my fumbling, prepubescent way, that I was a demon changeling, the kid who would fuck them up, all of them, for the rest of their lives. An abscess that would never heal.

As an adult, I understand about the seizure, although I never had a seizure again (roughly 60 percent of children who have idiopathic seizures never have another one). Even then at the age of the eleven I was quick to suspect that I had not *actually* died and come alive again. And anyway, even if I had, resurrection is a shitty deal. Because I was returned to this mortal sphere exactly the same as I left it. My first reincarnation was no marked improvement from the original model.

And I realized that my particular flawed brain would not change appreciably on its own. So I created the dialogues in my head, the rules, the obsessive running. It is the only way I know to do it, to fake like I'm an ordinary person. I sleep in a garage and I go to work and I say stupid shit to people so that they leave me alone but I never lay a hand on them. I pay my taxes and keep my dreams to myself and if people touch me I may howl like a talk show host but I don't take a kitchen knife to them.

After half a lifetime, this game is second nature.

SIX

I shower and dress and drive to campus. The class I teach meets on Tuesdays and Thursdays, which means that I don't have to teach or go to the office today. Days that I don't teach I work in the library, researching for my dissertation. When I climb the shallow steps to the library I pass through a mist of cigarette smoke around the pebbled ashpits. The smokers chatter like blue jays.

Upstairs, I unlock my study carrel and sit down. I square the edges of the stack of books, arrange a yellow legal pad in front of me, line up my pens. Then I pull over an Old English dictionary and a pocket verb guide. On the other side of the legal pad I smooth out a copy of an Old English manuscript page. The Xeroxed copy of a vellum manuscript is smudgy and gray. I take notes, looking up words, declining verbs.

My life is like an encyclopedia, a structured taxonomy of proper social behaviors and daily functions to which I adhere like a human-sized strip of duct tape.

The filigree of ancient Latin script blurs.

I put the pen down and push over the pile of books. They slither down the desk, collapse like a minor avalanche to the floor. The thin volume of German philosophy sits isolated on the shelf. But I don't know what else I can discover by opening it to the missing page again. The book was never checked out. I don't have any way to place a mind behind the missing page. Only the evidence of its absence. And I burnt the page itself.

I don't know who wanted me to find the body. I do know I should leave it alone, leave it—fuck, call the cops, be done with the whole hideous thing already. But how do I do that without ruining everything I've constructed over the years?

If I can figure out *who* it is, or at least *why*, I can go to the proper authorities then.

But how do I find out anything? I've arrived at a dead end. A dead end—I grimace and rub my fingers over my temples. My head hurts.

The dead body. That's it. That unsheathed carcass once possessed a mind. The mind holds its own secrets in death. How does a person go about deducing the physical identity of a body when the obvious things like a wallet or dog tags aren't likely to present themselves?

I figure a cop would go back to the house, look for trace physical evidence, receipts, clothing tags, shoe size. Collect forensic samples. And wear sunglasses at night. That's what they do in those cop shows, anyway.

Cop shows. The police. I think the police department keeps public records of people who go missing, or at least they do for kids. Those flyers of missing kids are plastered all over Walmart entrances.

I type quickly, pull up the Akron Police Department webpage. Ah, yes. A link for reported missing persons. I scroll through the lists of names, only opening up the files on male names with ages between twenty-five and fifty-five. Clicking on posters with pixilated faces staring blankly back at the world, looking for features that might belong to a man who is only a vague impression of porous, wax-slick skin, attached lower earlobes, and gray-streaked lank brown hair. I read through descriptions. Tattoos, scars, complexions, eye and hair color.

Then one of the posters makes me pause. James A. Sims, Caucasian male, thirty-four, brown hair, blue eyes, no scars or tattoos, epileptic, no permanent address. A note at the bottom of the poster claims that MP could not contact his only known living relative, a sister. The face in the grainy photograph is several years out of date. Wide, unfocused eyes, a button-down shirt, a thin neck with a prominent Adam's apple. I squint and move my face close to the laptop screen. His earlobes are attached.

His neck is so thin. The shirt hanging on a frame that must have been underweight. I close my eyes and try to remember the corpse but all I see are rough brown-gray spinal knobs, whitish pink flesh clinging to the underside of the skin.

I realize how stupid I am. I wasn't paying attention. I'm not an investigator. Whoever left the notes for me was not asking me to solve a crime. It was the string dangled in front of the bored cat. Cats don't care who dangles the string. They only care that they are the ones who demolish the string.

My fingers move across the keyboard, opening new searches. Websites devoted to butchering. The correct way to hold a hunting knife. Directions for killing and draining an animal. Slit the jugular. Or sever the spinal column at the weak area where it joins the skull plates. My fingers go to the back of my neck, press against the skin at the base of my skull.

The thing is, I don't even know what the *point* of that message in my mailbox was. What was I meant to figure out when I went to that house? *Who* killed the man, or *how* he was killed? The how is easier. At least, it's easier for me to remember the look of that skin, the shredded edges as if a serrated blade had chewed through the skin. Of course it would be, for a person of my proclivities and neural condition. How would I possibly be expected to deduce human motivations? So I think this is what I'm meant to see and understand—the killing itself. But that seems so pointless. What possible motivation could a person have for tempting me into the dark recesses of my broken mind with a trail of once-human breadcrumbs?

I wonder if I could kill a person. An odd thought. It's one thing I've known since I was ten, that I could kill a person. But not like this. Not using my hands to wield their dooms, not putting my fingers on the body and carving into it. The thought of that—a part of me does want to know what it feels like, to slice through skin like my mother slices through a pink ham, the thick meat ripping at the toothed knife blade. I shiver. And then I realize that I don't want to kill anyone. I want to feel what it is like, but I don't want to wake up the next morning knowing who I am, knowing what I've done, for the rest of my life. I already know how it feels to walk everywhere, to run, to sleep, with the weight of it like a homunculus crouched inside your chest. I don't think I've inhaled fully since I was ten years old.

I slam the laptop shut and stand up. It's a bit of a relief, actually.

To know there are limits to my depravity.

The house on Allyn Street is a clapboard two-story, built in the 1950s when the city burgeoned with textile and tire factories. The Chevelle's idling engine vibrates through the coiled springs supporting the driver's seat. My hands grip the wheel, even though the parking brake is on. My knuckles are white. I swallow and close my eyes. Not looking at the house, at the boarded-over window. Not thinking about what lies inside that room, on that narrow metal-framed bed.

I felt strong, realizing that I didn't want to kill anyone, that staring at the mutilated body didn't send me hurtling past logic and the ability to think in the future tense about consequences. And because I felt strong, I came back. But now my body is undergoing some strange physiological reaction.

When I got out of the psych unit, the shrink who put me on a low dose of anti-anxiety medication didn't wait long enough. The new meds, combined with an antipsychotic that hadn't cleared my bloodstream, sent my nervous system into overdrive. I felt my brain dissolve. Ants crawled through my veins. My blood went sluggish and my muscles got lax and heavy, but my skin shivered and my heart raced. I felt like a hummingbird trapped in a polar bear's body.

I feel like that now. Like metal toothpicks prick up and down my arms. My skin twitches but the muscles are dull, leaden. I want to know who he is, the man handcuffed to the bed in the room with the Victorian bureau and the dusty floorboards. I can't move. Can't slow my heartbeat.

Well. I'm here anyway. I reach for the door handle. Anything that happens, from this point forward, I have done by opening this door. I know this is true, but nothing feels real. Even the air when I climb out has the weightless blank quality of a dream.

The house's side door is still ajar and the dark slit between the wood slab and frame makes my stomach feel strange, like I might throw up or start laughing too loudly. The house is like a cracked eggshell, all the ripe insides turning rotten.

Afternoon sun shines warm on the side of my face. When I close my eyes briefly it turns my eyelids the color of pink Zinfandel. I shouldn't be here, not in daylight. Shouldn't be here at all.

I open my eyes and pull the door open.

The house is dark, the thick stench of decay so strong that the air feels soupy. Instead of heading for the stairs I look around the first floor. A few empty rooms at the front of the house. My breath echoes faintly. The house feels still, frozen.

Empty.

The kitchen windows are all boarded over, leaving only dark behind. A tar-thick black that presses against my eyes. I get out my cell phone and touch the screen, shine the small bluish light around. The kitchen is full of shadows, gaps in the counter and cupboard blocks where the sink was removed, the refrigerator pulled out. The holes look like the result of some monstrous botched surgery, empty electric outlets staring up at me like black eyes. When I take a step into the kitchen the linoleum crackles under my sneakers like cornflakes. A gray blanket. I kneel down, careful to keep my fingers off the blanket. With the edge of my cell phone, I nudge it. Drag out a corner. It's just a blanket left balled-up in the corner. When the fabric loosens it releases a sweet rotting smell like old urine. The stink is as sweet as caramelized sugar but pungent, spicy. My eyes water.

A rustle. A small plastic baggie in the folds of blanket. When I move the blanket I see a twist of tin foil with a lump of caked yellowed gunk that looks like rosin, a faint powdery residue in a halo around it.

In the corner something glints in the watery glow from my cell phone. I go over and kick it lightly. A backpack, but not like a college student or a hiker would carry. It's pink with shiny appliqué pieces, a cartoon picture of a black-haired girl. Some cartoon character for kids.

Stephen watches cartoons sometimes and I have seen it briefly when he flips channels. The name comes to me then: Dora the Explorer.

I look around. No one would have a kid here, surely. Would they? Who would leave drugs and a kid's backpack? Someone who left in a hurry. Obviously.

There are no more rooms on the first floor and no more objects to poke at, so I head upstairs. The stairwell closes around me like crushed velvet. I run the back of my hand against the wall to keep my balance in the stygian dark.

The first door is still locked, the second one open. When I click on my cell phone and shine it around I see the bed, but for a second I think the man is gone. Then I see the white glare of the cell phone's light glinting off a handcuff, the bloated blued-white of skin, and I realize that he is still there. But someone has dragged a sheet over the corpse.

The smell in here is rancid, so thick that it coats the inside of my mouth and when I swallow I can taste rot.

Dark stains in small coin-shaped spots on the sheet. When I shine the light on them they look like oil, not blood. I think the blood has mostly drained from the body. Maybe a spleen burst open from the pressure of bloat, or some other organ gave way to decomposition.

I cough a little and bury my face in the crook of my arm. I think about the blanket downstairs, and the backpack. The contradictory treatment of the body on the bed—someone shackled him and skinned him; someone covered him with a sheet.

There are signs of habitation here, but the detritus below, the body in the bed, and the sheet over the corpse point to different people. To someone dark and rotting of soul, and to someone childish, scared. Someone unable to call the cops but driven by a desire to put the ravaged body to rest. Someone human.

According to the missing persons report, James A. Sims was mentally disturbed and had no fixed address. The unlocked door and the condemned sign on the front of the house must mark a temporary crash pad for transient people. Or, did mark it. Until someone—one of them?—turned it into a deranged artist's studio.

And the next camper discovered the house was already habited, if not by the ghost of the violently deceased, then by the ghost of future cops, detectives, and forensics teams.

A drugged-up homeless person with a Dora the Explorer backpack has more sense than I do. I don't want to touch the sheet, release any more of the rot into the air, and there is nothing left for me to find as far as I can tell. So I turn to leave. But when my hand closes over the door handle, I see something on the back of the door. I hit the screen of my cell phone so that the light brightens.

Someone has written on the back of the door, scrawled in blue ink across the once-white paint.

O, that this too too solid flesh would melt

"Sullied," I say.

My voice startles me.

For a second, breathless, I imagine the sunken eyeholes of the corpse turning in my direction. The whole world waiting for my next words.

I cough again, swallow, and duck my chin against my neck. I put my cell phone in my pocket and leave, pulling the door shut behind me. But I can still see the words in my mind, that sharp downward slanted print. *O, that this too too*—it's from *Hamlet*, of course, but most copies of the play use the word "sullied." There is some disagreement about which word Shakespeare intended, which word is a copier's error. I have always preferred "sullied."

But it occurs to me as I go carefully down the dark stairs that however sullied the corpse, it is inarguably less solid and will slowly disparate into parts, the liquid leaching out, gases escaping, the drying remains shrinking in on themselves until they turn to dust.

All flesh that was solid once will melt.

When I get outside the sun seems too bright. I stand blinking and put my hand over my face. Does my skin smell like rot? I can't tell. I can't smell anything.

It's too hard, the sunlight. My skin feels exposed. I'm a fool for coming back. I don't know what I thought I would find.

I don't know how—God, *how*?—my mystery murderer knew I would come back. Or were those words there before, and I just didn't see them?

My memory is unreliable and I'm so used to relying on my mind, the cold mechanisms of it flawless as steel and hard as adamantine. It's all soft in my head now. Disintegrating.

I cross the street to the Chevelle and pull my keys out. My breath suddenly comes so fast that my vision clouds over and my muscles soften, as if they've turned to tapioca. I sag against the hood and close my eyes, the black painted metal under me sturdy and sunwarmed.

When I finally open my eyes I look out at a world not terribly changed. The house across from the secret mausoleum has a red and blue rental sign hammered into the front lawn. Dirt is ground into the cracked sidewalk so that it looks like ribbons of black. The houses on either side of the street are running to decay, blank faced, obtuse. Blind to the defiled relict in their midst. Or does each slant-poled edifice hide its own cankerous secrets?

I turn over my left hand, look at the cell phone. I know now that my own spore will not be so noticeable, not if the house is or was being used as an ad hoc homeless shelter. And there are the words on the door. People study handwriting, specialists do. City detectives could analyze the strokes and determine the author. No one would know it was me who made the call. No, they will. They will trace the call and I have no reason at all to be here. But still, there is evidence there. I should call. My thumb presses the 9. But why me? How am I complicit in this? It was done for me, with me in mind, at the very least. I press the 1. I don't want to know the answers. I want to have never found that pink message slip. I want to go back to the garage and wake up innocent. I don't care if I was bored. I was good, or at least, I wasn't standing on the cusp of damnation with nothing but air underneath.

"Mickey?"

I freeze.

And look up, slowly.

He is wearing a hooded sweatshirt with the hood pulled over his head and he is no longer haloed by the kitchen light, but I recognize him anyway. That sparrow-frail build, the diffident stance, the pale skin.

Aidan is on the sidewalk, hands in his jeans pockets, looking at me from under his hood.

"What are you doing here?"

I turn my phone over, slide it into my jacket pocket. I straighten up.

He doesn't back up. Doesn't turn his head to look across the street in any startled gestures of guilt. I think that all of those cop shows are wrong. No one starts confessing with the reckless abandon born of stage directions.

I wait for him to glance inadvertently to his left, toward the house across the street. He doesn't move, just keeps staring at me. It's like a western, the showdown scene. Only it's really cold and my nose is running. I wipe my nose on my wrist.

At my gesture, he takes a few steps toward me, stops before he reaches the car. He puts his head to the side like a sparrow spotting a worm. "Is this about what I said? The murder?"

I don't say anything. He has no tells, no subtle tics or movements in the direction of the corpse not a hundred yards away.

"You know I didn't mean to scare you or anything. I mean, I'm not saying you're scared, but if you came here because—" He breaks off. Then he says, "How *did* you know where I live? Did your brother tell you?"

"My brother?" I didn't intend to say anything but the words are startled out of me. And then, "You live here?"

He scratches his nose with his thumb. "Well, yeah," he says. "He came by a couple times."

"You *know* know him. My brother." I thought it was just a meeting at a poetry event. I thought Aidan was obsessed with me. But no, I'm being foolish. It would make so much more sense if it's my brother he's after, at least from a sexually motivated perspective.

"That doesn't—nothing makes sense." I didn't mean to say that out loud. I push myself off the hood of my car. "Why would I come here about a murder?"

He just looks at me. Shrugs. "Why else are you here? I just figured you were, I don't know. Interested."

"Why would I be interested?"

He swallows, inhales. Says in a rush, "You're telling me a murder doesn't interest you?"

"Jesus," I say.

He blinks twice and looks down at the sidewalk. He doesn't look to his left. Or anywhere else. Then he says, "Okay. I just thought you were here to see me."

I point my finger at the for rent sign. "I'm house hunting," I say. "Real estate."

He smiles a little. Then he stops smiling. "I can't tell if you're joking."

For a second, I am transported—caught up in the hypothetical world in which I am not here playing corpse voyeur and amateur detective, but here for a perfectly prosaic and functional adult reason. A hypothetical world Aidan apparently finds at least partially plausible.

I think about what would happen if it were true, if I told my parents I was leaving the garage. Moving out. Becoming an independent adult.

"Maybe I am," I say.

"Okay." He shrugs again. "Well, you can come on up."

"What?"

He says, "Do you want to see it or not?"

"Do I want to see what?"

He pushes his hood back and rubs his palm over his hair. It's sweaty, dark strands like question marks glued to his forehead. "If you want to rent it," he says, "shouldn't you see it first?'

"You *own* it?"

"God, no," he says. "I'm renting it. But my roommate moved out and I can't afford the whole rent, so—" He waves his hand vaguely at the house. I look over at it, study it for the first time. The house is large, a graying clapboard with faded blue shutters subdivided into apartments. Beside the front door a black mailbox has white stenciled numbers: 412½. It directly faces 411 Allyn Street.

"It's Apartment B," he says, watching me study the place. "The upstairs."

A wooden staircase trails up the outside wall to the upper-floor apartment.

"So, do you want to come up or not?"

"No." I shake my head and look away. I was joking, I almost say. I am here about something else entirely. Aidan never looked across the street. I won't look either. But the shaking is coming back. I feel panic climbing up my throat like a centipede. "I should—I need to go. I'm late."

He coughs and shakes his head. "Look, I'm really sorry if I scared you or anything. I didn't mean to."

"I'm not *scared*," I say. "I don't *get* scared." I wrap my hand around the keys in case it's still shaking.

"Okay," he says. "Well. You can come over if you want. It doesn't have to be about renting the place."

I don't know what an obsessed person looks like. He looks calm, his mouth relaxed. But I don't know what his game is. "Stop this," I say. And I don't know what I mean.

I turn away from him, fumble with the door, heave the heavy construction open.

When I climb in the car, his mouth moves. I can't hear him but I recognize the words.

Bye, Mickey.

He gives a brief wave with his hand.

After I drive off I realize that I have pushed the delete call button on my phone and erased the almost-dialed call.

SEVEN

I drive south, past my parents' house to the running trail in a metro park near the Cuyahoga Valley. My skin feels like it's going to crawl off my skeleton if I can't run fast and hard enough to pull my body back into some sort of order.

I think about the corpse, about the faceless homeless person who pulled a sheet over a mutilated body, a gesture so startlingly kind it makes my jaw hurt from clenching. I think about that stained sheet like a sacred shroud cast over a festering orgy of desecration. I think about the red and blue RE/MAX sign and Aidan's sudden apparition, a gray-hooded specter, a human *deus ex machina*. I think about my parents' garage and the stench of burning paper. I think about the smell of hot piss and how I stared at the wax-smooth skin of a man I had just murdered and wondered if I was supposed to feel something.

I run until the trail fades onto great slabs of slate rock, a vast shelf slanting up to a steep drop-off. Crouched at the stone lip of the precipice, I prop my hands on my knees, panting.

Scarlet and brown peaks and hollows of the valley spread out beneath masses of dark clouds piled against the western horizon. The whole earth is beneath me. If I could stretch my arms and lift off I would fly into the cold and limitless gray and be clean forever.

On the way back a low ripple of thunder curdles the air. The first drops of rain taste like rust and salt. I like running in the rain. The noise and the stinging slap of wet running clothes drown out everything else. I almost feel calm by the time I get back to the car.

When I return home I go through the garage into the house. I wipe my hands over my face and flick away the droplets.

The house breathes. Muted noises. Human voices.

I go through the kitchen and dining room into the solarium.

Stephen and another teenage boy I don't recognize are in the living room. The strange boy turns his head sharply, stares at me from behind plastic-framed glasses, his moist pink lips slack. Stephen ignores me and slouches his spine lower on the couch. He twiddles the control in his hand and his avatar on the TV screen jumps across a dark chasm.

"You." I point at the pale teenager. "Quit staring. And you. Where are the parents?"

Stephen says without looking at me, "I dunno."

A distant voice calls: "Mickey? Honey, is that you?"

I look at Stephen. "Thank you, brother. Your usefulness is overwhelming."

He shrugs.

The friend watches me, thumb immobile over the control. His eyes track me as I leave the room. I can feel the heat of his gaze and it itches between my shoulder blades.

My mother is in the basement sorting laundry. The fresh cottony scent of her detergent has seeped into the kitchen.

I stand at the top of the stairs, resting my palms against the doorjamb and looking at the carpeted wooden slats descending into shadow. Beneath the smell of the laundry detergent, I taste lingering traces of stranger scents: dust, macaroni and cheese, urine. I haven't gone down those basement steps since that day when I was ten years old and met my first corpse at the bottom. Harmony of the spheres. I swallow a hysterical laugh and back away from the basement. I sit on a stool at the kitchen island and wait for her to emerge from the basement with a plastic laundry basket on her hip.

She smiles when she comes up.

"Hi, there." Her smile fades. "You're wet. You should dry off before you catch a cold."

"Did you ever want me to move out?"

She falters. "What?"

"Of the garage. Do you and Dad have these fantasies where I'll suddenly be like, Hey, I'm a fully grown woman with a PhD. I think I'll rent a two-bedroom condo in Cleveland for a while, maybe go vegan and raise some cacti."

"You want to raise cacti?" She sets down the laundry basket and puts her arms around her middle.

"Of course not," I say. "You're missing the point."

"No—no, I think—oh, honey, your father and I have talked about it, of course, but—and you *are* doing well. Recently. I mean, at least from what I've seen, especially in the past few months, you've seemed—happier." She shakes her head. "But you know we love having you here. That's not a problem. There's no need to—you should never feel like your father or I would ever pressure you to do anything, or to make decisions out of a need to. . . Sweetie, I'm saying you should move at your own pace. Don't ever think we would pressure you to do things you're not ready for."

I smile a little. I am getting cold, just standing here with the basement door open. I rub my arms. "God, you make me sound like a recovering cancer victim." I wave a hand to forestall her anxious protests. "But I get the message. Thanks. I was just wondering."

I go into my garage and shut the door and sit down on the mattress. My sneakers leave dark wet patches on the concrete. My cell phone is lying on my pillow. I have four missed calls, and two messages. Three of the four calls are from Dave. One is from a number I don't recognize.

I listen to the messages. The first voice is so quiet I unconsciously lean forward to hear better. But even without hearing the words I recognize the voice.

"Hey, Mickey, it's Aidan. I got your number from your brother. I just wanted to apologize again if—" Some words are lost altogether as the sound of a siren goes by in the distance. "Sorry," his voice says in my ear. "I'm—walking to class and it's loud. Anyway, that was all I wanted to say. Bye."

I delete the message and stand up to stretch and shower. I just can't figure out what he's after.

The next message comes on and even with the phone lying on the bed I can hear the digitalized squawking. My brother is not one for dulcet tones.

"Jesus *fucking* Christ, Mickey," he's shouting. "Just got a call from your new fucking *boy*friend! Did you put Ro*hyp*nol in his drink yesterday? God in *fuck*ing heaven, babe, he had, like, fifty questions about you, does Mickey do this, why did Mickey come see me, did you give her my address—"

He's laughing but he's not usually so loud if he's not angry. I pick up the phone but don't put it to my ear. My thumb covers the delete key. I wonder why he's angry, but then think that maybe he brought Aidan home for his own purposes and for the first time in his life has been cockblocked by a sibling. The thought almost makes me smile. But I remember that Aidan's interest in me has nothing to do with the sordid minidramas of suburban American life and I swallow hard.

Dave is still talking. I push my thumb down. *Message deleted.*

I am almost finished stretching when my cell phone starts buzzing again.

I pick it up. "Are you mad at me or something?"

He sucks in a breath, and I think hearing my real voice startled him. From the short silence I can tell he was working his way up to a dramatic crescendo for my voicemail and I've broken his rhythm.

When he starts talking, he sounds normal, his voice light and happy. "*God*, no, my darling. Why would I be *mad* at you? I just don't want to see that sweet little boy—*crushed* by your machinations. Do you like that? I think *machinations* has the right *mech*anized feel—"

"Don't do that." I hate when he gets metaphysical. Or maybe it's metapoetic. Meta-anything, really. "I didn't do anything. Not to him."

"Not to him." Dave's voice mimics mine so perfectly that it startles me. He's always been a good mimic, but in his mouth my voice sounds so—melodic. Feminine. It disconcerts me. I always feel like my voice should sound more like broken glass. "That's not the real problem, though, is it?" He's back to his normal voice. "The *real* problem we find ourselves confronted with is your little *sojourn* this afternoon. Into the bowels, as it were, the belly of the beast. The beast, in this metaphor, being our metropolis, the summit of our acme, Akron. The point is—"

"You're high." I should've figured that earlier. I pinch the skin between my eyebrows. "Christ." I hate it when he is like this.

"*High*?" And he's shouting again, suddenly. I move the phone away from my ear. "What the fucking *shit* does that have to do with anything? Are you *try*ing to distract me? We need to discuss why you would hunt down little Aidan, if that's even what you were doing. What else could you be doing there? *What else were you doing there?*"

His anger pisses me off. He knows how much I hate yelling. I hear my own voice rising to match his, fighting back against his decibels with my own. "I was looking at his fucking rental property. I'm moving out. That's what!"

There's a short silence.

Then Dave says, "No you weren't."

"You don't know everything about me. I'm not a pet rock, I'm not a fucking joke, the kid who never grows up, never changes—I change. I grow up."

I see corpses and I don't melt, I don't collapse into madness.

He laughs. "No you don't," he says. "Who's telling you this? Is it Aidan? Did he tell you you were a joke?"

Oh, God. I am different. I feel something weightless and buoyant in my chest. I put a palm against my heart and feel it beating, steady and solid.

I just realized where that strange fantasy about moving out came from.

I have looked into the abyss and nothing has crawled out to take up residence in my mortal shell. I have seen my second corpse and I am not descending into a replay of the madness after I encountered my first.

I say, "No. This is me talking. No one else. Me."

Dave says, "Well, good. I'll fucking slice his throat if he does. No one talks to you that way."

I smile at that. "You do. Sometimes."

He starts to laugh again. "Okay, touché, you got me on that one, babe. But you know I love you. I would never do anything to hurt you."

"Quit yelling at me, then."

There's a brief quiet. And then, in a whisper, he says, "Anything for you, princess." And then he starts laughing loudly.

I hang up the phone.

After my shower I still feel anxious so I go out to work on the Chevelle. The car sits under the slanting raw wood carport roof and it smells faintly of sap and cold soil. The hood propped up, the smell of axle grease and WD-40, the gravel chips crunching under my sneakers like broken teeth—it feels good. So after I replace a spark plug and a couple of worn cylinder heads I keep tinkering, finally decide what the hell, I'll replace the whole intake manifold. I'll have to order parts online.

While I lie on my back on the gravel, my hands caked in grit and oil and the smell of burnt rubber and oxidized steel all around me, I think about Dave and wonder how he sees me. When he first came back to Ohio he kept asking me to move in with him, kept saying that I was an adult now and it was time to act like one, not to keep hiding in the garage like I was ashamed of something that happened when I was ten. And when I was eighteen. Well. Any time I left the house, basically. He stopped asking after a while.

I think about my mother's delicate panic. I wonder if they are right. They probably are. They know me better than anyone, apart from my childhood shrinks. The accounting of my life is a simple line in the ledger of human history. It does not add up to much.

But the man in the house on Allyn Street is already dead. It seems to me there is little that I can do to make things worse, to fuck up his life any more than it is already fucked. And if I do nothing, whoever targeted me with that note might try again, might kill someone else. If I do nothing, I might become a proxy murderer. If I do something I could save a life. There is a Jewish proverb that if you save one life, you save the world.

I have, by the mathematics implicit in that proverb, already wrought the destruction of the planet. If I pull anything from the ashes of my own deeds, it will likely be some pernicious, mutated thing not capable of saving anyone.

But at least I will have done something. I wonder if there is some way to balance a ledger with a single column.

I wash my hands with orange-scented grease-cutting soap, rubbing the granules into my skin around the nail beds. Then I sit on my mattress and pick up my phone. I scroll through missed calls and hit dial.

After two rings, Aidan picks up. His voice is quiet, but it tilts up at the end with curiosity.

"Mickey? Is that you?"

"Were you serious?" I say. "About needing a roommate."

There's a short silence. "What do you mean?"

"I want to know if you're serious about wanting a roommate."

"I guess so," he says. "I like where I live. It's really close to campus." Each word sounds like he's pronouncing it while taking another step onto crackling ice.

"You said my brother told you about me. Did he tell you about my other roommate? The cutter?"

"Yeah." Another pause. "Look, I don't—"

"Are you scared of me? Scared to live with me, I mean."

"No."

That one word is the only thing he says that sounds confident.

"Okay, then," I say.

"Okay then, what?"

"Okay, I'll move in with you."

"*What*?"

"If you're okay with that."

"Geez," he says. He starts to say something a couple times. The silence stretches.

"I can pay rent," I say. "I have a job, and I have some savings."

"Oh," he says. "I mean, yeah. No. That's great."

"Do I have to sign a lease?"

"Not really. The landlord gives us month-to-month leases here. You just have to get credit approval. But you have to sign this asbestos waiver. I think the house was painted before 1970 or something."

I have no idea what he's talking about. "I might screw this up," I say. "After the last time I tried moving out. I mean, I'm going to try. But I'm just saying."

Aidan says, "You don't have to worry. I'm not like that."

I know that he is nothing like my former roommate, who was ordinary in an almost cartoonish way. Aidan is no caricature. The problem is, I don't know *what* he is. I don't know if he is an unstable but relatively legal citizen, or if he is a more publicly polished version of me, something truly demonic.

"I don't even know why I'm doing this," I say. "I just—"

"No, I get what you're saying," he says. "After the last time, you're careful. That makes sense. But it'll be fine. Do you want to stop by and see the apartment? See your room?"

"No," I say. "I live in a fucking garage. I'm not picky."

He starts to laugh. It's a soft sound like water gurgling down a drain.

I wait until he stops laughing. "When should I move in?"

"Whenever you want," he says. He breathes in a couple times, easing the laughter out of his voice. But his words sound stretched, broadened, like he's still smiling. "I have class pretty much every day. Just tell me when you're moving in and I'll skip. I can help you. I'm stronger than I look."

"So am I," I say. "But you probably guessed that from my macho swearing. I think I'm going to move later this week. I'm busy tomorrow."

"Oh," he says. "Wow." And he starts laughing again. I have no idea what I said that was funny this time. "This is pretty sudden. Kind of strange."

I don't say anything.

He says, "Strange in a good way. I'm pretty happy about this, Mickey. I think this is going to be fun."

Fun. Jesus. I hang up the phone.

I am surprised to find that my shirt feels damp, that sweat sticks my hair to the back of my neck. My pulse feels steady but my body is producing adrenaline as if some atavistic part of my brain is already feeling the chill breath of some terrible fate.

After a few seconds, when I feel less flushed and sick, I get up and go inside.

My mother is in the kitchen with her laptop open, probably sharing recipes online or whatever she and her cyber ladyfriends do.

"I'm moving out," I say.

Her head jerks up. She pushes the lid of her laptop closed and just sits there at the island. Then she says, "Oh—oh." She smiles. "That's really—that's surprising. But, but it's good. I'm really proud of you."

I look at her.

If Jack the Ripper had lived in a garage instead of overcrowded London, if he had run eight miles a day in the rain and sleet and snow of northern Ohio, if he had gone for weeks at a time without interacting with another human being, no history book in the world would print his name.

I wonder if my mother has any idea what I am risking. She should, but then she works so hard to construct her mental fairytales about me, playing like I am a slightly difficult but fundamentally normal daughter.

I haven't killed a man since I was ten, but my last roommate exited the apartment we shared with a gash in her thigh, blood gushing between her clenched fingers as the paramedics strapped her to a gurney. My ability to play the game is remarkable. I follow the rules, I strip away distractions, I live by the law with greater asceticism and fanaticism than Saint Anthony practiced in his Egyptian tomb. But as in any game I do lose forays from time to time, and with each loss the tension inside me grows. A slow erosion of willpower. The odds are good that I will end up in prison, my name splashed across CNN or, worse, indexed in the history books. I know my parents see what they want to see in me: a decade of calm, controlled behavior, an unpleasant but generally ordinary individual. They don't know—I can't let them know—that the best my parents can hope for me is that I die anonymous.

"Are you—are you *happy*? About this decision?" My mother is looking at me, a frown wrinkle between her eyebrows.

I don't really understand what she means. The decision to move out or stay in my garage has nothing to do with happiness. But I suppose without the context of a cryptic Nietzsche quote, a corpse, and a mysterious hooded stranger with a walleye who keeps turning up, she has very little to work on in terms of deducing my motivation.

"Sure," I say. "Definitely. Yes."

EIGHT

The next Sunday I pack my books and clothes into cardboard boxes, duct-tape them shut, and load them into the passenger seat and capacious trunk of the Chevelle. The sky glows like a fire opal, cream lanced with sizzling gold and pink and blue. Frost sparkles over the slate roofs of houses.

For a second, I sit with my palms on the steering wheel, my boxes piled around me. Ready to drive away from my parents' house.

My cell phone vibrates in my pocket. But I don't pick it up. I know it's Dave. I don't know why, but he's been weird about my decision to move out. At first he yelled and said that I had promised to move in with him whenever I was ready to move out. Which I never did, I'm sure of it. I don't know why he was lying to me. He lies to everyone, but not to me. But then he called back and apologized and said he was just scared for my safety.

"It's not a good place," he'd said. "What about the neighborhood? It's sketchy, is what it is." He laughed and his voice got singsongy. "A cesspool of crime. Gang warfare. Genocide, even. Pedophilia. Incest. Mori*bund*ity."

"That's not a word."

"I'm writing a poem. It's about the word moribundity. Call the Oxford English Dictionary."

"Jesus."

"But I'm just—I just *care* about you. I care about my baby sister, all grown up and on her own but *still*. God. I mean what if something *bad* happens?"

"It's fine," I said. "Everything is going to be fine."

The phone stops vibrating. I take a breath. And I put the car in gear. Say, not quite out loud, "Everything is going to be fine."

But even I don't believe that.

I drive through the city until I reach the glass and brick buildings of the university. Manicured sports fields and parking garages give way to cracked asphalt and pulpboard-windowed houses. Buicks with starred windshields hump the sidewalks and a kid with a basketball dives across the street in front of me. I have to step on the brakes hard.

When I pull up into the driveway by Aidan's apartment, I look over my shoulder. In the light of day the condemned house's roof sags in the center, concave with gravity. A house gravid with death. There are still no cop cars out front. I wonder why no one has reported the smell, but it's cold enough that there aren't many people just walking around outside. And you can't smell it unless you're inside the house.

I drag a basket of clothes out of the Chevelle and, balancing it on my hip, weave my way up to the unstained wooden staircase. One of the slats still has a pink width measurement inked into the grain. The stairs smell piney, raw, a lingering hint of sawdust and sap.

I pull the apartment key from my jacket pocket. Aidan stopped by to drop them off yesterday. I pretended I wasn't home. He left them with my mother.

The door at the top of the steps opens on the kitchen. The kitchen floor is yellow and brown linoleum. The sink basin is streaked with white and yellow lime residue. There is a full-sized refrigerator and a small metal-legged table with two folding chairs. To the left is a twenty-something male's version of a living room: flatscreen TV, hi-fi sound system, three racks of CDs and Blu-ray discs, and an aging mauve couch with yellow foam crumbling through the weave. On the far wall a large window framed by dirty white drapes looks down into the frost-rimed street below. A kid in a bright red insulated coat runs between parked cars, and a second kid with a hooded jacket rides by on a scooter. When I look left, I can see the taller brick buildings of the university and a fringe of bony tree branches and telephone wires.

Straight ahead is the balding roof of the house in whose inner sanctum lies a half-skinned body.

I go down a narrow hallway opening off the living room. A door opens off the left and another off the right. The door on the right is half open. I push it in and see a large bed, rumpled sheets piled on top. The beige walls are covered with sketches and prints of faces, hands, clusters of fruit, city skylines.

I pull my head back and push in the second door. It opens on a bare room with a wooden floor, a window without curtains, a metal bed frame. Another door to the right. I push through it into a tiny bathroom with chipped green tiles.

There is a cat standing in the sink, licking water puddled around a soap dish.

I just stand there for a second and stare at the cat. I don't know what to do with it, so, in case it's Aidan's and he doesn't want it escaping, I just shut the bathroom door so it won't escape.

Then I push my boxes into my bedroom and go back out into the kitchen. I look around for a trashcan and find one under the sink, two crumpled silver cans of Bud Light and a squashed carton of Chinese food leaking onto the bottom. I hunt around and find a bottle of Lysol spray. I spray down the sink and countertops and rub them with paper towels.

In the freezer I find a tissue-wrapped copper plate and a box of photographic negatives. In the silverware drawer are a box of matches, a set of paintbrushes, a can opener, and a corkscrew. I open the oven and there is a pizza box sitting on the middle rack. I pull it out. Dried, cold crusts and a round white plastic container of congealed garlic butter. Christ, he's disgusting. But my brother Dave is a bit of a slob, too. At least Aidan doesn't seem to be the sort who leaves his underwear lying around. I don't understand how anyone can stand clutter. It feels—unnatural. Unhealthy. Like you're shedding pieces of yourself in public.

I stuff the empty pizza box in the trash and pour half a bottle of vinegar in the stove, then dump in the remainder of a box of soda from one of the cupboards. White foam expands and crests.

After I strip-clean the kitchen I go back to the bedroom and climb over stacks of boxes. I open the bathroom door. The cat has brown and black tiger-striped fur and yellow-green eyes. It turns and looks up at me and its pink tongue curls around its thin pink nose. I hold out my hand. The cat thrusts its head up, arching into my palm. I pick the cat up. Its throat crackles, the vibrations translating into my ribcage and rattling my bones.

At my bedroom window I stand like Nero with the cat draped over my shoulder. The evening sun breaks through a shelf of clouds and catches the myriad cracks and smears on the pane and turns it to molten ore. A sheet of burning fire illuminating the grungy street. After standing at the window until I recognize the creeping muscular ache of obsession, I blink and turn away.

I sit cross-legged on my neatly-made bed with my laptop open in front of me. I have folded and hung all of my clothes and stacked my books on the shelves. When I shut the closet door, the bedroom is empty except for a bent reading lamp and the single bed. The windowpane fits crookedly in its wooden frame and consequently exhales cold air. I am huddled in a thick sweatshirt that says Alcatraz on the front. I think the sweatshirt used to be Dave's.

I hear a noise through the bedroom wall, the apartment door opening. The jingle of keys. Double thuds as he kicks his shoes off.

It is quiet for a bit. Then I hear his footsteps in the hall. They pause in front of my door. And then retreat.

I figure he doesn't know how to approach me, doesn't want to startle the tiger in its cage. I should set the tone here. Establish the rules of conduct. I get up and go out into the living room.

He is on the couch, slouched so that his curved spine rests in the crack between the cushions, his neck propped up on a crushed pillow.

His jeans are stained and there is a crumpled button-down shirt lying on the floor. The TV burbles quietly. He is cradling a can of beer on his bare stomach. The winter sun leaking through the window glitters like warped glass on his skin. He is thin but there are traces of muscle across his bare shoulders, his wasted-looking chest.

He turns his head when I come in.

"Hey, Mickey!" His smile stretches the skin under his eyes, pushes his eyebrows into flaring dark streaks. "I thought you were going to call before you moved in. But then I saw your car outside."

"I parked in the back." A narrow gravel alley beside the house leads to a communal lot between this house and a couple others, each also subdivided into apartments. Rather than paralleling on the street, I chose to park in back. The idea that I would worry about the safety of the neighborhood per se, as my brother fears, is patently ridiculous. But I do admit to some flutters of anxiety on the Chevelle's account.

"Yeah. But it's pretty recognizable, even for a junker."

For a second I don't know what he means. And then, thinking about the gravel lot out back, I understand and a blinding rage seizes me.

The lot, with its zoological array of rusting-out behemoths, looks like a cross-section of the death of the American auto industry. The Chevelle is the second oldest vehicle in the gravel lot, seconded only by a 1970 pea-green Buick station wagon so ugly it looks like a renegade prop from a low-budget Stephen King film.

After a long silence, I say, "It's pretty recognizable."

"Yeah." He just keeps smiling, his eyes wrinkled to slits. I don't know what he's enjoying so much.

"It's a matte-black restored 1970s muscle car," I say. "So yes, it's recog*niz*able. What are you, some kind of vehicular philistine?"

The smile falters at this. He scrunches his nose and rubs his forehead. "I guess I don't know much about cars."

"And you called it a junker."

"I just meant—"

"And put a fucking shirt on. I didn't sign on for any randy Art Students Gone Wild experimental living project."

He drops his hand and laughs. It's a surprised and happy sound. "Geez," he says. "Is this all about your car? I'll never say anything bad about it ever again, cross my heart. And I'm sorry about the shirt." He reaches for the shirt and shrugs into it, buttoning it halfway. "I got paint all over myself today." The cat sidles around the corner of the hall and minces into the room. It twines through my legs, drapes its tail across my ankles.

Aidan notices and with the hand holding the beer motions to the cat. "I forgot to tell you about the cat. It's not mine. My old roommate left it. We can chuck it out if you want."

"I don't mind it."

He watches me. Then he turns his attention back to the TV, lifts the remote and turns up the volume. He takes a drink and when he lowers the beer a yellow liquid runs around the lid. I can smell it from the hallway, a pungent, bready smell.

"Your brother said you didn't like animals."

"I like them okay."

"So it's just people."

I nod.

He grins again. His eyebrows tilt upward at the edges when he smiles, an odd muscular contraction that makes his face demonic. "It's okay," he says. "Your secret's safe with me."

I don't know what he means.

But I'm not here just to play happy roommates.

"That house across the street," I say.

He takes another sip and glances up. Drinking could be a delaying mechanism, but he looks barely interested. "Which one?"

"That house with the yellow tape. The condemned house."

"Oh, yeah?" He grins. "I think it's a *crack* house."

I don't say anything.

He frowns. "It's okay," he says. "I mean, since I've been here there hasn't been much crime. I think it was, you know, condemned a while ago."

"Oh good," I say. "For a minute there I was concerned for my safety." He's not taking any bait at all. Fine. I can play that game, too. "I'm going to the store now. To get food. Do you need me to get you anything?"

He waves the beer at me. "Nah, I'm good. Thanks."

"I'm going to try here," I say. I am almost surprised to hear myself say it. "I'll pay my rent on time. I'm responsible that way, with numbers and schedules and stuff. I like cleaning, I like the smell of bleach and all, so I'll clean the kitchen, but you're going to have to keep your own shit picked up at least. And I don't go shopping unless I have to, so don't expect me to play housewife and buy you food or make you meals and don't expect me to talk to you all the time or whatever."

"No," he says.

"And if you have parties I'll lock myself in my room and open the window but if they stink up the place I might throw stuff at them and start screaming cuss words or something."

His mouth twitches but he doesn't say anything, just watches me.

"I'm not some nutjob who's never lived on her own. You don't have to worry about, you know, anything weird like that. I have zero social skills but I won't *do* anything."

He still doesn't say anything.

"I didn't kill my last roommate."

The laugh-light flickers out in his eyes. He straightens up. "I know. You didn't mean to hurt—"

"The only guy I ever killed—"

"I *know*." He looks at me. He's not smiling. "I won't ever do that sort of thing. Okay? I'm not like that. Your bedroom is yours. I won't go in it. I don't cut myself and I certainly don't mo*lest* people. Promise."

I shrug. "Okay. That's okay, then."

He nods. "Got it. And you don't touch my stuff. The film in the freezer stays in the freezer. And don't eat my food, but you can drink the beer if you want. And you can clean the kitchen and living room but don't go in my room, okay?"

"I hate beer."

"Do you smoke?"

I shake my head.

"Because I sometimes smoke."

"That's okay. I like that smell better than what you smell like now."

He looks at me and then smiles again. "We'll be okay," he says.

I don't know how to respond. If Aidan is my corpse artist he is too subtle to let me read it in his face. And anyhow I am terrible at reading faces.

At night, after the apartment falls into silence and Aidan's husky breathing comes from the bedroom across from mine, I slide my feet into my sneakers and go out, holding my palm against the kitchen door's latch to silence the click as the door closes.

This time, instead of my cell phone or the tiny flashlight on my keychain, I am holding a real flashlight, a slim penlight that I found in the toolshed behind the garden at my parents' house.

It's dark but the downtown heart of the city is not quiet or dark. There is no hush of wind through pine needles, no creak of telephone wires like in my parents' suburban paradise. A pinkish smog hangs over the skyline. Voices, distant music, and ambulance sirens pitch and fall like a tidal pool.

When I am about to cross the street, a car turns onto Allyn and rushes toward me, headlights burning funnels into the fractured dark.

I stumble back onto the sidewalk and look carefully before I cross the street.

I make sure to slide inside the condemned house before clicking on the flashlight.

The minute my flashlight glows white in the dark, I hear a quick scuffle and a sharp crack. Then the sound of hard panting.

I walk into the kitchen, my back to the wall. It occurs to me that I should be afraid, that I might be attacked. That I could be killed and flayed.

But underneath the patina of fear that coats my skin like a candy shell is something hot, vivid, burning in the pit of my stomach. I am excited.

The noise comes from the kitchen.

The flashlight beam picks out the empty, crackled linoleum, and then the glint of the backpack. And a woman, clutching the backpack against her breasts like it's a baby.

She's huddled under the counter in the hollow left by a missing appliance, maybe a dishwasher. In the sharp glare of the flashlight she blinks up at me, her skin shimmering like moist creosote, eyes flaring white with terror.

I spread my free hand so she can see the harmless pink skin of my palm.

"I'm not going to hurt you," I say. "I just want to know about the—the body upstairs."

She makes a gargling noise. I move the light slightly and see the shine of mucus or saliva on her chin. She has a gap between two yellowed eyeteeth, the middle teeth a blank space. Her tongue thrusts pink and moist between her lips, ballooning them out. The tip of her tongue curls and then retracts and then thrusts out again. Plum-colored skin under her left eye twitches.

I sigh. I recognize her frailties. Years spent kicking the heel of my sneaker against a chair in a psychiatrist's office have familiarized me with the physical evidence of any number of mental disorders. The waiting rooms of those places are like carnivals of the mentally disturbed.

The dregs of Thorazine and olanzapine, the heavy-duty drugs used to treat schizophrenia, float around the bloodstream, infecting it with myriad glitches and twitches like a fragging computer screen, symptoms of the cure rather than the disease. These twitches are called tardive dyskinesia and God knows I'd rather believe the FBI had hired space aliens to kidnap me than twitch like a short-circuiting motherboard.

She watches in silence when I come up to her. Her head jerks to the side.

I crouch down in front of her.

"Don't worry," I say. "I just need to know. The man upstairs. The dead body. Did you put the sheet over him?"

She groans, a sound like a constipated moose.

And then she flies up, her limbs a whirlwind. I scramble back.

She rushes by me and the door slams.

I'm alone in the kitchen with nothing but the fresh smell of aconite and ammonia and the old reek of decomposition.

At least I know what the witness looks like. And, I think, looking around the empty kitchen, at least she remembered her blanket, drugs, and Dora backpack this time. Her night is looking up, even if mine has turned to shit. Without her—well, hell, even with her, given her mental condition—I won't be any closer to identifying the killer. I click off the flashlight and wait for my eyes to adjust before going back to the apartment across the street.

My feet are quiet on the wood stairs and I turn the key carefully in the lock, easing the door open. But when I creep inside the apartment is quiet, so quiet I can hear the faint hum and gurgle of the refrigerator.

If Aidan is still in his room, he is no longer snoring. But nothing moves. No creak, no rustle of fabric. I imagine that he is lying there, awake, listening to my furtive creeping. I wonder what he is thinking. If he knows where I went. And I wonder if he has made similar journeys himself.

I ease my feet out of my sneakers and my bare feet are invisible in the dark as I go back to my room.

NINE

I get up at six the next morning. Shower. Dress. Instead of driving, I walk to campus to teach my first class of the day. I can see advantages to living so close to work.

Sometime after midnight last night the temperature dropped and rain turned into a heavy wet layer of snow. Frozen sludge covers the fields between the academic buildings. The sidewalks have been salted and grit under my shoes. The sky hangs low and bruised, pregnant with rain and ice, grieved to precipitation.

I don't remember much of what I lecture, but from the Plasticine expressions on my students' faces they don't notice anything out of the ordinary, or really anything at all. After teaching, I check my e-mail in the grad student office. Then I work in the library for five hours. I was supposed to finish a translation of the manuscript pages last week, but I've done no work on my dissertation at all since finding the corpse.

I finish the translation and go back to the apartment. Everything seems brighter, sharper, inside. Even shadows are razor-edged. I don't know if it's just the scintillation of the unknown, the sharp tang of death and disaster haunting every corner of the cheap construction, but every minute in the apartment, every moment since my decision to move out of my parents' garage, has felt like holding a live butterfly in my cupped hands, something frantically alive and almost unbearably fragile.

I think I like the way I feel.

Aidan is at the sink draining a pot of spaghetti.

I sling my backpack by the door.

"Hey," he says. "I made enough for two. You want some?"

"Yeah." The word sounds bald, awkward. I don't know what else to add. I could thank him. That might be the polite thing to do. But I didn't ask him to cook for me. So I say, "I'm pretty hungry."

"Good."

He pours the drained pasta into two bowls and takes them to the kitchen table. I edge behind him and wash my hands at the sink.

"Do you drink wine?" he asks.

"What?"

He points to a cheap bottle of cabernet with cartoon animals on the label. I shrug and he pours wine into two plastic cups. He sets one cup on the table near me and takes his cup and a bowl of pasta and goes to the living room. He stands in the doorway and shifts his weight. I sit down at the table and reach for the cup and drink for a long time and then set the cup down. The wine eases through me. Settles in my stomach like a warm fist.

"You can sit."

He breathes out and comes quickly and sits down at the table across from me.

He looks at his plastic cup. His lips part like he wants to say something.

I hold myself still.

"How was your day?"

I say, "Shit."

"What?"

I spread my hands. I don't understand how people can do this—the talking. The meaningless mutterings. "Are you going to just pretend you didn't hear me leave last night? Is this some—is this normal? I mean, I'm serious here. I don't understand you. But can we at least—can you just, I don't know, talk about *real* stuff. Say things that are true and that *matter*."

He shuts his mouth. Looks down at his bowl. Then he looks back up. "It's not my business where you go." His thumb plays with the edge of his bowl, traces shapes on it. "You know? I mean, I don't want to know. I'm, we're both adults."

He sounds awkward, his words stiff, like they are uncomfortable in his mouth.

"Fine." I wave my hand. "So you're not curious. That's your business. But I am curious about you." I point my fork at him. "I want answers." What I really want to ask is, Did you kill and skin a man in the abandoned house across the street? But if his answer is no, I'm no closer to the truth and that much closer to a phone call to the cops and a lifetime playing with Play-Doh in a room that smells like SpaghettiOs and vomit.

"Start with that murder thing you said at my parents' house," I say. "What's that about?"

"My—you mean, my mom?" He sits back in the chair. Puts his fingers over his mouth, and then buries his hand in his lap. "I didn't think you were interested. You didn't sound particularly happy about it at your parents' house."

"I'm not interested. If your mother died ten years ago and the cops never solved the case then there's nothing anyone can do about it. Which begs the question: Why bring it up? Why corner me, a total stranger, and start going on about solving murders?"

I lean forward. His head moves back.

If anyone sketched the two of us, I would look like a lion and he would be a gazelle transfixed between terror and oblivion.

"Even by my abysmal standards of normal interactions, that's bizarre. So talk."

He clears his throat. Then he looks down at his bowl. He lays his fork down and reaches for his cup. He drinks, and then takes a deep breath.

"Okay. So, well, the thing is, I was a kid when my mother—" His voice catches. He takes a breath, carefully. As if he's tasting the air. "My mom died. Eleven years ago. She died of asphyxiation in a massive house fire. We—my sister and I—were at my father's house when it happened. The police found two separate origin points for the fire, so they figure it was arson. The case was ruled a homicide but it wasn't ever solved."

I lean back in my seat.

"Okay."

"Okay, what?" he says.

"Okay, I get it. You want me to find the asshole who killed your mother and you want me to go Son of Sam on them. Blow them to kingdom come."

The skin on his face slackens. "Wha—no! No, of course not. I don't want—you don't kill people."

He says it as if I've proposed that the sun rises from the west and he is correcting me, gently but firmly.

"You don't know that." I drain the rest of my wine and set the empty cup down. A droplet shivers on the rim before racing crookedly to the chipped plastic tabletop. "My brother told you that but he also told you about the guy I killed when I was ten, and about my last roommate being hospitalized. You're hoping I'm like some personal gorgon, able to be unveiled at your whim and turn your enemies to stone."

"No."

"Then what?"

He leans forward. His fingertips whiten on the edge of the table. "Your brother said you can't feel pity or, well, and you can't *like* anyone. And I saw you at your house. What you said to your mother. You tell the truth because you don't care how it feels to the person you're talking to. I want the truth. That's all. I want someone who will find out the truth and tell me."

I look at him. "So you already know who did it."

His eyelids droop. He lowers his head. His shoulders rise when he takes a breath. "No," he says. "I don't know. I want you to find out." His voice is a whisper. But I can hear him and I know that he is lying.

"This is stupid." I stand up and take my empty bowl to the sink. "Why would you stalk me to my parents' house just to ask me to tell you who killed your mother when you already know, or at least have a pretty good guess?"

"I *don't* know." He slams his palm flat on the table. The sound startles me and I jump.

His breathing is uneven.

I grip the edge of the sink.

"I'm sorry," he says. "God, I'm really sorry. It's just, my dad and my sister act like—well, they don't ever talk about it and they never talk about anything, or go visit—I mean, my family never gets together. Not all of them. I think we need to bring everything into the open, to really talk about what happened, if we're ever going to deal, you know? Only, I was really young when it happened. Sometimes it feels like everyone else *knows* while I'm just guessing. Maybe no one knows what really happened. But I *need* to. I need to know the truth and deal with it. I need to talk with sister and my dad about stuff instead of everything just, you know, festering."

"Go visit who?"

"What?"

"Your family never visits who?"

Aidan rubs his forehead with his palm. Then he smoothes his palm over the back of his neck and drops his hand to the table. He looks at his upturned palms.

"I have a sister in an assisted living facility. She sort of lost it when my mom died. No one ever visits her or talks about her. Like she doesn't exist anymore."

For a while I stand at the sink and watch him.

I was right. His story isn't interesting. The family secret that keeps them all apart is either the fact that his assisted-living sister killed their mother and then tried to off herself, or the mother killed herself and tried to take the sister with her. It won't take much time or energy to figure out which it is, and, if I do figure it out, the knowledge won't change anything. It occurs to me that I could probably do this, solve his family's sordid little mystery. It's a finite group of suspects, unlike the Case of the Corpse Across the Street.

But his broken family isn't my problem. And I have bigger things to worry about.

"You're right," I say.

"I am?" He looks startled. "About what?"

"About why people engage in small talk. Real drama is pathetic. It's almost worse than discussing the weather. Why do people always talk about the weather? It's October in Akron, Ohio. The weather goddamn sucks. There's nothing else to say about it."

He looks up at me and smiles.

"I wonder if you could get a job just telling people the truth," he says. "You know, saying things no one in their right minds would say but people need to hear anyway."

I don't know what he's talking about. But at least he is talking. It gives me an idea. Maybe this is the game. Maybe I have to solve his personal drama in order to figure out his relationship to the house across the street. If he met me at the poetry reading, then he's been aware of me—interested in me—since before the corpse became a corpse.

I leave the kitchen and go back to my bedroom and come back with a yellow legal pad and a pen. I put them on the table and he looks up at me with his eyebrows raised and his lips parted.

"Pertinent information. When you're done, put it on the counter."

"Seriously? You—you don't have to, you know." He smiles a little, raises a shoulder. "I mean, I know this is my problem. What you said, it's just—pathetic drama. My issues. I know that. And I know there's probably not anything you can do."

"I can ask around. No promises. But you obviously want to know, so—whatever. I'll do it."

"Okay." He picks up the pen. Rolls it between his fingers. Then he says, "No, this is a stupid idea. It really is. I don't know what—I mean, it's not like it's going to change anything."

"No," I say.

He clicks on the pen. "I'll tell you what I know."

"Okay."

He frowns and when I turn to walk away he says, "Hey."

"Yeah?"

"For real. Why are you doing this?"

"I don't know." I grin. "What is the expression? For shits and giggles? I never understood what that means."

He looks at me. And then presses his lips together and bends his head to the legal pad. Whatever he sees in my face, it is not, apparently, the hungering need to know about murder that has infected my dreams now for weeks.

I shut my bedroom door behind myself. The cat tangles between my legs. I pick him up and he settles like a mink across my shoulder, his purr vibrating against the tendons in my neck. There is a coin-sized spot of pain behind my left eye. It burrows like a cyst into my eyeball and my head flickers with hot-cold light. I lie down on the bed, curl over on my side. The cat turns in a circle and then lies down, cupped against the hollow of my stomach. Its sleek brown body rises and falls with my breathing.

I see a bloody footprint on the floor. Another on the stairs. My eyes hurt. The walls are shadowy and lean inward. There is blood everywhere, glistening. The basement is a hellish grotto lit by a moon made incarnadine. I can feel blood caked under my fingernails. Someone is lying at the foot of the stairs. A high-pitched voice is cackling, giggling, crazed. I realize that I am dragging my fingernails down my skin, shredding strips of flesh like paint peeling from a wall. The hysterical cackles pour out of my throat.

I startle awake suddenly. Shadows lie thick and brown around the bedroom. My mouth tastes like chalk dust.

I roll over and the cat squawks and wakes up and stretches, arching its back, the fur bristling. Dying sun burnishes the fine hairs along its spine.

I get up and go into the bathroom and bend over the sink, cup cool water and drink, then splash water over my face.

A noise to my left startles me. I look up and see Aidan lying on the sofa with one arm crooked behind his head. He lifts his head from his arm and looks at me. "Everything okay?"

I shove the cat off the counter. It falls on its paws, but grunts when it hits the floor.

"Mind your own fucking business."

But I am surprised to find that my voice comes out a rasping whisper. I am hoarse.

I need to get out. I put on my shoes and run across campus and down busy roads, my sneakers splashing through gray slush, the air nipping at my exposed face and neck. My mind submerges into a misty calm and I don't have to think.

In particular I shut out the truth that's been rattling around my ribs like a hard nut, a truth I've never told my parents. The truth is, my version of crazy isn't just manifested in a dislike for being touched, in a propensity to say the word "fuck," or even in my utter lack of empathy for other humans. No. At night, I dream about the basement where I killed a man. I dream about my brother's afterbirth lying in its steel bowl like violence floating in pain. I don't know why my parents let me get close to human organs and blood so soon after I mutilated a corpse. My mother told me that she thought it would be good for me to see birth, a new baby. To be reminded of life. She should have known better. She must have been able to see that it isn't *life* that fascinates me. My parents, my therapists, my brothers—everyone knows I dream about those two events. Here is what I have never told them: in the dreams the basement pools with blood and it is my brother's newborn body that I am mutilating on the floor.

When I wake up my jaw muscles ache. I am so worn out, so unutterably weary of the fight against my own perversion. The truth is that I don't know if I can make it. I don't know how long I can keep from cutting someone's skin and letting all the sweetness run out.

I don't think about this truth during my run.

After I finish the run and shower, I pad barefoot into my bedroom, rubbing my long wet hair in a towel. The windowpane flickers gold and crimson. It's only when I go across the room and look out the window that I start to think about the truth. And the truth lunges at me and swallows me whole.

TEN

I tried this almost ten years ago. The living-on-my-own thing, I mean. It didn't work out so well. I am thinking this while I sit with my elbows crooked around my knees looking out my bedroom window. The oil smears from myriad fingers pressed against the glass over the years collect light and fracture it like crystals. Red and blue and white and yellow, tiny Christmas lights dancing across the dark. The cop cars silenced the sirens a couple minutes ago but the ambulances are still there and blue uniforms move jerkily through the colored strobe lights. A silent, deadly disco dance.

The apartment door slams. Footsteps pound across the floorboards and my door bangs on its hinges. I look around.

Aidan is sucking in air hard, gripping the doorframe. He sags against the fulcrum of his fingers and the tips whiten. He leans his head back.

"I didn't do it," I say. I turn my head and look back out my window. My hair falls around my face and hangs over my bent arms and the twin humps of my pale knees.

"God," he says when he gets his breath back.

"He didn't have much to do with it either."

Aidan comes inside the room. He is breathing hard.

I keep my eyes fixed on the glittering spectacle below. Billows of inky smoke from the wood frame house across the street. The stretcher has been shunted into the back of the ambulance. Along the street half-naked people wearing flimsy cotton pajamas or hastily thrown-on coats and boots stand ankle-deep in dirty snow, agog and salivating with curiosity.

A knot of cops is gathered around a clipboard. The pajama-clad voyeurs cluster around, heads nodding, shoulders hunched up around their ears in the cold. I guess the cops are collecting names, interviewing witnesses. One of the neighbors turns and points up at our apartment.

Shit.

Aidan says, "What—what happened?"

The sirens came. That's what happened. I saw the reflected flares of firelight and smelled smoke when I got out of the shower. I went to the window and stood looking down at an inferno. Arson. An accelerated burn, oily tar-black smoke coiling into the air. Shattering glass. Cops came. Atonal screams as metal overheated, wood beams cracked.

My eyes dazzled. Flames licked hungrily at the night sky. The next thing I knew I was outside. Holding out my palms to the fire. Rags of flame against the dark canvas of the sky. People screaming, wailing. A girl in blue flannel pajama pants clutching a bottle, her pale hair flaring incendiary white. Gusts of flaming debris. Delicate moth wings of newspaper, veined red with flame, disintegrated suddenly into ash. Cordate shells of curled plaster. I stood in a melting puddle of pewter silt. The crackle and patter of falling rubble. The wooden house shrieked like a frail woman in the halcyon arms of a violent and insatiable god.

I say without turning my head, "A fire."

"Yeah, I can see. There's smoke everywhere, and debris and cops and—and why are you naked? Is that—is that ash in your hair? What's—were you *down* there?"

When I stood at the window looking down at the fire, all I could imagine was the heat of the flames. A gold and vermillion bacchanal. I only wanted to get closer. I imagine it must have caused a stir. I didn't notice at first. Until the cops came and someone tried to touch me. I remember the plasticky smell of the blanket the cop was trying to put around me. And I realized I was standing in a melting snowbank, naked, my skin flaring gold and crimson in the great light, my hair swirling in heated updrafts, a silvery dust of ash settling on my shoulders and upturned hands.

So I pushed away the blankets and the cops and went back across the street and upstairs to the apartment, and I shut and locked the door and went into my bedroom. I stood at the window while the fire hoses stanched the living flame. The reek of smoke drifting over the street.

They found the body. With their masks and breathing apparatus they climbed through charred timber and glinting shards of glass. Sullen flares of red and orange amid the wreckage. They came out with a stretcher carrying a zippered plastic bag over a lumpy shape the size of a small child or a charcoaled corpse, a body reduced to its concentrate.

"Why were you down there?" Aidan asks. "Why did you go down there without—um." He stops talking.

Someone pounds at the apartment door.

Aidan turns his head and looks behind him.

My lips are dry and stick together. "That'll be the cops."

Aidan rubs his palms over his dark bristling scalp. "Oh, God. Okay. Are you going to talk to them? Mickey?"

"Because it was beautiful," I say.

There is a silence. Another bang at the door and the muted sound of a strident voice.

"What? What was beautiful? The fire?"

I rest my forehead against my knees. Aidan's feet echo on the floorboards. I hear the metal click of the lock turning. They come in with cold air and smells, smoke mostly, but other human odors too, like deodorant and Mexican food. The clatter of hard-soled shoes in the hallway outside my bedroom door.

"—need to speak with her—some connection to what went down."

Aidan says something about shock and the fire. The cop says he wants to know if I saw who started it. If I saw anyone run out of the house. If that is why I went running outside.

"I think she just went down to watch the fire," Aidan says.

"She must've seen something or she knows something." The cop lowers his voice. "She came running out like a—well, she just comes tearing out, you know, stark naked, and she runs up to the house and she's standing there—"

"Like a conductor," I say, lifting my head. I can feel the grit caked in my sweaty skin. "Like Beethoven conducting his ninth symphony. Deaf enough to hear."

"What?" One of the cops is a woman.

"I'm crazy," I say. "Not guilty. You're wasting your time."

Aidan is behind the cops. He says, "She's not crazy, exactly. But she's, you know, telling the truth. She has some mental—"

"Some mental *what*?" says one of the cops. "Problems? Like starting fires?"

"*No*," Aidan says. "I mean—not like that."

"And who are you?"

"The roommate," Aidan says.

"Name?"

"Aidan," he says. "Devorecek."

"Spell that."

"D-e-v—"

The other cop says, "What sort of mental problems does your girlfriend have?"

"*Room*mate," Aidan says. "We just live—it doesn't matter. She's not a pyro. It's, like, emotional issues. Not criminal issues."

"So why'd she run to the house? She connected to the body we found inside? Emotionally?"

"No, it's not like that," Aidan says. "Wait, what body? I thought that place was empty."

The guy cop goes closer to Aidan. Aidan licks his lips nervously.

Strands of hair are glued to the sweat on my face. I comb them away with my fingertips.

I climb off the bed and stand up. The cops twist their heads around and stare at me. The male cop's eyes shift and he backs up a step. But even the female cop is staring.

I hold my arms out, palms cupped up like when I stood in front of the flames. "Is this why you came up here? You want to see this side too? The back wasn't enough?"

The female cop says, "All right, that's not funny." She turns to the male cop. "Wait outside."

I walk up to her until I'm only inches away. I can smell her, a scent that's half smoke, half perfume, a sweet, acrid stench. Saliva fills my mouth. I swallow hard, trying not to gag. I can feel the coldness in her uniform, the heat of her skin.

"Step back," she says. Her hand goes to her hip. "Step *back*."

"I thought you wanted this. You came *look*ing." My breath stirs the fine hairs by her ear. "Can you see me well enough now?"

"Step back," says the male cop. I look over at him. He has pulled his gun, a stubby weapon with an oddly shaped square barrel. A Taser. He holds it like a real gun, forefinger on the trigger, the other hand bracing the fist.

I wonder what it would feel like to be shot with that much voltage. If I would feel the pain as much as any normal person would. My heartbeat picks up. I move over to him. My skin is cold. His eyes struggle not to look down at me, to see my nipples hardened by the cold. "Step *away*," he says.

"I don't kill people." I go close to him. The skin on his neck is leathery, the color of old bologna, moist and plucked-looking. "I don't. I didn't kill him. Okay? That wasn't me."

"Step back or I will restrain you," he says. "Do you understand me?"

He's talking loudly like he thinks I'm partially deaf in addition to being mentally deficient.

"I'm not stupid," I say. "And I'm not an *arsonist*."

"Leave her alone," Aidan says.

The male cop looks at me and then he lowers his gun.

My heartbeat slows. The room is cold and gray, evening shadows creeping across the floorboards. The shattering gold light is gone now.

I take three steps back. "I didn't start the fires."

"Put some clothes on."

"I didn't."

"Just tell us why you were down there."

I lick my lips. My tongue is sticky. "To watch." It comes out a whisper.

The cops look at me. And then the male cop says, "Well, that was pretty stupid. Wasn't it."

"I guess so."

I wonder who hated him so much, the mutilated body in the house. Or who loved him. The knife peeling skin from its frame like a painter stripping a canvas.

They ask my name.

I look at the floor and hug my elbows against my ribs. The smell of the fluid on my hands. His hair on my knuckles as I brush it aside and touch—God, it's gone. The corpse is burnt, shuttled away in a blue medical examiner's van. My body feels weightless.

I hear Aidan telling them my name. My parents' phone number. The male cop has already turned for the door.

The female cop says, "All right. We'll be in touch if we have more questions." Her voice lowers. "You may want to reconsider housing options, potential roommate situations. Can't be that pricey around here." She snaps her book shut. Aidan follows her out. I hear their voices in the hall and then the snick of the outer door.

He comes back, his footsteps slow. He comes in, leans his shoulder blades against the doorjamb, and puts his hands on his head again, his gesture of helplessness. He slides down the frame, legs splayed out, and says, "Oh, my *God*."

I blink and lower my hands. "What's wrong?"

"What do you *think* is wrong," he says. "You just flashed half of Akron and I—I think I just talked two cops out of arresting you for murder and arson."

And then he bursts out laughing. He starts laughing so hard he gets hiccups.

I laugh too. The sound startles me and then suddenly we're both laughing. My stomach quivers and I feel sick and I can't stop laughing.

I gulp and get quiet first.

I look at my roommate. He's inside my room, sitting on my floor, cackling like a demented loon. I think this is the closest I've ever been to him. Close enough to see the dark prickle of beard on his jaw, the shadowed indentation on his upper lip. Underneath the delicate scent of turpentine his skin smells palely of Ivory soap. Turpentine is an accelerant. But he doesn't smell like smoke. His skin smells clean.

He stops smiling. A delicate pink stains his cheekbones. "Geez, Mickey," he says. "You could maybe get some clothes on sometime soon."

I cross my arms over my breasts and frown at him. "Why? I thought you were gay."

He opens his mouth. "You did?"

"You came over to the house with my brother. You said you *knew* him."

"I do—I mean, I *just* know him. We just talked at that poetry reading and somehow my art came up and he wanted to see if I was any good. He came by the studio a couple days later and we got talking. He asked if he could see some of my older stuff, and it's here at the apartment so I invited him over. That's when he told me about you."

I laugh.

He squints at me. "What's funny?"

"Nothing. It's just, he wanted to see your art? *He* was stalking you."

"Come on, Mickey. That's not stalking. Look, I knew what was going on, okay? I told him I wasn't interested and he was cool. And anyway, what does it matter to you?"

"It matters because I thought you were—I thought that it wouldn't matter to you. My being a girl." I shrug. "Or being crazy. Or naked. But I guess it does."

"No, no," he says. "I'm sorry. You're right. You deserved to know. But it doesn't matter, it really doesn't. You being a girl. That's fine." He laughs again but it sounds harsh, uncomfortable. He avoids my eyes and his are all shiny. "But the naked isn't—I mean, I could be Elton John—okay?"

This is another thing I don't understand: how crazy is sexy to some people. Most people who meet me randomly realize I'm likely to go off at the slightest provocation, cussing, throwing things, slamming doors. They call me a bitch and they avoid me. But sometimes my brother or someone will introduce me to a person and explain that I have mental problems. And then when I lose it and fuck up I see this look—this glassy-eyed look—the same look all the pajama-clad gawkers had, gazing at the fire. A ravenous, rapt look.

I turn around suddenly. My stomach is still trying to heave the turkey sandwich I ate earlier, from being so close to those cops. I recognize the feeling tingling behind my eyes, in my chest. I'm angry. Pissed off. *Furious.*

I yank open my closet, pull out a pair of jeans and step into them.

"I don't start fires." I grab a T-shirt and tug it over my head, pull it down. "I don't randomly attack and kill people, like some out-of-control—I mean, some idiot starts a fire and burns an already-dead corpse and I'm the crazy one. Some stupid bitch cuts her legs for fucking *fun*, and *I'm* the crazy one."

"Mickey, come on, I don't think that, okay? If you mean your roommate, about the cutting thing, listen, I'm sorry about that and all, but it wasn't really your fault. Dave told me about her and I know—"

"I *am* fucking crazy," I say. "That's not news. I mean I'm not out of control, I didn't *do* those things. I didn't *try* to kill her." I pull my hair out of my shirt and loop it into a loose knot at the back of my neck. I come back and stand in front of him.

"I know," he says. "Dave told me. I know she let you cut her. You went too far. You called the cops. You saved her life. You weren't trying to kill her."

"No." I look up at the ceiling. "Shit." I don't understand why I'm so angry.

I say, "She knew I liked it. The blood. I liked watching her cut. She was in the bathroom with her leg up on the sink and she had the razor snicking through her skin and I came in and she saw my face. She saw I liked it."

"Mickey—"

"She held out the razor and said, here, you can try it."

He makes a noise like he's going to say something else.

I put my hand over my mouth and then pull it down. "I didn't cut her. I never touched her. I stood there and watched, but I didn't touch her. I didn't lick her blood. I didn't do any of those *psycho* things she said I did. I just—I just fucking *watched*. But she was bleeding a lot and I thought she might—you know, be in trouble. So I called the EMTs."

I lower my head and look at Aidan. He's staring at me.

"The guy I killed when I was ten—"

"My God, shut up, Mickey. You push a pervert wannabe rapist down the stairs and he breaks his neck. Jesus. That was the sanest thing any ten-year-old could do. No one blames you for that. *No* one."

I come to the doorway and crouch down. "I was going to say the guy I killed when I was ten was the only crazy thing I've ever done."

I don't know if he's noticed that he sat up straighter and leaned his shoulders forward when I crouched down. The skin between his eyebrows wrinkles. "No," he says.

"Yeah. Yes. That was pretty crazy. You know what I did when he fell down the stairs?"

He's watching my mouth move, frowning at the shapes it makes like he's trying to read a foreign language.

"I went down the stairs after him."

I remember what really happened. I dream about the stairs a lot, but the dreams are always different than what happened. In reality there was no blood. Just the guy in his shabby pants and yellow polo shirt lying there with his head toward the basement floor and his feet halfway up the stairs. I noticed the smell when I was edging my feet around his hips. The dark wet spot spreading on the front of his beige pants. And then I climbed down to where his sagging fat face lolled to the side, his eyes half-open. I was only ten. I didn't know that eyes stay open when you die. No one had told me that. In the movies, people die with their eyes closed. I was fascinated by the shiny white gleam under his half-closed eyelids. I put my hand out. I pushed my fingertip against an eyeball. It was moist and pulpy like a skinned grape. I pressed my fingernail into the eye and watched the pinkish viscous liquid well up.

"Like slicing an aloe leaf," I say. "That's what it looked like. Have you ever seen aloe sap?"

Aidan doesn't say anything.

"Anyway, the point is, I remember the whole thing and I didn't feel—anything, except maybe curious—when I saw a dead body. And I'm not 'blocking' or whatever. The shrinks, everyone tried to come up with reasons for why I am the way I am. There's no reason. The guy was dead and I felt curious, that's all. I wanted to touch a dead eye. It was sort of—" I try to think of the right word. *Electric.* "It was a buzz."

His eyes shift. He's looking at me strangely. I don't know what the look means.

"You think you know me. You think I'm a broken person who can be fixed, or, or the result of some terrible tragedy. But that's not me. You don't know *shit* about me."

His lips part but he doesn't say anything. And then his eyelashes tremble and sweep shut. When he looks up again his eyes are glistening. He roughly brushes the back of his hand across his cheeks.

I stand up and go into the bathroom and slam the door.

I rinse my mouth out in the bathroom and splash cold water on my face until I feel less like throwing up. When I come back out, he's gone.

I flop down on my bed. Lie still for a while watching headlights sweep over the ceiling. The fire trucks and ambulances and cop cars have long ago cleared out. Normal city sounds, rap music and tinny TV squawks and car horns, drift up. When I rest my palm across my left breast I feel the solid kick of my heart and it is slow and rhythmic. My heartbeat is not accelerated.

After a few hours of lying still staring at the ceiling I get up and walk out of my bedroom. Aidan's bedroom door is shut but lemon yellow light haloes the inside of the doorframe. The cat is in the kitchen, lying on the counter. He gets up and arches his back and grunts when he sees me. I open the silverware drawer. There is a fruit paring knife. I feel the matte handle, the faint glisten of steel in the shadows. I put my left hand on the cat's head. The cat bucks its skull against my palm, its purr humming like machinery. I set the blade of the knife delicately against the underside of the cat's jaw, where the soft down fur meets in a Vshape.

The cat squeaks and licks its lips and tries to pull its head away, but my left hand cups its skull in a strong grip. The cat struggles. The knife doesn't waver.

And then I scoop up the cat and go outside. The night air is biting cold. White flakes drift, uncertain, from the pink-tinged sky. Frozen tree limbs creak. The cat struggles and I let him go. He jumps out of my arms. His paws thump softly on the wooden slats. He bounds down the stairs and disappears into darkness.

I drive the knife blade into the soft pulpwood. When I cup my cold hand around my neck my pulse is slow and steady. Nothing has changed.

I am still sitting on the steps in the cold when my phone rings. I sit with my thumb over the delete button. The number looks strange to me, even after all these months. For more than ten years my older brother has had a 212 area code, and now the number has the familiar 330 Akron area code. I wonder why he moved back to Ohio. It occurs to me that it's odd I never asked him. We talk on the phone all the time, we always have, but we never seem to talk about things normal siblings would. I grin a little, imagining the two of us trying to hold an ordinary conversation. *How was your day? Oh, it was fabulous—I got my hair done! How was yours?*

I pick up the phone. "What?"

"Hey, babe. Come meet me."

"Where?"

"My place," he says. "Come over. I want to show you something."

I close my eyes and rest forehead on my knees. "Why?"

"Because I *said*," he hisses. And then he stops talking. For a second there is silence. And he laughs, the sound of wind chimes in summer. "My darling, we live, like, *ten* minutes away from each other now and it's like we're strangers. We never see each other." His voice softens. "Did you ever think that would happen? I mean, in a million years. The two of us. We used to be in*sep*arable."

"We haven't seen a whole lot of each other for a long time," I say. "You moved away. I grew up."

"Grew up." He sighs. I hear him suck on air. The static sound of an exhalation. I imagine the smell of his cigarette smoke. "Do you think it's inevitable? The inevitable encroachment of adulthood?"

His voice sounds like smoke and chocolate. Older and raspier and exactly the same.

The basement. The first cigarette Dave ever smoked was in the basement. This was when I was ten, when the man was still living with us. He was at work that afternoon. I found Dave in the basement looking through the man's things. Dave found a crushed red and white Marlboro pack in the inside pocket of a corduroy jacket. He spun around when I came to the doorway.

When he saw it was me he smiled and held up the carton. "Did you know he smokes?"

I didn't really know what cigarettes were. Neither of our parents are smokers.

We sat on the couch and he struggled with the lighter. His forehead contacted in a frown as he rasped his thumb across the spin-wheel again and again trying for a spark. When he got the struggling flame he held it out to me. Wanted me to put the cigarette in my mouth first.

"Why?"

"Because," he said. "It looks fun in the movies. I think you'll like it."

I put the cigarette in my mouth. It tasted like bitter paper. He held the flame to the end and said, "Breathe in."

I did and felt the hot smoke coiling in my mouth and pressing down on my lungs like a child's fist. I coughed. Handed him the cigarette.

"You don't like it?"

I shook my head.

"Well, you will."

"Why?"

He smiled and took the cigarette from me. Held it in two fingers and put the butt to his pursed lips like a socialite. He inhaled delicately, swallowed a cough. His cheeks and the edges of his nostrils turned pink. "Smoking," he said, "is addictive. It means that you are a smoker now. That you like to smoke. When you grow up you'll smoke."

"Really?"

He took another drag, rolled the smoke in his mouth, breathed it out and coughed. Nodded.

I held out my hand for the cigarette. But he held it away from me. "No, no, no. Now I want it. I'm a smoker now."

"Because of me?"

"Yes," he said. He sat down on the couch next to me and sucked again at the cigarette. He breathed out, slowly. "They cause cancer, you know. I suppose I'll die of this."

I sat next to him and watched him. I didn't know what cancer looked like.

He held out the cigarette. "Okay. You can try again. Just a little breath, all right?" And when I did, watching me blink and try to swallow the smoke, he said, "Mom always said she didn't want us to smoke. Because smoking kills. But it's okay. I want to do the things you do. We'll always be partners. Right?"

A few months later I would kill a man. But he didn't know that then. I did like that cigarette, the first one that we smoked. I have never smoked again but I like the scorch smell. It's just that I'm a runner and so I worry about things like lung capacity and VO2.

And I worry about things like whether he was telling the truth. I know now that Dave was lying about the nature of nicotine addiction, but I have never been sure whether he was telling the truth about his smoking because I'd done it first. I do know that our whole lives, neither one of us has ever gotten in trouble alone. Not even when I killed that man. Oh, he didn't have all the medications or the psych unit stay, but he saw his share of shrinks. At first, our parents took him to their therapist for family talks. Dave said it helped him, so he started going once a week. After each visit, he smiled, cried a bit, told our parents he felt safer, saner, healed. In private he raged, spittle collecting in the corners of his mouth. Never at me. Just in general. He hated those visits so much. But he went so I wouldn't be the only one with the weekly visits, the medication, the strained silences.

"Look," I say, "I'm not coming over. Today was kind of a—a long day."

"But everything is—look, babe, I need you. I've got something to talk to you about."

"No," I say. "Not tonight."

He sighs. I imagine him stubbing out the cigarette, the black and red scorch mark it leaves like an exhausted eye.

I don't want to hear him try to convince me to come over. I don't want to hear what he has to tell me. I hang up the phone and wonder where the cat has got to, if it will die of exposure or get hit by a car, and if either of those deaths is better than the quick clean slash of a knife blade.

ELEVEN

When I wake up in the morning my hair smells like smoke, and the cotton pillowcase is gritty with fine ash.

I get up and trip on the yellow legal pad lying on my bedroom floor. Aidan's notes. Because I don't want to think about the smell of smoke or the house across the street, I sit down on the edge of the bed and read through them. His handwriting is as neat and evenly spaced as if he wrote in time to a metronome. I've noticed also that while he's not particularly clean, he is often tidy, the sole exceptions being during moments of intense artistic creation when he will strew a room with paint and turpentine and the accoutrements of his art.

His mother's name is at the top of the yellow paper: *Barb Devorecek, 53, d. 06-23*. Below he has listed the names of his father and two sisters, and three additional names with the notation "former clients of B.D." by them.

I stand up and go to the window. The burnt house is a ragged shell with black scorch marks on the sagging roof. Yellow crime tape is wrapped around the house like some Tim Burtonesque nightmare Christmas present. I don't know what to do now. The county medical examiners have the charred remains of the body. Any evidence of handwriting is gone and after yesterday, after my first physical confrontation with Akron's finest since I was ten years old, the last thing in the world that I want to do is draw more attention to myself by asking too many questions. They will investigate. And I will just watch the story unfold on CNN like every other American with a TV tray and a microwaved dinner.

My hands feel empty. I put my palms lightly on the cold glass and tell myself that the mystery is still there, that I still have a puzzle to solve. But I don't. It's been wrested from me by the same invisible hands that shoved me face first into it last week.

I hear the creak of the shower faucet and steady thrum of water against the fiberglass hull of the shower stall.

And realize I still have one more lead. I have my relentlessly disinterested roommate. It would be tidy if he were the killer. But he never looked at the house or brought up the subject of corpses without any hint that he enjoyed making them. He acted genuinely freaked out after the fire. And while he's not stupid, he doesn't seem as book-clever as I would expect a German-speaking Shakespeare-loving sadist to be. But what do I know. Solving people is not my forte.

The cold case.

I turn away from the window and grab my laptop, pull over the yellow legal pad, and hunt under my bed for a pen. I *can* solve Aidan, of course.

I get online and look up Aidan's mother's name and read through the initial news story—a local woman found dead in a house fire—and the obituary. According to the obit, Mrs. Devorecek worked part-time as a child therapist, often working from her home. A credit to the community, a loving wife and mother, she was survived by her former husband, her two daughters, and her son. A close friend of hers started a scholarship in her name for poor inner-city children to study music.

Grabbing a pen, I scan Aidan's notes for the friend's name but it doesn't appear on the list. I jot it down: *Judith Greene*. Then I go back to the reports. A few months ago, the city reopened the case. It had been classified a homicide but no one was ever arrested. One of the children was present at the scene, an adult daughter named Stella. Unavailable for questioning—found in catatonic state—institutionalized. No viable leads.

. . . *After a potential lead regarding the investigation into the unsolved death of Barbara Devorecek, a local woman found dead in a house fire ten years ago, Akron city police have re-opened the case.*

But after the news update, there is no more information.

I chew on the end of my pen and think for a while.

Then I close my laptop, slide it and the legal pad into my backpack, and leave for work.

Because I taught yesterday, my schedule today is open. I have office hours and I need to research, but I have some time before I have to go to campus. I drive around for a bit, circling through the streets that carve dark gouges through the snow heaps and the grim cement and brick towers. Gusts of smoke from sewer grates pass like wraiths through the maze of downtown.

I pull over finally near one of the old churches, St. Bernard's. An elegant gray stone building with soot-blackened saints keeping watch from the ornamental buttresses. A plastic laminated sign affixed to the front doors reads "Soup Kitchen Mondays Wednesdays Fridays at 11 A.M."

I have driven by this church before and noticed the sign, but without much interest. Until now. I have to park on a steep sloping alley and I yank on the parking brake. I check my watch as I go up the steps of the church. It's ten-thirty.

A few volunteers inside are setting up folding tables. I can tell they are volunteers because they wear nametags that read Volunteer.

"Hi, can I help you?"

A woman comes hustling over, her ponderous chest swaying under a thin beige sweater. She's tying an apron around her waist as she comes.

I do intend to look into Aidan's mother's death, but it seems pointless not to at least try to find the homeless woman, my last shred of potential information about the corpse and his killer. Not that I expect much.

"I'm looking for someone," I say. "A—" Shit, what's the politically correct word for a homeless drug addict with mental problems? "A woman with a—ah, a Dora the Explorer backpack."

"A what now?"

Her brows bunch over her eyes, gray hedges against the light in her irises. She is wearing tan slacks and a beige sweater, both wrinkled and faded, and threads of gray hairs cluster around her temples. But she has a piercing in one nostril and I think that at one point in her life she thought of herself as beautiful.

I know I need to explain what I need better, so I take a breath and start again.

"I ran into a woman—she wasn't, she doesn't have a home. It was pretty obvious."

"You're saying she was homeless."

Oh, that one is easy. "Right. She's homeless. She carries a Dora the Explorer backpack and she has symptoms of tardive dyskinesia."

"Tardy what?"

"Not—look, she's been on schizo meds. Lithium, Thorazine, you know, the stuff that makes you twitch like you've got St. Vitus's Dance."

"Saint Who? What are you talking about?"

"Come on," I say. This is bullshit. She works with homeless people, she has to know what I'm talking about. I blink and pluck at my nose and move my tongue around my mouth, feeling my teeth, my lips.

The woman moves her head back, her eyebrows going up.

"Like that," I say. "Do you know who I'm talking about?"

"Okay," she says. "Yeah, that could be a lot of people. Is she a regular here?"

"I don't know," I say. "I'm looking for her. I think she saw something—"

"Whoa now, are you talking about, a crime? She's wanted for questioning?"

"No, nothing like that," I say. But I can't think of another story to fill in the blank. "Not like that. I just want to—talk to her."

The woman rubs the back of her neck and shakes her head. "It really could be a lot of people. With a backpack?"

"A cartoon character—it's bright and shiny. Pink."

"Oh, pink." The woman thinks for a minute. "That kind of sounds like Desiree."

"Desiree."

"Hold on a sec." She yells toward the back. "Carmen! Hey, Carmen, get over here."

A woman comes over, thin, hobbled by a long straight jean skirt and a baggy brown turtleneck. She's wearing thick wire-frame glasses and she pulls them off when she comes up and rubs twin kidney-shaped reddish spots on the bridge of her nose.

"What?"

"Do you know Desiree?"

"Yeah, she comes in sometimes. Why?"

"She have a pink—what kind of backpack now?"

"Dora," I say. "The Explorer. I think."

"Yeah, that's Desiree," glasses-girl says. She puts her glasses back on, tucks her hair behind her ears. The lenses magnify her eyes like a grasshopper's. Oversized and childish, they stare out at me.

I pull out my backpack and scribble my name and phone number on a card. "Can you call me if she comes in?"

"Why?"

But she takes the card.

"Just please, call me. It's important."

"I'm not sure that's—" She looks up at the larger woman. "I mean—"

The larger woman shrugs. "I don't think there's a rule against it. Just to tell you if she stops by?"

"Yeah."

"I'll give her your card. How about that. Then she can contact you."

"She can't," I say. "Are you an idiot? You work with these people. God, it's not like they've got a cell phone charger in one hand and the latest iPhone model in the other."

The larger woman blinks a couple of times. But she doesn't cuss me out or raise her voice. In the same flat tone, she says, "I'll have Carmen give her your card, but I'll give you a call too. Fair?"

"Thanks," I say. "That's good."

When I leave the wind is shrill, singing atonally like some old-world seer calling down doom on the mortal sphere. The air smells like encroaching winter, old smoke and dead earth, and I wonder how the fire was started, and who started it, and why Aidan's mother died in a house fire that must have burnt like a Viking pyre and lit the neighborhood with aureoles of gilded ash.

The fourth floor hallway of the humanities building with its buzzing runner-lights and speckled linoleum seems unusually festive. Someone tacked a paper chain made of orange and brown construction paper links along the blank wall in front of the stairwell and shreds of cotton now adorn the bulletin board. I push into the graduate student office to collect my books for class and see equally cheap decorations have exploded across our office space as well.

I drop a note in Telushkin's mailbox informing him that my next chapter will be late, and rip up a pink slip informing me to phone the dean at his earliest convenience. Then I head to the library. In my study carrel, I open my laptop and get online. The medical examiner's office is downtown, about a block away from the university campus. I write down the address, realizing I've driven by the unprepossessing concrete block and glass building a hundred times. It's crammed between parking decks, the marble-faced courthouse, and high brick buildings with fluted windows and lawyer's names on brass plaques.

I wonder if the autopsies are performed at the actual office or if the medical examiner has to go down to the hospital's morgue with a briefcase full of surgical knives in one hand and a Starbucks in the other. I imagine some young resident doctor who barely passed her exams trotting in expensive heels toward a steel table on which rests the burned and flayed husk of my corpse.

I blink and shake my head and go back to researching, draft notes for my dissertation chapter. I study for hours and close up the laptop when my eyelids start to feel gritty. I rub my fists against my eyes and crack my neck. Then I swing my backpack over my shoulder, lock up the carrel, and walk downtown to the banks of lawyer offices and courthouses.

The medical examiner's office smells like polyurethane and Calvin Klein perfume. It's clearly just an office. What little solid flesh remains of James A. Sims resides elsewhere.

I take a breath and walk toward the front desk. A large woman wearing chunky gold jewelry and a papery smock blouse sits behind it, flipping through *Dog Fancy* magazine. She hands me a form without looking up when I ask for an information release.

I print "Barbara Devorecek" in the slot labeled *Name of the Deceased*. When I finish filling out the form I pay three dollars and the woman puts the form into a manila folder and tells me the information packet will be mailed to my address within the week.

I have reached the lobby door when she says, "Hey, hon? Ah, Miss Brandis?"

I turn around.

Her hooked, lacquered fingernails hover over her keyboard. "This case is an unsolved homicide. We don't mail out information on current cases, okay?"

I go back to the desk and lean my elbows on it. She smells musky, a scent like chalky clay. "Unsolved?" I remember reading about this in a newspaper story.

Her computer screen is tilted up and I see a name followed by a list of vital statistics. Stella Devorecek. Height, weight, current residence. The current residence is an assisted living facility. At the top of the screen it says "material witness."

I keep my eyes unfocused, traveling the wall behind her desk with its mundane calendar featuring Ohio's covered bridges and a small crayon drawing done by a juvenile hand.

"It just means the investigation was never completed. It happens more than you'd think. It could be any reason. Sometimes they know what's happened but a material witness can't be located or interviewed. Or sometimes it's something else. It can be anything."

I touch my thumbs together and look at the child's scrawl behind her. "Can I ask something?"

The woman's chair creaks as she sits back, turning away from her computer monitor. "What would that be, hon?"

"I know about the two fire sources but that could be coincidence, right? Or an accident. I mean, why is it an unsolved homicide instead of, like, just involuntary manslaughter?"

The woman's tongue touches her lower lip. She lifts a hand and jiggles the thick gold ring in one earlobe. "I don't know where you're getting your information from, honey. I can't tell you any of that stuff."

"Just, can you please tell me why it's been classified a homicide, and not just a, a tragic accident?" I pitch my voice low and work a tremulous quaver into it. My eyes flicker to her computer screen, to the tiny print, and catch on the word "asphyxiation." *Cause of death, asphyxiation. Secondary causes of death, 48 milligrams of zolpidem tartrate, partially metabolized, and 30 milligrams of fluoxetine hydrochloride.*

The woman looks back at her computer screen. "I can't print off the coroner's report. It's the rules, okay?"

I lean against the countertop and put my fist under my nose. "Okay." I hiccup. I want to look like I'm crying but really I'm trying to block my nasal passages. The office has a bitter lye stench from printer toner and air freshener.

"Are you okay?"

"Yes. Thank you."

"I'm sorry."

"It's okay." I push away from the counter and walk out slowly, dragging the balls of my feet. When I push through the doors I stop and straighten, easing my spine and facial muscles out of the posture of feigned suffering. Cars hurtle past and a cop stands on a street corner smoking. Raveling threads of steam twist from sewage grates. I turn my wrist to look at my watch. I need to put in another celebrity appearance—look, look, a pose, a profile shot!—for my weekly office hours.

As I walk back to campus the name that has been eluding me snaps into my brain. Ambien. My mother used to take sleeping pills after Stephen was born.

I head east to the campus library and go inside and log online. Zolpidem tartrate is indeed the generic name for Ambien. I type quickly and discover that fluoxetine hydrochloride is the generic name for Prozac. The recommended daily dose of Ambien is about four milligrams. I tap the desktop with my fingernails, thinking about how many pills it would take to overdose, and thinking about premeditation and mental instability and the nature of good and evil.

After a bit I emerge from the library and climb down the stacked steps overlooking a dry fountain in the middle of the bricked central walkway on campus. A student coming out of a building adjacent to the library turns to his left and his movement catches my eye. It's Aidan. He walks quickly, headed away from me, his hands in the pockets of a gray sweatshirt. His dark head bobs through clots of students like a button floating downstream.

I hesitate. Then I jog down the steps and follow him.

He cuts behind a building and steps up on a cracked cement loading ramp and goes in through a gray industrial door. I look around and see a blue sign that tells me this is the art building. I put out my hand. The metal door is cold.

Inside I go down a long, shadowy hall. The corkboard covering the walls has been chewed by tacks and staples. The hall opens into a foyer area with a faded brown couch and a few planters. A twisted metal wreck lies in the center of the room under a skylight. Speckled sunlight lies like a cancerous skin across the metal sculpture. I walk into the center of the foyer and look around. Copper statues, prints of anime cartoons and acrylic life-size paintings of crucified, full-breasted women line the walls.

Aidan is not in the foyer. I don't know where he went.

The foyer is empty, so I go over to the drinking fountain and drink. Then I fill my hands with water and feed the crisp brown palm tree next to the drinking fountain.

I wander back into the foyer and sit on a brown couch. The stiff cushion rises and there is an unrolled condom between the cushion and the couch arm. I don't touch the condom. I unzip my backpack and take out a textbook.

Two students come into the foyer, but they don't come near me. They head for the elevator and stand around arguing while waiting for it to arrive.

"I'm not going out with Lindsey, it was just a movie."

"How am I supposed to believe you? How?"

A finger pokes my scapula. I startle. My lungs airless, my skin hot.

And then I swallow a couple times. Breathe. And, calmer, twist around. He's leaning his hip against the back of the couch, wearing a white long-sleeved thermal undershirt under a brown paint-stained smock.

"What are *you* doing here?"

The corners of his mouth pinch into a smile. His solitary good eye glitters.

I can still feel the imprint of his finger on my shoulder. I imagine the clean snap of bone if I wrench his finger out of its socket. I swallow again and clear my throat.

"I saw you leaving the library."

He tilts his head to look at me with his right eye. Then he comes around the side of the couch and sits down at the far end, near the arm. The condom falls out and he picks it up and stretches it like a rubber band.

"The greatest lie is the lie we tell ourselves."

"What?"

He points two condom-wrapped fingers at the book I've been reading. It's a book of selected readings by Nietzsche, translated into

English. I picked it up at the library, not really sure what I could hope to discover in reading it.

My roommate, who apparently knows at least his more basic Nietzsche, says, "'The greatest lie is the lie we tell ourselves.' He said that, right?"

For a second that seems to stretch like rubber, creaking with the pressure, I don't say anything.

He waits, and then says, "What are you really doing here?"

I study him for a long time. But I still can't see anything in his face. I wonder if his very innocence is the most perfect mask.

"I'm reading." It's the truth. He didn't ask *why* I am here.

He flips the condom at me. I flinch and it hits my shoulder. I fling it off me.

He laughs. I flinch again.

He stops laughing. He looks at me. Then he stands up. "I'm in the middle of class. I need to get back. Follow me."

I follow him down a narrow hall with brown tiles. He pushes through two heavy metal doors at the far end.

We walk into a long, low room that looks like a factory warehouse, full of hulking metal machines and stainless steel bench tables. Fluorescent lights buzz overhead.

"Do you know what a print is?"

I see other people standing at the counters. I can't see what they're doing. "No."

He walks across the room and I follow several steps behind. In the middle of the room are two large metal presses, round steamroller wheels each with a crank handle. I put my hand against one of the smooth curved sides of the roller. "Don't touch that," he says sharply.

He goes to a table near the water tray, bends and opens a thin drawer, and pulls out a copper plate. He brings the plate and two plastic tubs of paint over to a counter stacked with jars of paintbrushes, rags, thin metal spatulas, paint-stained stirrers. He finds a rag and drapes it over my shoulder and pretends he doesn't see me back up a step, startled. "Hold that," he says.

I look at the copper sheet I am holding in my hand. It has fine lines etched into it, small scarred wedges, but I can't tell what the picture is.

"Where do you want me to put this?"

He doesn't say anything, just drops a glob of blue-gray paint into a pile of deep reddish-brown paint. I rest the plate on the countertop, put the point of my chin on the top edge, and watch him. He pours viscous oil onto the chalky piles of paint and then mixes the paint with a wooden spatula, folding the slippery oil and stiff peaks of paint together until it becomes a thick liquid the color of boiled sour cream and beets. He moves quickly, his hands confident. His thermal undershirt cuffs dangle threads between his fingers. He puts his right wrist to his mouth, holds the cuff between teeth, and pulls the sleeve back. He looks sideways at me.

"A little help?"

My backpack is heavy and hurts my shoulder. I look around the room for someone to help him.

He says, "I meant, can you pull my left sleeve up for me?"

I stare at him in silence. And then I reach over. His skin is cold. I realize it is cold in the drafty warehouse room. My skin feels prickly and hot. I tug his sleeve back.

"Thanks."

He takes the print from me and lays it on the tabletop and starts smearing paint on top of it with even strokes. He works paint into every line in the copper plate, stroking smoothly. His face is tense, contracted. After he covers the plate in paint, he starts scraping it off again, using the edge of the spatula to peel off curls of sludgy paint.

When the copper plate has been stripped clean, he goes to a narrow metal tray. Sheets of rag paper float in about two inches of water in the tray. He lifts one of the water-supple papers over his arm and goes to a heavy metal press in the middle of the room. He says, "Bring the plate over."

I pick up the plate by the edges.

He takes the print and smears paint over it, then sets it down on the press table. He sets the rag paper over the print, spreads a towel across the top of the rag paper, and winds the handle of the press until the heavy round press has rolled over the entire paper. Then he lifts back the towel, which has gotten crushed flat, and he peels up the rag paper.

The front of the rag paper has an old man's face on it. The old man is looking to the side as if something has caught his attention. Soft bags under his eyes, tiredness in the lines dripping down his face, but there is still a faint spark in his eyes, a brittle, clear light. I bend forward and see that the face emerges through small dashes of lines, plum-colored shadows that sculpt the wrinkles and hollows in the face. The light in the eyes, the face itself, are only white paper.

"You're really good."

"Yeah," Aidan says. "I'm awesome." The muscles by his mouth contract into a smile. His eyebrows slant up, a laughing devil.

He takes the sheet over to a corkboard and pins it up with two yellow thumbtacks. Then he splashes kerosene over the copper plate and scrubs it into the fine lines with a small toothbrush from a Folgers coffee can. Swirls of paint mix with the kerosene and run off onto the metal countertop, an oily pinkish liquid that looks like grease and blood. When he finishes, he throws the rag into a bin full of other smelly, paint-smeared rags.

"That's a fire hazard, you know."

"In French," he says, "*hasard* means luck."

I look at him. At his crazy eye dancing sideways while the other one remains steady. "No. It means chance. Not luck."

"Well. Chance, then. Maybe God gives you chance and you make your own luck."

I stare at him.

Someone comes by and says, "Hey, Devorecek, get moving. You've got twenty minutes to get another print out."

Aidan looks over his shoulder at the person and lifts a hand. He turns to me. "Can whatever you have to ask me wait?"

"It already has."

He hesitates. Then he says, "Okay. Talk to you later. Now get out of here. Can't you see I'm busy?" He winks.

Outside the icy wind smells of pine leaves and dry soil, but I can still taste kerosene. It tastes like rotting sunlight.

He comes in that night smelling like pine sap, kicks off his shoes against the baseboard and shucks off his gloves. He goes over to the fridge and catches sight of me. I am sitting cross-legged on the floor in the living room grading a set of midterms.

"So what was it?"

"What was what?"

"Your question."

I set down the exam and the red pen. "I wanted to know if your mom took sleeping pills or antidepressants."

Aidan leans into the fridge and emerges with a carton of orange juice. He pours himself a glass and leans against the kitchen counter. He holds the glass in both hands, thumbs touching. His lower lip pushes out as he studies his thumbs.

"I don't know."

"You don't? You don't remember if your mom was on antidepressants?"

He looks up. "Miranda would know. My older sister. You could ask her."

I just watch him for a while. Then I pick up the exam.

He says, "What?"

"I thought you were the one who wanted to know."

He takes a breath. Sets the cup down on the counter. He comes toward the living room and stops in the doorway. "I do."

"Okay then."

He shoves his hands into his pockets. "She had those orange prescription bottles in the medicine cabinet. And she took pills with her coffee in the morning. I don't know about sleeping pills at night. Miranda would know."

"All right."

He stands watching me grade. Then he says, "What is it? Did she—did she take sleeping pills before the, um, the fire?"

I set the exam down and look up. "Yeah. A hell of a lot, apparently. Ambien *and* Prozac."

He pulls his hand out of his pocket and wipes it over his mouth. Turns his head to the side. Then he lowers his hand and inhales, slowly.

"So what else have you found out?"

I don't know what he expects me to say. "Just what you already know. The fire looks intentional. Your mom had lots of partially metabolized meds in her system. Don't know if she set the fire or if someone else took advantage of her sleeping like Rip Van Winkle."

The skin near his mouth tightens but he doesn't say anything for a while. Then he nods. "Okay. Well, thanks for letting me know." He hesitates. "I think I'm going to—I've got this project I'm working on. I'll be back late."

I raise my eyebrows. "Yeah? Well, ah, parting is such sweet sorrow."

He laughs a little. He collects his shoes and pulls a pack of cigarettes out of his pocket as he walks out the door.

I don't hear him come back until two or three in the morning. The apartment door creaks and wakes me up. I lie there listening as he stumbles and catches himself on the counter. A few minutes later I hear him vomiting in the bathroom. A faint tinge of something sour seeps into the air.

TWELVE

The intake manifold for the car has come in and I stop to pick it up on my way back to the apartment. It's more expensive than I thought, and I realize I won't have much money left to make rent. For a second, I think about asking my parents. But I can't. Because this is about being an adult. I figure I'll see if Aidan will be okay with buying all the toilet paper for the month. I'll get it next month.

When I get back to the apartment I try to explain this to Aidan but it is hard to talk to him. He didn't say anything in the morning and now he's in the throes of some artistic frenzy. He crouches on his hands and knees over a flat board laid out on the kitchen floor. The board is covered in a thick red gel. He plunges his hands into a can of yellow paint and splatters the yellow across the board in a descending arc. When I wave my hand in front of his face, he blinks and wipes his chin on his shoulder. A dab of yellow paint sticks to the corner of his mouth.

I point at the paint mark on his face. "Did you hear what I said?"

He rubs his knuckle over the corner of his mouth. "Yeah. Don't sweat it. You can just give me rides sometimes."

I freeze and stare at him.

He grins up at me.

"*Fuck* you," I say.

I go into my room and slam the door on his voice pitching in consternation. He tries to follow me.

I open the door in his face, a check in my clenched fist. His paint-covered fingers leave red and yellow half-moon marks on the walls.

"I didn't mean anything, I swear. I'm sorry. It was just some random, some stupid comment, okay? I'm really *sorry*."

I throw the check at him and shut the door again, leaning against it. It takes me a long time listening to his frantic jabber and his knuckles on the thin plywood door before I understand that he is under the impression that I took offense at the crude sexual innuendo in his comment.

I open my bedroom door. His eyebrows are slanted in tragedy. "Seriously, Mickey, I'm a shit. I *am* and I'm *sorry*."

"I'm not pissed," I say. "Forget the whole thing. Misunderstanding."

His eyelashes descend and he stands with his hands at his sides, the bony joints of his shoulders pushing through the fabric of his stained T-shirt.

"I said it's okay."

He bends and picks up the check where it has fallen. Paint smears the paper. He smoothes the creases in the check, and folds it and puts it in his back pocket. "Well. Okay, then."

I don't tell him that I thought the pun on "rides" was funny. It's the idea of having another human being sitting in my car that terrifies me.

I watch him turn back and go into the kitchen, and kneel by the paint-splashed board. It occurs to me that, regardless of his relationship to the corpse across the street, at the very least Aidan is telling the truth about how he feels about me. He is genuinely not afraid of me and, for reasons I can't begin to understand, he does not believe that I am a latent killer. I feel a flicker of curiosity and realize that I *want* to solve his mother's murder. I want to find out what forces wrought that mind.

Instead, I go running. But this time I'm not running for the purity of it, for the escape. I'm running with a destination in mind. The huntress stalking her prey.

No one from the soup kitchen has called. I didn't really expect them to. So I need to follow up on Desiree of the Drugs and the Backpack myself.

The air tastes crystalline, gusts rattling bare branches. A freezing mist crusts my skin like a shell of cold pearls. My sneakers strike the concrete with hollow thuds, loud in the preternatural stillness. I jog through the deserted campus and head south through abandoned parking lots behind the performing arts center, down a curving road with no cars idling at the forlorn red lights.

The southern sector of campus is bifurcated from the main campus by a valley through which runs a train track. The curving road I follow loops down under an overpass, and the tracks spool out of shadow. Under the overpass a blue tarp is folded next to a black trash bag. Some homeless person's lair.

I once heard a speaker at the university talking about the homeless population in Akron. He claimed that many of them sleep rough under the bridges in winter. And it looks as if he may actually be right. The speaker also claimed that the city of Akron is plagued by the homeless but that seemed to me a strange assertion. I doubt that most upstanding citizens have ever seen or spoken to a homeless person, except for the ones who lurk by freeway exit and entrance ramps with their cardboard signs, and the most interaction that occurs at those interchanges is a strenuous avoidance of eye contact. It seems to me that the homeless may instead be plagued by the rest of Akron's population. I stop and look at the accoutrements of a migratory life. The thick smell of unwashed body, but a certain cleanness to the life lived pressed up against the shadow of not-being. I wonder if the person whose sole shelter is a blue tarp will die of exposure. It annoys me that normal people have already decided that this individual, this human-shaped absence, can die, but that I with my morbid fantasies should be despised. Sympathy is illogical, but if people are supposed to be sympathetic they should at least practice it consistently.

I wander for a long time, hunting down the trace of the homeless. But I don't see any sign of Desiree. I think about how easily people die of exposure, of disease. How fundamentally not hard it is to be killed, through murder or through apathy.

After my futile search for my one link to 411 Allyn Street and the corpse inside, my witless witness, Desiree of the Dora the Explorer backpack, I head back to the apartment to shower and change and go in search of my only other puzzle piece: Aidan's past.

When I climb into the Chevelle, I slide the key into the ignition and for a second just listen to the throaty rumble of the engine. It's a new car with the manifold replaced. I think it even gets better gas mileage, but it's hard to tell when a good day averages about seventeen miles to the gallon. I let the engine idle for a minute, exhaust billowing out behind the car and smudging the sky like ash. I want to know why Aidan hasn't told me who he suspects in his mother's death, which character on the Clue board of his past he thinks he's protecting. There isn't a logical reason for him to be so shy about it. As he said, it's not like I'll care one way or another. But for whatever reason, it doesn't seem like he's going to tell me.

I power my way through Akron's salt-whitened streets, looking for a road called Brown. The house fire from which Aidan's mother's corpse was dragged a decade ago occurred at 2136 Brown Street. The street itself is narrow, a cracked sidewalk running jaggedly through mounds of grayed snow studded with upturned trashcans and crumpled beer cans. The houses perch on small stamps of thinning grass, porches sagging, roofs rain-buckled and sun-bleached. Because this area is crowded with low-income housing, I am surprised to find the lot without any problems. The house has not been rebuilt. Aidan's old house was a yellow Cape Cod, and the shell of the structure is now singed and streaked with black, a gaping hole in the roof near the chimney. The plywood tacked across the door has been stamped with large pink letters that read Condemned.

There is an obvious synchronicity between Aidan's decade-old murder and the more recent corpse, but so far I can't see any *sense* behind the inexplicable parallels.

I pull the Chevelle over to the side of the road and park. The bitter air nips at my skin. Hugging my arms against my chest, I climb through overgrown weeds to the front door. A black-painted mailbox sits above a white doorbell. I lift the lid of the mailbox, but it's empty. I breathe in deeply, but the house does not smell of char or death.

I step backwards off the front porch and crane my head back, studying the house. It's a typical layout, so the floor plan probably involved two bedrooms, a kitchen, a bathroom, and a living room on the first floor, with a narrow attic above and a basement below. With three kids, two girls and one boy, the extra bedroom on the ground floor probably belonged to the girls, the attic above to the boy.

The report claimed that the fire had two points of origin. Given the singe near the chimney, it is safe to assume that one point was the attic. The other point was the master bedroom, facing the street on the left-hand side of the house. The wall here is buckled, the siding blackened, the window long ago shattered, boarded over, and taped shut.

I turn and head back to the car. My face is numb and my nose drips.

"Excuse me? Excuse me."

I stop and turn around, wiping my sleeve under my nose.

A fat woman has come out of a tiny brick house to the left of 2136 Brown. She is wearing pink slippers and hugging a faded pink cardigan around her breasts, which bounce like melons in a sack as she waddle-runs to me.

"Excuse me!"

I wait and she arrives finally, panting. The top of her head barely comes up to my shoulder and I can see pale skin through the garishly-dyed red hairs sprouting from her scalp. When she moves her clothes give off a faint odor of cat litter.

"Hi," she says, wheezing. "I saw you looking at that house."

I don't say anything. My fist, clenching the ignition key, rests on the car door's frame.

"I've lived here for twenty-three years. I used to be neighbors with the family. A very sweet family. It was terrible what happened." She stops and looks up at me as if expecting me to comment. When I don't, she sucks in a breath and says, "If you don't mind me saying it, I don't think gawking is very respectful. That woman was a saint."

A light flickers in my head. "Are you Judith Greene?"

She says, "Oh! Did you know her?"

After a slight pause, I say, "Yes. I was a—she was my therapist."

Judith Greene tilts head. The cream-colored rolls of fat on her neck dimple. "Oh, I'm sorry I said you were disrespectful! I thought—I mean, you know how kids are these days. Every Halloween it's the same, you know? Do you want to come in? It's real cold out."

"No. Thanks. How well did you know her?"

Judith Greene's bulbous eyes stare up at me, the whites branched with veins and tinged pink, the irises the color of pale amber, yellow washed in gold. "We were like *one* soul trapped in *two* bodies," she says.

Her whole body quivers in its pink sweater.

We stand in silence, our breath startling and dark in the clear sky.

"What about her kids?"

She says, "Yes, they were beautiful children. Miranda was so talented, and that sweet little boy. He used to watch my cats. I wish I knew what became of them. It was so terrible, what happened. I think we all needed to—you know, move *on*. And you know, with the divorce, they were already living with their father."

"What about the other one?"

"The other one?" She licks her lips. The moisture glistens. "You mean Stella. She was—Barb loved her so much."

I look at Judith Greene. "Loved her more than the others?"

"No, but with her—*disability*. You know how it is. We love the ones who need us in a special way."

"Disability?"

"With her, you know, her *mental* condition."

"Oh," I say. A sister with a mental disability. A fire. I almost smile but it's not particularly amusing. "Yes," I say. "I know how it is."

She reaches for me and before I can move, she squeezes my bare hand. Her palm is clammy and soft. "You know, I sing with a choir and we are doing a performance to raise money for a scholarship in her name—you've probably heard of it. The Barb Devorecek Memorial Scholarship?"

I swallow. My mouth tastes like rotten fruit.

She says, "Let me get you a card with the information on it. You should come. I think you'll really love the performance."

And she turns and scuttles back to her house. I stand by the car. I bend forward, resting my forehead against the cold metal frame. I wipe my sweating palms on my shirtfront. She comes back waving a bookmark-shaped flyer. I take it from her, fold it into my jeans pocket, and open my car door before she can touch me again. Shielded by the metal and glass door, I say, "Okay. Thank you. I'll be there."

I'm lying, of course, but she forgot to ask my name so it doesn't matter.

When I slide in, I see her lips forming a question. I crank the ignition, slam off the parking break, and roar away from the curb.

She stands watching me until the car reaches the end of the street.

At the next stoplight, I pull the legal pad out of my pack and find the list of names Aidan wrote. I circle the name "Stella" three times in red ink. The way Aidan told the story, it sounded like this sister is in an assisted living home because she was injured in the fire, or because she was psychologically unhinged by it. Or maybe that's just how I heard it. I wonder why my mind didn't assume she was already a mentally sick violent criminal. And then I think about Aidan's inexplicable friendliness, his utter lack of fear or discomfort around me. I wonder what Aidan considers acceptable in human relationships. How he defines normalcy, or innocence.

I call Aidan's cell as I drive. He doesn't pick up. I leave a message.

"Your psycho sister," I say. "What exactly is wrong with her? You've got to give me the details. I'm kind of new at this detective business, so you've got to help me out. Okay?"

When I get back to the apartment, I notice a dark figure sitting hunched over on the wooden staircase outside the door. I hesitate, but then I recognize the shaggy fringe of caramel-colored hair under the knit cap. I head for the stairs. He looks up when my sneakers rattle the slats. His cheeks are chapped.

"What the hell are you doing here?"

He scrubs a knuckle under his nose and then sniffs hard. "My school had this field trip to the university's polymer science building."

I look at my baby brother and remember the dean's imperative pink slip from yesterday.

"Oh. Damn." I should have looked. I wave my hand at Stephen. "Get your ass out of the way. I have to unlock the door."

He stands up, dragging his heavy backpack with him, squeezing himself back against the railing. I edge past him to unlock the door and push it open. The kitchen feels warm after the frigid outside air. I put my backpack in my room and when I come out he is standing in the middle of the kitchen floor like an island of teenage angst.

Since he hasn't been to the apartment yet, I say, "Hey, why don't you go check out my room. It's in the style of early modern rustic, the college years."

He nods once and shuffles obediently down the hall. I check the fridge and pull out two sodas, a bar of cheese, and a carton of eggs. I fry scrambled eggs and melt cheese on top, scrape the eggs onto two dishes, and set one of the dishes and one of the sodas in front of the couch.

"Hey, scrawny. You hungry?"

He comes out and slouches on the couch and looks at the food. Then he picks up the soda.

I lean against the kitchen sink. "So."

He pulls off his hat and holds it balled in his hands. His straw-stiff hair crackles. "So what?"

I pick up the dish of eggs and start eating. Around a mouthful, I say, "So you must have a real reason for coming over. Spit it out."

He squeezes the hat and looks down at the eggs. Then he takes a breath and shrugs his shoulders, and picks up the dish.

"That tour was frigging boring. We did it when I was in *middle* school."

"God," I say. "The appalling *nerve* of some people. But seriously. What's the deal?"

He doesn't say anything for a while. From the street below someone screams an obscenity and a car horn blares. He bends down and unzips his bag. He roots around and then pulls out a textbook, which he opens. Slotted in the textbook is what looks like an old Polaroid.

"I found this a while ago. I was looking for a baby picture for this stupid school project we have to do. I was going through some of Dave's old pics, like, in the basement."

I can't see the picture from the kitchen, and I don't feel like going into the living room where I'll be able to smell his teenage body odor and deodorant and the cafeteria and perfume scents lingering on his school clothes.

"You know, my telepathy just isn't what it used to be."

He looks down at the picture like he doesn't quite know how to explain it. Then he stands up and holds it to me. I don't move, so he takes another step, still holding it out.

"At first," he says, not looking at me, "I thought it was, like, a picture of Dave."

I can see the photo from here. It's a baby picture, your normal sort. Fat kid with crazy black hair, the hippy-looking mother squeezing the hell out of the kid, who's laughing up at her. I can't for the life of me think why he'd guess Dave, except that Dave and I are the only other kids in the family.

"Well," I say, "if that *was* Dave wearing a ruffled pink onesie, it would sure explain a lot."

Stephen pulls the picture back and studies it. Then he glances up at me from under his eyelashes. A little smile twitches up the corner of his mouth. "Yeah," he says. "I guess it would."

He slumps back on the couch. I finish eating the eggs and rinse the dish in the sink.

"Do you remember that?"

I shut off the water. Shake my hands and then wipe them on my jeans. I don't know what to say. I understand what he's asking. He's asking the same thing all those years of shrinks asked. Stephen was born late in the year that I was ten. He doesn't remember before that, just like all the shrinks I had to visit didn't know the pre-killer Mickey, either. So of course they want to know, Was she always like that? Is there a genetic flaw in this child? Or are we witnessing some psychotic reaction to a traumatic event?

I raise my arms slightly. "What you see," I say, "is what you get."

He frowns down at the photo.

"No, you stupid ass," I say. "*Here*. Me. Right now. Who I am now. I don't give a fuck about people, about *any*one. It so happens I was born this way, but it wouldn't matter anyway, if, you know, something made me this way. Point is, this is the way I am. So whatever is weighing on your young mind? You should probably take it somewhere else."

He looks up at me. "Does Dave ever ask you for money?"

There is a silence. I notice cracks in the plaster wall behind Stephen.

"I don't know," Stephen says. He's talking quickly now. "It was sort of weird. He called my cell phone which is, like, weird on its own, and then he starts talking about this really strange stuff, like, he kept asking if I understood the heart of *God* or some bullshit like that. Then all of a sudden he asked if I still had the birthday money Grandma and Grandpa sent me."

"Do you?"

Stephen shrugs. We both know the answer. Stephen is a packrat. He saves everything. "I sort of lied and said I'd spent about half. I mean, what does he need *my* money for? The only thing I can think is he's, you know, doing drugs again, or—I guess *still*, maybe. Right?"

There is a faint convex shadow on the wall. Like the house has imperceptibly sagged with the years and the drywall is slowly caving between support beams.

"Probably. Don't give him your money, okay? If he calls back, just tell him I've got him covered."

"Are *you* going to send him money? Mickey? Do you send Dave money?"

I don't say anything right away. Then I look at Stephen. "Either way," I say, "he's my problem."

Stephen looks uncomfortable. He shifts on the sofa. Looks down at the photo again. "He's my brother, too."

"No, he's not."

Stephen looks up, surprise etched around his eyes, his chapped mouth.

I wave my hand briefly, erasing the words. "I mean, he's like, what, fifteen years older than you? He's old enough to be your fucking *father*. Forget him. Okay?"

"Forget him."

"Well, whatever, just don't worry about him."

Stephen watches me for a minute. His lips squeeze together. Then he slides the photo back into the textbook and closes up his backpack. He stands up. "I like your—um, your TV. This is a cool pad."

I watch him make his way to the door. He stops by the door again. "I'm glad we had this talk, Mickey."

I laugh. "This wasn't much of a talk, little brother. You should raise your standards."

He shrugs a shoulder, hesitates.

"Well. Bye."

I hear his feet trundling down the steps. He jumps off the last two. I go over to the living room window and watch him jog across the street. I watch until the knit cap bobs out of sight around a corner.

Then I go into my room and pull out my cell phone. I sit for a long time. A slow pulse of pain tightens my scalp. Pressure increases, steady as a heartbeat. After a while, I call Dave.

The phone rings for a while. When he answers, he sounds groggy like he just woke up.

"Wha—Mickey?"

"You're a fucking pathetic loser," I say. "What the fuck are you on? You can't hit your seventeen-year-old brother up for cash. You utter *shit*."

"Oh." He coughs, spits. "Hold on, babe, you've got the wrong—I would never do that. Okay? Never. I mean, maybe I did call him, maybe I made something up about—but what else could I do? I've called you how many times since you've moved in with that pretty art creature? *How* many times? And you never call me back."

When I don't say anything, he says, "Twelve. Did you, can you fucking believe it? My own sister."

"I don't know what you want from me."

"Nothing. I'm sorry, babe, it was nothing, it was, I was just really fucking lonely, you know? And our darling parents, well, dearest mum is so sweet it gives one cavities and you know I have *such* father issues, and I—"

"You can call me. I'll talk. I'm—" The word sticks. I swallow. "I'm *sorry*. Okay?"

"Oh, Jesus, come on, babe, don't be such a fucking martyr. I'm not asking you to do anything—just a few words, the pleasure of your company, not anything so terrible, is it? Is it?"

"Don't," I say. "Just—try not to be such an asshole."

He laughs. "What about your lovely roommate? Do you speak to him? Do you gossip like starlings about his poor dear murdered mum? His *feelings* regarding the great loss?"

I hang up on him. The phone falls to the floor. I sit and stare at the fallen phone for a long time. Then I get up and go for a run.

Early evening. The frozen crust of earth purls with trapped melted snow. The scent of snow, of wet crumbling tree bark, of exhaust. And under it all the sharp bitter smell of scorched wood, melted rubber, overheated metal, the last traces of an apocalyptic fire. Overhead an exuberant, limitless arc of night swirls with dazzling white stars.

I run hard. The pounding rhythm of my feet, the whisk of breath. The trail winds its way down and the gurgle and lap of water rushes through the dark. I come out on an outcropping of rock and see a flare of ice-white foam, water cascading down tumbled rock, glittering in the moonlight.

Just like last night, Aidan doesn't come home until almost two in the morning. He stumbles against the edge of the kitchen counter and whispers, "*Ow*." I lie in the dark listening to the muted fumbling noises as he trips taking off his boots, his jacket. His keys fall on the floor. Finally his bedroom door creaks and the night grows quiet again.

In the morning I make coffee, set a red-capped bottle of ibuprofen next to the pot, and write *dumbass* on a napkin, which I fold creatively behind the pills.

He comes into the kitchen rubbing his eyes. He notices the bottle and gives a cracked laugh. "Thanks, Mickey. You don't have to."

"Damn straight," I say.

I watch him sit carefully at the table, lowering himself as though his joints hurt. He sets the bottle of pills between his palms and drops his chin toward his chest.

I watch the creases in his face, human hieroglyphs of suffering.

I go to the refrigerator and get out a carton of milk. Pour a glass for myself and one for him. I set one glass in front of him. He reaches it for it. My hand remains touching the cool surface. His fingertips brush mine. He glances up, surprised.

"Your mom was a child psychologist."

"No."

"What?"

He reaches for the glass. Cups a pill into his mouth and then drinks. When he lowers the glass the skin around his eyes looks frail as parchment. He rubs his wrist across his milk-glazed mouth. "I mean, she wasn't really a doctor or anything. She was a 'play therapist.' She mostly just played with kids."

"Yeah? Interesting choice of career."

"She used to work in a daycare."

I go to the cupboard and pull out a bag of bagels and put one in the toaster.

"Till your sister was born, you mean."

Aidan coughs a little and takes another drink of milk. He sets the glass down, puts his hands on the edge of the table. He picks at a hangnail, sucks his finger. "No," he says. "Till she was diagnosed."

Outside the living room window the street buzzes with life. Car horns honking, people calling to each other.

"With what?"

He takes a breath. "Autism. She's severely autistic. She used to be pretty high functioning. She regressed after the—" He swallows hard. "—the fire."

The answer surprises me. Autism seems so garden-variety damaged compared to the more homicidally-inclined psychiatric diagnoses I was expecting.

I think for a while. Then I say, "Did you know that I went to about a thousand shrinks of every stripe and color when I was ten?"

He raises his eyebrows, looks up at me.

"Wouldn't it be weird if I'd gone to your mother?"

Aidan doesn't say anything for a minute. Then he says, "I think I'd have remembered that."

"Not really. You would've been, what? Four? Five years old?"

He looks down at the kitchen linoleum. Then back up at me. "Did you?"

"What, go see your mom?"

He nods.

Silence drags on. I let him listen to the quiet, the distant city sounds, let him realize that deep down he's been thinking this all along. Wondering.

I say, "No."

The skin around his eyes and mouth shifts. A dark light flaming behind his eyes. I realize that I was an idiot, that I can watch emotion unfurl, implode like a dying star, and still not know what it means. I smile. My mouth feels bruised, sore. "I'm going home today," I say. "May be a while. Don't wait up."

He smiles, but lines drag at his mouth.

I drive to my parents' house.

THIRTEEN

Archeology, the meticulous examination of sediment and bone, appeals to me. But human archeology is more complicated. How many layers of a self are there? The human capacity for self-deception is infinite.

When I walk up toward the front door I can hear a student playing the piano. I open the door and see a high school student's skinny back swaying at the piano. Sunlight streams through the leaded glass windows and paints rays of yellow across the mirror-clear black lacquer finish on the piano. The student plays like a metronome. She chops out phrases of Chopin like a chef slicing vegetables. I stand in the monastic sterility of hardwood floors, brown leather couches with fuzzy gold pillows and a glass-and-black entertainment set. I wonder if my life feels to other people like this music feels to me. Disturbing, off-kilter. Technically perfect, but tonally wrong.

My mom is sitting on a stool on the opposite side of the piano. She sees me walk in the front door, and her eyes track my movements. I go through to the kitchen, and in the kitchen I stop facing the basement door. I put my hand on the doorknob.

I breathe in, hold the breath, and let it out, softly.

I turn the knob.

The stairs creak under my feet.

I stop halfway down but there is no sign of damage, no stain, no lingering scent of death. My imagination plays tricks on me when I sleep.

I shake my head and go more quickly the rest of the way down the stairs.

The basement apartment has a pale green carpet. The walls are goldenrod yellow. I stand and look at the countertop, the microwave, and through a small door a bedroom and a tiny bathroom. The last time I was down here was the summer of the fat college student who would become the first corpse I ever knew. He taught me to play cards. The summer he lived with us, he and Dave used to play cards together down here for hours.

I go into the bedroom. The white-painted bookshelves still hold copies of Dave's books. He moved into this room after the college student's death. Dave lived here till he graduated from high school. Since then, my parents haven't rented the basement to anyone. I know that the upstairs photo albums are full of typical family pictures, and I also know that the photo Stephen found wasn't one of them. He got it from Dave's personal collection.

I pull a box painted with red and orange geometric shapes from the bookshelf. The box smells of cedar and candle wax. Inside are stacks of Polaroids. I sit on the end of the bed and spread out the photos like playing cards.

Dave used to collect photos like some people collect trinkets, a shot glass from every Hard Rock Café, the rookie cards of every Cleveland Indians player. The photos from the cedar wood box are mostly of him. Like pictures of him at three years old running down a shoreline, the taller figures of our parents in the background, only black silhouettes against the sun.

One of the pictures makes me pause. Dave is not in this picture, just a fat baby splashing in a kiddie pool. I look at the one-year-old me, all tubby belly and constipated expression, and wonder why Dave kept it.

Most of the rest of the photos are of Dave, or of him and me.

I sift through them and don't know what I'm looking for. I squint at the pictures and wonder if it's possible to read flawed DNA from a photograph, but I don't think it is.

I don't remember some of these pictures. Others I do remember. There is a picture of me at six years old, blowing out birthday candles. A party hat is on my messy hair, my eyes sparkling. It looks like a nice picture. I remember that birthday, but what I remember best was my mother walking in on us, on me and Dave in the kitchen, later that night.

I don't remember consecutive events. I remember flashes. The sizzle and flare of light. Giggling. Holding a match in my fingers. Dave's hands closing around mine. Fire blossoming in my palms. The sweet dark smell of cooking flesh. My mother said later that Dave told her I was experimenting with fire. Dave explained that he caught me and was trying to make me stop. I remember how she was crying when she smeared yellow ointment on my hands. I remember how she hugged Dave, her tears and snot dripping into his hair as she said, "You saved your sister. Thank you. *Thank* you." I shuffle the photos together, tap them into a neat square, and set them back in the box. Then I go upstairs.

The piano student has left but the piano lid is open. I slide onto the bench seat, which is still faintly warm. I finger-pick, reading the sheet music still propped on the piano and sounding out the Chopin phrase by phrase. My fingers ease into the music as I play it through a second time, listening to the resonance and melody, the complex tonal variations, steel strings pitched at perfect tension and resonating at certain frequencies. I bring the student's butchered black-and-white performance to sudden life.

When I stop, I lift my head and notice that the windows are dark, that I am playing in a shadowy room with the only light coming from the hall between the kitchen and living room. The house is quiet except for the creaks and hums of old pipes. And a faint, husky sound, like uneven human breath. I frown and slide the piano shut, and go into the kitchen. My mother sits at the island, perched on a stool. A large ledger, curling receipts, and a few slit-open envelopes lie around her. Her elbows are propped on the tile surface of the island and her hands are shielding her face. Her shoulders move in spasmodic jerks.

I stand in the doorway for a while. I don't think she hears me. But then she gulps and sniffs and moves her elbows off the countertop, and presses the sides of her fingers against the corners of her eyes, probably so that she won't smudge her mascara. But when she turns her head to look at me, her mascara is already smeared and caked in the fine creases by her eyes.

"Oh, hi there, honey. I didn't hear you."

Her voice is thick with mucus. She tries to smile.

My shoulders are hunched, my hands fisted in my jeans pockets.

We don't say anything for a while.

Then she gets up and collects the receipts, folding them inside the ledger and snapping the ledger shut. "It's late. I should start supper."

"Are we, like, poor or something?"

"What?" She turns to me. Then she looks at the ledger and sniffs again and smiles brightly. "Of course not. We're doing fine. I'm just—being stupid."

I think she means about finances, and I think, Shit. Because I was going to ask for money. I don't know if Dave was serious or not about needing cash, but just in case, I figured I'd hit up the endless well of parental love, expressed in twenty-dollar denominations. Usually I give him some of my stipend money if he's running low, but I'm not the ATM I used to be now that I have to pay monthly rent and utilities.

I go over to the fridge and open it and look for something to eat.

"What are you here for?"

"I forgot something. Came to get it. Is there enough of that pasta for me to have some?"

"Of course. The marinara is in that container there. By the eggs."

I carry the plastic containers to the counter and fix myself pasta and sauce, heat the plate of food in the microwave.

"So is everything going well? Your classes?"

I glance over at her. "Yeah. They're okay. My classes, I don't know. The students are so gullible. I could tell them anything and they'd believe me. They're a bunch of rats in a box waiting for someone to start experimenting."

She smiles a little, gets out a saucepan and slices butter into it. She crushes a clove of garlic. Papery garlic shells litter the countertop.

"Mom?"

She turns to look at me. Her face, creased with dark mascara, looks like a Greek tragedy mask.

"Do you remember me always being like this?"

She doesn't answer right away. She blinks and gets a skein of green onions out of the vegetable drawer in the refrigerator. I pull back against the sink when she passes me.

She says, "We didn't notice anything right away. But we wouldn't. I mean, all babies fuss and poop their pants. You start noticing their—well, I suppose you would call it their personalities—later."

"But then you noticed."

She slices onions into the sizzling butter. "I don't know."

The microwave dings. I pull out the plate of pasta. Iridescent patches of oil glisten on the steaming sauce. I get a fork out of the silverware drawer and blow on the pasta.

"What do you mean you don't know?"

"Well, I suppose I noticed things that—made more sense later."

"After I killed that guy."

She doesn't say anything. I can't see her face from the sink. I assume that she's thinking about her answer, but then she puts out an arm, props it against the countertop, and her head drops forward and she turns it to the side, and I see that she's biting her lower lip and her eyes are closed tight. Tears stiffen her eyelashes.

I watch her cry for a while. Her chest hikes up and down, water pooling in the hollows under her eyes. She looks old when she cries.

Then her breathing evens out, and she wads paper towels against her face and blows her nose.

"So what are you crying about now? The same thing you were crying about earlier?"

She takes a few breaths. Like air is something newly discovered and she's tasting it, sampling it. Her face glistens. "Yes," she says. "The same thing."

"And it's not finances."

"No."

"Is Dad having an affair?"

She gasps and then laughs. The wrinkles on her face ease. "No, honey." She smiles and dabs at her eyes. "You don't need to worry about that. Your father and I have been through rough patches before. We'll work this one out."

I eat some pasta. Chew. Swallow. "So it's me."

She moves the sauce off the burner. "It's not anything. Sometimes I just cry."

"That's pointless," I say. "Most people cry for a reason, right?"

She pinches her lips together. And then she takes a breath and lets it out, slowly. She looks up at me. Her face is calm but her eyes sparkle with collected tears. "What's it like in your head? What are you thinking right now?"

I raise my eyebrows. I don't know what she wants me to say. "Nothing, I guess. Nothing important. You've got snot on your lip."

"Why do you think I'm crying?"

I squint at the pasta. "I just said I don't know. If I had to guess, I'd say because being around me makes you sad." I look at her. "But that doesn't make any sense. Because you've lived with me my whole life."

I watch as tears well up in her eyes again and spill over. Her eyes burn, incandescent. She doesn't wipe the tears this time. She says, "You never cried. When you were only three years old, I found you in the sandbox playing with toys and you had banged your head. Your forehead was bleeding, dripping onto your sandcastle, but you didn't seem to notice. And then one time I saw a little neighbor girl come over and take a doll out of your hand. You just watched her like she was a—a curious specimen."

I just look at her. I don't know what she wants me to say.

"Does it hurt you? When people touch you?"

I shrug. "It makes me feel—claustrophobic. Freaks me out, kind of. It probably feels like vertigo."

"Vertigo."

"I read about vertigo once and it sounded about right. I'm just guessing."

She nods.

She doesn't say anything for a bit. I notice that she's stopped crying. Finally, she dabs off her face again and tosses the wadded-up paper towel in the trashcan. Then she goes to the fridge and gets out a plastic-wrapped package of raw chicken breast. She says, "You were playing that Chopin so beautifully, such good tonal control. And I was just thinking about how you can play musical emotions you've never felt. And how I can't hug my own daughter." She starts slicing chicken breast on a cutting board. I watch the knife blade flash through the firm pink flesh. She says, "I went through a stage when you were about fourteen, when we were realizing that it wasn't going away—whatever it was—anyway, I went through a stage where—where I sometimes wished you had died."

She brushes hair off her forehead with the back of her hand. She gazes up at nothing and then shakes her head and starts cutting chicken again. "I didn't wish you had died. I just felt like my child had died, but wasn't dead. I can't explain it. I would wake up in the middle of night and realize I could never—never take my daughter shopping, or to the movies, or to—to *prom*. I could never—kiss my own daughter. Hug her. Talk to her." She stops talking.

"We're talking now," I say. "We're conversing."

She gives a sound like a cat choking on a hairball. She says, "I could be talking to the—to the *refrigerator*. I'm explaining why human beings cry. That's not—we're not *talking*, Michaela."

I don't know what she means. It sounds like we're talking, at least it sounds like it to *me*, but I think pointing that out will not exactly help.

"I just told you I used to wish you were dead," she says. Her voice is shrill. She turns to face me. "Do you feel anything? *Any*thing?"

Her face is stricken with sharp lines. I imagine that if I touched my fingertips to her face the skin would feel moist and cool like a hard-boiled egg. I could smooth my thumbs over the dark smears marring her egg-white cheeks like Aidan brushing paint over a mess of penciled lines. And suddenly I want her to wake up in the morning, startled, to realize that I was never born, that my whole life was just a bad dream that she has finally woken from and that the sun is warm on her pillow and she is happy.

I look down at my hands, cupped around the pasta container. The sauce has left an orange stain on the plastic. "I understand why you feel that way, I do. I'd be pissed, too. I'm not what any mother would wish for in the daughter department, so I—"

"Jesus!"

I stop, startled. My mother never swears. She looks brittle. The knife is wavering in the air. I watch the tip trembling.

"I'm your goddamn mother! I *love* you! Say something!"

Instead of making her feel better I have brought a wildness to her pink-stained eyes. I don't know what to say.

I just stare at her. At the knife. I wonder if she's going to stab me.

After a long time I say, "It's okay. You don't have to."

"I don't have to?" The knife wavers. "I don't have to love you? Do you have any idea what it feels like to hear you say that? Oh God. That's not what I meant. I love you. I do love you."

All of my life she's said this to me. I used to think it was odd but then Dave told me that she didn't know. She still doesn't. I don't understand how she can *not* know. She thinks that it's possible to love me, like I'm just some ordinary person who can be saved, or changed, brought back from whatever dark place I got lost in. But I can't be saved. No matter how much I want it.

"I wish—"

She blinks and looks at me.

I swallow. "Never mind. Thanks for the pasta." I put the bowl down on the counter.

She watches me as I leave. Streaks of mascara drip down her cheeks, a sad clown's eyelashes.

FOURTEEN

I intend to write some of my dissertation but when I get home all I can think about is the knife in my mother's hand. Tears. Human grief. I think about Judith Greene with her fat cheeks and tragic eyes. And I think about that blue tarp under the bridge.

It occurs to me that ordinary people kill other people all the time. But they don't murder solely from rage or from a delight in the act of killing itself. The depths of sadness, which I have never felt, are deep enough to kill, to drive people to unthinkable acts because they can no longer think. They only exist in a world of feeling and that feeling is misery.

I don't sleep much, drifting in a watery dreamscape where I am tangled in algae and reeds and when I drag my hand free of the water I see that my fingers are tangled in my younger brother's hair and I realize that I have been trying to rescue him but forgot my purpose and now he's drowned. The edges of my dreams leave me exhausted but hyper. My skin feels shrunken, like it hugs too tightly to my bones.

At five-thirty in the morning I get up and go into the kitchen. As quietly as I can, I slice cheese and pull out a packet of bologna. I butter two pieces of bread and stack together a sandwich, slice it lengthwise, and zip it into a baggie. I collect some carrot sticks as well. The homeless shelter and soup kitchen won't be open this early, which means anyone who slept rough on the raised concrete buttresses under the bridges will still be there.

A hoary sun cracks the slate clouds in the east and rain flares white against it. Past the southernmost dormitory and the art building, a steep hill drops down to the tracks. I jog across the parking lot of the academic building, stop in the weeds overgrowing the verge, and look down toward the overpass. The slope ends in broken shale and the metal stitching of train tracks.

Emerald green glass bottle shards glint through the brown crust of rust, old leaves, cigarette butts, and soiled trash bags. My sneakers creak on the cold gravel. I near the overpass and see that my guess was right. There is a veritable homeless domestic scene awaiting me. Broken bricks pin the edges of the blue tarp, and two hefty trash bags of clothes lie between the bricks, along with a man in a few overcoats and a yellowish beard.

I keep hiking down the tracks. He stirs when I pass but doesn't lift his head. His coat sleeve is empty.

I walk for a long time. I pass two people who are sitting together talking. They look up at me and raise a hand, nod their heads. I am uncertain what the protocol for greeting is, but I nod, awkwardly, and keep walking.

On one sloping concrete embankment I see a collection of trash bags, a shopping cart filled with blue plastic Walmart bags tied tight around their contents, and the object that caught my eye in the first place: a stained pink backpack, still shiny in the glittering golden dawn.

The occupant of this outdoor domicile is at home. A woman sits on the concrete by the cart, one hand on a cigarette, eyes fixed on the middle distance. She blink and turns her head toward me as I pick my way down the tracks.

She doesn't seem to recognize me, but I recognize her. Or at least, I recognize the pink bulb of her tongue as it pushes through the gap in her front teeth, pulsing in and out like a nervous snake.

"Hey," I say.

She mutters to herself and rocks. After a while she looks back at me. Her cheek twitches so hard her head jerks to the side slightly.

"It's okay," I say. "I'm not going to do anything to you. Look. I brought you a sandwich."

Her eyes wander away from my face and I realize that she is totally disconnected, that even the sandwich isn't reaching the lucid bit of her subconscious.

I reach out to touch her.

"No, no." Her fingers pluck at the air. "Don't be sweet. Don't be no. It eats the sweet."

"Sh. Hush. It's okay."

She warbles meaningless syllables to me. Spit drains from her mouth.

I say, "I won't hurt you. I don't lie, you can believe me." I don't even know what I'm doing, only that she saw the corpse, she is tied irrevocably to that world. But she pulled a sheet over him. I only want her to know—I'm not sure what. That I saw it, that I know who she is under the fracturing mind and social stigmatization.

But her eyes look everywhere except at me. So I reach out and I force my hands to touch hers, her skin the texture of old mushrooms, spongy and damp.

The heat starts in my palms. Pricks along my fingers, down my wrists, running like molten iron up the insides of my arms, burning in the hollows of my elbows. The sickness in my stomach makes my heartbeat kick faster.

She screams. Saliva slides down her chin. Her chipped and yellowed nails claw at my arm. Thin pink welts race over my skin like tunneling worms.

And then the fabric of her skin melts. Relaxes. Her eyelids close. I jump back as her body rocks forward, the joints folding, the limps collapsing. Startled, I think for a minute that I have killed her somehow. Then I realize she must be fainting or having an epileptic seizure. I grab her just before she hits the gravel. Her body is heavy and smells sour. The dampness of her armpits, her stale breath. I lay her against the cloth-sided suitcase. I check her pulse, which is butterfly faint but steady. She has fainted, not seized.

I look down at her. A shadow hangs over her lax skin and I can almost imagine the lips filled out with teeth, the wrinkles erased by reversed time. I imagine her resurrection, the eyelids lifting on clear and smiling eyes. She will get up and gather herself and her steady feet will take her to a warm lit place where some child catches sight of her, and reaching out desperate hands cries in a voice full of birthdays and bright Saturday mornings, "Mommy! Mommy!"

I stand over her in the cold morning and imagine a world in which she's some kid's home, and I am some mother's pride and joy. I see two people in her, but only one will wake up. It makes me angry, for some reason.

But I don't have time wait here for her to wake up. No time to witness her resurrection to a life more or less precisely the same as the one she's lived thus far. I look at my watch. I need to get to campus.

Coming here makes no sense. Bringing her a sandwich makes even less sense. I knew she wouldn't be lucid. A schizophrenic whose condition is severe enough that she was on the amount of medication necessary to leave behind those physical glitches, and who is no longer on any medication, would not by any means make a worthwhile witness.

I pull the wrapped sandwich and baggie of carrots out of my pack and set them next to her. The only thing I know about her is that, as tattered as her mind is, she still pulled a sheet over a dead body to cover his nakedness. I did not bring her a sandwich out of kindness. If anything, I think I brought it to her for the same reason that she pulled a sheet over the corpse. We are like the ancients who burnt grain at altars to gods who never answered, as if the blind obstinacy of ritual itself can inscribe some grace on the practitioner.

She is still unconscious when I climb the slope to the street above.

It is now after eight in the morning. A few cars pass by, and pedestrians with briefcases beep remote locks on their cars and enter banks and office complexes and fade into their quotidian lives. The torrid sky arches overhead and the ordinary masses pass me by like I'm invisible.

I change into a clean pair of jeans and a sweater, and I head back to campus to teach my classes. After teaching, I go up to the department offices, ignore another note from the dean, slot my finished chapter into Telushkin's mailbox, and venture into the grad student office to print out directions to an address I've scrawled on the yellow legal pad. The address is in Hudson, a preppy mostly Caucasian suburb almost half an hour north of Akron.

Hudson's downtown area is a preserved historic site with gabled roofs and quaint cupolas. A few blocks over I find a subdivision of large, generically prestigious houses, the plasticized grass and neat hedges an unnerving green beneath a fish-colored sky. I park on the side of the road near a No Parking at Any Time sign and get out, clutching the zippered edges of my hooded sweatshirt across my chest. I walk up a wide driveway toward a house with more windows than siding. I can see into the front hall through a floor-to-ceiling window beside an oversized polished-walnut door. The foyer has a sixteen-foot ceiling, a crystal chandelier, an antique hat stand, and a pristine bowl of fruit on a tiny polished maple table.

I press the doorbell.

After a long time I see a pair of feet descending a long staircase. A woman emerges. She is wearing ironed slacks and a black cardigan. She comes to the door, arms folded under her breasts, head tilted to the side, squinting. Her wrinkled expression tells me that she is annoyed to be answering the door to a stranger.

The door creaks open.

"Yes?"

"Miranda Devorecek?"

"Yes?"

"I'm a volunteer with Harvest Home."

Miranda's thin fingers end in tapered, French-manicured nails.

"Yes," she says.

"We're raising money for a Christmas party. Would you like to—?"

"We already paid," Miranda says. "I mean, we sent in our—I donated already. Don't you keep records of this?"

"Yes," I say. "But this party, we're collecting *extra*."

"I don't understand. You have a party *every* year and you've never collected extra before." Her lips are thin. When she pinches them together, her dark eyes seem to widen, heightening the shadowed contrast between cheekbone and jawbone. Her face is delicate, china pale, the eyes fierce and direct and identical to Aidan's, except that both of hers look straight at me. Her plucked eyebrows and elegant fingernails tell me that she is aware of the fact that she is beautiful. I wonder if she is equally aware that she is the only perfect product of her mother's womb, if she feels something due to the fact that her siblings are marred, broken replicas of her flawless form. If she feels guilty because of her unbrokenness, because she is better than her genetic inheritance.

"So, you're complaining about paying extra so your sister can have a happy Christmas? While you, what, drink four-hundred-dollar champagne at your Chase bank Christmas party?"

She draws her head back slightly. "Who told you I work at Chase?"

"You're a branch *manager*. And you're telling me you don't make enough to—"

"What the hell—" She shuts her mouth again. Her tiny seed-pearl teeth click together. She shuts the door in my face. I watch through the windowpane as she goes back into the kitchen. She reappears a minute later folding a slip of paper in a razor-sharp crease.

She opens the door and, pinching the paper between thumb and forefinger, holds it out to me. "Here. And Merry Christmas."

I unfold the check and look at it, licking my lower lip with exaggerated care. "This is—wow. Your brother just shut the door in my face."

"My—you approached my *brother*?"

I look up at her, widening my eyes in what I hope looks like innocence. It's not an expression that comes naturally to me.

"He's a goddamn *art* student," she says. "He's one of *you*. He's there practically every—he practically *lives* there. With her. Why would you chase him down for money? There's no way adult diapers and animal crackers cost what you people gouge us for every year. Me, I know what you're doing. The guilt card. I get it, okay? And, yes, I work seventy hours a week at a high-powered corporate office. I live in a big, sterile house. I never visit my—my sister. Okay? I know that. That's why I let you—why I pay the—why I pay what I do. Okay? Someone has to. But at the very least you could leave the family members who *care* out of your money-grubbing. All right? I've got cash and no heart, right? Well, my brother is—he's going to feel guilty now. You know what he'll be doing? He'll be sitting with her and feeling *guilty*. What is the matter with you people? What is enough? It's not money, it's clearly not actually *giving* a shit. So what do you want from us? *What?*"

She is breathing hard. Each inhalation draws thin lines in her throat. I watch the hollows between her collarbones. She stares at me.

"Thank you for your generous donation." I refold the check, put it in my jeans pocket, and turn to leave.

With my foot on the edge of the step, I look back. "Do you miss her?"

Miranda's thin lips part. Her eyes flare wide.

"I meant your mother. Do you miss her?"

There is a brief silence. Then she says, "Who the fuck are you?"

I don't say anything.

She says, "Wait—are you the roommate? Is that it? Are you my brother's mentally sick roommate? Is that who you are?"

I smile.

She says, "My God, I'm going to kill him."

"He wants to know what happened. He wants to know the truth. If you like him so much, why don't you want him to know?"

Miranda holds onto the door. Her knuckles are white as bone.

"My brother," she says, "has my mother's weaknesses. He has my mother's capacity for a naive innocence that borders on simple-mindedness. He adopts strays and perverts and broken people compulsively—you, of course, being a case in point. He has an obsessive personality. I don't think his desire to know exactly what happened to our mother is healthy or helpful. It just feeds his neurosis. He can't accept that some people are too broken to be saved. She was one of them. It's not like the last time was her first attempt."

I am startled and for the first time, I really look at Miranda. She just stares back, fierce and unblinking.

"So you don't think your retarded sister set the fire. You think your mom did."

For a second I think she's going to start screaming. Her mouth is pinched shut but she inhales, tendons standing out like bridge buttresses on her throat.

Then she slams the door.

FIFTEEN

When I get back to the apartment, Aidan lies on the couch with a sketchbook propped on his stomach. The TV hums softly with the lulling monotone of a BBC narrator. When I come in, his head comes up and he points a stick of charcoal at me.

"What did you say to Miranda?"

I am startled. My quiet little sparrow of a roommate has never looked so intently alive. The brunt of Miranda's rage is printed all over his thin skin, in the wrinkle between his eyebrows, the tight lines by his mouth. "Nothing," I say. "I mean, I was just asking questions. I apologize if I offended her, but I'm not exactly known for my finesse."

His mouth relaxes a little. "Well, in the future why don't you just ask me." He raises the remote and turns up the TV. "Hey, it's your favorite nature program."

"I don't have a favorite—what do you mean, why don't I just ask you? You never give me straight answers. You haven't been exactly champing at the bit to find out how my investigation's been going, either. The last I checked, your sum total response to my investigation is your dedicated attempt to ruin your liver."

The frown settles back between his eyebrows. He wipes the back of his wrist across his mouth.

"Okay," he says. "What do you want to know?"

His fingertips, pressed against the charcoal stick, are white in patches.

"Forget it."

"What?"

"I said forget it." I keep expecting to see that glaze of anticipation in his eyes when I talk about death, about murder and arson. I thought at first that he felt the same way I did about our cohabitational adventure, the sizzle of danger and death. But instead he just looks ignorant when

I mention the house across the street or the fire, and he looks physically sick whenever I bring up his mother. Circumstantial evidence suggests that he may be a killer. A mutilator of corpses. But nothing else in his behavior seems to tally with the external coincidences of his apartment's location and our sudden meeting.

As I lay awake listening to Aidan stumble through the living room last night, I realized that, while I don't understand ordinary, decent human behavior, I also might not be able to understand sociopathic behavior. The realization was strangely disturbing.

I go over to the television and manually turn up the volume.

"Move over. I want to watch this." I sit on the floor at the far end of the couch from him and open a binder full of digitalized illuminated manuscripts. The BBC announcer remarks in bland Home Counties tones about the deadly jaws of the crocodile. I laugh and when I look up Aidan is smiling too.

At night I lie awake in the dark and listen to Aidan come in, to his socked feet shuffle in the kitchen, the metallic creak of a can releasing, a hiss of air, a gurgle.

In the first amalgamation of Anglo-Saxon dialects, what we now call Old English, the word *doom* meant judgment. As if the ancient Germanic tribes had understood that fate was arbitrary, that acquittal and damnation alike fall on the unsuspecting regardless of their merit. But maybe our expression "impending doom" suggests that we understand something else, that all judgments are damnations, that there are no acquittals, no justifications, only tragedies. That once a person is a suspect they become guilty and carry their taint forever. I think Aidan wants me to tell him that his sister murdered his mother. I don't know why. He already believes it's true.

I fall asleep and dream that the cat has returned and is sitting on my chest looking at me with human eyes. The eyes are dark, black-lashed, luminous and tragic with hope. I realize that they are Aidan's eyes and I startle awake. I hear him snoring in the living room, the sonorous rasp a counterpoint to the low static of the television.

Once when I was young, about eight maybe, my dad got pneumonia. He lay on the couch with his head propped up on a rolled pillow and my mom canceled her piano students and even upstairs in my bedroom—I lived in the house then—I could hear the tinny rattle of the TV punctuated by his wheezy coughs.

I was squatting on my haunches on the white shag rug in the middle of my bedroom, cutting a doll's hair. I gripped the doll by its hair, her wide-eyed face and pinched waist spinning slowly, her tiny pointed feet dangling like bird claws. I sliced through the hair with a pair of scissors, and the doll fell. Yellow plastic hair scattered across the carpet. I picked up the doll by what was left of her hair and sheared it again. I don't remember why I was cutting her hair that way, like some demented hangman passing the time at a cosmetology school. The door banged open and Dave came in. He was wearing a camouflage G.I. Joe thermal shirt. He grabbed the doll and wrestled the scissors out of my hand, pinching my thumb. He cut her head off with the scissors. I remember the chewy, gnawing sound the blades made in the stiff plastic. He gave me the scissors and the doll, and I grabbed hold of the cuff of his shirtsleeve and I cut his thumb. I would've kept sawing away at his thumb, but he screamed and Mom came running down the hall. I hid the scissors behind me. Dave tucked his thumb under his fingers and put his hand in his pocket.

"Mickey? Sweetheart? Dave, what happened, what did she do?"

Dave said, "Nothing."

Mom looked at me and at my decapitated doll. I picked up the doll head and looked at the warped eyes. They looked startled.

"Honey? Are you okay?"

"I didn't scream."

"I know," Mom said. She bent to touch me, kiss me, something. I put the fist holding the doll head between us and she stopped short.

She pursed her lips and then said, “Play nicely, please.”

When she left, Dave said, “Hey. You want to play outside?”

It was February. A brief thaw had started to melt the heavy icicles and every few hours another sheet of softened ice would slide off the roof and shatter on the wet lawn. But it was still only a few degrees above freezing. And Mom had been very particular about us staying inside once Dad got sick.

“Mom said no.”

“Don’t ask, don’t tell, that’s my policy,” Dave said.

“Why would I tell?”

“I don’t know,” Dave said. “Maybe you’re a quisling.”

“What’s a quisling?” I cut my doll’s head in half again, right through the painted blue-rimmed eyes.

“A weasel,” Dave said. “A tattle-tale.”

When I didn’t answer him right away, he said, “So yes? Or no?”

“Okay.”

“Cool. Hurry up. Before Mom gets back.”

I hadn’t realized she was leaving. Dave said she was going to the store. We went downstairs and I put the scissors in my back jeans pocket. I liked having scissors near me. When I looked at things—the photograph of our smiling faces over the stairwell doorway, the fern in the planter on the landing, the defrosting package of chicken breast on the countertop—I imagined the sounds they would make with the scissors chewing through them.

Dave pulled on sneakers without tying the laces and put his arms through a camouflage jacket that he loved because, he said, it made him “butch.” He put me into a snowsuit. It felt bulky, like I was waddling in a comforter. I didn’t like the feeling. His hands were cold and sticky.

“Don’t touch me.”

“Shut up.” He pulled a hat over my head and tied a scarf around my neck. Strands of hair got stuck in my eyes and across my mouth.

Dad said something from the living room but then started coughing so we couldn't tell what he said. Dave turned around and put a finger to his mouth. His eyes shone like the sun refracted through prisms.

He opened the door softly and we went out. A sugary-white ice covered the yard and cracked like eggshells under our boots. I thought we were just going to play in the backyard but Dave wanted to go down the street to the cul-de-sac where a new house was under construction. We weren't allowed down that way.

We trudged down the sidewalk, lifting our legs high to pull our boots free of the melting bog of ice and snow, robotic moonwalkers. My scarf rested against my lower lip. It was wet with mucus and saliva, slowly freezing over. I could taste the icicles forming against my mouth.

The site smelled fresh, like wet paint and sawdust. The mud in front of the house was churned up, crisscrossed with ridges from backhoe tread, the gashes filled with sloshing icewater. Coils of red plastic tubing lay across the bare dirt.

The basement had been dug and concrete poured, but the house frame hadn't been erected yet. Rainwater had filled the basement during a heavy storm and then a shell of ice formed when the temperature dropped overnight. Pine needles and gravel sprinkled the white ice-crust. Dave ran to the low concrete base wall and screamed, "Don't try to stop me! I've got nothing to live for!"

He stopped at the edge and looked over his shoulder at me.

I didn't say anything.

He jumped in. The ice sheared apart. A wave of silty, brackish water lapped over the edge of the pit. He shrieked from the cold. I went over to the edge and looked down. Hair plastered to his skull, he rose up out of the water, pinched blued eye sockets, pink flares on his cheeks. An ancient water god rising from a dark world. He held up his arms and said to me, "I'll catch you, Mickey. Jump."

I said, "I don't want to."

"I dare you to."

I just stared down at him.

And ice-cold fingers closed around my ankle and pulled. Or the earth heaved under me. Anyway, I went down.

Crazed darkness rushed up at me and I was plunged into a biting cold. Thrashing arms and yelling. Dirty water gushing into my mouth.

He was yelling something to me.

"Scream," he was saying. White flecks on his lips, mud splattered across the pale dome of his forehead. "Scream, you fucking bitch, scream!"

I didn't even have the breath to laugh.

And then Dave clambered out of the pit, slogging waves of water lapping in his wake. He bent and hauled me up after him. I emerged into bitterly cold air, drenched, shivering inside my snowsuit. I clamped my arms around my sogged stomach and sat on the muddy slide of earth sloping away from the concrete wall.

Dave looked down at me and said, "We better get you home. Before you get sick or something."

Mom was in the foyer when we tramped inside, dripping mud and water and shedding pine needles. She grabbed me and I said, "Don't touch me." But she was not looking at me. She said, "How could you? How could you do this to me?"

Dave said, "Mom. I'm sorry." His voice hiccupped. He sounded like he was maybe crying. "It's my fault. She wanted to play outside. I shouldn't have let her. I should've watched her closer."

My teeth were chattering. I looked at Dave looking at Mom, then up at Mom looking at Dave.

She said, "You're grounded. Don't ever do something this stupid again."

Mom unwrapped my scarf and sodden hat and mittens and pulled off my snowsuit like shucking a butterfly out of its cocoon. We tramped mud through the hallway to the stairs in the living room. Dad levered himself up on one arm.

"Don't start," Mom said. "He's grounded."

Dad coughed into his fist. He looked at Dave. "I told you," he said.

"She jumped," Dave said. "I'm sorry." His eyelashes were clustered with droplets of water.

Dad lay back down again. "Don't be too hard on him," he said to Mom. "It's not his fault. She's unpredictable."

Mom was looking at Dad. I looked at Dave and saw a grin split his mud-spattered face. It disappeared when Mom looked down at him. His chin quivered.

She sighed. "Take off your clothes and dry off, sweetie. I have to give Mickey a bath."

She herded me into the bathroom and shut the door. Then she cranked on the spigots in the bathtub and pulled my shirt over my head. When my head came free from the wet material, I saw that she was looking at me with a strange expression on her face. She leaned toward me and her voice was a whisper. "Don't ever do that again, okay?"

"Okay."

"I'm not mad at you. I'm just mad because you could've gotten hurt. I don't, I couldn't live with, if you got hurt—Mickey, honey, you can't hurt yourself. It hurts *me*. Okay?"

"Okay."

And I climbed into the hot water that lapped over my skin in a pale imitation of the dark icewater. I imagined the mingling of the two waters, cold and hot, dark and clear. Silt floated in the bathwater like insects caught in amber. When I looked up my mom was watching me. Her eyes looked soft, charcoal-smudged, and her mouth curved sadly. She cupped her palm against the crown of my head. I realized that I didn't know what she was thinking, that I had never known and that it was something beyond my ability to imagine. And I realized then that I would never know why people said things, never understand why people did what they did.

The worst part is that I don't understand any of it, the motivations or the feelings, and so I don't even know what I lost, back before I had anything to lose. When I was just an embryo, the chemicals in my brain arranged themselves in some unholy order and deprived me of any great depths of loss. In the same move, they stole my ability to fully experience anything on the other end of the spectrum of human emotions. I don't think I will ever be truly excited or genuinely happy, so long as I remain obedient to the dictates of legal, ordinary behavior.

I lie in bed listening to the sonic quality of Aidan's profound sadness and rest my forearm across my eyes. I wish I knew what it was like, either grief or joy. The best feeling I ever get is when I run. Sweating hard, muscles burning, it's not really a *good* feeling, but it's okay. It feels safe, like I'm strong and controlled and disciplined. Like I am not on the brink of taking a knife to the person waiting in line behind me at the grocery store. How do normal people do it? How do they feel such joy from a touch, a look?

I close my eyes and touch my opposite shoulder with my right hand. I imagine that I put my arms around another person and it feels like the serotonin release at the end of a long run, the exhausted comfort of knowing that, for right now, at least, I'm safe.

SIXTEEN

The next morning I find myself coasting to a halt in front of the familiar burnt-out shell on Brown Street. I lean my chin on the steering wheel and stare at the house.

The short red-haired woman comes to the door when I knock. I hug my chest for warmth. The mucus in my nostrils has frozen. She peers up at me and then the door opens all the way. Her house is thick with warmth and smells like microwaved pasta and tuna and flower potpourri.

"Come in, come in. *You*," she says, pointing a marshmallow-fat finger at me, "were not at the choral performance."

I stand in the entryway. A fat black cat with jade eyes comes down the stairs one step at a time. It stands watching me, its thin tail ticking back and forth. She hustles into the kitchen and comes back with a sheaf of red and green flyers.

"Handel's *Messiah*," she says. "Have you ever heard it?"

"Yes."

"It's so beautiful. You have to come. It's the Advent Festival, we perform all the Sundays leading up to Christmas. All right? Now, come in. In here."

I go into the living room and sit on the edge of a couch that sighs and sinks under me. It is covered in a flower-printed drop-cloth. A gray cat comes in and settles on my lap. I put my hands under its belly and feel the pulse of viscera, the rumble of a purr. I imagine sliding my fingers around its throat and strangling it quietly while she talks. She is in the kitchen calling to me but I'm not paying attention.

She comes back with a mug of hot tea.

"—so sweet," she says.

I take the tea and sip it. It is so sweet, but I realize that she was probably talking about Aidan or one of his sisters, or possibly his dead mother.

"—every single day," she says, and digs her clenched fist into the soft flesh above her left breast. "Just an *ache*. Right *here*. I'm sure you know what I mean."

I nod.

"So what did you want to ask me?"

"You mentioned that they were all at their father's house," I say. "That night."

She nods, watching me.

"Even the retarded one?"

She flinches at my term. Her soft jowls are the color of tapioca. "Oh," she says.

I pinch the underside of the cat's chin with my fingernails. It jerks its head and slides off my lap and scampers away.

I set my tea on my knees and lean forward, watching Judith Greene. Her eyes move around the room, the figurines on the mantle, the photographs of smiling children and unsmiling old people.

I clear my throat.

She puts a hand to her breast again, pressing her palm on it. I watch the rise and fall of her little fat hand. "I hadn't—how *is* she? Stella, I mean. After that night, she was so, it was so—she shouldn't have had to be there."

"She's in a home," I say. "Assisted living for the mentally or physically disabled. It's called Harvest Home."

She nods as if she knows this.

"Why was she at the house when the others weren't?"

Judith Greene shakes her head as if chasing away a mosquito. "I didn't—I don't know. We found her when—the paramedics came. I was the one who called the fire department, you know." She looks at me sharply when she says this last part. I don't tell her that I already know, thanks to the 911 call being public record.

We are quiet for a while. I think about her phrasing: She shouldn't have had to be there.

I say, "Thank you for the tea and company." She looks up at me and remembers her face and smiles, but it looks like putting on a mask. Her eyes are still far away.

"So, Handel's *Messiah*? I'll come. This time I mean it."

Her smile carves dimples in her cheeks and forms rolls under her chin. "Oh, good. It's so beautiful."

She follows me to the door. I escape into the cold and hurry to the car. Her scent seems to linger in my clothes and on my skin.

As I drive away from Judith Greene's cat litter-scented hovel, I think about the pristine cleanliness of Aidan's sister's house. So when I pull into the gravel lot behind our apartment building, I'm surprised to see Miranda's silver Audi bumper-kissing our dented industrial-sized trash bin. It's like I've conjured her with the force of my imagination.

I grab my backpack out of the car and trot up the stairs. Inside, their voices tangle together, viola and violin in a sudden crescendo.

"—so fucking immature!" Miranda's voice careening into soprano range.

"*Me* immature! You're the one who won't talk about anything, oh, like it's really mature to just completely rewrite history, pretend nothing ever happened. You can pretend you never had a mother but you can't pretend *she* doesn't exist, because she does and she *misses*—"

"And, what, my moral shortcomings give you permission to give my name and address to every psychopath in the greater Akron area? Do you have any idea what—"

I slide off my shoes and rest my backpack near the coat rack, and walk into the kitchen.

They are standing in the living room. Miranda is dressed in a charcoal gray pinstripe pantsuit. The tucked waist on the suit jacket, cream-colored silk shirt underneath. Her smooth dark hair, her perfect dark eyes.

Aidan is standing close to her, his back to the window. An opened sketchpad lies at his feet, his charcoal sticks scattered on the carpet. His eyes move when he sees me. Some expression crosses his face, some tightening across the forehead, the eyebrows slanting down at the sides as if he's sad or anxious.

Miranda twists around to see what has disturbed him. Her coral-pink lips, twisted in mid-sentence, freeze.

We just stare at each other for a second.

Then I say, "Hey. What's up."

Miranda pushes her brother aside and strides across the living room. Her thin heels make hollow clunks through the balding carpet. She puts her finger in my face. The fingernail is glossy and rose pink.

"*You*," she says, "need to back off. Get out of my family's business and *stay* out. Do you understand?"

"Miranda," Aidan says. He reaches for her arm. He grabs her wrist but instead of digging his fingers into the tendons to get her attention, he slides his hand down and wraps his fingers around the fleshy part of her palm. His face is a stark contrast to the tenderness of the gesture, angry ridges across his forehead, between his eyebrows. "Settle down. Okay? She's a friend. Come on."

"A friend? A *friend*." Miranda lets out a laugh. She inhales and her shoulders relax. She takes a step back. She does not pull her left hand out of Aidan's grip. "When will you understand that the pervert who hangs out by the used games store is not a *friend*, Aidan. These people need treatment. They need to be kept—"

Aidan says, "Shut up."

She shuts her mouth. She takes her hand out of his and turns to look at him. Her mouth is pinched so tight that fine wrinkles radiate from the edges of her lips. She straightens the collar on his faded shirt.

"I have to go back to work. You get this—this *friend*—to stay away. You understand? You need to get away from these, these needy people. And do not entangle me in your quixotic stupidity any more. You hear?"

She looks over at me, and then she bends over and takes her purse from beside the couch. She walks out. Her heels echo all the way down the stairs. Aidan stands in the living room. His face is flushed. He puts his hands in his pockets and goes over to the window, watches her pull out of the driveway.

He says, "Sorry about that."

"Quixotic."

"What?" He looks over his shoulder at me.

I smile at him. "Quixotic. That was a nice expression. Your sister's kind of all right."

He wipes the back of his hand over his mouth and then stretches his shoulders. "Kind of all right. Come on. She's *terrifying*." But he grins while he says it.

I don't know what to say.

He goes into the kitchen. I watch him pull the last orange out of the fruit basket and peel it. He drops the rinds in the sink and I open my mouth to tell him we don't have a disposal. But I can get rid of them later easily enough. And I've already been enough of a shithead to him today.

I hear myself saying, "Look, I'm sorry about your sister. I really am. I won't do that again."

He carries the plate of sliced oranges into the living room and sits down in front of his opened sketch pad. He glances up at me. "Don't worry about it." He watches me for a second and then he smiles.

I go over to the couch and sit down.

He reaches over and turns on music. R.E.M. at the height of their late-nineties glory.

"Oh God," I say.

He grins at me and cranks up the volume. Michael Stipe is singing something about losing his religion. Aidan squints like he's thinking about some impromptu karaoke. I have heard him attempt this before in the shower and he is not exactly vocally gifted.

I grab his plate of oranges and pick up a slice.

"I'll kill you."

He laughs. "With an orange and your ninja skills?"

"You shouldn't underestimate the strength of my desire not to hear you singing," I say. But I don't pitch the orange slice at him. I just stick it in my mouth and suck the juice from the bitter white pith.

He grins and bends his head to his drawing pad. Under his breath he starts whispering, "—me in the cor-ner."

I turn my head to watch what he's drawing. And as his hand sweeps over the page I notice his arm. His sleeves are pushed up past his wrists. Four yellowed bruises with dark red half-moon crescents carved into the center of each bruise stagger across the pale inside of his arm. I remember his bandaged fingers when he came over to the house for Stephen's birthday.

"Hey," I say. "Tell me about your sister. The fucked up one."

He stops sketching and reaches over to turn down the music. "Why?"

Because he walks around with battered arms and fingers like most people wear a well-worn T-shirt. Because I can't tell if he accepts damaged minds or is dangerously drawn to them.

"Because I want to know about her," I say. "Because of that." I point to his arm.

He looks at me with that blank dark eye and then bends his head again.

"Because she's retarded," I say.

"Listen," he says, and flips a page on the sketchpad. He's not yelling, like Miranda, but his voice is taut, trembling at the edges. "She has autism. So quit saying 'retarded.' And there's nothing to tell. You want to know when her birthday is? She's turning thirty on Tuesday. She wears a diaper. She hits people. If she gets her hands on a sharp object she jams it into whoever touches her. She's a fan of eighties hit bands like Queen. Oh, and she *loves* the color yellow."

"You don't hate her."

"I adore her."

He flips the pad up and pulls a clean page down.

"Okay. Your *other* sister isn't your mother's biggest fan ever," I say. "We did discuss that, in between her telling me to get the fuck out of her house."

His pencil tip hovers over the page. Then he digs it down and draws a strange geometric shape. He wiggles the pencil, sketching, shading. "Yeah. I heard."

I rock a little on the couch and wonder if there is another orange in the refrigerator. "What about you? You a big fan of your mother?"

"She was hard to live with," he says. "I didn't hate her, though."

"Hard to live with how?"

He's drawing a foot. I watch the arch, the tendons, the protruding anklebone, emerge.

I realize my bare feet are resting on the carpet. I pull them up onto the couch and tuck them under me. He erases part of the toes and with a few clear lines he transforms the foot into a cloven hoof. He doesn't look up at me, but I can see his lips curl up in a smile.

"*Ass*hole," I say. And grin.

He puts his pencil down and rolls onto his side, propping his head on one hand. "What?" he says.

"Your sister said you were kind of like her. So, what made her hard to live with? She was a sucky artist? Or she liked nineties hits?"

"Hey, I'm a terrific artist and the nineties *ruled*."

"Har har."

Aidan rolls his pencil across the devil hoof drawing. "She was really emotional. You'd have hated it. Crying, laughing, wiping her nose on her sleeve. That sort of thing."

I open my mouth but Aidan says, "And no, I'm not like *that*. But the sad thing. I get down sometimes. Miranda thinks I'm—"

He doesn't finish his sentence.

"Going to off yourself like your mom tried to do?"

He looks over at me.

"Your sister spilled the beans about your mom's psychiatric history. Said she tried to kill herself a couple times."

Aidan rubs his fingers in the nubby carpet pile and studies the balls of lint he collects. Neither one of us likes to vacuum. "Mom was bipolar. When she was down she talked like she wished she was dead. It wasn't her fault, but it really bothered Miranda. You know, to think Mom *wanted* to die. She didn't like that."

"She hates your mom."

"Hate's part of love," he says. "Hate is what happens to love when it gets sick."

I raise my eyebrows and sit back on the couch. "Geez. It's raining outside, but it's a lovely day in here with Mr. Sunshine."

He shakes his head, straightens up and reaches for his pencil. He glances up at me and smiles. Then pretends to pick his nose with the pencil. I laugh.

"So now your turn. Tell me about your house. What was it like growing up with you?"

"Oh, it was marvelous," I say. "Being as I'm such a delightful person—a saint, really. My family members have often told me they feel they should have *paid* for the privilege of living with me." I lick tacky, drying orange juice off my fingertips. "To be honest, I'm not the right person to ask. I'm a fucking lunatic, so the rest of the world looks crazy to me."

"*And* you cooked the dog."

"Right. I cooked the dog." I think. "I also stockpiled matches and tried to start the house on fire. It was raining, though. Go figure." I still don't know why my mother thought I would like a surprise party. They all screamed *Surprise!* a dozen of them, little eight-year-old girls in sparkly dresses, shrieking, giggling, eating cake and ice cream and party mints. Mom wouldn't let me leave, kept telling me to smile and have a good time. And yes, stealing the matches from the kitchen and trying to burn the house down was an overreaction. But like I said, I didn't know what I was doing and the rain put out the matches that I tossed under the front porch as soon as I'd lit them. "And I stapled my fingers. And this one time I put my mother's bras in the freezer and all the frozen meat in her underwear drawer."

"*What?*"

I smile. "Okay, I'm kidding." I am not, of course, although technically it was Dave and not me who stapled the webbing between my thumb and palm. The scar is faded now and the only time I can see it is when my hands are very cold and turn pink, the scar stays pale.

Aidan gives me a strange look and then he looks down at his sketchbook and starts drawing again.

"What's that look for?"

"What about Dave?" he says. "He's a little, I don't know. *Off.* Right? And I don't mean because he does drugs. I mean, there's something a little—"

He stops talking and for a while is quiet.

"A little what?"

He bites his lower lip and then erases a line. Studies the page. Sketches soft hash lines and then erases another line. "A little *sado*."

I look at the dark bowl of Aidan's skull, the lines of his shoulder blades like thin wings under his almost-translucent shirt. I wonder what Dave looks like to other people. Most people only see his public self, the laughing, teasing, slightly zany self. A few people see glimpses of his other self. I imagine he must look to them like a brightly colored moth with the faintest aureole of flame crimping the edges of his wings.

"Right?"

"Right, what?"

"I mean, Dave's sort of—out there. At least sometimes. Am I right?"

"Hey, at least he's not a psychopath."

"Mickey! What is this?" Aidan frowns and turns his head to look at me. "I tell you all about my family. And now you're, what, *protecting* him?"

I laugh.

He looks at me. His eyebrows peak and his mouth goes down at the corners.

"Jesus, are you serious? Fine. What do you want to hear? Do you want me to tell you he's a raving lunatic? How can I say that? How would I even know what a raving lunatic *looked* like?" I notice that my thumb is folded tightly against my palm. Maybe because I was just thinking about the staple thing. I unclench my hand.

Aidan says, "That would be a start."

"What's that supposed to mean?"

Aidan picks at the carpet weave with the sharpened pencil. "You know what Dave told me about you?"

I shrug.

"He told me about you pushing that guy down the stairs when he tried to—you know. But he also said—well, he said that you were the one who cut your roommate. But, well, you said you didn't touch her and you don't lie. But the thing is, I think your brother knows the truth, too, that you didn't do anything to your roommate, that she was a total psycho. Because you tell him pretty much everything else, so why wouldn't you have told him that? So he, well, he just blatantly lied about you, and anyway, even if he didn't know the truth, he really made it seem like you were sort of temporarily stable but basically unpredictable and dangerous."

I raise my eyebrows. "Gosh, he wouldn't *dare*. Except—oh, right, that's the truth."

"No, it's not true. That's my point. Telling me was stupid and unnecessary and, worse than that, it was just *mean*."

"Are you insane? In what universe am I *not* unpredictable and dangerous? Christ."

Aidan breaks the lead tip of his pencil. He looks at the ragged wooden end of the pencil and then he sighs and lays the pencil across his sketchpad. "He's just—he strikes me as the sort of person who might make up a story about someone just to watch other people react.

Which is kind of mean. You know? I guess I'm saying I don't like him. Okay? I don't like your brother."

"Terrific. You don't like my brother. I pretty much detest him. But then, I detest the human race. What's your point?"

"I think you have a weird thing with your brother. I don't mean, like, sexual or anything. I just mean that he's sort of—and you believe what he says, even when he lies. And that's, like, sort of what abused people do. You know?"

I laugh. "Are you kidding? You've got to be joking."

He looks at me. His crazed eye dances.

I don't like looking at it. The eye makes me feel sick suddenly. I swallow and look down at the cigarette-burned weave of the couch. "Yeah, he's like you said. He's—he can be mean. But, God, he *gets* me. Okay? I can't hurt him accidentally because he'd be ready for it. I think you're the same way. And that makes you the only two fucking people in the whole world—" I stop talking. And realize that what I am about to say is the truth. I swallow. "You're the only people," I say, "who would be *ready* for me if I did something. You wouldn't let me hurt you. So I guess I feel safe with you. Because like it or not, I *am* unpredictable and dangerous."

Aidan rips off the top page of doodles and crumples it in his hand. He pushes himself up on his left hand and with his right he throws the wadded paper into the kitchen. It hits the rim of the trashcan and falls to the floor.

He looks over at me. "You want to meet her?"

"What? Who?"

"My sister," he says. "Stella. You want to meet her?"

I rub my hand over my mouth. "No."

He watches me.

"No," I say louder. "*No.* If I see her I'll fucking kill her. I'll stab *her* with some sharp fucking object. I'll rip off her fingernails one by one and I'll dig out her eyeballs and choke her with them. I don't want to meet her. I don't—"

"*Hey*," he says.

I realize he's been saying it as I've been talking but I didn't hear him.

"Shut up. Stop."

I close my mouth.

"This is what I mean," he says. "This. You were nice to Miranda, in your own way. You were polite anyway, and for you that was, like, being Mother Teresa. Especially when she was so rude to you. And you don't hate Stella, you just want to hurt her like she hurts me. I don't think your shrinks were right, okay? You're not unpredictable. You're not some pre-serial killer, and you're sure as hell not a joke. You're not going to do anything you don't want to, and you don't *want* to hurt people. So you don't have to be afraid with anyone. Not anyone. Okay?"

I look at him. But he won't look away. His one good eye won't shift. The pupil doesn't even move. I end up looking away first.

After a while he gets up and goes into the kitchen and picks up the wad of crumpled paper and puts it carefully in the trashcan.

SEVENTEEN

The next morning, a Saturday, I run then get in the Chevelle and, instead of going to the library like I usually do, I head away from campus. Turn north onto the freeway and churn my way through slushy snow to Hudson.

Harvest Home is in Hudson. A sprawling, single-story facility with brick and white daub walls, a sprawling, mostly empty parking lot, and sliding glass doors that open in front of an overhang with clearance high enough for an ambulance. I know this because an ambulance currently sits under the bricked overhang. The lights are turned off. It looks routine, no desperation. But maybe there is never desperation here. The inmates are already rubbish, pushed to the edges, swept into a neat pile. Maybe one more or less does little to upset the cosmic balance.

I imagine the hallways smell of urine mixed liberally with pureed baby food. I sit in the car and contemplate going inside. Approaching the front desk and asking for Stella Devorecek's room number.

One of my therapists had a Down syndrome client. The girl was twice my size with flat, coin-shaped eyes. She was kneeling in front of a toy box in the waiting room the first time I saw her. I went over to a chair and climbed on it to wait while my mother filled out paperwork. The girl lumbered to her feet and came over to me. Snot was crusted on her short upper lip. A diaper crinkled and wadded between her legs when she walked. Before I could react she put her arms around me and leaned her hot, damp face against mine.

They pulled me off her in only seconds. When I was taken into the therapist's room I looked back at her. Her mother was cradling the oversized girl, but the almond-shaped eyes gazed blankly back at me, the flat button nose oozing blood and mucus. She wasn't crying. I came out an hour later and she was still there, arms wrapped around her mother's neck, a slick of mucus running into her open mouth. She waved bye to me when I left.

I sit in the Chevelle and tap my fingers on the steering wheel. I finally make up my mind to go inside, and I turn the key in the ignition and drive away instead.

Miranda Devorecek comes to the door quickly this time. I can hear noise, silverware and tinkling laughter, and there are Audis and Toyotas packing her wide driveway. She halts when she sees me.

I put my foot across the lintel. "Hi."

"Oh, God. Look, will you please go away? I'm having—well, obviously you won't care about that. If you don't leave, I will call my brother."

"Your brother?" I grin. "And what would he do? He's no Sly Stallone. I mean, he *might* win a fight with a Chihuahua. Maybe."

"I'm asking you nicely."

"Which is weird," I say, and move forward. She backs up and I slip inside. "When you think about it, I mean. Insane people tend not to respond to niceness, the banality of civilization, and you know I'm—what did you call me?—right, one of *these people*. So why ask nicely?"

Someone comes into the foyer holding a tiny crystal cup of a pink fizzy drink. The woman has straw-colored hair and is wearing a casual lavender shirt and tan slacks that easily cost a couple hundred dollars.

"Oh," she says.

"This is my brother's roommate," Miranda says. "Mickey, right? I assume that's short for something." Her thin mouth is wrinkled like she's holding vinegar in her mouth. "She's here for the party."

"Well," I say, "not really. I hate parties. The last one I attended, I tried to burn the house down afterward."

The woman in lavender stares at me. Her eyes flicker to Miranda, who looks at me steadily. The skin under her eyes looks blue.

She says, "That was quite possibly the most insensitive thing anyone has ever said to me."

"Really?" I smile. "Could I have some punch, maybe? It would make a nice contrast to the tea I had the other day with that disgusting old woman who used to be your neighbor. The one with the cats who sings in a choir."

"Judy Greene?" Miranda looks surprised. She raises her chin slightly. "You can follow me to the kitchen. The punch is in there."

I follow her to the kitchen, walking past the glare of the lavender-shirted woman. A room opening off the foyer is thronged with women in fake-casual clothes and bright-colored paper bags full of tissue paper. Most of the bags are silver and pink.

"Wedding shower?" I say. "For you, or someone else?"

"Someone else."

"Oh, that's right. You're divorced, aren't you? I read about it on the Internet."

She inhales but doesn't say anything.

We go into the kitchen, a long room with a red baked clay tile floor, stainless steel appliances, and fake wood beams across the ceiling. A crystal bowl of fizzing punch sits on a table flanked by pink and silver napkins and paper plates and platters full of tiny cookies covered in powdered sugar.

"I assume this is your revenge. For what you overheard me saying about you yesterday. I can only say that I'm sorry you overheard. That was—impolite. However, I stand by what—"

"Tell me about your mother."

Miranda stiffens. Then she turns away from me and goes over to the table. She ladles punch into a plastic cup and turns around and hands it to me. She glares at me, and I am startled again by how eerie it is to be stared at by Aidan's eyes, only his eyes in her face are twinned, synchronized, perfected.

"Some people," she says, "deserve to die."

I take the punch and sip it. It's frothy and citrusy. "This is good."

"Thank you." She can't help it. The words slip out. She looks irritated. "She was one of them."

I almost choke on my drink. I thought Miranda was insulting me. I swallow and lower the cup. "What?"

"I answered your question. Now please leave."

"Well," I say, "that was sort of a bizarre answer. Could you explain it?"

"No."

I take another sip, then drain the cup. I look around for a trashcan.

"Plastic recycling is in the cupboard there."

I go to the sink and rinse the cup and then put it in the bin Miranda points out to me.

"Your old neighbor thinks the sun shone out of your mother's ass."

A pink stain spreads across her face.

"Is this what you're into? Dredging up pointless *gossip*? You get off on the salacious details of other peoples' lives, other peoples' pain?" Her voice trembles. "Get out of my house. *Now*."

I want to ask what she means by salacious gossip but she has a point. Asking more is just prurient interest at this point. They were just kids, Miranda and Aidan. Nothing they think they know has any more truth than the other person's, and neither of their truths are helpful. Her brother thinks their autistic sister committed a crime and he tortures himself daily for loving her anyway. Miranda, on the other hand, believes that her mother committed suicide and she spends her days pretending she is a damaged shell of a human being so that she doesn't have to admit that she's stronger, better, and more whole than her own mother.

I shrug and walk toward her front door. She comes after me and reaches around me to yank the door open.

I turn in the doorway. She is very close to me. Her skin is a poreless matte and she smells faintly of orange peel.

I say, "For the record, you're more like your brother than you think. And you don't deserve to be punished."

She inhales. Her blue-veined eyelids close briefly.

I leave and when I look back, she is leaning against the door, holding onto the edge with both hands.

The sun is setting when I get back to campus. I park and walk toward the library. The cracked slabs of the sidewalk cant drunkenly, exhausted by a season, a lifetime, of freezes and thaws.

A group of students is clustered around something on the sidewalk ahead of me. When I get closer I see that they are staring down at something hidden by the overhanging shrubbery. The knot of people takes up the whole sidewalk. I stop and look around for options. To the left is a thick slide of brown mud, and I'm only wearing sneakers so I don't want to wade into it. When I look back at the group of students, someone has moved and I see that they are looking down at an animal, growling and writhing under the bush. I look with more interest.

One of the students, a guy in blue and yellow athletic sweats, turns and sees me watching. He moves to the side. The animal is a brown cat writhing and meowing in a puddle of shit and blood.

EIGHTEEN

The cat looks like it's been hit by a car or run over with a bike. Either way, the cat has dragged its broken spine across the sidewalk from the parking lot, leaving a smear across the concrete. The animal shows its pink spiny teeth, yowling.

When I move forward, a girl notices me and makes way. "Oh, my God, isn't it the saddest thing ever? Can you imagine? We don't even know what to do. Derek went to go see if he could find cardboard or something to put it on so we can take it to the vet or whatever."

The thing is, I recognize it. The yellow eyes, the patches of caramel and mocha-colored fur. The cat I found in the bathroom sink when I moved into the apartment.

I look up at the kids. They seem so young, their cheeks pink-tinged in the gusty wind as they stare lusty-eyed at the distressed animal, their mouths warped into shapes of distress or disgust.

"Shit." I sigh and shift my backpack more securely over my shoulder. I nudge the Zips athletic guy with my elbow and he takes a step back, his bullish head swiveling on a golden-brown neck.

I kneel carefully. The fur on the cat's hind legs is matted with runny diarrhea. I reach out to turn the cat over so that I can see the ruined bowels better. The cat snarls but then when my hand brushes its flared whiskers, it starts suddenly to purr. The cat butts its wedge-shaped skull against my hand. I cup my hand, rub my knuckles once along the smooth side of its cheek. Its rough tongue strokes my finger.

"Oh God," says a girl behind me. She sounds like she's crying.

The Aztecs—and I think this is true of many cultures—believed that eating certain parts of their victims, like the heart, imparted the essential qualities of that person. If this cat has an essential quality, it is trust, or forgiveness. The cat looks up at me and I touch its warm chest, its vibrating, rumbling ribs. My fingers feel the cool, slippery coils of pink small intestines. The cat cries once and keeps purring.

When I touch its head I remember driving the knife into the pulpy wood of the stair. I still have that knife. It's in my backpack. I think it's Aidan's knife. I saw him slice open a tube of paint with it. But I've held onto it ever since, like a talisman. Like if I held onto it, I would remember how I didn't kill the cat. But now I will have to anyway.

I feel them around me, the students gathered close at my elbows. I don't want to get out the knife in front of them. I don't know how else to do it. But it's up to me. I did this. I am the one who is the cause of its suffering, even if I'm not a useless moron standing around mordantly luxuriating in its pain like the rest of them.

So I bend over and pick up the cat, gather up the limp hind limbs and the frantic scurrying front legs, the dripping shit and blood and bile and matted fur and purring vocal chords. Warmth bleeds through the fabric of my shirt, and I can feel a dampness against my stomach. The cat cries when I cradle it in my arms.

The cry makes me feel dizzy. But the dizziness doesn't make sense. This is just a cat I cast into the night a few weeks ago to remove any unnecessary temptation, to prevent myself from giving in to my darker side. I didn't care then about the animal. Or maybe I did. Maybe I sent the cat away to save it.

I am surprised to find that I'm having a hard time breathing. My chest moves, but air doesn't seem to flow in or out.

A cat's skull is small, the neck vertebrae delicate as a china teacup. I grip the head in one hand, the other fist tight on the neck, and wrench the cat's neck. A snap. The head dangles loose, a broken bone inside loose skin. The thick tangy smell of wet fur and feces.

Sticky fluids, blood and diarrhea, drip between my knuckles and paint stripes down my leg. The students look at me. Their faces are Klee paintings, void eyes and tombstone maws.

Their horror pisses me off. I raise the body of the cat in my two hands, proffered like Abraham lifting up his son to his god. "What?

Did you want to let it linger? Do you get off on its suffering? Are you fucking *animals*?"

They jabber frantically, screeching and squawking and flapping away. One trips on the edge of the sidewalk, flails, and steps back into mud, foot sinking with a squelch, an ooze. They yell, and one girl's face is covered in tears and her eyes shine like burning worms.

And I turn and run off, awkward. The backpack heavy and banging against my spine, the cat too light in my arms.

I get back to the apartment and only then realize I am still carrying it. What do I intend to do? Bring it inside?

Shit.

I look around. The industrial-sized garbage bin in the back parking lot.

I walk around to the parking lot. But I can't let it go. The eyes are still open. Green-yellow. Staring.

I want to apologize to the cat. I want it to close its eyes. I hate how death does that, steals even the silence of closed eyes. It just keeps fucking *watching* you. It stares at you as you descend into jibbering madness, watches your mind escape out the back door while your hands are covered in blood and viscous fluid from a severed eyeball—

Shitfuckshit.

I'm kneeling on the gravel and it's sharp in my knees like broken teeth. I claw the backpack open. The knife is in my hand.

I want the cat to stop watching me. The smell of it. The shining smell of viscera and iron-scented blood. The clean snap of its bones. I wish I didn't like the sound so well. The feeling of it.

Stop it, I say. I scream at the cat. *Fucking stop it.*

The warmth of the apartment flushes against my skin. I look like a ravaged golem, the cat diarrhea turning tacky and blood drying in flakes.

I walk into the kitchen. My body feels buoyant, a jellyfish floating in a saline silence. I can't tell if I'm dreaming. Aidan comes home. I hear him at the door behind me. The kitchen light is off. A pale rain-washed gloaming leaks through the large living room window.

My hands are buried in the kitchen sink, rinsing the knife.

He sees the knife lying in the sink, the faucet running uselessly. Some sticky red substance crawling towards the drain.

"Mickey, what—? Is that—is that *blood*?" He won't stop nattering away. "I'm not trying to be *nosy*, but I think I've got a *right* to know why my knife's got blood on it and is rusting in the sink."

My back is to him, head bent, hair fallen down in front of my face and he comes up behind me and I move my head, a curtain of hair falling over my shoulder. He reaches out, his fingers in the fall of hair, and I turn into his hand.

We stand that way in silence, his palm electric against my skin. And then I move with the quickness of a thought, a blink, a flicker. He makes a small hitch in his breath.

I stare at him and the lines of his face and neck are as sharp as awl-etched copper. He looks down at himself, at the rough black knife grip jutting from the sticky brown-red smear on his shirt. I put a hand against his chest and jerk the knife back. He makes a sound like a scream, only faint as a kitten's cry, and falls to his knees. He hits the linoleum with a dull thud.

I hold the knife under the water again. Turn the faucet handle to hot. Scrub it with lemon-scented suds. Then I dry the knife on my jeans and lay it blade-open on the countertop. I step over him and say, "What did you fucking *think* would happen."

I startle awake. I'm sitting in the corner of my bedroom, my arms wrapped around my knees. There is a knife in my hand and I'm shivering. Have I been dreaming? Hallucinating?

My dreams are always filled with death. The problem is, my memories are too. Sometimes I have a hard time differentiating them.

Once when I was little, but this was after I killed that guy, so let's say I was twelve, Dave and I went down to the park near the corner of Rose and Exchange Street. He went to play basketball and I sat cross-legged on a park bench reading a book while listening to the dangling rusted chains of the baskets creaking in the wind.

A girl about Dave's age came up pushing a baby stroller. The kid was wailing, snot pouring out its squashed-looking nose. I put my finger in the book to mark my place and watched them come up to the bench. I pushed out my jaw and lowered my eyebrows but she didn't stop. Didn't even look at me. A basketball bounced across the grass and hit the wheel of the stroller. The girl looked around. "Hey!" she said. "What's *with* you?"

Dave came jogging across and scooped up the ball. "Sorry," he said, grinning down at her. He pointed a thumb in my direction. "But you might want to think about moving the kid somewhere else."

"Oh yeah? Well, it's a free country, buddy. In case you hadn't noticed." She put her hands on her hips. She had a belly ring, and her shirt rode up when she put her hands on her hips so that we could see it. I watched her with interest. Dave balanced the ball on one hipbone, ran a hand through his longish hair. He knew he looked good and he liked to get girls to come on to him. The girl pushed out her lower lip but her eyes got wider and curious, not squinty and angry.

"That's my sister," Dave said. "And she'll eat that kid of yours if you don't shut it up. You think I'm joking but I'm not. I'm telling you for your own good."

"Oh, whatever," she said. But she looked over at me. I was sitting neatly like a little Buddha, a heavy old hardback copy of *The Iliad* on my lap. I looked back at her, unblinking.

"I'm serious," Dave said. "Really." His voice had taken on that warm, soft tone. The earnest, almost husky cadence that had everyone from teachers to parents to hormonal, post-adolescent girls melting. *Believing*.

"You're crazy," the girl said, looking sideways at me but talking to Dave.

"Crazy?" Dave shook his head. "*She*'s the crazy one. My little sister here killed a man a couple years ago. Just because he tried to touch her. I'm just saying, for your own sake, that you might want to move that kid."

The girl glared at Dave and grabbed the stroller. She pushed it over the bumpy grass, glancing over her shoulder at us. Dave bounced the ball twice, caught it again, and sat down next to me. He leaned his elbows on the ball and rolled it to his knees and back.

"What book is that?"

I tipped the cover to show him.

"Blood and guts, the original version," he said. And giggled. He rubbed the back of his hand under his nose. Then he reached over. I ducked under his hand but he grabbed my hair anyway. He held my head with his fingers knotted in the hair at the nape of my neck. Then he put his other hand over my mouth and said, "No biting. Don't bite, now, little girl."

I bit him so that he would move his hand, a pinch, not a real bite. He giggled again and pulled his hands away. I shook my head and opened the book and started reading again.

"What?" he said. "Am I *boring* you?"

"You're annoying me. There's a fine difference, but those with acuity can tell the difference."

"Acuity. Do you even *know* what that word means?"

I rolled my eyes without looking up at him.

"So," he said. And stopped rolling the ball. "Should I have left it here? The little victim? The cute little kid with those big, delicious, juicy—"

I hit him with the book.

He laughed.

"I don't eat people."

"You might. Someday."

I didn't say anything. Then after a long time, I said, "I wouldn't *eat* people."

He shrugged. "You never know. They might taste good. Jeffrey Dahmer thought so. He was like you. He was antisocial. But he dated people. He liked them. Then he ate them."

I was quiet for another several seconds. "That's stupid."

"What is?"

"Eating your girlfriend."

Dave laughed. "Well," he said. "You'll never know."

"Why?"

"Because of how you are. No boys will ever date you. I'm pretty much the only person who'll ever love you."

"How come?"

"How come what? How come I love you?" He held the ball out and tried to spin it on a finger. It fell and he caught it, hugged it to his stomach. Looked over at me under a fall of dark hair. "Because I can. No one else can. But me, it doesn't gross me out that you might someday eat people. See what I mean?"

I laughed. "Okay. So, what would people taste like?"

"Maybe like chicken, only stringier."

I grinned. "Oh, and maybe a fat person tastes like bacon."

"Maybe," he said. "I think it would be tangier. Like that venison we had that time that Uncle Randy killed the deer. Remember when we ate that deer?"

"Yeah. But why would a person taste like that?"

He shrugged. Seemed to lose interest in the conversation.

I shook my head and opened my book again.

He rolled the ball restlessly over his legs. Then he stood up and bounced the ball at me, but I was ready and I pulled my book up and the ball bounced off harmlessly.

"I'm going to go invent the cure for cancer and take over Mesopotamia," he said. "You okay with waiting here?"

"Whatever."

He went off dribbling and weaving around the ball, graceful as a professional player. I turned a page and went back to reading.

At that age, I didn't know there were limits. Things I would only ever be able to dream of. At that age, Dave was still able to make me believe that no bogeyman of children's nightmares was beyond my capacity to become. In any event, Dave never mentioned that Jeffrey Dahmer was murdered in a high-security prison. I found that out when I was older, when I realized that human laws would keep me moral, if only because I could never survive in a prison.

I rock back and forth and wonder if there is any way to halt this process, or if I am fated to complete the transformation, if I am some murderous chrysalis, a nightmare creature struggling against human bondage towards an inexorable and terrible freedom.

Aidan bangs into my room.

"Mickey! What have you done? Is this—is this *blood*?"

I'm sitting in the corner of my bedroom with knees hugged against my chest.

"Hey! You've got to answer me, okay? I've *got* to know why my knife's got blood on it, why it was lying there rusting away in the sink."

I open my eyes and push my hand through my hair. God, I'm tired. "Go away."

He comes into the room. The knife in his hand. Dripping dishwater on the scarred hardwood boards.

I push myself back. Backbone pressed against the wall. "Don't come in."

"What the hell is going on?"

I put my head down on my knees. You've been through this before, I tell myself. In the dreams. You can see how it will play out. It's not the end of the world. It's not like you haven't done it before.

"Just tell me." He crouches down. Trying to make himself eye-level with me, modulating his voice like he's talking to a fucking head case or something. "You've got to at least tell me someone's not dead. Okay? Do you see my point here, Mickey? That I've got to know? Are you even listening to me?"

I lift my head. "Yes. Yeah, I'm listening to you. Now get the fuck out."

He holds the knife. It drips pinkish water.

The silence goes on for a long time. Long enough that I can smell him. The faint smell of human under the turpentine.

My heart feels stiff, the muscles struggling to contract, to expand. "No one is dead."

"Okay. Good. No, that's good. Okay. So, whose blood is on my knife?"

My arms are wrapped around my legs. I can still feel the heat of its skin, the oily texture of its fur.

I look up at him.

"I killed our cat."

We breathe. In and out. In and out.

"Our cat?" he says. "You mean, the cat that you said ran away? Like, *weeks* ago?"

"It did." I swallow. "I didn't lie."

"Okay." He sits back on his heels. He puts his free hand, the one not holding the knife, over his mouth. "Okay. What happened?"

I say something about the students. My voice seems to be coming from far away. It sounds like when Dave mimics me, like someone reciting poetry in a voice meant for singing lullabies.

I tell him about snapping its neck.

And then I am silent.

After a while he says, "What about the blood? The knife?"

"Oh," I say. I close my eyes. "It's just—look, you said I didn't want to hurt anyone but that's—oh God, I do. I want to—I can't even *think* about—I don't want to, you have to believe me. I don't want to let him get control of me yet."

"Him?"

"Satan," I say.

Aidan's mouth twitches.

I wave my hand impatiently. "The Tempter. You know, in medieval plays—never mind." My skin feels frail. "I don't hear voices or anything. It's just an—expression. I don't want to—turn darkside. Not yet. Not *ever*, but I don't think I can—I can't put it off forever."

When I open my eyes he's staring at me and his face is a collection of sharp lines with rage printed in them. He sees me looking at him and his face flushes slowly. He opens his mouth like he's going to yell. Then he takes a breath and holds it, lets it out. "Okay. Let's try this again. The knife."

I say, "I couldn't—help it."

He just waits.

And so I tell him what I did to the cat.

When I stop talking he closes his eyes briefly. "My God, Mickey."

Another short silence.

"You had to kill it," he says.

I look at him. "What?"

He is frowning, thinking hard. "I get it, about the cat. You had to kill it. That was—it wasn't, you know, what you said. It wasn't you going—darkside. The cat was in pain. But then—using the knife. Why did you do that? What made you flip like that?"

I want to tell him. I *intend* to tell him. It felt like panic. And rage. Mostly hatred. I hated it for making me a killer, again. I open my mouth to explain but my tongue feels thick. I close my mouth and shrug.

"You don't know?"

I shrug again.

He is silent. Then he says, "You said that I got you. Like your brother gets you. Right?"

I don't answer. I don't know what he means.

He puts the knife down. I watch him, confused. And then he gets up and comes forward.

My eyes widen.

"No—what the—*no*!"

He kneels down next to me.

"Don't you fucking dare," I say. I look at the knife, lying about two feet away. "Get the hell away from me or I will stab you in the face."

He puts his arms around me.

I hold my breath. Close my eyes. It doesn't matter. It doesn't matter.

Fuck.

I lunge for the knife. He wraps his arms tight around me and holds on. I strain against him, shove myself back with my legs. We both slam against the wall. I wrench sideways. He clings on, gets a leg across mine. Jerks back on my leg and pulls me off balance. I fall forward. He tips over and we crash down together. Lie panting. My eyes fixed on the knife. I get an arm free and my fingers reach for the blade. He pulls hard, holding me back. I make a straining noise.

"Please. *Please* get off me."

"No." He's breathing hard.

"Get off or I'll stab you in the eye. I am not kidding."

He laughs, breathless. "You're not going to stab me."

My face is pressed against the floor. I turn it to the side. Pressure on my cheekbone. I close my eyes. Lie slack. And then tense and lunge for the knife again. But he doesn't let go. He grabs my flailing arm and we wrestle in silence until I fall again and he lies on top of me, arms wrapped around mine. I feel sweat on my face. The walls move forward gently. Pulse. The flesh floor breathes. I gag.

He pulls my hair back.

Jesus. I close my eyes and swallow. Hot spit pools into my mouth.

I swallow rapidly, twice. And then gag. The taste burns.

"Why are you doing this to me?"

He holds on and I throw up. He lets me get a hand free to wipe my mouth. I spit and then try to pull away. He grabs my wrist and holds on again. We fight until I throw up again. I lie with my face near the vomit and try to calm down. Everything stinks.

"You—fucking pervert," I say. "Your sister? The one who knocks you around when you go visit her? Remind me to send her a fucking *gift* basket."

Aidan laughs. His breath hot on my neck. I jab an elbow back but he moves. My skin is feverish and sweating, my tongue is dry and tastes like bile. I blink and drop my head, rest my cheek against the floor. "*Please* get off me."

And he lets me go.

I scramble away on hands and knees and crawl into a corner. I gag and spit and wipe my mouth with my hands. "You rat bastard asshole!"

He gets onto his knees and watches me. His good eye is dark and grave, his walleye tugged like a restless compass needle towards an uncertain pole.

He gets up and goes into my bathroom. He comes back with towels and starts to clean the floor. He stops briefly and then glances up at me. I've scrambled onto the bed, wedging myself into the corner, the knife gripped in my hand. He bends down, his bare neck thin and white, the knobby vertebrae in bas relief. He wipes up the floor. Goes back into the bathroom to rinse out the towels. Then comes out and scrubs at the floorboards. I watch him squirt cleaner fluid and then scrub with the towel. The acrid stench of bleach drifts through the room.

My fingers are squeezed so tight around the handle that they tingle.

"What the *hell* is wrong with you?"

He says, "Are you okay?"

"Am I okay. Am I okay. What the hell do you *think* I am? I fucking—I want to—"

He looks at me. "But you're not going to. Okay? You're not going to do anything. You're going to put the knife down and feel like shit and *deal* with it."

"I *am* fucking dealing with it! I was fucking *dealing* with it before you *assaulted* me!" I hold out my free hand, the one not gripping the knife. "Look at this, you asshole! Look at my hands! I'm—" The tremor is visible. Each finger quivering like a leaf stirred by an unseen wind.

He looks at the shaking hand. Lines crease by his mouth. "Now you know what it feels like," he says. And he bends his head and starts to scrub the floor again.

I blink. "What? Like what feels like?"

He gestures with the vomit-soaked rag. "Guilt," he says. "Or grief. Whatever you felt when you killed the cat. I don't know. The point is, you're going to have to learn how to feel things without going—you know. Without taking it out on whatever makes you feel that way. You have to learn to feel *shitty* and just keep feeling it and not do anything. That's what people do. They just—bear it."

He stops talking.

I stare at him.

He points at me. "So don't ever do that again. Don't freak out with the knife like you've crossed some invisible boundary and it's too late. It's not too late. You're not Satan's bitch just because you had to put a cat down. You're just a person. People feel bad. You just have to learn how to feel like hell and go on." He stands and balls up the rags. He carries them into the bathroom. I hear the hamper lid shut. A cupboard door closes. The sink faucet runs and then is shut off. He comes in. "You want any dinner? Or not yet?"

I open my mouth. Close it. He shrugs and walks out. I hear the silverware drawer bang in the kitchen. I peel back my fingers. The knife falls onto the blankets in front of me. My hand is sweaty and pink. A headache prickles behind my right eye and my stomach feels clammy, but my heart rate is slowing, evening out.

I stand up.

He's at the freezer holding a bag of frozen chicken patties. He turns when I come in. "Mac and cheese and chicken patties? Yes? No?"

I swallow hard. It can't be worse than what I just felt. I go up to him and lean in and kiss his cheek. His skin is cool. I back away quickly, bump a hip into the counter edge. I fold my arms tight across my chest and look at the wall behind his head.

"Do not," I say, "attempt to reciprocate, or I will really and truly stab you in the fucking eye and I am quite serious about that." The refrigerator hums, starting to defrost as the freezer door stands open. The skin around his eyes tightens. For a long time he is quiet.

And then he smiles. "Okay."

He goes to the cupboard and takes down a cardboard box of macaroni and cheese. "Do you add milk or water to the cheese mix?" He squints at the packet of powdered and chemically-enhanced cheese.

"I think you use milk."

"Crap. I think our milk went bad."

"I told you we needed more milk."

"Yeah." And he looks over at me. "Me too. Okay?"

I don't know what he means, but he flushes and I feel faintly dizzy myself.

NINETEEN

Thanksgiving is next week. The first serious signs of winter have crept in and hunkered down. I run under flat gray skies stacked with clouds like steel-hawsered frigates. Cars tires froth through a salted slush thick with wet leaves, cigarette butts, and other detritus.

On Monday I come in from my run and see my cell phone lit up on my bed, ringing. Dave's phone number blinks on the screen. I ignore it and shower.

After my shower I check my voicemail. When his familiar voice picks up I realize how long it's been since I talked to him. Weeks, probably. Maybe a month. Even when he lived in New York I never went this long without talking to him.

I wonder why I've stopped returning his calls or picking up. I'm not paying attention but I focus when he mentions a copper band. I realize he's asking about a mystery, if I have made progress in my Sherlock Holmes impression on Aidan's familial drama.

"—Because I don't want to sound cliché, but you really were made for greater things. I mean, watching you run around after that boy's late lamented *maman* is like when I see the Dalai Lama on a *bill*board advertising fucking peace or some such asinine shit. You're meant for mountains and goddamn *yaks*. Do you know what I mean? Your art student's mommy died bloodless, it was a fucking Angela *Lans*bury murder."

Something cold settles in my gut and I shiver. My thumb hits the delete key before I am even conscious of making the decision. I slide the phone back under my pillow.

And then I take a breath. I pull out the phone and call him.

He picks up right away. "My darling!"

"Sorry I haven't called."

There's a brief, awkward silence. I never noticed before how easily we talked. There was never anything uncomfortable between us, not like when I try to talk to other people. Dave's mind is like an Olympic athlete, preternaturally quick, prescient in its ability to seize on my fragmented thoughts and make of them something coherent.

I clear my throat. "Are you going to Dad's thing?"

Our father has an annual party for faculty members. The notes about this event have been appearing regularly in my mailbox at work.

He laughs. "Oh, I love it. Are you inviting me? And will we go? And will we join the common throng and will we whisper and giggle like all the beautiful morons in their feckless fancy?"

"I hate it when you start alliterating. Are you coming or not?"

He stops laughing. "Listen," he says. "Don't go there. They sap your soul, doll. They drain you of everything vital, everything beautiful."

I sigh. Maybe he was always this hard to understand, but for whatever reason it seems like recently everything he says is moving light years faster than I can follow. He used to be the only safe person in my world but now the only thing I am thinking is that Aidan is so much easier to talk to. Even though he is an utter enigma to me, Aidan is easier to read than the brother who has always been my other self.

"I know," I say. But I don't want to listen to him anymore, so I hang up the phone.

And I stare at it where it lies on my pillow. "I know."

That night I don't sleep, just sit on my bedroom floor with my laptop propped on my knees, writing a dissertation chapter. The semester is almost over and I have no dissertation draft to show for it. I have no murderer, no longer even a corpse. I have failed at everything. My fingers feel stiff. Even the joints are exhausted.

Tuesday morning sneaks in the window while I'm still sitting on the floor with my laptop open. My neck is stiff, my ass is numb, and my eyes ache.

I get up and look out the window. The street below my bedroom window lies hidden under a white Precambrian mist. I decide to go for a run and hope it will wake me up enough to teach my classes.

I pull on a Gore-Tex running jacket, not looking forward to the run this morning. It's not quite December and the real cold hasn't sunk in yet. The temperature still hovers in the upper twenties, but it's a wet, relentless cold that makes your teeth ache.

Aidan is in the kitchen watching coffee percolate when I back come in from my run. He stands with his arms folded over his chest, leaning against the wall, his eyelids dropped to half-mast.

He rouses when I come in. "Hey, Mickey. Your dad called me. He wanted me to tell you to come tonight. Something about your dissertation director being there, and you need to be able to pull off a social gathering if you're going to be an academic, and he's been leaving messages all week."

I strip off my jacket and hang it on a hook by the door. "Yikes."

Aidan tries a smile and his jaw cracks when he yawns. "Yeah. He said he's left messages at your office and tried your cell phone but you didn't answer, and he doesn't know if you check messages."

I untie my shoes and peel them off my cold, wet feet. "The thing I would miss most," I say, and, when Aidan blinks at me, "if I were to wake up normal someday, the thing I would miss most is how you all overcompensate for my deficiencies. It's so very restful."

Aidan grins a little and swings his head side to side in exaggerated annoyance. Then he makes a sudden lunge for a cupboard. I startle, but he's just pulling out a mug. The coffee has finished its last dying gurgles and the pot is full.

My father, like many academic administrators, spends the semester freezing salaries and the holiday season hosting end-of-semester shindigs designed to release accumulated tension and grease the wheels of faculty-administrative collaboration. I have no desire to attend this evening, but I've avoided Telushkin long enough. At some point I should remind him what I look like, at least to the extent that he'll be able to pick me out of the lineup of graduates at commencement, assuming I actually graduate some day. But, God, parties are annoying. They are not something I do well.

The thought of desires and annoyance makes me think of Desiree. I have taken her sandwiches a couple times in the last few weeks. She never says anything, not anything more significant than jumbled words, although she no longer panics or faints when I make sudden movements. She likes the color pink, apparently. She is taken by shiny things, though only for short amounts of time. She smokes cigarettes to the filter and then rips apart the filter as if she's looking for the secret to immortality. I have discovered nothing else useful.

I move around Aidan and pull out a jar of peanut butter, and grab grape jelly from the fridge.

"So?"

I glance up at Aidan in surprise.

He's clutching his coffee mug. Steam beads on his eyebrows. "So are you going to go?"

I shrug.

"What," he says, "you don't *love* parties?" He laughs at the look on my face. "You should go. And you can invite me. You know, like, as your escort?"

Over the rim of his mug I can only see the slant of his eyebrows and the crinkles by his eyes. It strikes me as odd that I am so familiar with his facial expressions that I can read only half of his face so easily. I know his face better than I do the faces of my family members. I wonder why that is.

"Of course," I say. "Let the plebeians revel in our love. They will write sonnets to us."

He laughs.

When I finish making the sandwich, I pull on jeans and a sweatshirt over my running clothes and collect my backpack. Then I put the sandwich in a baggie and collect another baggie of vegetables. I zip the food into my backpack and leave.

Clouds swarm dark over the morning sky burgeoning with storm.

I head for the car parked behind the house.

"She walks in darkness."

I startle so badly that I almost drop my car keys.

He emerges from the shadow behind the industrial trash bin and something in the stale smell of trash and the crisp wet darkness makes me think of a tarnished Beowulf trailing seaweed and smelling of monster blood.

I suck in air.

"*Fuck* you," I say. "And it's 'beauty' not 'darkness,' you Neanderthal."

My elder brother laughs. He swings his hand at me but I duck it.

"Where are you going?"

"What are you doing here?"

We talk at the same time, but he answers first. "I haven't yet visited my sister's abode, the spider's nest, as it were. Stephen has. He told me that you gave him the personal tour. I felt—left out." He comes forward into the pale of light by the rear door of the first-floor apartment. "It's really quite lovely. Very do*mes*tic."

"I still don't understand what you're doing here. Did Dad send you to break my arms if I don't show up tonight or something?"

He laughs. His bare throat gray in the dark.

"It's not like you would do what I told you to. Not anymore. Is it?"

It's a strange thing to say. I can feel my heartbeat under my ribs.

"I've got to go."

"Take me with you."

"No." And because the statement is so bald, I laugh and turn away from him and jog down the sidewalk. I think I hear his footsteps behind me but I doubt my brother can keep up. It surprises me how something as simple as running—an action *Homo sapiens* adapted for particularly, the speedy lope of the two-legged creature across the plains—seems so challenging to most people. One time, when I was a couple minutes late for an appointment with Telushkin, I didn't shower first. Just showed up in his office slick with sweat and breathing hard.

He asked how many miles I had run that morning, and when I told him he shook his head and said he could never run like that. I had laughed. He is potbellied, his skin slack on his bones. He seemed to think the laughter was offensive.

I squat on the glass-speckled gravel and hand over the sandwich. Desiree talks to me about blue and cops and words that seem to be either Klingon or some archaic form of pig Latin.

She glances over her shoulder. She freezes for half a second, then wrenches her head to the side like she's been struck. Her fingers splay over her forehead. She starts to moan.

I look around and see my brother.

For a second I don't do anything.

Then I jump up. For some reason I'm angry.

"I told you not to come, you fucking asshole."

He laughs and gravel skitters under his shoes as he comes down the slope. "But I was curious, my darling." He stops and looks around, his fingers playing with strands of his hair. His eyes travel over the backpack, the shopping cart, over Desiree bobbing her chin and patting her forehead with her palm, rocking back and forth. I can't tell if she's having some sort of attack or just greeting my brother in her planet's native language.

I stand up and brush the dirt and grit off my jeans. Then I march away from Desiree, heading back toward campus. Dave doesn't follow right away but then I hear his footsteps behind me. I think about breaking into a run. I know he can't keep up with me, but he somehow figured out where I was going. Like maybe he's followed me before. I try to think if I've ever seen him but I know I haven't. And I would sense my brother's presence. I know I would.

I let him catch up with me.

He falls into step, his breath coming fast. White gusts swarming into the pearlescent air.

"You shouldn't smoke so much."

"What?" he says. "What's that apropos of?"

I don't correct his grammar. "You're too young to be so out of breath from such little exertion."

"Aw. I think you're *worried* about me."

"I always worry about you," I say. And then, because I can't stand it anymore, the sound of his panting breath or the smell of him, like cigarettes and the warmth of his aftershave, I break into a run and leave him behind.

I pull up to the driveway of my parents' house at five-thirty that evening. Aidan's rusted yellow hatchback Tercel crunches up the drive behind me. I still don't know why I agreed to bring him. There is already a neat collection of shiny cars along the cobbled street, year-old Audis, convertible Mustangs, even a cherry-red Porsche GT2. No one embraces the most cliché iterations of midlife crisis like academics.

I lead the way to the porch and open the front door. Light floods out into the gray-blue twilight, followed by a warm swirl of cologne, hair gel, wine, sizzling butter, cinnamon. Laughter clinking like wine glasses. A glitter of color, rustling fabrics, and the flash of rings and bare skin in the living room and solarium. I wind through, Aidan in my wake. The Persian rug underfoot, a stained glass panel in the dining room reflecting flickering flames from dozens of candles.

"Michaela! Michaela, come over here."

I turn to see who's yodeling my name across the room. My dissertation director, wearing a mustard-colored corduroy jacket, sweeps his arm over his head. When I turn back, Aidan has abandoned me. He threads his way through the throng in the direction of the fireplace. When I stand on my toes, I see why. Stephen is sitting on a folding chair near the fireplace, shoulders hunched, headphones on, a plate of shrimp and prosciutto balanced on his lap. It occurs to me that my quiet roommate is, in fact, closer in age to my younger brother than to anyone else in this room. Excepting me, of course. I don't tend to think of Aidan as young.

My dissertation director's breath smells sweet. He crowds in too close, wheezing and chattering about career plans and my dissertation chapter.

"—And have you met Dr. Scott Renfield? Visiting lecturer from Purdue I was telling you about?"

A thin man is standing beside Dr. Telushkin, gazing into the middle distance. When Telushkin says his name, the thin man raises his eyebrows and looks at me. His eye sockets are sunken, the skin over his thin cheekbones delicately puckered like the crust that forms over boiled milk.

He reaches out a hand.

I wipe my palms on my thighs, shift my weight back. "Right," I say. "Dr. Renfield. You, um, you wrote that book on Chaucer and financial reform."

"That's right. Yes." He rolls his lips together when he talks and makes a moist kissing noise. His rejected hand wanders back to himself, smoothes his tie and fingers the tie pin. "Won an NEH grant with that project."

I don't know what to say. I hear myself saying, "That's—prestigious."

Prestigious. Terrific. I cough into my hand and look around for Aidan. But I don't see him with Stephen. I wonder if he's gone to the dining room to collect food.

"I'd like to talk about your project, if you have time. Bob tells me wonderful things about your work."

He's looking at me, eyes bright and wet-looking in the worn palimpsest of his face.

I look down at the floor. Pick at my thumbnail and glance up at Telushkin. "Yeah, well, his work is in folklore, so he, um, he tells tall tales for a living so, you know. Grain of salt."

The professor from Purdue rolls his lips together. Telushkin clears his throat.

I smile. Try a short laugh.

And their faces ease into jocularity. Telushkin puts his hand on Renfield's shoulder and they both chortle, fake, belly-rolling chuckles as if what I've said is the most hilarious thing they've ever heard.

Then Telushkin says, "Get you something to drink, Scott? Michaela?"

I shake my head.

Renfield turns to look after Telushkin when he waddles away.

I exhale and back up a step, preparing to worm my way out of the crowded room. A woman in a sleeveless black dress is standing right behind me. Her arm brushes mine. I flinch away and swipe at my sleeve but the instinctive act makes the backs of my fingers brush her bare shoulder. I swallow hard. Her shoulder is palely freckled like a bird's egg. I want to scratch my fingernails into its melon-cool surface. I grip my fists and turn away from her. My tongue feels dry and swollen, a ball of panic wadded into the back of my throat.

My father is standing near the piano, isolated in shirtsleeves and a loosened tie, the god at home coming faintly unraveled at the seams. Light glistens on the lenses of his glasses, turning them opaque and white. A woman in chunky turquoise jewelry comes up to him, smiling, but he doesn't notice. His face is aimed away from her, turned in my direction, the white ovals of his lenses fixed on me.

I wonder what he is thinking. His daughter, the academic, being singled out for an introduction to a visiting scholar. His daughter, the antisocial basket case, quivering and twitching and sweating after a two-minute conversation.

My fingernails press into my palms until I feel a faint tickle, the splitting of skin. I duck my chin and head for the kitchen.

The kitchen table is laden with platters and dishes and crystal-clear scarlet Jell-O moulds and mounds of crusty bread and fruit trays and the scent of butternut squash and nutmeg. A woman at the sink turns around. She is familiar, someone who comes to help my mom throw her semiannual bashes for dad's private-box-at-sporting-events colleagues.

"Hi there, Michaela."

I nod and slide around the island.

Aidan comes into the kitchen. He stands with his hands in his pockets. Grins. “Having a blast? Saw that guy chatting you up. What do you think? You could pull off the whole trophy wife thing, right?”

“Fuck you.”

Mom comes into the kitchen carrying a platter of hors d’oeuvres.

“Oh Aidan, I didn’t see you. I’m so glad you—oh, honey, there you are, your father wondered where you’d—do you think you can you take the plate out when you go back to the living room? Aidan, have you met people yet?”

“My mother,” I say, folding my arms across my chest and leaning my hips against the island countertop, “is decompensating. Notice her decreasing linguistic control and scattered concentration.”

“Oh honey, not today.” Mom sets the platter down with a sharp crack. The woman at the sink starts rinsing off some green leafy garnish and clipping fronds to set along a plate of cold cuts. Congealed fat seams the pink-purple slices of beef. The salty tang of cold meat makes me swallow. I push my hands into my jeans pockets.

A voice in the living room slices through the burbling murmur. The murmur pitches headlong into hilarity. It sounds like a revel, an orgy perhaps.

Mom smiles. “Oh, that sounds like Dave.”

“I didn’t know Dave was coming,” Aidan says.

Mom heads into the main room, her treble voice reaching for her firstborn son. Aidan follows her out into the living room.

I had meant to head for the garage and wait out the party but I decide to wait and see Dave. I don’t have to go back into the living room to find him, though, because he always manages to find me. I ease a cheese and pimento triangle from the corner of an etched glass platter and slide onto a barstool by the island.

The woman by the sink looks over at me but doesn’t say anything. When she finishes decorating the platter I say, “That looks really great.” She looks at me and the skin across her forehead smoothes out.

She starts to smile. I worry that she might take my compliment for an invitation to tell me about her grandchildren's tonsillitis. So I say, "I mean, for predigested subcutaneous fat deposits from hormone-injected animals."

The smile is eclipsed by tensed muscles. Her eyelids fall. She takes the platter into the other room.

In the living room, Dave's voice rises above the hubbub, followed by a tide of laughter. He says something else, and there is a sudden hush. My mother's voice steps into the silence, soft, gentle. Soothing the waters troubled by whatever verbal mischief Dave's restless brain has come up with. I reach across the island to the abandoned stacks of mini-sandwiches.

I am eating my third mini-sandwich when Dave comes in. He enters from the doorway behind the stool and I see his reflection emerging from the evening-shadowed windowpane over the sink.

"My adoring public kept me. I apologize."

I brush crumbs off my thighs. "I regret to be the one to inform you, but your public are maudlin fools and senile collectors of plaster shepherdesses. You may want to reconsider boasting about their approbation."

He laughs. When he leans on the counter his skin smells strange, cloves and chlorine and rotting potatoes. A sweet and rancid reek. I want to ask him where he went after I left him by the train tracks. I wonder if he's been skulking around the homeless under their bridges all day, because he smells faintly sour, as if he's been sweating or hasn't showered recently. But for some reason the question, which is the sort of banal shit we usually natter about, seems laden with something darker. I don't want to answer any questions about what I was doing down there, who Desiree is, or why I am bringing her sandwiches in the early morning.

"It may interest you to know that your opinion is in the minority. Your humble servant was recently featured in *The New Yorker*." His shirt is gray silk, and sweat patches darken under his arms.

A glimmer of movement in the windowpane. I watch another form materialize in the rose-tinted murk, an indistinct shape with diffident shoulders, chin sunk toward a concaved chest. Strange that I recognize him immediately—a man identifiable by his lack of definition.

"No, no," I say. "You are premature. Bring forth your accolades when the time ripens."

"What?"

I swivel on the stool. "Papa," I say. "Was he glorious? Has his fame shed light upon the noble name we share?"

"Your brother is an artist," our shared paternal member says from the doorway. His hands in his pockets. Rolled shirtsleeves, the knot of his burgundy tie loosened. A faint sparkle of light refracted by sweat at his temples. "There's no need to mock."

Dave looks from me to our father. He smiles and his tongue traces his lower lip. "You misunderstood us, Dad. Mickey is my *big*gest fan."

"Oh God," I say. "That's defamation of fucking character. You write like Gertrude Stein on Nyquil."

Dave laughs hysterically. Tears well up under his eyelids and he puts his palms over his mouth, gasping. Dad shakes his head and turns back to the living room.

Dave blows out and leans close to me. His breath stirs strands of hair fallen across my face.

"We've lost him. Alone again. You and me, against the world."

When I don't answer, Dave says, "But not anymore. Is that it? But, where is your most faithful paramour? I saw him out there. He seems happy. You seem very happy together."

"I really don't know what's wrong with you today."

"Poor baby." His fingertips brush the ends of my hair. I move my head away but he grabs my wrist. His fingernails are long and I can feel the pressure of their half-moon shapes against the tender skin on the inside of my wrist.

Then he loosens his grip, as if he's just realized how tightly he's been holding on. He turns up my palms and we watch white crescent marks in the thin underarm skin darken with suffusions of blood. The nail bites cross fainter ruffled pink strands, healing scars from when Desiree scratched me in the throes of her fainting fit about a week ago. He frowns slightly, turning my wrist toward the kitchen light.

"He drinks," I say.

Dave looks at me.

The pain bores hot and sharp behind my right eye.

I smile. "He's so tragic. It turns out to be a story by Tolstoy, not Dickens."

"But living with you would drive anyone to drink," he says. His voice is very soft. He is interested. His hands slacken their grip as he leans forward.

I pull away, drawing my shirtsleeves down over my palms. "I didn't drive you to drink."

"No. But my soul is made of tungsten, my heart of carbide."

He reaches for me again, and I catch his wrist and bend the fingers back. "Don't."

He smiles at me and I pull away from him. Through the kitchen window the sky flares vermillion behind a fringe of fir trees. Our shades pass like gossamer across the sunset-tinted windowpane as if we are nothingness, or are pure essence.

The house finally settles on its haunches after the exuberance of human laughter fades to silence. Aidan gets up off the living room couch when he sees me. He looks from me to the empty door behind me.

"Where's Dave?"

Stephen, on the couch still, is holding a bag of Lay's potato chips. "He left a while ago. While *you* were still holed up in the garage." He points a potato chip at me.

"Nicely done." I nod in genuine appreciation. "Our *paterfamilias* still hasn't found the cojones to mention my failed attempt at socializing."

Stephen sucks his bottom lip but doesn't respond. My father, who can hear me from his liminal position in the dining room doorway, says nothing.

Aidan and I leave. He gets in his car and I get in mine.

I beat him home.

Strobe lights, red and blue, lance through the darkness. Behind me I hear Aidan's brakes squeal as he double-stomps them. Our house is under siege.

TWENTY

My heart seizes up like a fist. Blue and red whirling lights dazzle across my skin. Paramedics hurry from the lit ambulances and cop cars through the doors of the first-floor apartment. The house is broken open like a shredded tulip, a windowpane shattered and glass glittering under the glaring white light anchored to the roof of a police car. The neighbors, our dark familiars, line the sidewalks and stand hesitant in front doors, eyes like boiled onions and teeth set whitely between moist slack lips. People all over the front lawn.

The air is cold. I am already out of the Chevelle—the driver's door hanging open—and running through the gridiron of cop cars. Voices screaming. Aidan's voice behind me, high-pitched and frantic.

Yellow tape strung from the mailbox post to the front porch clings to my skin as I break through it. I fling it off.

The front door to the downstairs apartment stands ajar. Dark silhouettes move around inside the lit apartment, passing around a single still shape. Halfway across the yard to the front door a weight hits me. I slam into the ground. Something cold and heavy pins my face down and the dirt smells like metal and rotting fruit. I grunt and arch back, lashing my elbow up into the body on top of me.

"Let her up."

The weight lifts off.

My mouth is sticky and dirt cakes my tongue.

A cop with a face like a slice of Spam, pinked and moist. He bends over me. He is chewing gum, and his pores reek of fermented hops and latex. He grips a gun in both hands, the nose downward-angled, a professional bend in his knees. His small pupils fix on me.

He is talking but I can't tell if it's to me or to a woman wearing a brown creased suit who stands next to him, a city detective badge swinging from a cord around her neck. Through the open apartment door the kitchen light shines like leaking blood onto the sheet ice caked over the cement stoop. A man is crying by the doorway. The woman in the brown suit is swiveled on her hips to stare at me but from the angle of her torso I think she was questioning him a second before.

I scramble to my feet and wipe dirt from my chin. I wait. But the cop just stands there. So I brush past him and go up to the door. The man standing on the stoop wears gray sweatpants and an OSU fleece jacket. Golden licks of light on his sweat-sheened skin. He snivels. He looks vaguely familiar and I think he must be the apartment's inhabitant, that I have passed him while taking out the trash or heading to my car.

The woman in the brown suit is demanding something from him, a sharp cadence repeated.

"No," the crying man says and sniffs hard, wiping his palm across his chin. "I swear to *God* I don't know who she is. I don't recognize *anyone*."

I climb up onto the stoop next to him but don't break through the yellow tape across the open doorway. The wind tangles in my hair. The air fresh smell of snowy cold is tainted with an acrid stench, ammonia and bleach mixed with something sweet and salty.

The kitchen linoleum, a crackled, heat-warped skin, the twin of our floor above. Framed by quotidian kitchen appliances—an old Whirlpool dishwasher, a dented Kensington refrigerator—sits a metal folding chair. A hand armed with scalpel instead of brush has sculpted this body, this teak-skinned, ash-eyed, naked woman. Her breasts, like jam-filled silk, dangle above arms cradling an obscene mass of pinkish-gray small intestine, lumpy ridges of large intestine lying coiled in the crook under a slit of rib. Duct tape wrapped around the back frame of the chair and across her ribs, just under her breasts, holds her upright in a seated position. Her neck and head bow to gravity and her curved spine, her gently bent arms, are masterstrokes. She is a visceral Madonna, an impious pietà.

A dizzying familiarity, as if this scene has been acted out a thousand times. I knew who it was before I saw her. The minute I saw the lights, I knew who I would find.

Desiree, the woman to whom I gave a peanut butter and jelly sandwich not ten hours earlier, and who, not quite two months ago, in one brief gesture of humanity, signed her fate.

A hot sour taste and a sharp pain in my gut. The importance of paying attention this time. I feel the cops around me, watching me. My heart is pounding. I want to stare at her but I can't afford it. I hold some terrible noise shut in the back of my throat, some yell or scream.

I make myself study the room, the position of the body. I notice odd aspects of this human artwork: the duct tape around her throat. A slit throat, maybe. The bruised darkening around the skull. Body hung upside-down to drain. That would explain the bloodless intestines

But not here. No blood pool around the chair.

Where, then? The railroad tracks? Or—

I feel like I'm going to fall down. I hold very still, breathe, and think.

And I know how she was hung. I see those butchering sites from the web flashing behind my eyelids. How do I remember them so clearly? I feel as if I have seen them somewhere else.

I turn away from the doorway, stumble off the cracked cement stoop. The ground under my feet is uncertain.

The pink-faced cop face asks questions. Do I know her. Did I kill her. Where was I. I don't know what to say so I don't say anything. I want to ignore them but the cops surround me. One puts a hand out when I try to slide past and get back to the car. Then the meaty cop comes up behind me. His palm slides over my wrists as he cuffs me. Mucus-thick sweat coats my skin.

The backseat of the cop car smells like cigarette smoke and vomit and piss. A nub of stubbed plastic where the interior handles were removed. I always wondered if cop cars were modified or created fully formed, a vehicular Athena emerging from the cranium of Crown Victoria. Enlightenment comes at the oddest times.

My heartbeat is unsteady. Sometimes it feels as if it has stopped altogether and I wait in silence for the knowledge that I am still alive.

Streetlights striate the darkness, swiping yellow across my legs, sliding up my body and disappearing into darkness.

In daylight, I have run and driven past the sand-colored edifice with pale stacked steps and shining plaques of fallen public servants. Tonight the car takes me underneath the glimmering edifice. The cop car burrows into a cement parking deck, gnome-globe lights casting sickly prickles across chipped plaster walls. A steel door. The smell of industrial bleach.

A small room with a metal-framed table, a chair. He uncuffs me and leaves me alone in the room. A while later the woman in a brown suit comes in. A young cop in uniform behind her carries a Styrofoam cup of coffee. He puts it down on the table.

The woman slaps a buff-colored folder down on the table. The folder is stenciled with the letters C.A.P.U. and the seal of the city of Akron.

The woman leans across the metal table. In the strange naked light her extended palm looks like uncooked chicken flesh.

"Detective Sandra Smith," she says. "Crimes Against Persons."

When I don't offer my own hand she draws back and folds her hands in front of her. She puts her lips together neatly, but other than that small motion her facial expression does not change. She stands with one leg slack, a confident posture. Standing is unnecessary. Her confidence is unnecessary. I already know that—Jesus, the clichés are endless. The other shoe has dropped. The straw has broken the camel's back. The fat lady has wound up her high notes. I am metaphorically fucked.

"Why don't we start off with your name. Would you state your full name, please?"

The words *start off* ripple, seeming to undulate through the mote-strewn air. *When you're old, you're smart about stuff and you don't get caught.*

The smell of bleach. Bleach and ammonia.

I swallow. My fingernails press against my palms. The smell of—the smell in the kitchen, Desiree's body, but the smell lying thick in the kitchen was not blood but bleach. Her death was quick but her after-death, the arrangement of her mortal coil, took longer, a meticulous marriage of aesthetics and pragmatics. I realize that her corpse is forensically mute. No evidence, if any existed, of my proximity to her, my hands on hers, my fingerprints on the plastic baggie of her sandwich, wherever it is. She was killed far from her lair, far from our contact, her body purged of my spore. But she was killed underneath my home. Or, underneath mine, and that of my strange-eyed, innocent-faced roommate.

"For what?" My voice surprises me, a hoarse whisper. I swallow.

"You're a person of interest right now, not a suspect. You don't need a lawyer, though you have a right to one. If you want one we can get a lawyer down here. But we're just going to ask you a few questions, figure out how you fit into the equation. All right? Let's start with your name."

She is staring at me so intently that her gaze feels like fingers pressing against the skin over my cheekbones. I want to look away. I want to jump up and smash her head into the stainless steel table edge. I squint slightly to force my gaze to hold hers, to hold steady, to appear sane and ordinary. "My, my wallet with my ID got taken at the desk when I came in. I'm, I mean, that's me."

The detective's fingernails are squared off, blunt and lacquered shellfish pink. She taps the nails of her first two fingers and her thumb together. She comes over to the table and takes the cup.

"You want tea? I can get you some."

"No. No, thank you."

She nods and takes the cup. Sips. She presses her lips together to dry them. She sits down. "You know why we brought you in?"

"Because I ran—I mean, I contaminated—"

She smiles and shakes her head once. “That doesn’t matter. You didn’t go into the crime scene itself. But you seemed pretty upset. Did you know her?”

“Know—?”

“The woman. Do you know the victim? The woman on the chair?”

It occurs to me that it would be entirely helpful at this point to be able to roll names off my tongue with the ease with which I can parse Old English syntax.

But names don’t mean anything, except as methods of psychological control. I read a study that said we call people names—and you can see this in nicknames, but it’s true in general, too—so that we have a handle for them. So that we can own them.

What, besides a name, do we ever really know about a person? About a family member or a friend you could say something, maybe, some personality trait or great deed that belonged to them alone and that defined them.

But all I know of Desiree are the things she carried with her. And that she was a person underneath it all, and that she respects the dismembered dead.

“She is someone’s mother.”

The detective sets the tea down. “What was that? Whose mother?”

“I don’t know. But she could be. She could be anyone’s mother.”

The detective reaches for the cup again. She sips her coffee and watches me above the Styrofoam rim. “Theoretically, I suppose so. Do you know for a fact that she is a mother?”

“No.”

“How do you know her? Is she an acquaintance? Someone you’ve seen her around?”

“Around where?”

“Anywhere.”

“I didn’t look at her face for very long.”

"Mm. But you started yelling before you saw her. You got out of your car and came running across the lawn yelling. Were you worried about her?"

"I told you—I mean, I'm telling the truth. I don't know her."

"Did you know she was inside the apartment? You seemed very intent on getting into the building."

"No, it was—it was because of the fire."

"The fire?" She sets the cup down again and puts her palms on the table. She leans forward. The tops of her freckled breasts press out against a cream-colored buttoned shirt.

"The house across the street. I saw the ambulances and police cars and thought of the fire."

"You thought there might be a fire?"

"No. No, it just, it looked like when the house across the street burned."

"And so you went running *toward* the house?"

I look away from the detective. "There was a body in that house that burned. They brought out a body on a stretcher. And I thought someone should see—"

The silence goes on for a while.

"Should see what?"

I pull my gaze back to her dark eyes, but her pupils are fixed, the muscles around her mouth and nose tense and I can't read her face.

"If there was someone in the apartment, too."

A tap at the door.

She pushes off the table and smoothes a strand of hair behind her ear as she goes to the door. She opens the door, and I smell sweat and beef. I look over my shoulder. A blue uniform shoulder. They talk in low voices. It is a man.

The detective comes back in the room and the cop follows her in.

"Miss Brandis, do you recognize this officer?"

I look up at the cop, my eyes tracing up his body. A hand gripping his belt, the knuckles dimpled, a mist of dark hair across the knuckles.

His uniform is neat, but wrinkles crease next to the buttons where his belly strains at the fabric. His eyes, I notice for the first time, are fanned by fine wrinkles, and the irises are the color of hazelnuts. He scratches his cheek and his fingers rasp on bristles.

"Yes," I say.

"You do?"

"Yes."

"He says he recognizes you from his investigation of the fire."

I remember his face when I stood in front of him naked. The way his eyes tried to fall, his eyelids to cover the pupils, to veil his shame, or mine. I let my own eyes drop now, my eyelids descend.

"Yes."

"I'm sorry, could you speak up?"

"I just said yes."

"Do you remember running toward the fire?"

The cop clears his throat.

The detective looks over at him. She links her fingers loosely and raises her eyebrows. Her facial muscles are relaxed, her shoulders are back.

"You acted like you knew who was in that fire, too," the cop says. He clears his throat, a harsh rearrangement of phlegm. "You seemed pretty excited."

"I didn't," I say. "I just—the fire—"

"You like fires?" The detective taps her finger on the edge of the table. Acrylic ringing on metal. "And ambulances. Emergency vehicles. They're exciting, aren't they? You like to get involved. Pretend you're part of it all. You like the feeling of—what is it? Risk?"

I swallow. "No."

They both look at me. The room is warm. The uniformed cop touches his neck, runs a finger around his collar. A bead rolls down his neck. The detective remains still.

"No," I say. "Maybe. It's not that, it isn't. I have a, a thing, like, a condition."

"Condition," the detective says.

"I'm sorry," I say because it seems the sort of thing people say in such situations.

The detective's fingers unfold. She says, "We just have a few more questions. No one is accusing you of anything. We're just going to ask and you can tell us the truth. Did you kill the woman?"

"No."

"Where were you coming from, when you drove up?"

"Home. A party. My parents—"

The cop says, "I just talked to—"

"Thank you," the detective says. Her tone is sharp. The cop wipes a finger over his upper lip. I realize that they have called my parents. They have heard what alibi I have.

I let my spine touch the back of my chair.

The detective asks me more questions. Her tone remains even when addressing me. After a while she says, "Thank you for your help, Miss Brandis. We may have more questions. You will have to remain in the Akron area for a while. You understand that, right?"

"Yes."

"Okay." She gives me her card. Says to call her if I see anyone I don't recognize around the apartment.

The cop takes me upstairs. He doesn't touch me but when I stand at the desk collecting my wallet, car keys, office keys, and the few coins that had been in my pocket, he clears his throat. "Do you have someone to come pick you up? You want to make a phone call? I can take you home but—"

I look over at him.

He wipes his palm over his mouth. "You need a phone?"

"I don't like riding in cars with people."

"I know," he says. "I figured. So you want to call your friend, or, or anyone else?"

"I mean, you're being nice to me. But you don't have to. I'm not retarded. No rule in the Boy Scout handbook about being nice to crazies."

He looks at me and then he says, "Yeah. You doing okay? With all that in there, you okay with that?"

"Yes."

"All right. Well. You going to make that call?"

"You can take me home."

"Oh," he says.

"I mean, it's okay if you take me home. If I can sit in the back. Behind the window."

He smiles suddenly. "Okay," he says. "That's okay. You just let me know if you need out or anything. The doors don't open from the inside."

"I know."

He smiles. The pads of flesh over his cheekbones press his eyes into squints. He leads me down scuffed linoleum corridors to the wide industrial metal-sided doors that open into the parking deck.

He drives me back to the apartment and opens the door for me like a gentleman. "You take care. Okay?"

"Yes." My palms are wet. My head starts to hurt. My act of innocence, my masterful performance, sweeps over me in a tide of shaking and cold sweat. "You too. Thank you."

"Yeah," he says. "Anytime. Be good."

Aidan gets up from the couch when I come in. He comes quickly into the kitchen and stands in front of me.

"You okay?"

"Yes." I go over to the kitchen sink and run the tap. Wait for the water to heat. I pour lemon-scented dish soap into my palms and scrub my hands into a froth of bubbles. I wash my arms up to the elbows. The lingering smell of ammonia and blood. My hands feel alien, as if they belong to some other body.

"What was—what did they want to know? What did they, did they ask you questions?"

I turn off the tap. Look over at him. My hands drip into the sink.

"They asked me why I ran into the apartment. If I knew her. If I killed her. I answered them. They let me go. Do you want to ask? You want my answers? What will you do then?"

He looks at me, his upper lip drawn taut against his teeth.

"What does it matter to you? Whatever I say, what does it matter? The only thing that can change is what you believe. So what do you think? Did I do it? Am I a fucking killer? Did I *do* it?"

He inhales. He looks at me for a long time. And then he shakes his head once and goes into his room. His door shuts.

TWENTY-ONE

The apartment is dark and cold. I feel for the light switch. The room smells of Jack Daniel's. The thermostat is set to fifty degrees Fahrenheit.

An easel sits in the kitchen. The wet paint catches at the light, dark orange and pale yellow dabs dissolving and mingling. I can't tell what image struggles through the rush of paint strokes on the canvas. The silence is frenetic.

I go into my room and empty my backpack of the contents, laptop, Bic pens, loose-leaf notepaper scribbled with library call numbers and notes in various archaic languages. I take the laptop into the living room. A newspaper lies on the couch. I move it to sit down, then see the date on the paper. I set the laptop on the worn carpet and open the newspaper. The mutilated body found near the university campus has been identified. The victim was an indigent woman named Desiree Morehead, fifty-two years old, of no known address and with no living relatives. Forensic evidence suggests she was killed elsewhere and brought to the house. The location of the murder is unknown but is likely to be nearby. No information is available on how she got into the house or who killed her. The apartment's inhabitant had an alibi and did not recognize the body. The police are soliciting information from any person who may have seen someone entering the premises that day, any person who may have been in the vicinity, hanging around or acting otherwise suspicious, in the days leading up to the murder.

My parents called this morning. My mother couldn't believe that something like that would *happen* and I wouldn't *call* her immediately. Didn't I know that she *worries*?

I didn't tell her about my foray into the bowels of the Akron Police Department last night. And she never asked about the woman, if I knew her. I don't know if she is afraid to know the answer or if it just doesn't occur to her to wonder.

For a long time I sit on the couch and try to feel something—anger, maybe. A clean rage. Or fear. But the numbness that feels like cotton in my veins instead of blood is different from my usual disinterest in other people. It's a colder feeling, like a sickness in my belly. I sit with my hands pressed between my knees and wonder if something broke in me when I saw her. I can't remember how she looked when she was alive, the shapes of her face, the color of her eyes, or how she smelled.

And I refuse to think about her dead.

I fold the newspaper up and put it in the recycle bin. I work in the living room for three hours. Aidan does not come home. His painting dries unfinished.

My roommate, for the first time in our brief acquaintance, does not seek me out, does not talk, does not say anything and especially does not ask what he does not want to have answered. I come home each night to a silvery mist of non-words with absences and non-meanings between them, pulsating, breathing, a shivering fabric of nothingness.

I research online. I sit in the university library and read ancient books and trawl through less ancient databases. I read archaic lexicons and memorize morphemes.

I come home to the silence. I call my brother but he hasn't answered his phone since my evening in police custody. I sit on my bed and read and try not to listen to Aidan's cramped silences. I try not to think of all the decisions that have led me to this place, try not to think about the fact that there is nothing that I can do to make my brain chemicals different.

Downstairs the apartment has been cleaned and evacuated. Another red and blue RE/MAX sign sits out front, this time for the apartment below. Melting snow softens the soil and the last shards of broken glass sink deep into the earth. The temperature creeps above thirty-five degrees.

The air smells like spring but it's a lie. Winter hovers over Lake Erie, waiting. Those of us born in this state live with the smell of freshening earth but believe only in that unseen slavering icy predator to the north.

I run in the melting snow and get a head cold.

My mother calls again. The family makes an annual pilgrimage to Michigan for the Thanksgiving holiday. I usually decline, but my mother is strangely insistent this year. She says she is worried about me, worried about how dangerous my neighborhood is. But there is something else that worries her. I can't tell what it is, only that her voice is strung like a violin string on the point of snapping.

The Chevelle's exhaust system breaks with a roar like a wounded dragon. In the distance between the apartment and my parents' garage no less than three cars speed pass me with a middle finger on display in the driver's window. I spend most of Saturday on my back on ice-crusted gravel trying to figure out if I can remove the muffler and have the crack welded, or if I need to replace the whole thing.

My mother brings me hot cocoa, and stands under the carport and asks if I'm coming with them.

I wipe at grease crusted over my chin and say, "Okay."

She nods a few times. But she doesn't leave. She just folds her arms under her breasts and watches me. Her breath is visible in the chill.

Because the Chevelle is still up on cinderblocks at my parents' house, I climb into the family car for a seven-hour trip to the grandparents' house. My family always makes it a four-day adventure, full, I am sure, of familial warmth and gastronomical delight. I stopped going a few years after I moved into my parents' garage.

I sit on a bench seat in my mother's minivan, trying to read history textbooks while Stephen crunches on peanut butter crackers in the seat ahead of me and my parents sit silently in their respective seats up front.

My grandparents' Michigan housing development, built in the late seventies, is all brown siding and ugly brickwork. Snow packed around blackened trees, stunted houses on frozen lawns. Thick glassy icicles fringe my grandparents' eaves. Stephen runs up to the front porch and jumps and knocks his red mittens against the icicles. They crack and shatter into the snow, a fine dust of ice shards puffing up like the detritus after a small explosion.

The family greets relatives in the living room. I go to the kitchen.

My grandmother bastes a glistening turkey, its skin blistering and crisp. Steam skims the carcass, vapid dancers rising to mist on the goldenrod-yellow oven hood. She notices my gaze and smiles at me. "It's fun with all you kids here. Thank you for keeping me company here, sweetie. Our little kitchen time."

The overhead light is dim and the room is quieter than the crowded living room.

I look at my grandma. She's wearing a pink jogging suit and the jacket is tight across folds of soft fat around her middle. I wonder how those pounds of human fat would look if the skin was sliced with a thin blade. Pale yellowish-white curds slithering out. A flash of memory. I remember flinging my arms around her waist when I was small enough that the top of my head reached her bellybutton. I try to think what hugging my grandma would have felt like. I imagine it would feel like Jell-O trapped in catgut. But I can't remember. I blink and decide that I fabricated the memory altogether.

I lean against the sink and try to think of something to say. We must share genetic material, although we couldn't look more dissimilar. For some reason my mouth aches with wanting to say something.

"Your mother said David was with someone now?"

This is news to me. I rub my hand over my face. "We'll never know if he is."

Dave still hasn't answered my calls, but he stopped attending our grandparents' get-togethers years before I did, shortly after he moved to New York.

My grandmother looks worried at the brusqueness of my tone, so I make my voice sound lighter, happier. "Casanova said he couldn't come this year. And by this time next year, whoever this someone is will be just one more broken heart on his Wall of Shame."

"Oh, he's not so bad." She smiles. "He's an attractive, successful young man."

Sometimes I think my mom's parents live in a world constructed entirely of 1950s musical sets in which the people they meet are as likely to burst into choreographed song as to snap their fingers and say, "Jeepers!" My grandmother, for instance, talks about Dave like she is under the impression that he is a high-powered workaholic who gives a single pink rose to his female, blonde, Anglo-Saxon dates.

And I wonder again why my mother, raised in this Technicolor Rodgers and Hammerstein set, decided to marry my father with his genetic predisposition for Shakespearean-level tragedy, stages soaked in blood and the entire cast strewn, limbless, around.

My father's parents were Jews from Eastern Europe, curators of exquisite suffering repressed until it fused with their DNA. My grandmother came from a poor rural Jewish community in Hungary. She spoke Hungarian and German but not Yiddish, so she could never talk to the other women in her congregation. She met my grandfather in a tobacconist's shop in Harlem, New York. He was that rare type of Jew—German-speaking and so broke he couldn't afford shoes that weren't held together with twine. She married him. My dad says that his only memories of his father are of a man whose wool overcoat smelled like cigar smoke and who sat and stared silently at the radiator while his wife yelled in German. My grandfather knocked up his wife, left for a year, came back, left again. Turned up two or three times in a decade, drunk and passed out on the apartment building's front steps. My grandmother took him in, made him a spicy boiled cabbage soup, then yelled at him. The only German words my dad knows are curses liberally mixed with threats of violence.

It's not my mother's fault that she gave birth to reincarnations of horror condensed to its purest, most elemental form. And it's not her siblings' fault that they are now related by marriage to a mostly mysterious heritage of immeasurable psychological trauma. I suppose I shouldn't blame them for finding us so incomprehensible.

My mother's whole family is really and truly ordinary. They are rural, under-educated, white Protestant Americans. Most of them are rednecks. I mean hunting rifles and jackets and Ford pickup trucks. Fishing trips. Budweiser by the gross.

This one Thanksgiving my mom's older brother, Uncle Randy, wanted to take us hunting. My parents tried hard to swallow the blind panic. Fluttered. *Oh, not Mickey, not a girl*, they said. *She'd far rather play with Jennifer's Barbie dolls*. Ignoring my rapt eyes, my sunlit voice begging, pleading to go. Dave, winking at me, turned to Uncle Randy and cast down shy eyes, clasped his hands behind his back, and said, diffidently, that he wouldn't mind going.

Uncle Randy took Dave, a scrawny fourteen-year-old, and our oversized brutish cousins. They were gone for the weekend. We drove down to Uncle Randy's house to pick Dave up on Sunday afternoon.

The deer carcass swung from the garage beams. Huge slabs of dark meat, white ribs. The smell of blood, but the ribs so white, clean as teeth.

Later that night, he snuck into my bedroom and told me about the hunt. About the slaughter. How Uncle Randy had closed his fingers over the handle of the hunting knife, directed his boyish tendons to tighten, to slice the skin at the backs of the knees and down the jaw, to sever the tough, meaty carotid artery, to jerk the edge of the blade through the rubbery jugular veins. They sliced the skin and peeled it.

Like a thick, meaty banana, Dave told me. Then they removed the organs. Liver and kidneys they packed in wax paper in a tray. The bowels were left with the bones and the skin. They hung the body to drain it.

As he told me, his breath hot on my face, I could picture every step of the process as perfectly as if I were watching it, doing it, in person.

After he told me about the hunting trip, Dave had leaned forward in the dark. He smelled of soap and laundry detergent. *I'm sorry they didn't let you go,* he whispered. *Maybe next time.*

They never let me go on a hunting trip. I can't really blame them for that, either.

"And you, young lady."

I blink and look up at my grandmother. She points the turkey baster at me. A droplet of grease dribbles down its side.

"What about me?"

"One of these days *you'll* be showing up with some young man. All it takes is the *right* one."

I just look at her. "The right one to what?"

Now she looks confused. "Well, to be the right one," she says.

We stare at each other in silence.

And then I burst out laughing.

She gives me a warped, tight smile and turns back to the turkey. Her skin is wrinkled and the light catches at its scaly patterns as she spoons broth over the bird.

The rest of the aunts and uncles and cousins come over the next day. No one says anything to me. I have always tried to play nice around the relatives. It means a lot to my parents. Mostly I just interact as little as possible. I know my way around the suburbs of Michigan pretty well from all the running I do when I'm here.

When I come downstairs after breakfast the next morning (having avoided the meal with its requisite chatter and cluttered table), the relatives are all in the living room going through their stage performances. Aunt Janine rattles on about the management position my cousin Jason got and Aunt Linda goes on about Jennifer's boyfriend who was a roadie and traveled with Green Day or something.

I sit down on the stairs so I can look down into the living room through the railing. An uncle cradles a bowl of pistachios between his thighs and pops the shells apart with his dirty thumbnails. His belly strains against his Michigan State sweatshirt. He cites baseball scores with a male cousin while the women glance up at the stairs and lean towards each other to talk in unmoderated voices about their offspring. I can tell by the way they talk about their daughters' dance performances and their sons' careers that they don't think much of me, with my eight years of college, zero work experience, and fewer than zero romantic experiences, fit for nothing but to live in a garage or the spare bedroom of an emotionally fragile art student. Their opinions of me aren't high, but my revenge is perfect: I don't give a shit.

Thanksgiving dinner is a cacophony. Glass casserole dishes full of green beans floating in mushroom soup mix. Scalloped potatoes with steam rising from brown-specked cheese crusts. The electric knife dipping into the turkey breast, slitting the crisp skin so that clear liquid dribbles down its sides. Laughter, arguing, and a self-righteous ESPN announcer in the background analyzing a touchdown.

I sit on the end of the many-leafed table near Stephen. His left elbow is propped on the table between us and he turns away from me to talk to a cousin who wears braces and has zits the size of gumballs. They talk about SAT prep courses, a Kings of Leon concert, and Super Mario.

If I even wanted to talk to one of my many relatives, what topics of conversation would I offer? Somehow I doubt any of them would have many opinions to offer on medieval play cycles, or power-to-weight ratios in pre-1970s muscle cars.

My father is across the table and a few seats to my right. He eats silently. Knife and fork slicing turkey into small, bite-sized pieces. Arranging each forkful, bite of turkey, dab of mashed potato, single green bean. In between each bite he takes a sip of red wine. He and my mother are the only wine drinkers. Uncle Randy is on his fourth Coors.

My mother sits at the other end of the table. She gesticulates, her jaw moving, her eyes wide, laughing and chattering like a marionette with a hyperactive puppet master. She touches the arms and shoulders of her sisters-in-law, her mother, her father. They touch her in return. They lean toward each other. Their stories veer towards the hagiographic. Remember that time Joe drove dad's car into a ditch, oh my God, and Randy had to give him rides everywhere, and they ended up having such a good time, all that riding around town together, when Randy's pickup broke down they went and bought that Chevy *together*? And remember that time you opened that lemonade stand and I said to Harry, I said, she's going to be an *entrepreneur*!

My father gets up and comes back to the table with the bottle of wine. He sees me watching him and raises his eyebrows, tipping the bottle in my direction.

I shake my head and take another bite of turkey.

Stephen smiles at something his pink-and-white skinned cousin says and shifts in his seat, brushing hair out of his eyes. He lays his arm back down on the table. His elbow touches my hand. He doesn't notice. I bite hard on my tongue and put my hand in my lap and don't say *fuck*.

Uncle Randy gives a great bellow of laughter.

We all jump a little and look over at him.

My cousin Jeff is protesting. Laughing, but protesting. No way, he is saying. That pot he smoked in high school was the only pot he's ever smoked. Swear to God. Where's Aunt Cynthia? She can vouch for him, Christ.

My mother flushes like a hothouse flower unfurling after too long in the cold. She laughs. "We see through you, big guy. We see *right* through you."

"No way! I've always been a straight arrow. A goddamn straight arrow."

"Oh, please."

"Come *on*, Aunt Cynthia! I'm telling the truth. You'd think *you'd* believe me!"

A sudden silence.

The cousin next to Stephen turns from watching Jeff's protestations of innocence to stare at Stephen.

Jeff looks at my mom and blushes. Uncle Randy looks at my mom, then at my dad.

I look across at my father.

He is looking at his wine glass. He does not look up.

Beside me, Stephen bites his lower lip and looks down at his plate. The rims of his ears are dark red.

I clear my throat. "Of course she believes you."

Eyes swivel to my face, confusion printed on their foreheads. I feel my father lift his gaze from his glass.

I say, "As you so aptly point out, she would recognize symptoms of pretty much any serious drug use. Between my anti-psych meds and my older brother's recreational experimentation, I doubt my brother and I have left a single mind-altering substance untested." I give Jeff a cheek-aching grin. "Although before you base your entire defense on my mother's familiarity with crazies and drug addicts, you might want to remember that she's also more familiar with brilliant academics and artists than with total fucking *bores*."

I toss my napkin on top of my half-eaten turkey and push back my chair.

"Lovely meal," I say. "Lovelier conversation. A delight, as always."

I walk out of the dining room, out of the house.

An overcast snowy night. My socks leave dark patches in the snow. The cold aches in my bones. I go out onto the empty street. Tire ruts carved into gray snow. Salt grit piled by the sidewalks. A few chimneys breathe thin pale streams of smoke into the ironclad sky. I walk up the empty road. Icy snow packs in my socks. I take off my socks and leave them lying in the street. My jeans cuffs drag heavy against my ankles.

Time passes.

Later the sky darkens to pewter and shadows stretch dark over the silent suburb. Streetlights glow greenish and alien. I walk back to my grandparents' house. When I get close I notice one of the cars in the driveway is idling, brake lights red in the darkness. The car is a minivan. My mother's car.

Frozen trees creak in the dark and unseen telephone wires cry plainsongs with inhuman voices. I wade through ankle-high wet snow up the driveway and put my hand on the front passenger's side door. The windowpane is tinted and I can't see inside in the dark. I open the door.

My father, sitting in the driver's seat with his hands resting on the steering wheel, jerks his head up from the headrest.

"Jesus Christ."

"Nope. It's just me."

I climb inside and pull the door shut. The car radio is playing soft classical music, one of Vivaldi's Four Seasons. The car smells like sour fruit and burnt rubber, the wine on my father's breath and the old heating unit in the car.

I put my hands under my thighs and stretch out my feet toward the vent near the footrest. My toes are the color of raw salmon. The bones feel like they will burn through the skin.

"Are you still doing that?"

I look over at him.

He lifts his hand from the steering wheel and points. My feet.

"The masochism."

When Dave took me diving into the basement of an unconstructed house, he told our parents it was my idea, that I had jumped into the icy sludge and he had rescued me. It was maybe, technically, a lie but not a consequential one. I never noticed heat or cold like ordinary people and would often go outside forgetting a coat or shoes in the winter. Dave's lie didn't upset me, but ever since then my parents have labored under the misapprehension that I have masochistic tendencies. I hate inaccuracy. But I also hate repeating myself. People are morons.

I roll my eyes but don't answer him.

My father scratches his chin. His thumbnail rasps against a silvery haze across his jaw.

"What are you doing out here?"

He doesn't say anything for a long time and I think that he won't answer at all but then he says, "Not being there."

"Are you going to get divorced?"

He lifts his head from the seat again and turns to look at me. Our reflections in the front windshield waver, merge.

"It disgusts me," he says. "Your masochism. And also your 'insightful' comments that are really just puerile jibes intended to rile rather than communicate."

I look away from our reflections and at his face. The faint glow from the headlights turns his glasses lenses white.

"You wear those juvenile T-shirts, you run like a maniac. Every time I see you I see pain. And every other word out of your mouth is fuck. Nothing about you is beautiful or gracious. You are hard, judgmental, uncompromising, needlessly cruel. You are verbally sadistic to your mother who has done nothing but love you. You ignore the only family member who truly dotes on you—and I thank God for it. I would hide Stephen from you if you didn't do such a comprehensive job avoiding him. You're like a human cancer in my family."

He leans back and breaths through his nose. His papery eyelids slide down.

I sit and we listen to violins chirruping, trumpets caroling. Silhouettes pass to and fro behind the warmly lit living room curtains, the picture window acting like a shadowbox in the night. We are voyeurs of civilization.

I could tell him that Dave is almost as fucked up as I am. I chew my lower lip. The coppery taste of blood in my mouth. I wipe my sleeve over my mouth and frown and wonder if I live a life strung precariously between self-inflicted pain and the word fuck.

"Every time I see you," he says, and I look over at him in surprise. "Every time I look out my office window and see you crossing campus, or when I—when I walk by your classroom when you're teaching—"

I squint, stunned that he knows my teaching schedule, let alone that he has ever ventured forth from his aerie to seek me in my den of graduate student iniquity.

"—When Bob Telushkin or, or any of the other faculty talk about you—and by God, they talk about you—when I see you at the dinner table—"

White curds of dry spit cling to the corners of his mouth. He stops talking and wipes his thumb and forefinger across the edges of his lips.

I swallow.

He spreads his hand against the wheel. "Of all my children," he says, and his voice has the hushed and tremulous quality of a choirboy in the confessional, "when I look at you, I see the worst parts of me, my pride, my inability to say the words, the words I need to say to the people I wish, the people I wish that I could love. I see my lack of, of kindness. I see my hauteur, my intellect thrown up like a bulwark against laughter, humility, pain. You have so flamboyantly perfected my own weaknesses. That's what it is, what is so terrible about you. Do you know what it is? Your perfection. Your mother told me something tonight."

He waits but I don't say anything.

"She told me that I should say something to you. As if I could fix you. As if because of our shared—personality flaws, as if perhaps you would—listen to me."

I laugh. The sound is harsh.

He flinches and the loose skin over his neck contracts as he swallows. "But how can I," he says to his hands pressed against the steering wheel. "How could she think that I—how can I fix you? I—God help me—I love you the way you are. What a terrible cliché. And so inadequate. I hate being around you and I miss you, I miss you every day now that you're not living at home."

I look out the window again at the snow-grayed ground, the pitch-dark sky. Neither of my parents knows much about Dave's manic behavior, sexual exploits, midnight calls to Stephen asking for money.

They don't know that I make a conscious decision every morning not to take a knife to the university and peel the skin off the faces of the assholes in my office. That the decision drives me running down miles of road until my energy is spent on something other than mutilation. They fear us, they are ashamed of us, and they love us in almost equal measure, but they don't know anything about us. We are two creatures they made together but whose genetic material is more diseased than any ingredient used in our making. We are their Abel and Cain, the flawed, weak and murderous, the wasted flesh. Stephen is their Seth, and like the biblical Seth, he remains largely overlooked but will be, if anyone is, their salvation.

"You're not like me," I say. "I mean, you're a total bastard to Mom sometimes, but overall you're decent. Moral. You're nothing like me."

"I don't need to hear this." His voice sounds thin, flat, exhaustion stripping all tonal variation.

"And besides, it's a little creepy that you watch my class."

He doesn't say anything. When I look over at him, his eyes are closed again and his hands rest on his lap.

"You deserve better than me."

He says without opening his eyes, "If I deserved better than you, Michaela, I would *have* better. Parents deserve the children they raise."

"No one deserves us."

His cheek twitches. He opens his eyes but does not turn his head. His lips press together. He has heard the plural pronoun.

More to distract him from contemplation of the word than for any conscious reason, I hear myself say, "I thought I died. Remember when I had that seizure? I totally thought I had died and come back to life for, like, I don't know, a couple weeks at least." I smile and look at the vague eyeless reflection in the windowpane. "I used to believe in that shit, in reincarnation, or baptism, the resurrection of the damned into new life. I wanted to change so much. God, if I could change, I would. I don't fucking want to be like this. Every morning I lie in bed and pretend that this is the day, that I'm going to wake up normal. And the first thing I always imagine doing is giving Mom a hug. Always. I don't know why it's her, but it is. And I imagine that I'm, you know, hugging her, and I look over and there you are smiling at me, and, I don't know, proud of me and shit. It's the stupidest fucking thing to think about and I do it every day."

His head turns slowly, ponderously, toward me.

The loose skin by his mouth folds back as his lips part. His teeth are yellowed from years of coffee and illicit cigars. He looks both strange and familiar, an expression dawning on his face until his eyes, the wrinkles, the darkness in them, a hope-lit wasteland, a darkling paradise, looks like the photographic negative of my own face.

I shut my eyes briefly.

When I open them, the world has not imploded in the frenzied glory of Armageddon.

My palms leave damp prints on the car door handle when I press it open and climb out. The night air bites at my lungs.

TWENTY-TWO

We drive home the next day. I sit with the side of my face pressed against the cold window glass until we arrive back in Akron, Ohio.

"Are you going to stay here tonight?"

I look at my mom. She is trying not to sound happy or sad. I don't know which emotion she is feeling.

"No."

"But, well, okay but just—just be sure and lock your doors. I don't like you being alone in that neighborhood."

"It's okay."

"No, it's not." She sounds frustrated. She looks over at my father, but he's already asleep on the sofa, the newspaper layered like crushed moth wings over his chest. "When will Aidan get back?"

"I don't know," I say. "I'm not his babysitter. Oddly enough."

My mother doesn't think that's funny.

Rain falls in gentle gusts, pockmarks the dirty snow lying piled against curbs. Lamplight glistens yellowish against the icy surface of the snowbanks and the slick streets. I duck my head against a sleeting rain that stings my face and neck and jog up the stairs. They thud hollowly under me. I open the door and the apartment is warm and light.

A metal folding chair sits in the middle of the kitchen, facing an easel with a stretched canvas on it. On the counter behind the easel are a half-eaten apple, a can opener, a soup can, and a bottle of milk arranged on an upturned Reiter's dairy crate. My broken reading lamp has been removed from my room and it sits behind the dairy crate casting strange shadows, dark and downward slanted, across the fruit and kitchen utensils.

A toilet flushes and then Aidan comes into the kitchen. He stops when he sees me.

"Hey. You're back."

I don't say that the same is obviously true of him. He smiles a little, distracted but like he's happy to see me, and doesn't say anything about the stuff in the kitchen or the fact that he has stolen my lamp. He is carrying a yellow phone directory, and he pulls a pocketknife out of his pants pockets and flicks the blade open. He rips the blade through the phonebook's spine with a clean, practiced slice. Loose translucent newsprint pages flutter free. He folds up the knife blade against his thigh and puts it back in his pocket. Then he squirts globs of paint on one flat section of the phonebook. With a Popsicle stick he drips paint thinner onto the globs of paint and swirls them together.

He sets the phonebook on the metal chair and dabs the brush into paint and, with violent strokes, he slashes out the shapes of the brown-fleshed apple, the half-empty jug of milk, the can opener, the rusty can of Campbell's tomato soup, empty, rolled on its side. His hand is as neatly vicious with a paintbrush as with a knife blade.

I watch him paint for a while. Then I edge behind him and get to the fridge. I pull out a can of Sprite and pop the tab. The soda is cold and tingles against the roof of my mouth.

I look at the canvas and see that the off-white paint he used to sketch the objects was not an outline of the still-life, like I'd thought, but the shadows. He is dabbing ochre paint onto the canvas, and emerging from the gray-white shapes is the photographically precise image of the speckled and aging yellow apple.

"That milk is going to go bad."

He doesn't seem to hear me. He raises a shoulder to rub his jaw, eyes fastened to the canvas.

After a while I wander back to my bedroom. I get my laptop and go into the living room. I sit on the couch, balance the computer on my lap, and check my email, and then I download some iTunes.

When I finish the Sprite I get up and go into the kitchen. The linoleum is covered in dried paint, flecks of amber, ochre, sienna, bronze, puce, chartreuse. My feet crackle on the shell of dried color.

The still life leans against the sink cabinet. Its canvas surface glistens with wet paint. He is sitting on the metal folding chair now with a large sketchpad on his knees and his hand is moving lazily. I assume that he's wasting time, waiting for the paint on the canvas to dry so that he can start another layer.

But when I go behind him I see that he is sketching with a charcoal pencil, the slowly emerging lines forming a woman's face. The face has a strange expression, eyes stretched wide, lips slightly parted, as if yearning achingly for something just out of reach. It looks like my face but the expression is one I've never seen in the mirror.

I crumple the Sprite can and toss it in the recycle bin. I go into the living room.

"What?" he says. "No one's allowed to look at you?"

"Go fuck yourself."

"Trust me," he says. "I do that plenty."

I can't decide if that's funny enough to smile or not. I turn on the TV and flip through channels to find a PBS documentary on cheetahs. I've always liked cheetahs. I like watching them move, oil through water.

"How was your Thanksgiving?"

"It was charming," I say. "Idyllic, really. Charles Dickens called to ask if he could write us up as the sequel to his *A Christmas Carol*, but he decided in the end our family holiday was too sweet to be believable to the general public."

He laughs. I can hear the scrape of the charcoal across his paper so I know he hasn't stopped sketching.

"How about yours?"

"About the same."

I stretch my arms behind my head and yawn.

"To be fair," I say, "my family's okay. It's not their fault I'm an asshole."

"You're not an asshole."

There's a short silence.

"Well," I say. "I'm no picnic."

His hand stops moving. He looks up at me. "Don't do that. I know what I'm talking about, okay? It's not like you own majority shares of the asshole market."

The heat of his eyes makes me uncomfortable. I turn back to the PBS show. I watch the big orange cats snaking through long grass.

"Sad isn't the same as evil," I say.

Aidan slams the sketchbook on the counter.

I jump.

He walks into his bedroom. The door bangs shut. The windowpane rattles.

Then the door opens and he comes back out.

"You think you're the only one," he says.

I turn around and stare at him.

He's standing in his paint-stained shirt with his arms clenched around his chest. "You think you're the only one who hates people. Well, I hate them, too. And yes, I fantasize about dousing them in paint thinner and lighting a cigarette. I *hate* people."

The apartment is silent except for the sound of his ragged breathing and the quiet tinny British voice telling us to notice how the female cheetah has spotted her prey.

He sucks in a breath and looks down at the floorboards.

"Well," I say. "Happy Turkey Day to you, too."

The skin under his left eye twitches.

"So, what happened? You want to talk about it?"

He takes a breath, almost tentatively, like someone who's afraid of inhaling smoke. Then his arms unfold, and he comes into the living room and sits down on the couch and leans his head back. He pulls his legs up onto the couch. Brown and yellow flecks splatter his jeans legs. The bruises on the inside of his arm are also brownish-yellow.

"Let me see," I say. "Your sister with the big fucking house was pretty civil to me, considering what I said to her. I don't see her pulling any Addams family shit. Your father owns a used car lot, so yeah, he's probably kind of a douche, but I doubt he's Genghis Khan. My guess is you had a great big family dinner and everyone had a great time and no one went with you to Harvest Home afterwards?"

His face eases, the muscles going slack.

"Really? I was right?" I grin. "What do you know. I'm getting pretty good at this relating-to-people shit, you think?"

The tragic tilt to his eyebrows, the softness around his mouth. His expression is an artist's caricature that draws out the secrets inside a person and transforms them into some primary-colored, obnoxiously obvious distortion: Aidan's face is a caricature of innocence. And I understand suddenly. He is not crazy. He is sane, he is ordinary, he is kind. He is not—cannot possibly be—a killer.

And, honestly, there has never been any real evidence that he is the arsonist-killer. I suppose I have known from the time I saw his neat block-print handwriting on the legal pad, so different from the handwriting on the pink message slip. But I didn't think about it. I didn't think about what it meant.

I feel the emptiness of infinite space inside my skin. I never realized how much I wanted him to be the killer. It would have made sense. A mathematically precise equation. And also—and also it would mean that he was like me, that there was someone else with that need to slice skin, to extract suffering. I would not be so alone. But Aidan's not a killer. He's just a decent kid with an autistic sister and a dead mom.

I feel so stupid.

"Look," I say, and my voice sounds alien, sad. "See, I hate everyone, regardless of race, gender, creed, or orientation. I hate good people, like you, I hate bad people, like Hitler, and I hate ordinary shitheads like your old man and your sister. Hate has nothing to do with love, for me. You see the difference between us? The subtle distinction?"

He turns suddenly and reaches out his hand.

I stop talking. My eyes skitter sideways, watching his fingers track in slow-motion.

"No, don't." It comes out a whisper. "*Please*."

His fingers, cold, callus-ridged, brush the back of my hand where it rests on my knee. And then he slides his fingers around mine and grips tight.

I swallow, choking on a gag, and close my eyes.

There is a long silence.

And then I say, "I think I'm going to hurl." I make it to the kitchen sink before vomiting sugary bile.

TWENTY-THREE

I teach my classes and sneeze, wipe my nose on my wrist, and keep teaching. A new muffler comes in and I spend a few afternoons under my parents' carport fixing the Chevelle.

Nothing seems to matter. Dr. Telushkin tells me my latest chapter looks promising. The semester draws to an end.

Advent starts.

I see holiday wreath lights on the streetlamps downtown and remember the flyer for Handel's *Messiah* that Judith Greene gave me. 411 Allyn Street is wrapped in yellow tape and scheduled for demolition. There is only one thing left that I can do. It's like moving a pawn against an inevitable checkmate.

I tack the flyer up on the fridge but Aidan doesn't say anything about it. I'm not sure he even notices. He spends a lot of his time gone, and I'm not sure if he's drinking, or if he's visiting his sister Stella, or if he's painting oil canvases the size of a small bus in the art building.

Two Sundays before Christmas I sneeze into a gloved hand and stand on the sidewalk looking up at the wooden doors of St. Bernard's church.

Today there is no soup kitchen. The church is reserved for shiny happy Akronites only. I look down at the flyer in my hand. Today, Judith Greene's choir is performing Handel's *Messiah*. The church looks elegant, the stone weathered and dignified, the pillars by the double doors yellowed with age.

I walk up the steps and go in. The foyer floor is carpeted with a faded gray rug and the boards creak under my feet. A white-haired woman in a green and red cable-knit sweater sits behind a folding metal desk selling programs for five dollars. I pull a body-warm bill from my jeans pocket and hand it to her. Her fingers fold over the note, but the gloves covering my hand protect my skin.

Inside the sanctuary is dark and red candles gleam like dozens of eyes along the walls. Narrow stained glass windows line the walls and the stone alcoves are guarded by statues of saints with hands upraised in benediction. People cluster along the pews, some sitting on the faded tomato-soup-colored seat cushions, others kneeling in solitude, most clumped together talking in low voices and laughing. The room smells of old wood and talcum powder and candle wax.

I find a bench at the far side of the room that is empty. More people come in, most of them old women in plastic head-covers and middle-aged men and women wearing expensive camel-colored overcoats and smelling like perfume and sweet port.

After a while the doors at the end of the sanctuary close and everyone sits, muffled whispers and the rustle of clothes drifting around me. Doors to the side of the altar open and a straggling line of people wearing cheap white robes enter, holding songbooks in front of their chests. They shuffle to the front of the room and stand in three rows and begin to sing.

The stuffiness in my clogged nose evaporates. She was right, the crazy cat lady was right. Handel's *Messiah* is beautiful. The voices are stretched tight and woven together until they don't even sound human. Sweeping chords press up against the shadow-hidden peak of the church ceiling.

I close my eyes. When the choir reaches the chorus I hear creaks and rustles and I open my eyes to find people standing all over the sanctuary. I remain with my gloved hands crossed under my breasts, my knees pressed together, and I look up at the walls, at the stained glass winking with light from passing cars outside. The flickering bright-colored light refracts the church's gloom, bending dark into showers of garnet and gold.

A wooden shelf covered in faded red velveteen lies in front of my scarred pew. I put my dirt-crusted sneaker on the velveteen and wonder what it is for until I realize it is meant for kneeling, for penitence or supplication.

The music infects me. I can feel all my nerve endings lying against the outer rim of my skin. I get up and bend, my knees pressing into the faded board. When I lift my eyes I see the choir, the crucifix, and the soaring panes of stained glass behind them. Their voices etch the contours of the suffering behind them. I imagine hundreds of believers kneeling on this spot before me, learning pain through ecstatic imagination. Staring at these images of Christ, at the vivid welts, the bracketed ribcage, the pain-arched toes, they must have learned all the delicate flavors of soul-destroying love, the savory tang of immolation. The pure wretched agony of compassion.

On one glass panel a tortured Christ hangs on a cross and a flare of headlights gilds his body, illuminating dark streaks traveling in crooked lines like falling blood or tears. I realize that it has begun to rain outside and water weeps down the colored glass.

The air in the church is thick with human smells. I don't understand why the sound of human voices fills me with such happiness. When I can't stand it any more I go outside and sit down on the front steps, the stone cold under my ass, and watch rain slant down across the grime-darkened city.

I put my elbows on my knees and bend my head against the rain. I came here for a reason and I need to follow through, to finish off this investigation. It doesn't matter that the choir sounds like resurrection.

I grip the rain-slick rail beside me and stand, pulling my weight up. My knuckles turn pale, the bone jutting up, stretching the skin translucent as rice paper.

The stone, the sky, the city vibrate with hallelujahs.

Here's the truth. I know who killed Aidan's mom. I mean, it's not rocket science. I can get the confession to prove it. The whole story. The ugly explanation, the facts, the cold hard—whatever.

I stay on the church steps, leaning against the iron railing with an icy drizzle running through my hair. When the music dies inside the chapel, I go around the side of the church. The little alley slopes downhill, a row of cars parked by meters, bumper to bumper. A metal railing around a sunken flight of steps leading to the church basement door, from which the choir members will emerge after their stirring performance.

I walk down the steps and stand in half-lit shadow for what feels like hours by a small industrial door in a filthy stairwell. And finally the choir members come out.

A woman buttoning a coat and laughing with a tall man carrying a hefty trombone case. Another man yelling into a cell phone to goddamn *fix* it, what's the goddamn *problem*.

Judith Greene comes out last.

Like the others, she doesn't seem to notice me. The door shuts after her with a hollow clang.

I follow her up the stairs and she turns halfway, hearing me or sensing my breath on her. Her skin looks like the flushed, translucent flesh of a ripe plum in the cheap halogen light.

"Oh," she says. Her voice falls at the end as if she has come sooner than she expected to a place she knew she was heading all along.

"Are you parked in the deck?"

She looks at me for a long time. Then she turns her head with the drugged motion of a sleepwalker and gazes up at the sidewalk above, people hurrying down the slanted sidewalk, cars passing. "Yes."

"Then we're going to talk here."

Her eyes moves to my face. The whites are damp, shiny. "What—what is this about?"

I can't hear any of Handel's eerie, perfect music in her voice. Her voice just sounds hoarse, thick with sweat and cat piss. I take another step so that I am level with her, my head looming over hers. Her fat body takes most of the narrow ledge and I lean forward until she is pressed against the grainy, rain-wet stone wall.

"In the spirit of full disclosure," I say, "I should tell you that I killed a man when I was ten. Also, I got perfect scores on my SATs and on my graduate exams. According to the education system, I'm a genius or close enough to make no difference. According to my shrinks, I'm a borderline sociopath."

Her fleshy cheeks quiver.

"So keep those two facts in mind and bear with me. I'm going to ask you some questions. The first one is this: Do you know how wiped out you'd be if you swallowed 48 milligrams of Ambien and 30 milligrams of Prozac? Close to comatose, almost immediately. And do you know how long it would take to partially metabolize that much? Long enough to suggest you took the pills *before* starting an accelerated fire. Which makes sense, right? I mean, you wouldn't want the fire department charging in and you with one hand stuck in the Ambien bottle like the proverbial kid and the cookie jar. Right? But keep in mind that we're practically comatose already. Are we likely to be dashing upstairs and down like Wee Willie Winkie with arsonist intentions? And here's my other question. My roommate's autistic sister wears a diaper. What kind of person wears a diaper but has the wherewithal to start two fires that burn hot, fast, and are localized in places brilliantly compromising the structural integrity of the house?"

Her tongue darts out and sticks tackily to her dry lips. "What are you, what are you saying?"

"I'm saying it was murder," I say. "Or, if you prefer, assisted suicide. From a legal standpoint, there's not much difference. Is there?"

She says, "She was a *saint*. She was a beautiful soul."

"She wanted to die."

"*Yes*."

I look at her. She looks down at her small doughy hands clasped against her pendulous breasts held aloft by soft folds of belly fat.

"Van Gogh killed himself," I say.

She raises her head. Her eyes are glassy. She looks vague, unfocused. "Artists are tortured souls, too pure for this world."

She seems to hear that. She nods. “She belonged with the angels. She was so beautiful. She wanted to fall asleep. I was her best friend. Her best. The only one she told about everything, about how she, how she *felt*. And when Alan left her, and his new, his new wife. She said her children didn’t *need* her anymore.” When she inhales her breasts press against me.

I prop my hand against the stone wall behind her. To passersby we must look like lovers, my form bending over hers and her soft shape yielding under mine.

“Tell me what it felt like.”

She doesn’t say anything for a long time. Then she says, “I miss her *all* the time. She hurt too much. I did it for her. Not for me. I was the only one who really *knew* how much she hurt.”

“Tell me how you did it. The pill thing confuses me. That’s a lot of pills to swallow. Did she take them herself or did you give them to her?”

“It was—she didn’t want to know. I make my tea so sweet that she just—it was just like our normal afternoon tea. Just the two of us. I thought it was just the two of us.”

I stare down at her. I don’t know what she means. Then I realize that she means she only wanted to kill the woman. She didn’t intend to frame the autistic daughter.

I imagine the scene, the small fat lonely cat lady watching the suicidal friend of her pathetic youthful fantasies fall asleep on her couch while drinking tea. Then she starts the fires and goes home. Later, when the paramedics come and the daughter is found terrified and catatonic in the basement, it’s easy to watch from the front porch and cry and say nothing.

“You really fucked up,” I say.

“What are you—why would you say that to me?”

The stone is wet and prints itself against my palms like Braille. I think about what Aidan said, that people feel shitty and learn to bear it. “You think you did what you had to, but it wasn’t your choice to make. Maybe she wanted to die, but he didn’t. Her kid, the one who asked me to find out what happened to his mom. He thinks his sister did it. He used to love his mom. He wants to love his sister. And now he's all fucked up, not sure what to do or how to feel, getting plastered all the time. His sister's afraid he's going to kill himself."

Her breasts jerk and she gives a wet sob. "Why are you *saying* this to me? I didn't, didn't hurt anyone, I *loved* her! I *had* to—I miss her every *day*."

She sobs, wrenching noises like metal being ripped apart.

I remember Aidan describing his mother, laughing, crying, wiping her nose on her sleeve. And I imagine this shabby woman in her cluttered house singing Handel and sobbing. As if she crawled into the dead skin of the woman she loved enough to kill.

"Oh, for fuck's sake. Grow up."

I push myself away from the wall and wipe my hand on my sodden jacket.

"Are you—are you going to—are you going to call someone?"

She watches me, quivering slightly in the chill. A half-assed murderer too mundane to realize that she had held the lives of five human beings in her pudgy fingers, and she'd squeezed. She's a dimpled, fat Faust who sold her soul to the devil and already hears his cloak rustling in the wings.

I *should* tell the cops, but the thing is, I'm not sure she'd confess again. Without her confession there really isn't any new evidence to hold her on. She would walk. I don't care about that. What I care about is that if I tell Aidan that she killed his mother and then she walks, well, Aidan would still live in a world where his mother's killer breathed and ate breakfast cereal and drank crappy tea. Aidan with his fingers wrapped in frayed Band-Aids, his arms yellowed with bruises from a grown woman's childishly frenzied grip.

A sudden tiredness sinks over me. I knew from the beginning, I told him right at the beginning this wouldn't do him any good. The weird thing is, somewhere along the way I started to *want* it to do something, to matter to him. To make something better.

I lean my head toward Judith Greene. Her eyes slide away, her chin lowers. Classic defensive posture. I can almost hear the British narrator's voice in the background. *The prey freezes as the predator approaches.*

My breath stirs the stiff curls by her ear. "It would be pointless," I say, "for me to call anyone. They've already reopened the case. It's only a matter of time."

Her eyes widen and swerve back to my face.

I could tell her that the Akron police department is not really reinvestigating. They are only wasting taxpayer dollars trying to interview a mute autistic woman who they believe was witness to a suicide. But I don't.

Overhead the church bells peal out a Christmas hymn instead of the usual tolling of the hours. Spatters of rain flare white against the halogen lamp. And it occurs to me that maybe the answer to Aidan's sadness isn't telling him the truth. Aidan thinks that he wants to know the truth, but in reality he just wants to *feel* something.

I lift my chin, closing my eyes against pin-sharp beads of rain. Aidan is not the sort of person who is starving for revenge. All he wants is to sit hunkered down in one of those bright-colored plastic chairs, lining up crayons with his sister, finally able to feel a pure emotion, pity unadulterated by guilt, maybe, or love without grief. What if I could give him that?

When I open my eyes Judith Greene is watching me with wide eyes, her teeth sunk into her lower lip.

I grin at her. "Well, this has been nice. You have a Merry Christmas, okay?"

I turn and take the steps two at a time. My shoes squeak on the slick wet stone.

Aidan is lying on the couch with his head tipped to the side, his mouth slack, snoring.

I bend over him. My hair falls into his face and its touch wakes Aidan and his eyelids unfurl.

The skin around his eyes is swollen and the whites are pinkish, bloodshot.

"You want to know who killed your mother? For real, you want to know?"

He just gazes up at me with that one eye swiveling lazily, like a petal floating in a jar of water.

My lips are near his. My words are moist and print themselves on his skin, slide into his open mouth.

"She was my therapist," I say. "I didn't like her. But I like fires. Your retarded sister wears a diaper. She was playing with Lego in the basement. She can't wipe her own ass, far less drug a woman and start two fires with accelerant."

His one good eye watches me. Then, slowly, he raises his hand and wipes the drool off the side of his face. He blinks.

I straighten up and snap my fingers in his face.

"Hey. Wake up. You putting the pieces together? Huh?"

He swallows and then coughs.

"I was asleep."

"Yeah, no kidding. Do I need to go through it again, or you think you got enough to Miss Marple your way to your answer?"

He doesn't say anything.

"I killed her. Okay? I killed your mother because she was my shrink. It wasn't personal. I hated everyone, and I was on medications. You know. Loopy. So I killed her and started the fire. And that's the truth."

He licks his lip and then he nestles his head back against the cushion and closes his eyes again.

I put my hands on my hips.

"Do you not even care? All this—you're telling me you don't even *care*?"

His eyes remain closed, his face motionless. He inhales and exhales.

"Well," I say. "You are very fucking welcome."

I go back outside and down the stairs into great sheets of rain.

TWENTY-FOUR

Pulling up my collar against the rain, I hike across campus to the library. I climb up to the third floor and sit in silence among the stacks smelling mildew and carpet cleaner. Books printed in primordial dialects of English rise like buttresses around me.

What did I think would happen? Did I imagine a scene of tent revival healing? Or perhaps the meticulous denouement of a Sherlock Holmes mystery, filled with modest expressions of gratitude and some spurious violin music?

Well, fuck him. Just . . . fuck him.

For one of the chapters in my dissertation, I am writing about medieval morality plays, popular stage plays performed by traveling thespians during the time when the English language was being wrought from the bitter struggle between Anglo-Saxon and Norman French. In these plays characters named Everyman, Vice, and Virtue act out simple stories in simple words in order to pare down human behavior to its most basic elements. In these plays God and the devil lurk in the wings while Everyman wanders the stage boards, trapped between redemption and damnation and armed only with a vocabulary limited to two syllables. Illiterate audiences learned their own language and the nature of civilized behavior in two hours.

Dr. Telushkin worries that my interest in morality plays stems from my belief that human ethics is not complicated, that morality can be codified in a series of rote gestures and that all moral judgment can be expressed using juvenile vocabulary words like *good* and *bad*. Dr. Telushkin is right. I crouch in the library and my fingers trace faded typescript in search of the knowledge of good. Or evil.

Dark brands of light lance across the evening sky as I walk home. The rain has cleared and the clotted clouds glow russet from the setting sun, a rim of fire opal around a mud-thickened globe.

I go inside and see Aidan kneeling by the couch, his head resting in a crack between the cushions. He looks like the fraudulent mimic of a faithful churchgoer and laughter bubbles up inside me, but then the laugh catches in my throat. Something about the laxness of his limbs. I go over and put my palms against the side of his neck. The skin moist and cool.

I hook my fingers in the neckline of his T-shirt and yank back and he falls, slithers through my hands and thuds on the floor. Runny vomit stains the couch cushions.

He coughs and burrows his head into the floorboards.

I go into the kitchen.

A trash bag full of warped glass bottles, amber liquid still sloshing across the bottoms. An empty bottle of ibuprofen.

I pull out an orange cardboard box of baking soda and a plastic cup. I mix baking soda and water with a teaspoon and carry it into the living room. I put the cup on the carpet. Then I kneel over him and haul him up, his head lolling back against the couch.

His jaw is slack. He exhales. His breath smells like piss.

"I'm *drunk*."

His voice is a shredded whisper.

I tip his head back and pinch his nose, and his mouth opens. He puts feeble cold fingers against my wrist. I pour the cupful of soda water down his throat and force his jaw shut. One hand on the top of his skull, the other on his chin, I put my face in front of his.

"Swallow."

He does, his eyes widening slightly. Milky liquid bubbles out the sides of his mouth. He struggles.

I release him, and he chokes and gags and strings of saliva and water dribble down his front. I slap his face.

The crack of sound startles both of us.

He gasps. And then his throat clicks, and he curls over and coughs and then pukes hard. He throws up, his diaphragm sending him into spasms of vomiting. He chokes and retches for almost three minutes. I look at my watch while he throws up. His vomit is runny, frothing with bubbles and the occasional white, decaying disc of a pill.

When he's lying on his side making gagging noises but not spitting up anything else, I stand and go into the kitchen and rinse out the cup. I bring him a fresh cup of water and make him drink it. Then I carry the empty cup back and refill it. He lies on the floor with a cup of water by his head while I get out a spray bottle of Febreze. He groans and coughs and drinks water and lies on his side with his legs drawn up against his stomach while I carry the couch cushions outside to the trashcan.

When I come back in he gets up on one knee, a hand on the floor in front of him. He is struggling to his feet. His shoulders shift, strain. He stands as if growing from the earth one limb at a time.

"Mick—Mickey. I'm—I'm *sorry*."

I look at him. He is leaking fluids and smells rancid.

Something strange twists in my stomach. A feeling—I don't know what it is. I only know that I don't want to cut him. He is a sloppy reeking mess and I don't want anything or anyone to hurt him. The thought is so bizarre that I don't know what to do with it.

He puts his arms out. His fingers reach for me. I turn on my heel and his fingers snag at my shirt, but the years of running have made me fast and I am out the door so quickly that his fingers close on nothing.

A tattered plastic bag slaps wetly against the side of the industrial garbage bin in the gusty wind. I wipe the back of my wrist against my mouth. I figured it would help him if I told him a psychotic kid killed his mother. Take his mom off the hook, and his autistic sister. Give him someone he could hate without feeling guilty afterwards. But I was wrong. I'm always wrong.

I fuck everything up.

I put my hands around my skull and press. My head hurts.

I pull out my cell phone and dial my brother's number. This time I leave a message. I don't know what I want to say but I start talking anyway. "Okay," I say. "I did something bad and I don't know how to—I just, I can't do this anymore. I fucked it all up and I can't—I want you to tell me what to do so that I, or if I can just—"

My voice stops. I can hardly breathe. I stand in silence with the phone pressed against my jaw. I don't know what this is. Something hot and hard lodged in my chest, pressing against my esophagus. A shock of heat, like sudden fear, but what am I afraid of?

I hang up the phone.

Rain coalesces from a pellucid sky.

TWENTY-FIVE

I don't know how long I sit on the steps. When I lean forward my hair falls like a shank of half-frozen seaweed across my hands. Ice has formed around the tips like pearl building up around sand.

I don't know where to go or what to do.

I want to run but it's so cold. The only thing I have is my car. The keys are back inside. I don't want to go back in there. But I need my car. I need the escape. I push myself to my feet.

When I open the apartment door I see Aidan standing at the kitchen sink with a can of Clorox and a scrub brush. Empty glass bottles in a kitchen trash bag heaved into the center of the floor, carpet cleaner white and foaming on the worn living room carpet.

He pauses when the door opens, then starts scrubbing again. I watch the shift of oblique muscle along his ribcage. He doesn't lift his head.

The faintest plink of water droplets in the sink. But the faucet is turned off.

I don't intend to say anything and am startled when I hear myself talking. My voice is low and vicious.

"If you feel like shit, it's your own stupid fault and you know it."

He wipes the back of his wrist under his eyes and then yelps when the bleach cleanser stings his mucus membranes. His head swivels to the side. His eyelashes are wet and his walleye wavers without purpose.

I pick up my car keys and my backpack from where I dropped it earlier. I put the keys in my pocket.

He leans over the sink like he's going to vomit. He doesn't say anything. A string of mucus slides from his left nostril. He sniffs.

I want to leave. I don't know why I haven't left already. I balance on one foot, scratch the toe of my sneaker against the opposite calf. "Look, if I go—are you going to do that shit again?"

He puts his fists against his forehead and presses hard.

And then he says, "Go away. Leave."

I stare at him.

"What?" I say. "You're mad at *me*? Why? You wanted to know about your mom. So I'm a shitty liar. So what? I just said it because I thought it would, I don't know, *help*."

"It would help if you didn't fucking *lie* to me!" He's screaming now.

I back up a step, almost lose my balance.

"Okay." My backpack slides off my shoulder. I snatch it back up. "But the point is, your sister didn't do it. Okay?"

"Fine," he says. His voice cracks in the middle. "Whatever."

He turns his face to me. Powdery kitchen cleanser dusts his face in ghost-pale patches, sliced through with tear-tracks.

"I don't understand. What's your problem?"

I wait for him to say something but he doesn't, so after a while I walk out and lock the door behind me.

There's nothing I can do anyway. A normal person would know what went wrong, whether it's me he's mad at, or himself, or if it's something else entirely. A normal person would know the right thing to say or the right gesture to make that would calm him down. But that's always been my problem. I create problems that I can't fix because of my flawed neurons. I wouldn't mind so much if it was just me that my mind tormented.

My skin feels so tight I want to run, or cut it, or bang my foot against the wall until the sharp sting cracks the pressure and lets me breathe again. But I owe Aidan more than my own release.

I drive north to Hudson. The rain turns to ice and plinks like chimes against the windshield.

The reception desk at Harvest Home overlooks an entry way filled with white wicker rocking chairs and low bench seats with mint-green cushions. The walls are painted mint-green with a border of stenciled white scallop shells. All the healthy people who move behind the desk or hustle down linoleum hallways in rubber-soled canvas shoes wear pastel scrubs. I stand in the reception room and press my sweaty palms against my thighs.

"Hi there! Who are you here to see?"

She smiles widely at me. A woman with bright red lipstick. I stare at her lips. Harvest Home management has clearly read books about the psychologically soothing effects of mint green. Shouldn't her lips be green? Isn't red the color of hookers and sex? I am clenching a folder in my arms, the yellow legal pad and print-outs with details on Ambien and Prozac and arson. My skin is gooseflesh. I wore a short-sleeved shirt and left my coat in the car, but it's cold enough that even I feel it. The thermostat is below freezing outside and inside is barely warmer.

The woman comes around the desk to greet me and I turn the notebook toward her so that she can read the neat black letters that spell out Stella's name.

A few minutes later she trots beside me, smelling like hand soap and fabric softener. She's talking about the progress Stella has made recently. Aidan's sister is in a community recreation room. A big-screen TV and low tables covered in modeling clay, crayons, colorful wooden abacuses, and banks of computer monitors. Two of the inmates are hunched at computers, typing quickly. I recognize Stella even before a hand that smells of soft soap fingers my arm.

"There she is."

Stella's smooth dark hair is short and caps her skull. Her features are long and sharp and she looks like a raven. The skin around her eyes is pink and swollen. She's wearing a T-shirt and gray sweatpants and is lining up a row of crayons side by side. The color gradation is immaculate, a red-ochre next to a red-sienna next to a persimmon red and then orange, tangerine, yellow, pastel yellow, and white.

I watch from the doorway. The woman by me fingers my shoulder again, her nails light as spider legs on my skin. "Do you want to go in and see her?"

I shake my head. As I watch Stella, a thick strand of mucus eases down over her upper lip. I clear my throat. “You said she’s doing better. She’s still not talking, right?”

“Right,” the woman says. “But she’s drawing. Her therapist says she’s drawing her emotions and memories.”

“About the fire.”

The woman doesn’t answer for a minute.

I turn away from the door and walk down the hall.

“Excuse me, aren’t you here to see her?” Her shoes flap down the hall after me. “Excuse me!”

I stop and turn around. “Who comes to visit her most, besides her brother?”

The woman hesitates. Her red lips purse. They are candy-apple red. Her skin is burnt sienna-brown. “The Akron city detective, you mean? I have her name on file.”

“It doesn’t matter. Just tell her, the next time she comes in, that Stella didn’t start the fires.”

The woman looks at me.

“She sure as fuck didn’t give her mother twenty Ambiens and Prozacs. She isn’t guilty.”

“I thought she was just a witness.”

I blink. It occurs to me that the police detective can’t possibly be as naive as Aidan. The Akron city police department probably sees Stella only as a material witness. But their interest in her reinforces Aidan’s fears. The strange child is the dangerous one. Normal people are so stupid sometimes. They don’t understand that evil requires premeditation, silence, and complicity. No one creates evil *ex nihilo*. Truly bad people take others’ suffering or doubt or temptation and shape it like clay. Innocent people don’t have intentions, even if their unthinking actions wreak havoc. I like clean lines, clean smells. Innocence makes me feel sick. I don’t know how to judge it. It is neither good nor evil.

"Okay, then." I feel my fingers trembling against the folder I hold over my stomach. "You can still tell her, though. Just to make sure she knows."

"She's a detective. I'm pretty sure that's her job. To know."

I smile. She smiles back at me. I don't know why she's smiling.

A few flakes of snow drift aimlessly in the gray air. My breath fogs the windshield. I turn up the heat and sit in the car, shivering while I wait for warmth to creep out and thaw my bones.

My cell phone vibrates.

I wipe my hand over my forehead. My skin feels waxy and stiff, like a half-formed mask. At first I can't focus and then I realize it's Dave's number. I wonder why he's calling. And then I remember. That message I left, hours ago. God, how long? It feels like weeks but I realize that it's only been about six hours. I don't even remember what I said. Only that it felt like a broken kaleidoscope, all the fragments of colored glass cascading down around me and nothing to hold them back or sort them into shapes.

I open the phone and hold it next to my ear. The panic is gone now but I feel—muzzy. Like I've taken too many antihistamines.

He's jabbering, talking so quickly that at first I can't understand him. I'm too tired to deal with his mania.

And then I realize that what he is saying has nothing to do with Aidan, or with whatever feeling choked me earlier.

I sit up straighter. "Wait, can you—shit, slow *down*—you need what?"

Dave says, "I need you to kill someone for me."

TWENTY-SIX

I sit very still and listen with the phone pressed against my left ear.

"Mickey? Come on, come on, don't go silent. I know you called. You said you need help. Well, I need help. Babe, can't you see? This is how you fix things. This is what you were born for!"

"But—"

"Don't be so ple*bi*an. You know I'll never let you go to jail, I know you, right? Who knows you better than I do? I won't let anything bad happen to you. I've got this plan, it's perfect. This guy—this asshole—my dealer, right? He needs the money, breathing down my fucking neck, all the time, Jesus Christ, every second. I can't handle it anymore, I swear, Mickey, the guy's driving me fucking crazy. So I'm thinking, what can I do? And I know, right? I know this guy, he's got no real ID, fuck, I don't even know if he's a real citizen. He's not on anyone's database. You think the cops are going to care if this asshole dies? No. So you just need to kill him. I've got a gun. Cops can't trace it."

"You kill him then. If it's so safe, so *justifiable*."

The sarcasm is lost on him. He laughs, a short bark of sound interrupted by a dry cough. When he can talk again, he says, "Jesus God, Mickey. *I* couldn't do that. The moral imperative and all that. We're talking about the capacity to end another human life. It's like asking your librarian for a nice cut of beef, you can't do that. One goes to one's butcher for one's butching needs." He laughs until he starts to hiccup. "I'm kidding. *Jok*ing. But seriously, I'm the first person they'd look at. The cops, I mean. Fucker who owes the asshole ten grand? Are you kidding me? I've got to have an *alibi*. A *rock solid* alibi. And they'll never think about the kid sister, the college-attending kid sister. I swear to God I've thought this through, Mickey. It's going to work. It's the *per*fect crime. I *swear*."

Snow collects in a swarming lace over the windshield.

"You there? Mickey, come on. You there? Oh babe, don't do this to me. This is what you were *born* for. This guy, I promise, he's nothing. A total asshole. This guy would fuck his own grandma if it would pay him. He's as fucked as I am, a total junkie. A user. Probably has AIDS already anyway. And you—Mickey, think about it. This is a *gift*." And his voice cracks in a wavering giggle. "Happy Christmas, Mick! It's my special Christmas gift to you!"

"A gift? You're such a—why would I *want* to kill someone? How is this fixing my problem?"

"Mickey." His voice turns hard. Congeals. He enunciates. "Mickey. Listen to me. You told me you fucked it up. Well you haven't even *started* to fuck up. Do you understand? If you don't do this for me, you will fuck everything up, *every*thing. Because I'll tell. God knows I'll end in the electri—no, what is it they do in this state? I'll end up in*ject*ed but before I do I'll tell everyone. I'll tell the parents. I'll tell Stephen. I'll fucking tell Aidan. I'll tell everyone. I'll tell them the truth and nothing but the whole goddamn fucking truth."

I pinch the skin between my eyebrows. This time, he lets the silence lie in a thick haze between us.

I know what he means by *the whole truth*. He means the truth about me, which is bad enough, but also the truth about him. Which, really, doesn't leave me with many choices.

I say, "Okay. Fine. But, if I do it? If I do it, no gun. I want a knife."

I'm only half certain that I am saying this to buy time and to figure out a way to get Dave out of his situation without having to call the cops on him.

But Dave doesn't even question my willingness to kill. He gives a soft sound, a broken sighing cry that reminds me of Gregorian chants, of polytonic hymns in praise of the light.

"Yes," he says. "Oh fucking Christ. *Yes*."

I close the phone. It falls to the seat. My breath has created a white fog across the inside of the pane.

I drive south into darkness.

The snow fades and a moon glimmers a sheet of suspended cloud particles of dirt and chemicals.

My head replays the sound of my hand striking Aidan's face. And Dave's voice, a voice pitching like a stick on a turgid ocean, jabbering about how excited he is, and do I realize that this is my calling, my meaning, the thing I was *meant* to do?

My palms sweat against the steering wheel.

When I pass the exit for the university I hesitate. I think I should turn around and go back, make sure my asshole roommate hasn't succeeded in killing himself. I'm tempted to let Dave do whatever it is that he is intent on doing without risking legal or moral complicity in it.

But if I leave Dave to do whatever it is that he is intent on doing, while I may escape legal complicity, I'm not certain what moral abyss I'll have fallen into.

My breath is uneven.

The freeway dips and curves out around great hulking shoulders of earth, the bridge strung across the valley between Akron's hills.

I swerve to the side of the road, a narrow shoulder against the cement embankment of the bridge wall. I kill the engine and sit watching rain steam on the sloped hood. The rhythmic zip-zip of cars outside. My mind shies away from Aidan, from how I thought I could fix him but I made everything worse. The back of my throat feels tight like a wad of gum sticks in it.

I don't know what this is, but it feels like—I don't like it. The cat. The clean snap of fragile cat vertebrae under my palm. The hot stink of fur and blood and diarrhea. It felt good. It felt *great*. When I faced those gutless assholes, I towered over them all, braced my feet on the shoulders of the earth and loomed. I was their god. Accuser, judge, and executor.

I've read all the psychology books and I know that feeling, that euphoria, is common. Serial killers feel like God when they watch their victims suffer. That's why they kill. And I want to feel that again. And yes, okay, I know that, really, actually, in all truthfulness, of course I am no god. But fuck if I can't awe with the best of them.

If I stand up straight and unclench my hands, they will sizzle and catch fire and the world will burn.

I am prone to hyperbole. The excessive word. The grandiose gesture. Dr. Telushkin likes the way my pen sweeps prose aside in favor of a more epic sanguinity. He doesn't understand the truth. I know that I sound absurd, tongue-in-cheek, but really. Really, Dr. Telushkin. Look closer. That epic language? Life, death, the glory of it all? I am not made of dirt like a human being. I am not mortal. I am *mortality*.

I sit with my hands clenched around the wheel. Silence.

I wanted to be better than my genes. I wanted, God damn it, I wanted to be *good*, and I tried. I tried to take away Aidan's pain, to give him a scapegoat that he could fucking *hate* with a clean, hot passion. But did I save him? Did I save him *shit*. I forced that sound out of him, the vomiting and then that fucking wounded-animal *noise*. I can't do it. No matter how much I play the game I'll always be a hundred steps behind everyone else, at my most civilized still a galaxy away from normal. But maybe Dave is right. I can't fix sadness, or anger, or hurt in other people, but maybe I can at least—I don't know. Maybe I can exact suffering where suffering is truly deserved.

I open the door and stumble out. The air tastes filthy and a film of salt covers the car.

Oh God. Because maybe he's right. Maybe this is redemption, or as close as someone like me can get to it. Save my brother, kill a drug-dealer. It would be sort of funny if I felt like laughing.

The bridge hangs gray and cable-strung across a gaping chasm between two vast shoulders of earth. Slate-colored clouds overhead, weak lights strung along the bridge, the snow-covered hills pale under the moonlight. The cement buttress is cold under my hands. The bridge shivers with tremors of passing cars and wind and aging space underneath, the upholding nothingness that surrounds.

My breath fogs white in the vast, chill air. I bend forward and lean my forehead against the singing cold metal. It burns like ice or fire.

TWENTY-SEVEN

Downtown Akron is a crust of fairy lights. My eyes are hot ball bearings swiveling in their sockets. Car horns blare. People hate people. Cities prove this better than any philosopher. Homicide is humanity's most basic instinct.

I rub the back of my wrist against my eyes.

I wonder how they do it, the nameless, faceless assholes in thousands of cars inching their way into and out of the city where they have sweated in nameless, faceless cubicles for eight hours and will return the next morning to sweat again for eight more interminable hours. I wonder what they would say if they knew who I was. A murdering deity afloat in a sea of gray-suited, deodorant-slick banality.

Dave lives in Akron's so-called art district, a brick-paved neighborhood full of decaying buildings, populated by lovers and drug addicts. I find a parking spot at the end of the block. My palms slippery against the wheel, the gear shift, the dangling keys as I lock up the car and feed the meter.

A black painted metal door near a pawnshop. I buzz Dave's apartment number and after a while the lock clicks. I go inside and climb a narrow flight of swaybacked stairs. A thin brown carpet worn yellow across the treads. Each slat creaks.

Up three floors and there's a door ajar. Behind the door, a long warehouse room. The window at the far end is a warped pane of glass. The wooden floorboards are speckled with aged grime and boot scuffs. A low black couch. A mattress with a rumpled gray wool blanket and a ripped box of orange cheese crackers spilled across the sheets.

I find Dave in the bathroom. He's sitting on the closed toilet seat with his head bent forward, his spine curved, elbows on his knees and hands dangling limp from bony wrists.

"Hey."

He turns his head as if he's moving underwater. Hair hangs in his eyes. He puts up two fingers and scrapes the hair back, leaving comb-lines in the greasy mess.

His mouth spreads into a smile. When he smiles, the skin on his lower lip cracks. He wipes at the dribble of blood with the back of his hand.

A glint of metal on the floor near the trashcan. I go over and bend down, look closer. Then I reach for the roll of toilet paper and tear off a hunk. I use the wad of toilet paper to pick up the needle and drop it in the trash.

"What else did you do?"

He wipes his hand under his nose and laughs. "Isn't that enough? Or should I tell you it's not contact solution in that contact lens case."

He laughs harder when I reach for the case on the countertop. Open the green lid and see white granules like finely ground salt. I pour it down the sink, run the faucet. Rinse my hands in the tepid water and shut off the faucet. My fingers drip.

"Jesus," I say. "What the fuck is *wrong* with you?"

He frowns and his lips quiver, his eyes filling with tears. "I know. I know I know I know. I'm a disaster, a fucking federal dis*aster* site, I've got so much po*tential* and I've made a great big fucking *mess* of it all. I hate myself."

"I'm the only one here," I say. "You can quit trying out for *Hamlet*."

He blinks and the tears disappear. He grins at me. "Yeah? It didn't work for you?"

I roll my eyes.

He laughs. "Wait till you see what I got for you." He feels his pockets and then stands up. He puts the tips of his fingers against the wall as if to hold it, delicately, in place, then he goes over to a chest of drawers in the corner. He opens one and lifts out a pair of lacy women's panties, looks over at me with an eyebrow raised.

"I don't have an eternity to spend on your shit, you know."

"Okay. Okay. Geez. Here it is."

He comes and bows, hands held cupped in front of him, cradling a switchblade with a scuffed matte hasp. I pick it up, feel the heft of it. He leans over me, bent like a priest conferring the holy body on some reluctant acolyte. I pull my head back.

"Don't."

He ignores me and he places his hands gently around the crown of my skull. His breath huffs in my hair.

I reach up and put my hand around his wrist. My fingernails bite into the soft skin on the underside. I dig them in until I feel the soft skin give and he yelps and pulls his hand away. He puts his wrist to his mouth. His eyes shine.

I go into the main room. There is a small kitchen area and I open a cabinet, then a drawer. I find a box of cling wrap with one corner crushed in. "Give me a name, an address."

"Don't be so abrupt. *Sa*vor life." He claps his hands together. "*Life* is but a—" He starts to giggle and it turns into hiccups, then coughing. He coughs and then spits onto the floor and takes a breath, lets it outs slowly. He says, "Anyway, you don't need an address. I will take you there."

I put the knife in my jeans pocket and the roll of cling wrap gets stuck down the small of my back, hidden by my jacket.

"Fine. Let's go."

The street sings with febrile energy. Wind taps against my skin, flaps clothing strung across balconies.

He stops in the street and stands looking around. For a second I think he's lost. But then he blinks rapidly and says, "It's here."

I look across the street. A corrugated metal door padlocked over a pawnshop, the neon lights buzzing and flickering overhead. Beside the pawnshop there is a small cracked stoop. The metal door above the stoop is wedged open.

I put my hands in my jeans pockets.

He looks at me and grins. His teeth look urine-stained in the weird half-light of city smog. "Yeah?"

"I suppose the locale is appropriate." I don't know what he wants me to say.

He laughs. Scratches his nose. "Oh, I almost forgot. *Bait*."

"What?"

He reaches into his jacket pocket and pulls out a roll of twenties tied with rubber bands. "Get the bastard to open the door and let you in."

I take the money and look at the wad of bills. Not Stephen's money. Mine, maybe. But not Stephen's. Money my brother keeps in his wallet and hasn't spent because he doesn't need it. I wonder how much of my money has accumulated in his pants pockets over the years.

"You ready?" He wipes the back of his hand under his nose. "This is it."

I take the knife and push the release button. The blade flares open with a gentle *schick*. I close it against my thigh. "Yeah."

We cross the street and go inside. A pale yellow tile floor and a narrow flight of stairs, the rubber tread on the stairs peeled back and hanging loose. The floor tiles are streaked, faded, age-wounded, and the walls are spiderwebbed with cracks.

We stand on the tile.

"Here we go again," he says.

"No."

"Yes. Like before. Everything," he says, "*every*thing you are is because of me."

"Not everything."

"No one would believe you if it weren't for me." He flutters his fingers in the air. "I gave you your *voice*."

"Yeah? Well, no one would love you if it weren't for me."

He smiles. He leans forward and puts his hand around the back of my neck. His fingernails dig into my skin. I choke on a swallow. He bends his head against my shoulder. I can smell stale, unwashed body.

"*Get off*."

He kisses my shoulder and steps away. “This is ours,” he says. “He doesn’t have *this*. Aidan doesn’t. Your meat pet. Your little pretty boy. No one has this. This is ours. This is *real*.”

“Aren’t you supposed to be somewhere else, establishing an alibi or something?”

He licks his lips. His eyes glisten. He hesitates like he wants to say something. We both wait. We listen. I know that my brother has no real reason to kill the man upstairs. I know that. My brother may do drugs, but he has no capacity for addiction. He is, as he would be the first to admit, a god, a shaper and wreaker, not one who is wrought. Oh, I have no doubt that the actual facts of the case are true: the man for whom death waits is most likely one of those invisible people, stolen or purchased identity, habitual association with the lowest of criminal lowlifes. But I doubt that he holds my brother’s life in his hands. My brother is not the sort to permit such power to anyone besides me.

He wants me to kill that man for a different reason altogether.

“I should,” he whispers. “Yes.”

My brother turns and leaves. The metal door drifts shut behind him.

TWENTY-EIGHT

The stairwell is hot and when the door shuts it snuffs out the brief breath of rain-damp air. I go up the stairs. Gray smudges and fingerprints line the wall by the loose railing. Graffiti. The smell of ramen noodles, cigarette smoke, marijuana.

I stop on the stairs and turn and look down. The runner lights overhead buzz. My uncertain shadow shifts over the wall. The landing below is empty. I put the back of my wrist against the side of my skull, where inside a warm pain nestles. My molars ache. My jaw is clenched. The faint coppery taste of adrenaline. The pressure under my ribs.

The hallway of the fourth floor. A baby's cracked voice ululates behind a closed door. The muffled sizzle of TV. Human spore.

I go down the hall looking at numbers. At 403, I stop and put my fingers gently against the cool metal of the door handle. The door is locked. I put the knife into my jeans pocket and with one palm pressed against the bulge, I set the other knuckles against the door. Take a breath. Knock. Three times. Clean and sharp.

After a long time, I hear the creak of floorboards and the rasp of the spyhole cover being lifted.

Then the lock clicks and the door opens an inch and a half.

"Who the fuck are you?"

The room exhales a pale miasma of boiled cabbage and cum.

"I've got payment. From one of your clients."

I hold out the wad of twenties.

"You with the cops?"

"No."

The door opens and I go inside. I walk into the main room. A TV on a broken coffee table. A splay of glossy foldouts, empty cartons of Chinese, a few crumpled wads of tinfoil, and the magazine of a nine-millimeter semiautomatic.

"You want soda? Beer?"

"Coke, please."

He looks at me. He's wearing a thin, stained T-shirt and his belly sags underneath it, flaccid and hairy. A gun stuck in the back of his too-tight sweatpants. The skin over his balding head and the backs of his hands is freckled. He's so overweight that as he stands looking at me I can hear his breath wheezing, air exhaled through a moist sponge.

Then he says, "Coke it is. Coming up." His lower lip glistens with saliva. He's missing several teeth. He turns and goes into a small kitchen. He comes out with a can of Coke.

I put the twenties into his sweaty hand and take the cool can. Pop the lid and watch the run of sticky brown liquid. I sip. He snaps off the rubber band and thumbs through the twenties.

"Who's this from?"

When I don't answer, he thumbs through the roll. "Well, this is only three grand," he says. He pronounces it, "Tree grand." I wonder if the accent is put on.

I lick my lips. Show time. "Yes. I know."

I bend down and set the Coke carefully on the floor. I straighten, my hand coming out of my pocket with the knife hasp in the palm. I flick open the blade.

"What—?"

His hands go back behind him.

I raise the knife and put the tip against my own throat.

"Wait."

His hands reappear. His mouth is open. The room is very small. Sweat oozes around his nostrils.

"You know David Berkowitz, right?"

"David—what? Who are you?"

I say, "Berkowitz. Stay with me, please. You know who he is, right? Son of Sam?"

"The—the serial killer, right. Yeah, okay. So what?"

"You want to know the thing about serial killers?"

He licks his lips. "What?"

I press the blade, tipping it slightly against the skin. I feel the warmth of blood easing down my neck. The blood collects in the hollow of my collarbone. I lift the blade away from my neck.

"Jesus," he says.

"The thing is," I say, "that they suffer from an inability to imagine other people's pain. And you know what else?"

He swallows. His cheeks shiver when he shakes his head once.

"That lack of imagination? It works for themselves, too. See, most people can imagine pain even when they're not feeling it—their own. Someone else's. That empathetic experience makes them avoid pain. Both their own and other people's. You following so far?"

"What the fuck is this?"

"Okay. The deal is this. You can't threaten a serial killer. What can you do? They're not afraid of pain. They're not afraid of their own pain and they're sure as fuck not afraid of anyone else's, because they can't imagine it. In fact—"

I step forward and raise the blade with both hands, the one gripped around the handle, the other hand cupped under the end of the blade, supporting the meaty palm of the other hand. The basic grip for an up-thrust that puts all of the cutter's body weight behind the blow. The blade slices cleanly into his right shoulder just under the collarbone, angled up. The tip hits bone. He screams. The sound shrill and echoing.

"In fact, the only thing that feels *good* to a serial killer is someone else's pain."

He lunges at me. I let him come. His body weight tips me back. I shift to the side, my arms circling him like I'm hugging him around the body. I pull the gun from his waistband just as my spine and left elbow hit the floor. He's on top of me. I hook a foot around his ankle. Lever myself out from under him with my left elbow and the fulcrum of our wedged ankles. His sweat-slippery hands on my arms. I get a hand free and punch the knife at his eye. He screams again and flings up his hands to ward me off and I roll off him and scramble away. I snatch up the magazine from the table. I put the open knife through my jeans waistband and slam the magazine home into the gun. Turn my wrist to see if the safety is off. Then I ratchet back the slide.

I aim the gun at his head. He lies on the floor. Blood spreads over the T-shirt. A drop of sweat rolls off his upper lip and splats on the floor.

He swallows hard. "Don't—shoot. You can have the—money back."

"That's another thing about serial killers." I thumb off the safety and grip the gun in my right hand. With my left I pull out the knife. "You can't bribe them not to kill you. You want to know why?"

His head barely moves. His pupils zigzag, white-rimmed.

"It's because of what I said earlier. The problem with not being able to imagine pain is that the pain center and the pleasure center in the brain are actually the same place. Did you know that?"

His eyes quiver, focusing on the hand gripping the knife and the hand with the gun and the distance to the coffee table and the door. I wave the knife. The slim blade glints.

"Pay attention, please. We are about to do something beautiful. But it will require your full attention."

He glances back at my face. The pink tip of his tongue darts to his lower lip again. "Wh—what?"

"We are going to—embrace."

"Emb—what the fuck are you talking about?"

I wipe the back of my knife hand over the cut in my neck. The blood is sticky, drying. My neck itches. Watching him, I lick the back of my hand. Let my tongue linger on the gum of blood in the creases between my thumb and palm. His eyelids quiver.

"The money is irrelevant." I take a step forward. Not close enough that he can kick me or reach me. "I'll tell you what I want. I want to play a little game. The game goes like this: you get to pick, knife or gun. See, most people *can* imagine pain. The interesting part of this game is that you're a normal person. And a normal person is actually more afraid of a knife than of a gun. Isn't that weird? Your logical mind *knows* the gun will cause more physical structural damage to your knee. But that emotional, atavistic part of your animal brain imagines the blade of the knife slicing through skin, muscle, tendon—"

His fleshy throat moves convulsively.

"—and that imagination is more terrible and more real than the scenario in the logical part of your brain. Isn't that fascinating? The gift of being able to imagine pain, to empathize, is a fundamentally illogical gift. I do not have that gift. I am the enlightenment ideal—a purely logical, fundamentally rational being."

I look down at him. At that maculate sweating hide. I can strip that sallow skin one piece at a time, and with each blubbery shred, I could exact punishment.

"You won't survive."

I watch the words imprint themselves in his frantic eyes, on his doughy flesh. He makes sounds, kittenish mewls.

Sounds like—

—like Aidan made—

Like I made when Aidan—

Now you know.

I blink. Press the backs of my hands against my eyes. The faint smell of gun oil and metal.

I hear him move and my eyes open.

He's gathered his legs, half-rolled on his side, trying to rise.

He freezes. Stares at me. His jowls tremble. His tongue darts out, makes a dry, smacking noise on his fleshy lower lip. I smell the sweat oozing from his pores, the stench of pure terror.

In my head, I suddenly see the man on the basement stares, the urine stain on his pants. Then I am in the basement, standing by the corpse with half-closed eyes. And I remember the feeling. The power coursing through me. The sparkle racing along my nerve endings. *This* feeling.

I laugh out loud.

Time to quit fucking around.

I flip the safety pin so the gun won't fire and spin the weapon away behind me. It clatters on the floorboards. I pull out the role of cling wrap and before he can move, as the whites of his eyes begin to roll, I jump on him and wrap his face once, twice, three times in plastic. He begins to thrash and I jam the knife through one sleeve, pinning his arm to the floor. I grip the other arm, the one wet with dark blood, and lever it under my knee, then sit back on his upper thighs.

His head is banging against the floor, his chest bucking as he strains for air. A mist of condensation has spread across the vacuum-sucked plastic spread over his gaping mouth. His fingertips twitch and his legs are squirming under me.

"You have about two minutes," I say. "After that, I lose you. So listen up."

The agony in his face is like an El Greco painting, each line and shape exquisite with suffering.

Now you know.

My gaze flickers. Licks of flame race through my skin. His head rolls around. It sounds like a wooden ball on the floor.

Now you know.

I cough. Wipe my mouth with the back of my hand.

"Shit."

I get to my feet. The door in front of me. I shoulder it open and it swings shut behind me. I lean over in the empty hallway as if I'm about to vomit. Panting.

One of my shrinks told me that ordinary people rely on their gut to tell them the right thing to do. But my moral compass has no bearing, no consistency. I thought it would be the right thing to take the blame. Isn't that what Christ did? He took blame for human crimes and two thousand years later the churches still reverberate with hallelujahs.

But when I told Aidan that I had killed his mother, he didn't act like a man set free. And now I wonder what it will mean if I do this thing for Dave. I know what I am doing. I am finishing what I started eighteen years ago on the steps leading down into my parents' basement: interceding my DNA for Dave's crimes. He doesn't need this drug dealer killed. He *wants* him killed. That's different. I can only think of one reason why Dave would be so desperate for me to kill a man whose death doesn't benefit him in any material way. My brother gave me a knife to slice the skin off this man's bones. Odds are good that the knife I'm holding was recently intimately embedded between the carotid artery and jawbone of a woman named Desiree. If I kill this man and leave the knife on the premises I can provide a beautiful red herring, irresistible to city detectives who enjoy a neatly wrapped up crime with that ubiquitous non-motive that explains everything: criminal insanity.

I suppose Dave thought I would turn killer more easily. I imagine that he thought leaving me the tantalizing literary messages would be enough, that the image seared into my brain of that flayed body would tip me over the precipice. When I did nothing about the corpse, didn't even mention it, he burnt it down to protect his own identity. For all he knew, I hadn't even gone to look at the house.

He must have been confused, until I called with my frantic, gasped-out tale of muddled emotions from my confession to a crime of another in order to set Aidan free, and in which I failed and for which I sought some solace from him. And so Dave set to work, fixing his own problems, fixing my problems. Playing by the rules of the game that I had just established for him: I would not kill for pleasure. But for pointless expiation? I'm the stooge the whole world has been waiting for.

For the first time, I wonder what trade we really made all those years ago. It was a pretty straightforward setup. The man caught Dave doing something. Dave was scared, thought the man would call the cops or tell our parents. So he asked me to kill him. I didn't really think I could kill anyone. I just pushed him as hard as I could and he wasn't expecting the strength in my ten-year-old arms, the calculating cleverness of my ten-year-old brain that caught him at the top of a steep, narrow flight of stairs.

I thought I killed that man to give my brother innocence. In return I perjured a soul I had no real use for anyway since it was so flawed, so barely-human, in the first place. A fair exchange. But now I wonder. I know what I did back then was wrong but for the first time I wonder if I was both morally wrong and abysmally stupid. If killing that man did not set my brother free at all.

I turn and go back inside. My victim's eyelids flutter. I bend over him and yank the knife out of the floor. Then I flip the blade in my hand and slit the edge through the plastic, a quick twist of the wrist to catch the edge and then a fluid upward pull. The faintest scarlet thread wells up on his skin under the blade's tip.

"Listen."

His mouth strains, his throat making dry clicking noises as he gasps for air. I can't tell if he's conscious or not.

"Pay attention. Okay?" The skin on my face feels brittle, like the muscles are cracking, shattering. "It would be right to kill you. You're a human disease and I would be like a doctor if I killed you. A good person. You know? So don't think that this is mercy. It's not. Okay? It's *not*. This doesn't make me a good person."

His eyes find my face. He lies limp, staring at me. His breath rattles like pebbles in a bowl.

The knife blade snicks shut as I press it against my thigh. I get up and go outside and shut the apartment door behind me, and I wait to feel something. Guilt, grief, exultation.

Then I push through the stairwell door and emerge in an alley stained plum-colored by a watery crepuscular sky.

TWENTY-NINE

After I leave the drug dealer's apartment I wander the city for hours. A fierce dawn breaks through rainclouds and a faint smell of rotting trash hangs like a pall over the city.

I call my brother at eight in the morning.

"So you need to know," I tell him. I explain that I did not kill the man. "And, come on. You don't need him dead. Killing him is stupid, it's just plain fucking stupid and I'm not going to lose twenty years of good behavior for some total asshole. And don't worry, because I'll think of something else, okay? We'll figure it out. You're not going to ruin your life and mine and everyone else's by telling anyone anything."

"Mickey, chrissake, come on! He's *evil.* No loss to humankind. You kill him and you're still, what is it you want to be? A good person? You fucking are, you *are,* if you kill him. And darling, you *need* to kill people."

"No I don't. I did that once for you. And I'm not doing it again."

He laughs. He talks again, his voice wheedling up and falling into raging lows.

My head hurts. I yawn. After a while, I say, "Just shut the fuck up. You sound like a lunatic."

He swears and hangs up on me.

Wind skitters trash across the sidewalk. Cars zip past, churning slush. I hug my fingers under opposite arms, clenching my elbows tight against my ribs. I imagine some medical examiner slicing open my body and finding my blood slurry and thick as a cherry-flavored slush.

I am so cold my stomach muscles are twitching, I haven't slept in almost two days, and in the past twelve hours I have pissed off, terrified, and almost killed half of the people I know. But for some reason I feel—I feel okay. I didn't kill that man. I put the knife down and I left.

The phone buzzes in my hip pocket.

"You did it to yourself," he says. My brother's voice is brittle, the pitch strung tight and quavering. He's talking so fast that I don't understand what he means. *What* is on fire?

And then I laugh.

"You asshole," I say. "That's not even a joke. 'I set your car on fire' is a joke?"

"You had a choice, I swear, I told you I needed you to kill that guy. They'll find something, trace evidence, DNA, something. You had the chance. You could have saved me."

"The car is a 1971 Chevelle."

"I don't—are you listening to me? Are you fucking *list*ening? I needed you to cover for me just one more time, okay? I fucking *need*ed you and you didn't do anything, you didn't fucking do anything. I gave you everything and you could have saved me, you could have—"

My knuckles start to hurt.

"But," I say. "But I need my car. I can't—I mean, just give me the—" My voice breaks. "Just, can you, put out the fire or, or—"

"—but you didn't. You turned your back on me. So if you want it that way, fine. *Fine*. You want to destroy me? Is that what you want?" He starts breathing hard. "Jesus," he says, and his voice is high-pitched, almost childlike. "Why are you doing this to me? *Why*?"

"But my car," I say.

My cell phone illuminates. Call ended.

I press the phone hard against my ear.

My brother has never hung up on me before in our lives.

I want to find the right thing to say that will make time unravel.

Silence.

I stop walking. Someone pushes past me.

I sit down on the edge of the sidewalk with my feet in the gutter and lean forward and put my forehead on my knees. I put my hands over my head, holding the crown like it's fragile, like it might explode.

I rock.

Back and forth. Back and forth.

People call to each other. Brush past me. I cringe away. The noise makes my head hurt. A freshening blue sky. Car horns blaring. A siren wailing in the distance.

The headache throbs harder. I can feel each beat of my heart in the ache. People shove by me. Elbows, arms, everywhere the smell of cooking food, sweat, piss, the smells of soiled human existence pressing against me, bruising my skin.

I want to run away. But I can't run fast enough to escape this. I want—I *need* my car. Oh Jesus. If Dave tells the truth, the whole fragile construct of our lives will implode.

I put my fist to my mouth and bite my thumb to keep from screaming.

No air. Choking.

The dream again: falling into a void, into the vacuum pressure of a black hole.

I hate this fucking dream. The man on the steps. Blood. The taste of it in my mouth, coppery and sweet. In the dream I am pure rage, pure energy. Unleashed violence. In the dream there is no coming back. No more human left. Just the burning rage. The blood.

What I did when I was ten was wrong and I knew it and I knew that I deserved all those years of shrink visits and pills and boredom and rules. What I never fully realized was just how awful my crime was. The murder, that was wrong. Pulling out his eye was sick. It didn't occur to me until now that the one good thing I did that day, my attempt to save my brother, was the worst of all my crimes. I know I will be punished for that crime, too, today or some other day. I don't know if I can stand it.

I feel like vomiting.

If he tells, if our parents find out—I don't know what will happen. All I can see is Aidan bending over the couch like a person dying of some incurable grief.

I open my eyes.

And I get up and run.

When I go inside, Dave's apartment is empty.

I stand in the middle of the empty living space. Listening.

Then I turn and go towards the bathroom. And I halt in the doorway like I've run into a glass wall.

He's lying fully clothed, collapsed in the corner of the shower with one leg sprawled out onto the bathroom tile. The shower is running. The water smells sulfuric, pumps out in fitful gusts and rattles. His arms draped at his sides, scarlet strings running from his wrists down the stained grout, splitting like a forged river around crusts of mold.

He looks up at me. Whispers, "You were—gone so long."

I rest my head gently against the tile wall.

He tries to lift a hand. It flutters, the fingertips twitching. A small switchblade lies on the tile beside him. His lips move.

"—cops come," he's saying, trying to say. A dry tongue circles his lips. "Cops come, I'll tell them—it was you. It's okay. I know how much you want to—to—"

He still believes in his gift to me—the gift of the world *believing* in my psychosis. He was so fascinated by my pathology, by the way that I said and did things that startled ordinary people, appalled them, by how my mind galloped into dark places everyone else spends their lives hiding from. He thought I wanted to be free to live in the dark places. I know that I'm crazy, but I don't want to be a sociopath. I've only ever wanted to be normal.

I take a breath. "It's okay. I'm here now."

I kneel down, my knees on the slick tile. He reaches for me. His fingers are cold, his skin clammy. "Kill me," he says. "The—knife there."

The skin on his fingers is loose, a sack around a ridge of bone.

"No."

A long silence.

His tongue makes a sticky sound against the roof of his mouth. He says, "—want to kill yourself?"

The water eases his blood away, drains him. My head spins, a pulse throbs in my temples. A hardness under my ribs. We'd fade together. It would be neat, bequeathing our parents a shearing grief instead of the lingering wretchedness of court cases and newspaper stories. And I *could* do it. I am genetically predisposed to play the devil, having no natural talent, no capacity, no emotional propensity for kindness.

My lips are dry. "No."

"Then . . . what are you doing?"

His hand on my wrist. Ribbons of blood twine through our fingers. Water streams down his face like Christ's sweat.

"I don't know," I say.

"Don't leave," he says. "Don't—leave me—alone. Not again."

I slide my fingers out from his. My hands slippery with blood.

"Okay," I say. "I won't." I hook my hands under his armpits to budge him forward. The water pounds on my head, trickles down the back of my neck. I climb behind him and ease myself down, my back against the tile wall. His torso lying across my lap, his head against my breasts. His dead weight presses against my chest. His head lolls against my neck.

I fold my arms around his shoulders like a kid afraid of falling off a playground spinning wheel. Rest my chin on the top of his head. My hair falls down over his neck, tumbles across his chest. The water strikes the crown of my head and runs down us, turning my hair to snaking dark tendrils that blend and merge with his blood.

"Oh," he says. "Hey. Little sis. My good little sis."

My chest feels tight, airless. I want to run away, to shove off the weight. I hold tight.

Dave turns his face, burrowing the ridge of his nose and jaw against me. The pressure a thousand weights and tiny teeth tearing at my skin.

"You still love me?" he whispers. "After—what I did to your car. Still—love me?"

I can feel the thud of his heartbeat. One beat. Nothing. Another beat. The moments of nothingness stretch longer.

I say, "I never have."

The shower stall is rank with the sweetness of blood and the taint of lime, a strange milky musk. It smells like amniotic fluid.

And I think of Stephen's birth.

When I was let into the hospital room, the baby's kidney-colored body was being manipulated in latex-covered hands. The slick rasp of plastic over mucus-shiny skin. Stephen's first breaths were rusty. The obstetrician and a nurse moved on squeaky rubberized shoes around the room, checking the baby, measuring it, wrapping it up in blankets. The nurse came and laid the swaddled bundle of squalling infant on my mother's soft deflated stomach.

Come over here, my mother said. But my eyes went to the umbilical cord looped around the placenta.

Dave went over, leaned his hips against the mattress, his hands burrowed into the bed sheets, and bent his face toward the baby, cooing, making baby sounds at the bundle. My father stood with his fingertips resting on my mother's collarbone, his thumb making small circles on the back of her shoulder. My mother's skin was reddened, her hair clinging wet to her temples.

Then the nurse tried to lead me to the bed where my family rested against each other, limbs and fingers and eyes touching each other. My hand went to the cool plastic rail on the side of the hospital bed.

Don't you want to touch him? You can. He's your brother, my mother said.

I put my hands behind my back and sunk my chin toward my neck. A ten-year-old turtle drawing in on itself.

A few months later at one of my scheduled shrink visits I overheard my mother telling the psychiatrist that I didn't want to be around the family, that I withdrew from them, resented being made part of family dinners, family picnics.

But it wasn't that. It was never that.

My mother cries because I'm strange, but I don't understand that. As far as I can tell, she's never actually admitted to herself that I am psychologically different from ordinary people. She never even tried to understand. When I was a kid, I balked and shrieked and ducked but she didn't once ask how it felt when she tried to touch me. She never asked herself how scared I must have been, months after scraping a dead man's eye out of his skull with my fingernail, to be told to touch an eight-pound baby's face. What was I supposed to do? I can't read emotions very well but I'm not stupid. I knew by the looks on their faces that my family felt things I would never feel. I knew what I was capable of. So I put my hands behind my back and stepped away from the hospital bed. Then I turned and bolted out of the hospital room.

The smell of placenta and amniotic fluid clung to my clothes.

Dave came to find me. He always did.

I was sitting by a planter. The windowpanes were a rain-washed pewter gray. Shadows inched across the linoleum floor. Dave walked over to the seat and leaned against it. Tipped the plastic frame. Startled, my hands flared out, grabbed at the armrests. Dave pinned the chair against the wall with his weight, trapping three of my fingers. The bones ached.

"Stop it," I said.

He waited for a few minutes and then let the chair go. It settled onto all four legs. I rubbed at the pink welts in my hand. Then I reached up and took his hand. I dug my fingernails into the soft skin over the tendons at the base of his wrist. He bit his lip and when I let go, he gasped and laughed and rubbed his wrist against his stomach.

"Jeeeesus," he said. "Ow."

He rubbed my hair and went over to the window to look out into the rain-swept parking lot. I felt calm for the first time since we had come to the hospital. I felt evil. I felt honest.

Dave whispers, "Yeah, you do."

I don't remember what he's talking about. The water cools, a sluggish trickle pumping out over our heads.

A slow pulsing ache throbs against the edges of my eye sockets. I close my eyes and imagine that I'm far away, in a dark airless place with no smell except emptiness and nothing hurts and nothing matters.

THIRTY

"Oh God. Oh God. Dave, what did you—what's wrong with Mickey? Come on, wake up, Mickey. It's okay, I'm here, it's okay, just, I'm going to have to—oh, God."

The darkness sways.

The voice moves away, jabbering frantically. "—911 emergency, yes, I need an ambulance, emergency paramedics, right away. I don't—I think so, yes. Attempted suicide. Yes, probably. No, I don't know what he took, just—yeah. Hurry."

My eyes are shut tight. The light hurts.

But Dave shifts in my arms. His ribs press against mine as he inhales.

"*Ai*dan!" he breathes. "You *came*!"

Even faint as mist, his voice holds its silvery chime, its mocking incantatory lilt.

I open my eyes. My lashes are gummed and sticky.

Aidan's face hovers overhead, framed by the chipped pinkish bathroom tile. His eyebrows dark wings, a blue vein pulsing in his temple. His good eye burns, even his walleye steadied in the force of his glare. He reaches into the shower and cranks off the spigot.

Then he hunkers down in front of the stall, one hand splayed against the wall to steady himself. His solitary eye is not on Dave but on me.

"He said he took something. I came as soon as I could. He didn't say—he didn't say you were here."

"You're—a *saint*, a—veritable saint," Dave whispers. His bloody fingers reach out, trembling, and close around Aidan's wrist.

Aidan reaches across with his free hand and peels Dave's fingers off his wrist.

Dave's rejected fingers flutter in the air, questing for skin, for contact. They dance like butterflies across Aidan's forehead, touching his cropped dark hair, his forehead, his lips, leaving pink stains where he touches.

"So—pretty."

Aidan's skin is the color of old milk. His lips tighten across his teeth.

Dave gasps on a laugh. His fingers fall away. "Oh, don't be like that," he says. "I'm *dy*ing."

"No, you're not. I called the paramedics."

The bathroom shimmers, washed in silky rose light.

Aidan frowns and rubs his fingers on his kneecaps. "Mickey," he says. "You okay?"

When I don't answer, Dave says, "Do you know—did she ever—tell you why she killed him? Killed B-Bracy Hoff?"

Silence.

Dave starts talking again. When he speaks, even though he is barely whispering, I can feel the translated vibrations, each breath inhaled and exhaled trembling through my body.

Dave says, "*Oh*. Oh, yes, you don't know who Bracy Hoff is. Of course you don't. She—never calls anyone by name. You must have noticed. She read in some—book, has this notion that—she can set us free—if she refuses to—call us by name."

From somewhere far away, I hear myself say, "Don't do this."

Dave laughs. His head shifts.

"See? You think—you know her. You don't know *shit* about my—darling sister. You think she tells the truth. But it's all lies. She lies about Bracy. Why is that, babe? Tell—tell Aidan why."

Aidan doesn't say anything.

"*Tell* him."

And my hands tighten their grip on Dave.

"I killed him."

"Tell the *truth*."

"I killed him and I dug his eyeball out with my fingernails."

Dave says, "See, Aidan darling, everyone *thinks* that little Mickey—pushed Bracy Hoff down the, the stairs because he was—trying to—do something naughty to poor Mick."

I taste salt in my mouth.

"But the *truth*, the truth is that Mr. Hoff was a good man who—who caught little Davy Brandis with a penknife and a—and a box of matches, and he was doing something—to little Mickey. And when Mr. Hoff tried to reach the t-telephone, little Davy told—his sister to push—him and—and what happened then? Babe tell—tell Aidan what *happened* then."

A soft sound like a groan escapes. I bite my tongue until I can feel the creaking pain of it.

"She pushed him and—God Almighty, Aidan. You should—should have *seen* it. Like watching the—the birth of Venus, the a-awakening of Eve. More beautiful and terrible than—sin itself."

"Stop." Aidan's face is calm. The tears sparkle on his lashes, on the creases by his mouth. He doesn't move to wipe them.

"No," I say. "It wasn't like that."

"It was," Dave says. "It *was* like that. Our games. What games did we play? The cutting games. The burning games. Tell—tell him about playing Gestapo. God, our endless in*vent*iveness."

"Mickey." Aidan's voice is strained, pitying, gentle. Like he's talking to a little kid.

"Don't sound like that," I say.

"Mickey. It's okay."

I take a breath. Struggle to focus on his face, to make the words come out right. "I'm sorry I lied."

Aidan doesn't blink. "You mean about my mother?" His good eye is steady, watching me. "I know why you said that. For Stella. To protect her. It's okay."

"No," I say. "Your sister didn't do anything wrong. I did find out—it wasn't her. Okay? Your mother wanted to—your mother wanted to die.

She wanted to kill herself. Okay? I'm sorry. I thought if I told you—I mean, I thought it would help. I never say the right thing."

Aidan's fingers tap against his knees. "It's okay. You know . . . what I did, that wasn't your fault." He licks his lips. "I know you had to touch me, and all. Thank you."

"Well. I owed you."

Aidan smiles slightly and shakes his head.

Dave inhales. He reaches around and his fingers grab tight to my hair. He pulls hard. The pain is sharp.

"Someone want to *tell* me the fucking story?" he says.

The crusty slash on his wrist stinks like hot milk and copper. I put my fingers to his wrist, the nails resting against the edges of the slashed skin.

"Stop." Aidan stands up suddenly. "*Stop.*"

I pull my fingers away. Make a fist and press my knuckles against the tile wall.

"She won't," Dave says. "Look. See? She *won't.*" He drops his hand. Threads of hair tangled around fingers that lie, half-curled, across his stomach. "I tried though," he says. "To make her—astonishing. To make her famous. The dear Lord knows I *tried.*" A breath of laughter. "Few have done what I did, *offered* what I did—to the deity."

The creases by the sides of Aidan's mouth deepen.

I grab onto Dave's shirt, twist my fingers in the wet fabric. "Shut up," I say. "Shut *up.*"

Dave laughs once then gasps shallowly for air. His ribs against mine, his spine against my breastbone. "You don't—want me to tell him what I did for you? How I became *like* you—how I tempted you with the tenderest—morsels that you crave?"

Aidan's eyelids suddenly lift.

"Yes." Dave inhales. "The sacrifices—you are thinking of them? Wondering, perhaps. Well. I did it because—because blood pleases the god."

Aidan's eyes sharpen. His good eye swivels, focuses on me. "Mickey what is he—what's he *saying*?"

"The dead," Dave says. "Yes. Your suspicions are correct. I brought them to her—like the cat brings dead mice. A humble—supplicant."

"*Them*?"

I close my eyes.

"Oh, I have more—offenses at my beck," Dave says. His voice cracks with grief. "I *wish* I hadn't done it. Don't I—*don't* I, my darling? But—you left me anyway, growing smaller—on the horizon—locked in the—embrace of such a one as this—this goddamn artistic infant."

"No," Aidan says. "What are you saying? You murdered—"

"The woman, made a pietà of her. Yes. And the other—across the street. In the pretty room, inside the empty house. In *Xan*adu. I killed him in a dying—paradise and burnt it—to the fucking ground."

"Is this true?" His voice despairing.

I don't say anything.

"Mickey why didn't you say anything? To the cops? You should have, you can't just—I know he's your brother but—"

"She will never—hurt me," Dave says. "No matter what I do. Do you see that, little Aidan? She belongs—to me."

I open my eyes and look at Aidan. "At first I—I thought it was you."

Aidan looks at me unblinking and tears stand on his lashes and lie in the hollows of eye sockets and his upper lip. "What?"

Dave chokes, a bubble rising and popping on his lips, laughing silently through a mist of mucus and water. "Because my plot was—peerless. Because of proximity—and timing. When we met, when you told me your sad, sad tale of murders and, and *fire*—you became my—muse. You are the demon of my—loneliest loneliness."

Aidan looks at Dave for a long time.

"That woman who was killed. You *mutilated* her."

Dave says. "Sh, don't distress yourself. You're thinking now that you may have been wrong to have—saved my life. But I am not—like her, not like my dear sister. Not *sick* like her. I tempt, I tease, but I am only—vaguely dispossessed. I am not—crazy. I kill but am not a *killer*. I'm not compulsive, not a *psycho*path. I only ever harmed the hairs of—of heads no longer counting in the general consensus. Has there been—a hullaballoo? The civic voice raised in outrage? No. They don't *matter*. I would never kill a—kill a *real* person." He stops talking. And then his breath hitches. He holds it, and then lets it out, slowly. "But *you*. You, Aidan, darling. What kind of man are you? Mickey, she's going to—going to *crack* someday. Once she starts there will be no stopping her. Will you try? Do you realize that you should? You should stop her now. If you want to do the right thing."

Aidan makes a noise like a grunt. He looks down at the knife lying by Dave's thigh and his fingers reach out, touch it, and close around the handle. He looks around at the empty apartment behind him as if someone will arrive, leaping out at the last minute to free him from his dilemma. But no one comes.

"Do it. Darling, *do* it."

Aidan looks down at the knife in his fist. He swallows hard.

Dave reaches out and his fingers touch Aidan's face. Aidan jerks. The hand gripping the knife instinctively pulls back and Dave reaches over and grabs Aidan's wrist. He laughs.

Aidan gasps and yanks his hand back. It comes free, Dave's fingers slippery with blood and weak. Aidan's shirt cuffs are sodden and pink in finger-shaped stripes.

The knife falls from his hand and lands near Dave with a clink. Dave looks down at it. And then he picks it up.

"Well, well," he says, "will you lookie at *that*."

Aidan looks at him, the thin white skin on his forehead pleated. He looks like a confused child.

I feel Dave's muscles tense and even though I can't see the direction of his eyes I know what he's thinking. I know the burning fixation in his mind that won't forget the knife, that won't ignore the pulsing blue-purple vein in Aidan's thin neck, and that can't resist the increasing proximity between the two.

"No," I say. "*Don't.*"

I grab Dave's hand to force it down, dig my fingernails into his wrist. He's weaker than I thought. His arm falls heavy as a flank of meat. The point of the knife slices down cleanly into his thigh.

Dave chokes, gasps. His head bucks back into my chest.

I let go.

Aidan whispers, "Oh Christ." He stumbles to his knees, his feet, and runs into the main room. He coughs and then retches loudly.

A dark pulsing gush.

I push the weight of Dave's torso to the side. I press my fingers against the hot rhythmic spurts. I know there has to be a way to find the severed artery. My hands slip.

Dave tenses. And then, slowly, he relaxes. His muscles unclench. A tremor ripples through his left leg. His breath trickles out and then he inhales and holds his breath. He coughs once.

"*No,*" I say. I hit him in the chest and then in the face. A dark blood print across his cheek. "Come on. No. Please. No. Jesus, please, come on."

My chest is an empty cavity. I can't breathe. It hurts. A tight hard knot of pain under my ribs. It hurts like my heart has stopped beating and won't ever start again.

Noise swells into a sudden cacophony. Harsh strident voices in the hall. Fists bang on the door. Aidan's silhouette rises up in the living room, haloed in red and blue. The paramedics have come.

The bathroom fills with sound and smell and the heat of sweating bodies. They move in sharp, efficient gestures in the tiny bathroom space. Hairy arms and plastic hands reaching, pushing, pulling. Professional latex gloves pressing into his thigh, a rubber tube wrapped around his leg and pulled tight. When they lift Dave away from me his left arm slips, the hand falling with a thud to the floorboards. Black strands of my hair dangle from his thin fingers.

They haul Dave to the main room and strap him to a gurney. Aidan is hunched on the couch, his arms wrapped around his chest, rocking back and forth.

Blood and sulfuric water stick my shirt to my belly. The dream leaking into real life and this time I can't wake up. I want to cut something, to feel something, some pain worse than the choking airlessness. I don't know what I'm supposed to do. My lungs cramp. My hands are shaking. The floor is smeared with blood. My hands and shirt. The smell of it everywhere. My hand reaches for the knife where it lies on water-beaded tile. I rise, shivering, the air crystalline and empty around me. The room sparkles. The knife blade is in my fist.

One of the paramedics bent over Dave lifts her head. The skin on her forehead wrinkles and lines curve near her nose. Her upper lip lifts away from her eyeteeth. She looks like a cowering hyena hunched over half-eaten prey that has caught the scent of a starved lioness.

"You poor kid," she says.

And I realize that I have completely misunderstood the lines on her face.

The knife falls out of my loose fingers.

THIRTY-ONE

First comes the scarred tiling and the blue plastic curtains around a crinkle-papered bed at Akron General Hospital. Ten minutes to put three stitches in my neck, swab a little disinfectant, tape on a bandage. Then what feels like hours in the glass-walled waiting room with Aidan hopping up to dash outside and talk on his cell phone, talking, I think to my parents. The black print hanging over the plastic palm fronds in the waiting room: No Cell Phones in the Waiting Area.

Pressing my damp palms on my jeans knees. Rocking back and forth, breathing shallowly through my mouth. It smells like perfume and feces and hair oil. Swallowing spit. Quick trot down the hall, sneakers squeaking on the freshly-mopped linoleum. Bang into the women's, shoulder open a stall door, try to vomit but nothing comes up.

When the shakes calm down I go out of the stall and lean over the sink. Cup my hands under an automatic faucet that keeps failing. Rub my damp soapy hands over my face.

The mirror reflects pale skin, blank dark eyes. I want to see some expression on that face, some shift or tightening of muscles that will tell me what it feels.

Nothing changes.

I look down at the sink. I wish that I could throw up. Or cry. I want to be loud.

I wipe my hands on a paper towel and go back out into the waiting room.

Aidan's standing in the waiting room trying to look calm.

"You holding up?"

I look at him and then go over to the chairs and sit down.

The skin by his mouth crinkles as he sort of collapses into himself. He's trying, the poor kid is, to hold together the tattered threads of my life, of his life, of all of our lives, the strands of a shot-to-shit family that isn't his. I don't know why.

He sits down next to me, legs splayed out. He picks up a magazine and starts to flip through it. He has been calm, which surprises me. The wild panic of earlier receded and when they took Dave away he got up and came over to me. He picked up the knife, wiped it off on his T-shirt, and folded the blade up. I don't know where he put it.

He's controlled, peaceful now. Even his hands are quiet. The only noticeable change in his demeanor is the odd, almost proprietary way in which he answers questions. He says that my brother called us, that we went together, arrived to find him so far gone. With grief and some level of competence we joined him in the shower to staunch the flow or to (a hitch in breath) be with him to the end. He speaks in the plural as easily as if born to it.

I get up and walk over to the plate glass window. Thinking how many sharp objects are in the waiting room and how it smells of antiseptic but everything feels foul, gritty, infected.

My parents and Stephen arrive. How's he doing, my mother says, and doctors say, blood transfusions, and if he stabilizes, and so forth. Tissues. Snot dripping from the edge of my mother's left nostril. A nurse leads them back. They confer with doctors in a conference room. They are led behind the plastic curtain.

12:23 P.M.

My parents and Stephen come back from his room. They sit in chairs opposite the ones in which Aidan and I perch.

We wait in silence.

Stephen says, "So, um, what happened?"

My father clears his throat. He opens his hands and then closes them. But he doesn't say anything.

I clear my throat. "Are you hungry?"

They all look at me in surprise.

I say to Stephen, "You want to get something to eat? We could go find a cafeteria."

He licks his lower lip. Looks over at our father. "Is that okay?"

Dad nods once. He takes off his glasses, polishes a lens.

I stand up. Aidan looks up at me. "You want me to, you know, fill them in?"

"Yes."

"Okay."

Stephen follows me out.

The cafeteria is in another wing. It smells like old lunchmeat and stale coffee. We buy chicken sandwiches and sit down in a booth. Someone has printed in blue ink "Jason forever" on the laminate tabletop. I wonder if Jason wrote it, or if Jason was dying somewhere in the building as someone else wielded a Bic pen in defiance of the inevitable.

Stephen peels the foil wrapper off his sandwich. He lifts the top bun and pulls out slices of pickle, leaves them on the foil wrap.

He takes a breath and looks up at me. "So what happened?"

"He cut his wrists."

"He was on something, right?"

I take the wrapper off my sandwich. It smells like chalk. I wonder how old the chicken is.

"What kind?" Stephen asks.

I look at him. "What you're thinking. I found a needle in the bathroom. Don't tell Mom and Dad. Or, at least, don't tell them I'm telling you."

Stephen raises a shoulder, frowns at his sandwich.

I wonder when Stephen will find out about the puncture wound that severed the artery in his older brother's thigh. Or the rest of it, the whole filthy six o'clock news special. Aidan is stringing together some version for Mom and Dad. My mouth tastes bitter, like lye and rot. I can feel my pulse in my neck, in my forehead. Everything frantic under my skin.

I pick up the sandwich and take a bite. Chew. Swallow. My mouth is dry. I reach for my waxed paper cup of water. I wish I'd ordered juice. The water tastes like soap.

"Is he going to make it?"

"I don't know."

The silence goes on for a long time.

Stephen scrapes his fingernail along the laminate table edge. "So I'm going to apply to the University of Dallas. In Texas."

I cough and reach for the water again. Swirl it around in my mouth and spit it back into the cup. "You mean, like, for college?"

"Yeah."

I don't know what to think about his conversational gambit. "Well, you won't get free tuition if you go there, you know."

"Yeah."

I take another bite of sandwich.

"You should go to UT-Austin."

He looks up at me. "Why?"

"Because it's two hundred miles further away from here."

He smiles a little. He picks up his sandwich and looks at it and puts it down again. "Yeah?" he says. "Maybe I'll apply there too."

"What are you going to major in?"

"Biochem."

"Premed?"

"I want to be a dentist."

I laugh.

He looks up. His pale face flushes. "What?"

"Nothing. Just, who wants to be a dentist?"

He lifts a shoulder. "Teeth are interesting."

I shake my head. "You are weirder than you look. You know that?"

He bites his lower lip. Then he takes a breath. He says, "You have crooked incisors too."

"What?"

"Our teeth. We inherited crooked incisors. All of us. You have them, and Dave. I don't have them right now because of my braces. But they'll shift again unless I get more orthodontic work."

"Huh. I never noticed."

He says something so softly I can't hear him.

"What?"

"I said, I'm more like you guys than you think."

My heartbeat stutters. An icy trickle down my spine. I put the sandwich down.

I don't know what to say.

He looks up at me. His eyes fill with tears.

I know what I need to do. I just don't want to.

I wipe my hands on my thighs. Reach out and put my fingers on the sleeve of his jacket. The coarse cotton-blend fabric still cool from outside air. I press my palm against his arm, lay my hand flat against the slender bones under his jacket sleeve.

He looks down at my hand. He slides his fingers over mine. The feel of his skin like cold worms. I swallow a gag.

He grips my fingers in his.

The cafeteria is choked with sour food smells. I wonder how long I can hold still. But that's a stupid thing to wonder. I'll hold still as long as I have to.

He lets me go and I snatch my hand back. He wipes his palm under his nose then reaches for a napkin and blows his nose into it.

"I'm not really hungry," he says. "If you want to head back."

When we get back to the waiting room our parents and Aidan are still sitting in the same seats, not looking at each other. A few other people sit in isolated clots, heads bent, immobile.

My father looks like a stone effigy. The profiled head is so craggy, so chiseled that I expect a pigeon to come crap on it. Fluorescent lights shine oily and yellow on his glasses lenses.

Mom sees us and reaches out a hand for Stephen. He sits down next to her. She pulls a tissue out of her pocket and puts it against her eyes and sniffs. Offers him a tissue. He shakes his head and bites his lower lip.

My skin feels clammy. I go over to the window and lean against the cool glass.

"How long do we wait here if there's no news?"

"How long do we wait?" My father's voice is controlled, patient. "Do you have somewhere else you need to be, Michaela? Something else to be doing now?"

Aidan clears his throat and slides his spine down in the plastic seat.

I turn around, press my shoulder blades against the window. My father removes his glasses and pinches the bridge of his nose. He presses and releases and settles the glasses on his face again, tucking the earpieces behind his ears.

"I understand why you wanted Mr. Devorecek to talk to us," he says, "but you are far stupider than you appear if you think that we are not going to talk about this. If you think for one second that you can expect this not to—not to be *discussed*."

I blink, startled. Look at Aidan. He is slouched in the seat, fists burrowed under opposite armpits.

"I guess that makes me stupid, then. What the fuck are you talking about?"

A young child kneeling on a chair across the room is digging a plastic G.I. Joe action figure's head into his nose and then licking the snot off the plastic helmet. When I say "fuck," his eyes widen and dart up to my face. I glare at him. He just gapes back, saliva glistening on his lower lip.

Aidan gets up. "All right. I think I'm going to the vending machine. Anything for you, Mrs. Brandis?"

"No, thank you." Her nose is clogged and it sounds like she has said, *Doe thag you.*

"How about you, Stephen?"

"I just went to the caf with Mickey."

"Go get something else." Our father pulls out his wallet and folds a five dollar bill into Stephen's hand.

Stephen looks at the bill and then up at me.

"Go," our father says. "Aidan, please take him to the vending machines."

"Okay." Aidan nods at Stephen. Stephen gets up slowly and follows Aidan out. He looks over his shoulder at me, his brows peaked like slanted eaves.

Dad inhales and grips his hands around the armrests of his plastic chair. His knuckles stand up pale and crested, pressing through the fabric of his skin. "Start talking. I suggest you start with your lies."

Mom puts the tissue against her nose and lifts her head and breathes in, holds her breath, and lets it out. As if to swamp incipient tears with the infected air of the waiting room.

I look at the worn toes of my sneakers.

"Michaela."

I look up at him. For some reason my throat hurts. "You want the truth? Okay. Yes. He sometimes cut me. He burnt my fingers when I was six. Almost drowned me in that construction site. Yes to a million things we never told you about. But it was a game, it was just a game. See how bad it got before I yelled. Only I never yelled. I don't know why. I guess it's the crazy, some fun little trivia about antisocial personality disorder they don't tell you. The inverted pain tolerance. Caresses kill, burns don't register. He figured it out, that's all."

Dad makes a noise, half-cough, half-cry, and turns his head to the side. Mom sits still. Her eyes glisten but the tissue rests in her lap and she is no longer sniffling.

"Shit." I lean my head back. The glass is cold. "This is so pointless."

"Would it do any good to ask why you didn't tell anyone." This from my father, the dean, who, one supposes, has become accustomed to stating truths and not asking questions and so unconsciously flattens his interrogatives into declaratives.

I shrug. "It wasn't a problem." And raise my voice as the dean opens his mouth to protest. "Come on. I know you're going to bitch and moan about how it's abuse or whatever but it's fucking *not*. Okay? I don't care. I never cared."

Across the room the little boy swivels his thumb in his mouth, staring at me with wide, white-rimmed blue eyes.

I narrow my eyes and point my finger at him. "The word is fuck. F-u-c-k. You look over here again I'm going to go over and jab your eyes out with that fucking G.I. Joe, you little Aryan asswipe. Got it?"

He puts his thumb in his mouth and scuttles behind a planter.

"Oh, yes, why don't you deflect the conversation with a few more violent and repugnant remarks," my father says. "What do you think? Do you think we can come up with something grotesquely hilarious to describe what it feels like to find out your son has been abusing your daughter for twenty years and no one mentioned a goddamn fucking thing?"

"Jesus Christ," I say. "I'm fine. *He*'s the one in the fucking coma."

"Mickey, stop it."

Every head in the waiting room swivels. Aidan stands in the doorway with a bag of Doritos. Stephen is behind him.

Aidan comes into the room. He rips open the bag of chips and sits down. My parents blink like cats, slowly, with the skin around their eyelids as if their faces are imperfect masks. Stephen slides into his seat next to mom.

Aidan says, "You don't have to do that." In the sallow fluorescent lighting his skin looks mottled like cottage cheese, the sacs under his eyes sallow bruises. He turns to my parents. "She's *good*," he says. As if there is something weighty and sweet in the word.

"Oh God," I say. "Just shut up. Please."

My father grunts in negation but seems unable to find articulate sounds. His eyes wander the scuffs in the floor, the gouges and rubber streaks.

My mother sighs. The sound is like a leaf falling.

Aidan looks at me, lifts the bag of chips. "Want one?"

"Shit," I say. I push off the window and go over and sit next to him, lean forward, elbows propped on my knees. My head feels so heavy. I rub my palms over my forehead.

My father clears his throat. When he speaks his voice is soft, almost invisible. "I apologize for losing my temper. Can you at least—can you just tell us why you lied? Did you—did you think we wouldn't believe you?"

"I didn't say anything because, for the millionth time, it wasn't a big deal. It *wasn't*. It was just games. Just—games. And I knew if anyone found out they'd make this huge fucking deal out of it."

I get up. My muscles feel twitchy. I want to run. I go over to the window again.

Aidan says, "You get it, don't you? I know it's hard to hear, but you should know. She has problems, yeah, she may even have that antisocial thing. But the rest of it, the cutting, that's not—it's not her fault. It's *not*."

I spin around.

My father's head is raised, his eyes unseeing but fixed on Aidan. I don't like the way my father is looking at him. I hit my palms against my thighs and rock on the balls of my feet. My skin crawls. I feel like when I was on the anti-anxiety meds. I want to smash my face into the corner of the metal window frame.

"Not my fault? I mutilate dead bodies. Even if it's not my fault it's pretty fucking dire. You're, you can't just say words like that."

"You can if they're true."

"Oh come on. You sound like you ate a barrel full of clichés and then drank a quart of laxative."

They all stare at me.

I hunch my shoulders. "Look, what does it matter? None of this *changes* anything. Do you think I wouldn't change if I could? Oh, God, you don't deserve this, him or me, you really don't. Okay? Dad? No one deserves this."

Dad says, "But—"

"She lied because she loves him," Aidan says loudly. In the sudden quiet he clears his throat. "Sorry," he says. "I thought it was obvious."

I run out of the room.

THIRTY-TWO

David John Brandis dies at 3:58 P.M. without regaining consciousness. His death is ruled a suicide.

The obituary lists calling hours on Wednesday, December 28 at Westminster Presbyterian Church in Akron, Ohio.

The newspaper does not list the burning of a 1971 Chevrolet Chevelle, nor does it describe the snow-caked ghost yard near Firestone Park where the fire-scorched carapace is towed the morning of Tuesday, December 27.

The funeral is held Saturday at noon. New Year's Eve. The phone rings all morning and falls silent at 11:49.

The house creaks and murmurs to itself in the absence of human voices. I sit on the mattress in my parents' garage. I pick a hangnail on my thumb. Watch a tiny seed of blood emerge. I blot the blood on the yellow blanket beside me. Then I clasp my hands together between my knees.

The reception is held at the house. I listen to the cars pull up, the voices and clatters in the kitchen as caterers light butane-fueled warming pans and set out silverware.

Someone knocks on the garage door. I consider answering or getting up but my muscles feel sluggish. My throat hurts.

The door creaks open.

"Honey? Are you going to come in and get something to eat?"

My mother stands framed by a sugar-white cap of snow on the carport roof. The sky flames with dying light behind her, bronze and vermillion.

"No."

"All right." She stands in the open doorway. Her boysenberry lipstick has bled into the fine cracks around her lips. "Are you okay?"

Cold air snakes around my ankles. "Yes."

"Do you want to come inside?"

I open my mouth to say that the answer should be patently obvious. She is holding the edge of the door so hard her knuckles are bone-white, but her thumb rubs the edge of the door lightly, back and forth. My mouth closes. I think of all the little gestures she makes, the pauses and arrested movements. I wonder if it is my hand she is holding onto in her mind.

I swallow. "I can't—I don't want to go in there. I'm sorry."

"Mrs. Brandis? Where do you want the candles?"

Mom's shoulders tighten. Her mouth opens like she's going to say something to me. Then she smiles, a tight press of her lips, and nods. She turns her head to answer the person in the kitchen and moves away, still talking, explaining where she wants the mini quiches.

The door stands open.

I grip my knees.

Another car pulls up by the house and parks along the curb. A flock of starlings squabbling in the bare oak branches rises up, raucous, hoarse as a frenzied crowd. They rush, disjointed black streaks, into the bell-like dome of the sky.

Time passes.

Voices come near again.

I blink and look up.

My parents come out of the house, talking quietly. Sounds drift from the open kitchen door. The tintinnabulation of silverware and metal platters. The click of ice cubes. Human sounds.

My mother is talking in a low voice. My father stands with his fists balled in his suit jacket pockets, looking at the empty, oil-stained gravel. My mother comes close to him. She gestures in the direction of the garage door, then shakes her head. She presses her hands against her mouth. Her shoulders start to buck with harsh sobs. The cold wind presses her blouse against her skin. He puts his hands on her shoulders, smoothes them down her arms. She leans into him and he circles his arms around her waist and anchors her there. They stand against the stark outline of the setting sun, darkened shapes convergent like falling rocks caught by the weight of the other. Heavy with needing.

I get up and shut the garage door and go back and sit on the mattress. Press my hand under my ribs. It's so hard to breathe.

Aidan opens the door without knocking and walks in carrying a paper plate with thin black and gray lines around the rim. My mother's class showing itself even in disposable cutlery.

He sets the plate down on the concrete floor near me. A roast beef and cheese sandwich wedge, a slice of pickle, and a handful of mints. He is wearing a black suit and the pants have a cluster of vertical creases at the back of the knees. He turns his head, fingers a nick on the underside of his jaw.

He takes off his suit jacket. The underarms of his white shirt are faintly yellow. He comes over and lays down the jacket and then sits down on the mattress beside me. The familiar smell: Ivory soap, cigarettes, acrylic paint.

"So," he says. His left leg jiggles up and down. "Your mom wants you to eat."

I don't say anything.

Aidan waits for a while. Then he says, "Mickey, he's dead. Nothing you say can hurt him now. So when are you going to tell?"

I rub my hands on my knees. Look at the plate of food on the floor. The pink horseradish sauce is crusting along the meat.

"You need to tell someone. The truth, I mean. You need to tell the cops about Dave killing those people. If you do it, fine. If you don't, I will." He pauses, and then says, "And also your parents. They should know the whole truth."

A brief icy gust of wind sweeps in. Goosebumps stand on my bare lower arms.

He presses his hands into his thighs and stands up, slowly.

"Anyway. That's all I came to say."

He goes to the door.

"He—my brother was right."

Aidan stops and turns around.

"About me. And so what happened, when I—when I stabbed him—oh. Even if it was accidental—it *was*, but the point is—"

He watches me in silence for a bit. Then he says, "I know it's hard." He waves a hand impatiently. "All of that, yes, I understand. But right now. What you're really afraid of. I know what you're afraid of. But you don't have to be afraid. You're not the only one. It's not exactly easy having a big sister who assaults you practically every time you go visit. It's not easy loving her even when she—when she breaks my family into pieces just by being alive. Lots of people go through shit for the ones they love."

"It's not *hard*." My voice sounds old, cracked with disuse. "It's goddamn *awful*."

"I know," he says.

I look up at him. "You don't know. You don't fucking get it."

"No," he says.

"Shut up. You don't know what you're talking about. My brother isn't a serial killer."

"Mickey—"

"He didn't kill those people, you know, across the street, and the woman in the apartment downstairs—"

"Jesus God, Mickey, are you really going to sit there and take the blame for a murder you didn't commit again? How gullible do you think I am?"

"I'm not—just *listen*. He didn't kill those people because of any compulsion. It was clean, organized. He doesn't—he didn't *have* to kill. He did it for me."

He swallows hard, the nodules of his Adam's apple moving convulsively.

"Because he thought it would make me—I don't know. Free. Because he loved me."

"No."

"Yeah, I fucking know. Okay? I know that's sick. I know he was sick, even if he wasn't a serial killer. But I don't know—I don't know *why* or who fucked up who or if, if anything could have turned out differently." I pleat my fingers in the blanket pooled around my feet. Lean forward. "I—I didn't kill him—"

He says, "Mickey, don't. You didn't do anything wrong."

"*Fuck* you! Please." I am hoarse. I haven't talked this much in days. I swallow. My mouth is so dry. "Let me—say this. I didn't kill him but I—" I'm startled by a strange gasping sound that bursts out. I bury my face against my knees. "I should have." God, my chest hurts. It feels like it's being crushed from the inside. "When I was ten years old. I should've done it then. He's the one I should have pushed. I could have saved—everyone. I could have saved the world."

For once, Aidan is silent.

The silence is so stark that I lift my head.

He's just looking at me, his mouth partially open. His hands are curled at his sides.

"So how can I tell my parents about him? They are barely—I would kill them too."

I almost tell him, *If I unclench my hands the world will burn.*

My mouth tastes like burning paper.

Aidan looks down at the floor. The lines by his mouth are stricken so deeply I could lay a pencil in the creases.

He opens his hands, his fingers spread against his thighs. He closes them again.

After a long time, he walks out. The door stands open after him.

Days pass.

The spring school semester begins.

Normalcy and patterned behavior return. I still live in the apartment but most nights I spend sleeping on the mattress in my parents' garage.

I attend office hours and sit at my computer with my headphones in, my fingers on the keyboard, waiting to find words to type.

Stephen attends school. Plays video games.

My mother folds laundry and teaches Mozart to talentless teenagers.

The dean leaves pink slips in my mailbox and sometimes I ignore them. Sometimes I don't. When I sit in his office he is polite, his voice like chilled cream, and he asks after my dissertation, my health, my running habits. I answer his questions. When I leave his eyes follow me and I feel the weight of his gaze like cords tethering me to the earth.

The asshole drones in the graduate student office buzz, talking about weekend parties and grading student papers and which professor one should never take, or always take. They don't know anything about my family until Telushkin accidentally tells them. He comes into the office to ask if I've finished a chapter and says that he doesn't mean to rush me, that he knows I'm still grieving for my brother. For a few days my fellow grad students are quiet, awkward, their voices peat-smoky and conciliatory. Slowly, when I show signs of neither grief nor joy, they resume normal cadences and volumes.

In February I drive to Judith Greene's house.

The house still smells like cat litter and cherry-flavored cough syrup. She brings me a tiny cube of red Jell-O and a cup of Earl Grey tea with cream.

"Why are you here? Are you going to—tell anyone what I told you? No one will believe you. You used to be in therapy. You probably *are* crazy. Are you going to?"

"No."

"Then why are you here?"

I sit on her floral couch and a cat twines between my legs. I can see pink skin between patches of flaky white fur on the cat's spine.

The tea tastes bitter, almondy. I wonder if the cream has soured. I set the china cup in its saucer. Flecks of tea leaves swirl in the pale liquid and its rippling meniscus catches at the light.

"Because I want to know something."

She sits stiffly on her armchair watching me. She's wearing red cotton pants that are two sizes too small. Her flesh bulges against the fabric. When she walked in from the kitchen I could see the dimpled jiggling flesh of her ass and thighs.

Cat hair clings to her soft pink sweater. Her mascara is clumped. She scratches at one earlobe with her chipped pink thumbnail.

"What do you want to know?"

I look at her. And then I reach for my tea. It still tastes strange. I swallow and make a face. I don't know what to ask. I don't know why it matters so much to me to know the answer.

"Do you regret it? Killing her, I mean. Do you wish you hadn't done it?"

She blinks. Her finely wrinkled skin sags, dragging down the corners of her mouth.

"No," she says.

"But you miss her."

Her forehead creases. She looks up at me. "I *had* to do it. Alan left her and took her babies with him. And she was so, so—she couldn't—her *soul* was tortured. She couldn't *stand* it anymore."

I look around at her walls, the old sepia-tinged photographs of distant ancestors. Framed images of gay-looking singers.

"You cry a lot, don't you?"

Her little pink mouth opens and closes and opens again. "I don't—how—why would you *say* that to me?"

"No reason." I feel strange. Dizzy. The cat is rubbing its cheek against my calf and purring. I can feel its vibrating ribcage. "It doesn't matter. Forget it."

I sigh.

She says, "Do you feel all right? It looks like you're sweating."

She doesn't sound very sympathetic.

I raise a smile. For some reason I feel sad. I stand up. The close air in the tiny house is making me sick.

Before I leave, my hand curled around the doorknob, I turn back to her. She's watching me with those small bright eyes.

"By the way," I say, "I know you put Ambien in the tea. You're a fucking moron."

She swallows. Then after a pause, probably because I don't seem to be coming for her with a knife, she leans forward and says, "You deserve to die. You're not a nice person at *all*."

I smile. "Now that is the gospel truth. Yes." I lean my forehead against my knuckles. "Okay. Well. I'll come back next week, okay? Tuesday maybe."

Her small mouth opens. The yellowish enamel of her tiny crooked teeth. The soft hairs around the corners of her upper lip. She makes a soft noise like a grunt. Doesn't say anything else. A cat gives a rusty meow.

I go out and shut the door behind. Then I sink down on the front stoop and wait for the dizzy specks to clear. Trees sway overhead.

As I make my way down to the shiny red V4 Ford Focus my parents bought me, I watch the houses shimmer with watery luminescence.

My brother died because I killed him and I didn't cry, I won't ever cry, but somehow I think that Judith Greene is still more terrible, more wicked than I am. More alone than I am. If I am capable of feeling anything at all then what I feel for Judith Greene is pity.

I pull left off Brown Street and drive.

The edges of my vision sparkle.

A car's taillights flare red and smudged through a gray mist. A stoplight. I put my hand on the gearshift when I step on the brake, but this car is an automatic. Rain plinks against the windshield. A film of clouds shreds like crepe paper.

A car horn behind me beeps.

The light has changed.

The apartment lights glow in the darkness. I stand at the door with my keys in my hands and can't remember climbing the stairs. I let myself in.

A chair creaks in Aidan's room. He comes out into the kitchen with a paintbrush in his hand.

"I thought you were going to your parents' tonight."

I set the keys carefully on the countertop. They slither to the side, fall with a clatter. I frown at them.

"I didn't—don't feel well."

He comes forward. "Are you okay?"

"Yes."

"What were—I mean—" He stops talking.

"What?" I say. "What do you *think* I was doing?"

His walleye skitters sideways. Lines deepen in his throat as he inhales and holds his breath. He sets the brush down on the counter and presses his fists against his eyes. When he lowers his hands his eyes are incandescent.

"Nothing," he says. "I wasn't asking that."

"Then what?"

The corners of his mouth pull down. "I just, I was just *worried*. I don't know what to—how to make you feel better."

"I don't feel bad. I don't feel anything. Remember? Jesus, I thought we'd been over this." I swallow a yawn. "Sorry. I don't mean to—I'm sorry."

"Mickey, are you okay?"

I shrug.

He sighs. "Don't do that. Don't look like that, like it doesn't matter."

I don't know what to answer, what he wants me to look at him like.

Something shifts in his skin, in his eyes. He takes a step toward me.

I back up and run into the counter edge. The corner cuts into my lower spine. "What are you—?"

And he grabs my skull between his hands, each hand cupped over the side of my head, his fingers tight, his palms pressing against my ears so that I hear my breath echoing inside my head. The pressure aches through my skin. His fingers digging into my scalp are strong and tensile.

His breath smells of cigarette smoke and toothpaste.

I can see the faint pinpricks of beard along his pale jaw, the waxy white of dried skin on his lower lip. My chest hurts. Hot air trapped inside, afraid to let go, to breathe.

And in surprise I see pain on his face, a sudden contraction of his eyebrows, a look of seared agony in his eyes. He makes a noise in his throat and pulls my head into the hollow between his neck and shoulder. His cold jacket smells like sweat and the spice of turpentine and tobacco.

And then his grip loosens and I scramble back, banging into the counter again, sucking frantically at the air.

He looks down at the ground. He wipes his hand over his mouth.

I imagine what it would be like to go to him, to put my arms around him and hold on. I imagine that it would feel like screaming and like dissolving, like light fracturing into myriad pieces, endlessly expanding, endlessly diminishing. My hands start to shake.

I take a breath. "Ay—"

He looks up at me in surprise.

I swallow. "Ay—Ayyyy." Deep breath. "*Aidan.*"

We are silent.

He says, "My middle name is Christopher. That's three syllables."

I let out my breath. "*Fuck* you."

He smiles. He looks sad and, something else. A gentleness in his eye sockets, a dark warmth in the shape of his mouth. The muscular contractions of the face that portray the human emotion of compassion. I don't know what to do with that. I don't know why—how—anyone could feel compassion for me.

I go into my room but when I lie down my eyelids sink. Gravity pulls at my skin and gray rushes toward me and foams like ocean crests.

I hear Aidan moving around in his room. The smell of paints, the squeak and clatter as he tidies his things. The gush of water in his bathroom as he rinses his brushes. Then his bedsprings creak.

I get up and go to his room. Tap at the lintel.

"Yeah?"

I push open the door. His room is messy, rags and strips of tissue paper strewn across the paint-speckled floorboards, canvases stacked against the walls, a dismantled easel leaning against the bureau. The wide bed with its rumpled sheets, a stray belt lying like a curled snake on the sheets.

He comes out of the bathroom, his T-shirt in his hands. He stops short when he sees me.

"I want to sleep in your bed tonight."

He doesn't say anything.

"Without, you know, touching. But just—as friends."

"Mickey," he says.

"Can I?"

He looks down at his shirt. His knuckles are pale. The material is sogged and drips slowly onto the floor. Droplets pebble his bare feet.

I go over to the bed and climb in. My eyes keep wanting to close. The sheets are smooth and cool against my skin.

He goes into the bathroom. After a bit he comes out. I close my eyes and force myself to stay awake listening. I hear his bare feet scuff. And then the bureau drawer. He drops his jeans and the zipper clinks. The rustle of cloth as he pulls on pajama pants. He turns out the light and climbs into bed. The mattress slants. He slides his legs under the sheets and lies on his back. He puts his arms behind his head.

I force my eyelids open.

Moonlight grays the walls. Flashes of blue static electricity flare when he turns over to face me, the sheets rushing together, separating, crackling, decrepitating.

Pale light glazes his bare skin.

"I don't know what you're doing," he whispers.

"Me either."

"Okay." He puts his hand out. I see the darkness of it.

"No."

"Hold still. I won't touch you."

He tugs a strand of hair clinging to my sticky lip. Smoothes it across the pillow.

"Okay?"

"Yeah. Okay."

There is a long silence.

"So tomorrow's your late day, right?" He coughs a little. Swallows. "So since you don't have to go in early do you—maybe you want to go get coffee in the morning? Like at Starbucks or something?"

"Maybe."

He lets out his breath and turns onto his back.

"Okay," he says. "Well. Good night."

"Good night."

I lie in the quiet listening to his breath as it evens and deepens, the nasal roughness of a snore creeping into the lower notes.

In the dark I strain to stay awake and think about falling asleep. If I fall asleep I don't know if I will wake up again. And I drift into the waking dream, the ritual fantasy that is my private religion.

I lie in the dark and imagine that I sink into a well of drugged sleep, that my heartbeat slows, perhaps falters and ceases altogether. In the morning as pale sunlight creeps through the dusty windowpanes I will wake up. Some new breath will fill my lungs with a suspicion of joy and I will go get coffee with Aidan, where, grabbing for the sugar, I will spill some. And reaching across the table to brush the grains from my palm, his skin will touch mine and crackle like static electricity, like pollen in the air. Sunlight and air and skin, nothing more. And I will know that the sickness is gone.

I will laugh and get up and run out of Starbucks and I will drive home where I will come into the kitchen, flinging open the door, and my mother will startle, turning away from a pot of simmering oatmeal, her eyes flaring wide.

I stretch my eyelids and stare sightlessly into the dark in order to picture this scene, every detail of it immaculate and rehearsed. This is what happens: I stride into the kitchen and go to her and put my hands on her arms, feel the soft flesh give under my strong fingers. The warm squash of her breasts pressed against my chest. As I hug her, I put my mouth to her cheek that feels like velveteen and I whisper, "I love you. Mom, I love you." I whisper until the words infect her wrinkled skin, sink through blood and muscle and fuse to her marrow. She leans away from me to stare, her eyes dazzling in the morning sun. And the pale light touches our skin and turns it to fractured crystals and our sweat, our sweat smells of burnt sugar, beautiful in the ambered light as if every pore every cell is perfected and maybe it is.